RAPID DESCENT

GWEN HUNTER

RAPID DESCENT

MIRA

Recycling programs
for this product may
not exist in your area.

ISBN-13: 978-0-7783-2621-2
ISBN-10:   0-7783-2621-7

RAPID DESCENT

Copyright © 2009 by Gwen Hunter.

www.MIRABooks.com

Printed in U.S.A.

Acknowledgments

My Thanks To:

Mike Kohlenberger—raft guide extraordinaire, teller of great stories, and the real Jedi Mike. A guide who would never ever toss a client into the drink on the Lost Guide, but who has the skill to do it if he wanted. You are the only person I ever based a character on. Thank you for all you taught me about rivers, the history of the Appalachian Mountains and their ecology. It is because of you that this book exists at all.

Dave Crawford, owner of Rapid Expeditions in the Smoky Mountains, who gave us kayak instruction, kept us safe, took us rafting and had great stories. Thank you for all you taught me about myself. Because of you, I fell in love with hardboats and rivers, and I learned to relax.

Dave Shook of Old Town Outfitters in Rock Hill, South Carolina, and his son Cameron Shook, who came up with gear information and…um…have I mentioned the great stories? River people have a lot of great stories!

Sarah Bell of Green Rivers Adventures for the great trip down the Upper Green River. Loved the IKs— single-man inflatable kayaks! Ashlyn and Emily, you were great guides!

Leah McDowell, for the lessons in kayak rolling at UNCA, University of North Carolina at Asheville, and for introductions to so many people.

Becka Crawford, who named Rocking River.

Ralph Altman for being a friend since high school, and for being so gracious as I tried to pick up kayaking skills.

Robbie and Donna Ashley for the use of their pool while Rod and I learned to Eskimo roll.

CeeCee Murphy for helping me work out the accident scene where Nell is injured. And who loves rivers with "nice drops" of twelve to twenty feet...

My mom, Joyce Wright, for being my first and best reader, first and best fan, and for catching things I missed in the manuscript.

Jeff Gerecke, my agent, who keeps the future in mind.

Miranda Indrigo, my editor. Gifted with the broad view, a gentle—though thorough—editorial hand and an innate kindness. You have always made my books better, stronger, tighter and faster than my own limited vision.

And last but never ever least, thanks to my husband, Rod, who has supported my careers, my dreams and my writing. And who was willing to take on a new sport, a new lifestyle (river rat) and a new way to travel (RVing). I'm the luckiest gal in the world.

In memory of Delta

Who gave us love, guarded the house
and was an adventurer at heart.

PART ONE

1

Six Years Ago

Nell woke slowly, her eyes slit, blinded by sunlight. She blinked to clear the gummy substance away. Licked dry, cracked lips. Trees took shape overhead, fall leaves turning gold and red. Blue sky peeked beyond them and puffy clouds floated between. She was lying down. Outside. Lifting a hand, she encountered slithery cloth and held it up. It was her sleeping bag.

She eased an arm out of the bag and braced her elbow on the ground, then pushed. Her arm quivered, so weak it barely lifted her. Slowly, she sat up. The world rocked and whirled, dipping like a class-V rapid. A mallet thumped rhythmically against the inside of her head.

Nausea doubled her over; Nell reeled, retched, grabbing her head. Her pulse pounded. She retched again and again, dry heaves slamming around the pain in her skull, a wrecking ball intent on pulping her brain into mush. Intense thirst ripped at her throat. Her eyes burned, tearless. Shivers caught her. She clutched her head with a hand and the pain over her temple doubled. A pulpy knot rested beneath her palm.

Dehydration. Shock? Yeah, shock. Bump on the head, likely concussion.

Big freaking help, figuring out a diagnosis, she thought. She eased back down and eventually the nausea dissipated. Trees overhead stopped dancing. A bird called. Whitewater roared nearby. The air was cold and damp, the sensory stimulation as familiar as her own skin, yet nothing looked familiar from where she lay.

Beneath the sleeping bag, she fingered polyester fleece, smooth against her hand. Under that, she felt the ultrafine knit of water-wicking synthetics—her cool-weather, stay-warm-even-if-you-get-wet long johns.

Slowly, she turned her head and was rewarded with only a small increase in the rhythm of the hammer beating against her brain. The coals of a long-dead fire were close by. Four full water bottles.

Water. Nell slid an arm out and grabbed a bottle, pulled it back under the sleeping bag. With trembling fingers, she opened it. Managed to drink a few sips without losing much to the cloth of the sleeping bag. After a few minutes, her stomach settled and she drank half of the water. Her body sucked up the fluid, demanding more. But she waited, allowing her system to accept it. If she drank it too fast she might throw it up and lose all the benefit. She remembered that from wilderness first-aid class, or maybe it was the swift water–rescue course. She didn't remember why she was on a riverbank, alone, but if she could remember that much, the rest would surely come back.

Gradually, sip by sip, Nell drank almost all of the twenty ounces and capped the bottle. Slowly she sat up again, holding her head to keep it together, sure it wanted to fly apart. She was lying on a flat space in a tiny clearing, not more than ten feet wide and maybe twelve feet long. A shelter had been built over her, thin boughs of fresh-cut tree branches resting over a single, larger branch. She held her hand over the stone-ringed fire pit. It was as cold as it looked. Deadwood was piled nearby, but hadn't been used to feed the fire. Her kayak was overturned, hull up, resting atop her PFD, paddle, helmet, dry suit and kayak spray skirt. Her rescue rope had been used to secure the pine branches of her shelter in place. Her other rescue equipment, biners, pulleys, prusicks, were all piled together, half in, half out of the rescue-equipment bag. Near them was a cell phone, in pieces, turned on its side as if to dry out.

She reached an arm out of the bag and flipped the dry suit over. Each of the limbs had been sliced and the neck hole had been cut out, the gashes irregular, as if made by a rescue knife, slashing. The chest area was ripped and torn, punctured, as was the abdominal area. A sharp twig, dead pine needles still attached, was rolled into the neoprene fabric over the chest, which should have been protected by her flotation vest. It was twisted and snarled through several holes. A feeling of dread slid between her ribs with all the finesse of an assassin's blade.

She pulled the neck of her fleece shirt out and looked at her chest. Across her neck, ribs, abdomen and along her sides were field dressings, mounds of gauze held in place with elastic cling wrapped around her. Blood had seeped out and dried in the dressing. Her ribs and chest throbbed with each breath, and she had a feeling that if she coughed, she was going to hurt. A lot. She was cold, shivering, the skin of her hands white and puckered.

Nell looked around. First rule of white water—never paddle alone. But she *was* alone, and had been for a while, it seemed. Second rule of white water—you can only depend on yourself. It looked like she would have to.

Moving like an eighty-year-old instead of with her usual vigor, Nell peeled out of the sleeping bag. First things first, and the most urgent was the call of nature. Too weak to bend properly, she held on to a branch to rearrange her clothes, using the moment to inspect herself more thoroughly. She was covered with lacerations, punctures and bruises, sure evidence of being caught in a strainer. The feeling of dread increased. Finished, Nell pulled her clothes back in place and caught sight of her left hand. The plain gold ring brought her up short. Memories flickered. The feeling of alarm increased.

Where was Joe? She looked around the clearing. Joe had been here. It was his phone in pieces. His way of stacking firewood, with a package of corn chips nearby. Joe would never have left her alone.

Nell hobbled to the stacked firewood and bark. Kneeling, working by instinct, she positioned the bark, leaves and fibers in a cone, placed the kindling over it and took two Fritos corn chips from the opened pack. With the lighter she found beneath the chip bag, she lit the corn chips and set them to either side of the cone. The oil in the chips burned a long time and was a time-honored way of getting and keeping a fire started. The leaves and bark ignited and Nell fed the small flame with kindling until it could support itself on the deadwood. The blaze felt unbearably hot on her face and hands, testament to hypothermia.

Joe would be impressed at her recall of medical terms. He used them fluently, while she more often stumbled over them. She held her hands over the fire, warming herself, rubbing them gently together. They were bruised and cut, nails broken with filth crusted beneath them. She leaned into the smoke, holding her breath, letting the warmth seep around her head, through her snarled hair. Her face was chapped and raw, and the warmth felt wonderful. Rocking back on her heels, she took in fresh air for several breaths, then bent back into the smoky heat. And again. And again. Thawing herself.

When she was warmer, Nell rolled to a sitting position and slid her feet into her lightweight, neoprene river shoes with tough rubber bottoms, constructed to be worn by paddlers in cold water, and stood. The shoes were dry and warmer than her feet. Joe had left them beside the sleeping bag, which, when she looked it over, was both bags, Joe's and hers, one inside the other.

Nausea flirted with vertigo, and a cough threatened but held off. She crossed the clearing to the pile of supplies, strength returning more quickly now that she was moving, but pain bid for attention. Her head injury made the world sway drunkenly.

Beneath the cell-phone parts were two items—her rash-guard shirt, which Joe had somehow pulled off her body, and the Ziploc baggies that Joe used to keep sensitive electronics dry. They looked as punctured as her chest. Inside was a piece of paper, a letter with her name at the top. A shiver trembled through her, teeth chattering.

Shaking, Nell opened the ruined bag and let the plastic fall to the ground as she read her husband's neat, block writing.

Nellie baby,
    Don't know what you'll remember about the accident. Water went up fast just before we reached the Double Falls. The class IIIs looked and sounded like class Vs. Big water. You were out of position river-left, and elected to take the cheat. I was too far right and had to take the crapid.

Nell smiled at the river runner's term for a crappy rapid— a difficult and dangerous rapid, but one without a hoohaah component, without joy at the bottom. She touched the paper, her fingers sliding over the word.

    I was scared shitless when you weren't at the bottom, in the pool. The end of the cheat was blocked by

*a dead pine and you got caught in the strainer. Force
of the water had lifted your boat up enough so you
could breathe, but the tree was shifting, dragging you
down. I did a hairy ferry and took to the rocks, climbed
to get to you. By the time I did, you were bleeding pretty
badly and starting to slip under.*

Nell smoothed the paper. *Badly...*Joe with his perfect
grammar...

She considered the description of the rapids. The double
falls, the cheat—the easier drop taken by novices or
wimps—the mention of a pool. She remembered the trip. Joe
had planned it as a delayed honeymoon, kayaking on the Big
South Fork of the Cumberland River. Not a bad run, but not
easy, and not one they could paddle without a lot of rain. The
South Fork had notoriously unpredictable water levels. Not
a dam-fed river, rather, a rain-fed one, it was usually dry this
time of year, but the remnants of a late hurricane had stalled
over the Tennessee plateau and dumped a lot of rain. The
South Fork had been running big water—nearly 2500 cubic
feet per second, or CFS.

Her headache eased as she began to put it together, and
as the water she had drunk entered her bloodstream.

*I got you out of the boat but we had to swim the last
of the cheat to the pool. The water took a squirrelly curl
and it knocked you into a rock. You went out. Concussion. Shock. I'm so sorry, baby. I couldn't hold you. I
banged up my knee, getting you to shore.*

Nell looked around. They were river-right. Joe had gotten
them across the river in big water. Swimming. With a bad knee.

*I got us up the shore to a flat spot and set up camp,
made a fire, got you warm. I watched for other boat-*

*ers, but the weather must have turned nasty upstream
and no one was taking the river. It's morning now, and
you're still out and I'm getting worried. The water is
still too high to hike back, and my knee is swollen up
like a grapefruit. I'd never be able to make it up the
trail at the confluence and then the two miles to the
nearest house. So I'm paddling to the takeout for help.
I know—never boat alone. But I'll be careful. And I'll
get back to you. I love you.*

    Monday, 0800, Oct. 22

    Joe

Nell carefully folded the paper back into the uncertain
protection of the ripped baggies. She glanced at her watch.
It was 2:00 p.m.—fourteen hundred according to military
time, Joe's preference. The date displayed was 10–23.

Nell's legs gave way as her puny strength leached out. She
sat, landing hard, the baggies and her watch face all she
could see. It had been over twenty-four hours. Joe had been
gone more than a day. If she was where she thought, then
his rescue trip should have taken half the previous morning.
Help should have reached her this morning at the latest. It
was now afternoon, and no help had arrived. She looked out
at the water, still running high, perhaps 2000 CFS. There was
a large X made of tree branches—an emergency signal to any
passing boaters—only feet away on the shore. Joe's handi-
work.

Joe had gone out on the water alone.

Fear spiraled up, her heart beat at a painful, irregular
pace.

Her short fall had dislodged something in her lungs and
she started coughing, low, wet racking coughs that seared her
chest. Nell clutched her torso with one hand, her head with
the other. She had taken in water. Probably had pneumonia

to go with the concussion. She stared into the tree trunks, oak, poplar and sycamore branches, wavering for a moment with thin tears. She was too dehydrated to truly cry. Not that she had cried in years. Not that she would cry now. She closed her eyes, the world swirling, sucking her down.

When Nell woke again, her skin was hot and she was shivering. Only half an hour had passed, but her lips felt like sandpaper and her body ached. When she could sit up again, Nell scanned the clearing and her equipment. She was sick. There was no way she should go on the water. But Joe was out there… He hadn't come back. He was in trouble. Had to be.

Shoving the bag with the precious letter into her pocket, she pushed to her knees and stood, fighting the need to cough. She could cough later, be sore later, be sick to death later. After she found Joe. She focused on that one thing. Find Joe.

2

The most important element in finding her husband wasn't the state of her health, but whether her boat was still usable. She ran her hand along the hull, noting a few new scratches, but nothing major. Using her own body weight to test for cracks, she stepped up on the overturned boat and walked along it. It was sound. Forced to use both hands to flip the lightweight, forty-five-pound kayak over, she reeled and nearly fell as the boat rocked lazily upright.

She was weak. Too weak to be contemplating what she was planning.

In her memory, she could hear Joe's threat when he gifted her with the Pyrahna Micro Bat. "You ever boat alone and I'll kick your pretty little butt," he'd said, giving her that grin. Oh, God, that grin. Devil-may-care, skirting the edge of reckless but never giving in, so full of untamed life. She pressed the pads of her fingers against her burning eyes.

"I'll help you kick my butt," she whispered, "when I find you. After I kick yours for scaring me like this." Her voice was hoarse, weak.

Knowing she needed water, she upended the bottle and finished the last drop, capped it, and set the empty near the supply bag. The small, portable water filter was nowhere in sight, and she knew Joe had taken it, leaving her bottles. Which was smart, in case she had been too weak to make it to the river to filter some. She tucked two of the full water bottles inside the bag, and opened the fourth one to sip on. Joe had left her a large packet of trail mix and both of the dehydrated dinners they had brought, but the packages had somehow been punctured. Backpacker meals were similar to Meal, Ready-to-Eat, survival fare developed by the military and now made by several commercial companies and used by survivalists in the wild. Joe always packed a couple when they were going to be out overnight, just in case the fishing was bad. Along with the cell phone, these had gotten soaked and were bloated, the dehydrated food expanded with moisture.

She sniffed each of the freeze-dried packets and tore one fully open, pouring its contents into a metal cup, adding a little of her water to reconstitute it. Carefully, she placed a rock at the edge of the small campfire and balanced the cup on it. The ripped package went into the flames and she tossed the uneaten one into the torn baggie.

There was a smear of red on the baggie. Fresh blood. She inspected her hands. Several of the uncountable cuts on them had broken open. There were no medical supplies left. It looked like Joe had used all the cling and gauze on her already. Nell shrugged. She wouldn't bleed to death, not from these little things.

While the food warmed, she munched trail mix and considered the dry suit, but there was no way to wear it. She shoved it into the bow of the boat and checked the rigging. The boat was permanently rigged just for her, sculpted pieces of hard and soft foam along the rigging's hip and knee pads, the bulkhead set just right so the balls of her feet rested against it for leverage and steering. She had lost one of the hip pads, and she pulled the suit back out. Joe and she both boated with rescue knives strapped to their floatation vests, and she cut an oblong strip about four inches wide and two feet long from one of the legs; she folded it over until it was the right thickness and wedged it in place, securing it with a strip of duct tape. The parsimonious part of her cringed at further damaging the expensive suit. The realistic part of her counted it as just another element of the goal—finding Joe.

Shivers racked her. It could be cold in October on the Cumberland. She would miss the dry suit. Undeterred, she shoved what was left of it back into the bow. To counter the cold, she pulled the rashguard shirt over her head, feeling stupid that she had not thought of the warmth it could provide until now. Thus fortified, she dismantled the camp.

The rescue rope had been knotted through the tree branches of her shelter, and by the time she finished removing it, her hands were bleeding freely and stinging from pine sap. She coiled the rope properly and tucked it into her rope bag. Joe had taken none of her flipline, but she was missing two prusicks, webbing, and two carabineers—biners—used for rescue. Joe had likely lost his while rescuing her and had been smart enough to take hers.

An image hit her, Technicolor, surround-sound memory. Her hands. Holding the branch of a dead tree. Blood flowing weakly over her skin. White water rising around her, the river's might thunderous. Rushing and cold. The smell of the Cumberland was iron-wet in her memory. The roar of power damping any other sound. She was trying to attach a length of webbing to a branch above her, the biner and bright red flex sharp in her memory. She had tried to rescue herself. And somehow had lost the equipment. The image went no further, leaving her with only that single moment—tree, her hands, blood, two pieces of rescue equipment. And pain in her chest, up under her PFD. Where she had been stabbed by a branch she hung from.

When the instant of memory faded, Nell was sitting on the ground again, her white-water equipment before her, trail-mix bag on its side, some of the valuable calories spilled on the ground. Shivering, goose bumps tight on her skin, fever surely rising, she gathered up the mix and brushed it off. Eating it, she went back to work.

Her personal flotation device was missing a strap at the bottom, cut through by a sharp knife, but it would keep her afloat if she had to swim. The neoprene kayak skirt, the device that made boat and boater one and kept out water that would otherwise quickly swamp the small craft, was another matter. When properly in use, a kayak skirt was fitted around the rim of the opening of the boat and snugged around the boater's waist, making both a watertight unit. The skirt had been damaged and repaired with duct tape, which would make it stiff and harder than usual to fit over the rim of the boat's cockpit.

Nell pulled against the elastic neoprene, counting the tears. There were three big ugly ones and five smaller ones, all hidden beneath duct tape which had been applied to top and bottom. Nell felt her waistline and compared her wounds to the damaged skirt. The strainer must have punctured through the skirt, up at an angle beneath her PFD, and through her dry suit. Joe had obviously repaired what he could, but the duct tape restricted the elastic of the neoprene skirt. It might last for another run. *Might.*

But she had not lost her helmet and, miracle of miracles, she still had her paddle. Briefly, she wondered if she had dropped it when caught in the strainer. She had no memory of it in the vision of her hands. If she lost it, Joe must have recovered it for her.

Either way, she was good to go. But first, the river. She walked along the shore, checking out the flow, but the river curled away from her between the boulders lining the South Fork of the Cumberland. Balancing carefully, she climbed up one and worked her way upstream, jumping from the top of one car-, bus-, or house-size rock to another—the only way up or downstream, outside of the white water. Her river shoes gripped the slippery boulders. If she fell and busted her leg, she would be in bigger trouble than she was in now.

The water flow was still high and gave her an idea how difficult the trip was going to be. The roar of the water was like a jet engine. White water foamed and churned, hiding the undercut rocks, strainer-debris, sieves and other dangers.

The cheat was only a few yards upstream, still running with enough flow to take it in a creek-boat. She couldn't see the tree that had caught her, the cheat curving hard around a huge boulder, the rock the size of their bedroom in the apartment. Big water. Water that had already tried to kill her. Which made her mad, a much more useful emotion than the worry that niggled at the back of her mind.

Nell turned back downstream and walked past her campsite. Ahead, she saw a pair of young tom turkeys, standing on a spit of shore, drinking. With a flap of wings, they whirled uphill, racing into the scrub and out of sight.

Boulders and water-swept trees wedged between rock blocked her way. However, between two rounded rocks she found a glimpse of the white water downstream. The Washing Machine on the Big South Fork. From this angle, it didn't look too difficult. Dicey class IIs. It was impossible to hike farther. Nell headed back to camp, picking her way with care. Her breath felt easier, her chest pain was less. She could do this. She had to do this.

Back at the camp, Nell broke down the emergency X signaling for help. She tucked four lengths of flex into her pockets and scattered the branches.

Gathering up the last of her equipment, Nell strapped it on or tucked it in, wrapping the sleeping bags in their waterproof protection and forcing them into the stern. She stepped into the kayak-cockpit skirt and pulled it to her waist, her breath tight and painful. She couldn't hear the soft wheeze of her lungs over the roar of the water, but she could feel it.

She added a bit more kindling to the fire and checked the temperature of the Backpacker. It was hot enough to eat, though not hot enough to be tasty. Of course, no amount of cooking could truly make a dehydrated meal tasty. She scooped up the rice and bits of chicken with a camp spork. Energy flooded her with each bite and she felt better instantly. Joe had chosen the Santa Fe chicken and rice, her favorite. Dinner suitable for a belated river honeymoon. Grimly, she smiled as she ate, sitting close to the fire and absorbing the warmth.

Nell washed the cup and spork and tucked them into place in the kayak. It was much more full than usual, with Joe's sleeping bag, some of the equipment between her thighs instead of in the bow or stern. Using the empty water bottle, she carried enough river water up to douse the fire, first kneeling and drawing into herself a last bit of heat and warmth. When she could bear to, knowing that this meant she wouldn't be warm or safe for hours, she upended the bottle. The water gurgled and sizzled the fire out. She stirred the ashes, pushing the half-burned kindling into the mud. She had never added any of the bigger logs, and left the pile of deadwood and the ring of stones for the next camper.

As ready as she could be, Nell slipped on her damaged PFD, zipping the vest up the side and yanking tightly on the remaining straps. Each action sent shock waves of pain through her. She pushed the agony aside. There would be time for pain later. Much later.

She settled her helmet on her head, careful of the egg-shaped bruise, though there was no way to avoid it entirely. If the helmet shifted, she'd hurt, so she pulled the chinstrap more snugly than usual. Satisfied, she dragged the kayak to the shore, which angled down to the water. Before her was the Big South Fork of the Cumberland River and the pristine pool at the base of the Double Falls, but boulders bigger than cars blocked her view. From the sound of the rapids, she better be ready.

Every river has a scent, and the iron-tang of the Cumberland and of deep, rich earth and sap-heavy trees lining the banks and up the gorge walls filled her nostrils. A blue heron stood on the far shore, watching. Bending against the pain of her chest and the thrumming in her head, Nell wriggled into the white-water kayak, placing her feet against the bulkhead, wedging her hips in tight and snuggling her knees past the thigh pads.

She drank the last drop of water from the second bottle and tucked it inside the kayak body with the others. She made sure that everything was in place and secure, properly balanced, as the slightest weight shift affected the roll and pitch of the nimble little boat. She shoved the supply bag with its precious water and food between and under her thighs, and clipped it securely to the bottom of the boat.

She rolled the curled hem of the kayak skirt around the back of the cockpit hole, easing it into place with cold, shaking fingers. When the back and sides were secure, she took a breath for strength, leaned forward with her elbows at her sides, using her body for leverage, and folded the front of the skirt over the front rim, the skirt and the boat's emergency releases both in easy reach. It left her winded and aching and it was all she could manage—not a pretty entrance, but sufficient. And the repairs in the skirt held. She was watertight, at least for a while.

With a deep breath that banged around in her head and chest like a gong, Nell took her paddle in her right hand and shoved off with her left, sliding down the shore. Leaning back in a seal launch, she lifted her lower body and the bow as the kayak hit the water. Pain thrummed in her head and along her sides. Icy river splashed over her, the rashguard shirt providing some protection but not enough, water soaking through to her polyester sweatshirt as she braced right and left. With a directional sweep of the paddle, she guided the boat to the center of the small pool. The sound of whitewater was both behind and ahead, an enormous roar. Boulders and steep, tree-covered terrain rose all around her, forbidding and austere. It would have been beautiful if she hadn't been sick. If Joe weren't missing.

She swept with the paddle in the first half of a 360-degree turn, facing upstream, the Double Falls now ahead, with its rushing cheat visible. With another stroke that pulled her chest muscles into a short, tight spasm, she completed the turn. When she could breathe again, she checked the banks.

On the shoreline, what little there was of it, debris was piled against rocks. The scant foliage lay bent and low where it had been pressed down by rushing water, all evidence of the high water that caused the near disaster Joe had written about. She back-stroked gently to hold her place along the shore.

She located the current by the eddy line, a faint ripple of water. With quick, sure, forward strokes, Nell moved upstream, across the eddy at an angle, and leaned downstream. A single stroke and brace brought her into the current. It seized her boat and jerked her forward.

Ahead was the Washing Machine, a turbulent drop between two house-size boulders. The rapid was a class II, usually easy. Then came the El, a deceptive-looking, gnarly class IV. Though the rehydrated meal she had eaten sat uneasily on her stomach, she was glad of the energy it provided. She knew she would need every calorie before the day was over.

Nell positioned her kayak for the Washing Machine. Her

heart pounded with erratic fear that, until now, had never owned a place in her life. She studied the shoreline rocks. No sign of Joe.

He should have been back by now. He wasn't. There was nothing on this earth that would have kept Joe away from her. That meant that he was in trouble. And there was no one to help him but her.

She paddled forward with smooth strokes, into the churning water.

3

Nell shot between the two rocks and bounced down the Washing Machine, her Pyrahna bounding along the wave trains. Each time the boat rebounded, the jarring baited her lungs, teasing at the need to cough. Her ribs lifted and lowered with each breath, every paddle stroke burning with pain. She had raced through less than half the train of rapids when the coughing started. By the time she was through them, she was coughing steadily, her chest muscles tortured. The wounds on both hands had broken open. Even in the cold, her grip on the paddle was slick with blood. Still no sign of Joe.

The El roared up ahead. There was no time to reconsider.

Hands white and aching, her lungs on fire, Nell lined up for the El, paddling hard, spearing the water with forward strokes, glancing right and left for Joe. Nothing. No sign. The current grabbed the boat and yanked her forward. She was slightly off center, river-right.

The fifty-yard approach to the El was through squirrelly water, a boater term meaning that the water danced in unexpected ways, throwing the kayak up and down, requiring her to lean hard left and right, rocking up with hips and thighs and feet with each stroke, bracing the paddle against the water to maintain boat stability.

Her breath was tight, the air cold and filled with river

spray. Nell fought to relax, knowing that tension in a paddle stroke could change both her direction and speed, resulting in the kayak turtling over. If she flipped, weak as she was, she might not make the required Eskimo roll back upright. And a wet exit from the boat—pulling the skirt loose and swimming to the surface—might be deadly with water this big and this cold. Nell had never run the South Fork with water this high. She pushed that thought down deep and away.

The rock ledge of the El, with its swirling plunge, appeared, the water flow making it into a monstrous curl and drop. Her boat dipped into the hole just in front of the ledge. She dug in with steady forward strokes, pushing the boat toward the drop-off, her breath tight and painful, moving without her usual fluidity. The backward-moving water sucked the boat back upstream. She bobbed and paddled, leaning downstream, pushing with her feet against the bulkhead, trying to work through the current. This was the invisible danger. Holes would trap and suck down anything, paddles, boats, floating bodies, keeping them down and spewing them out later, at a time of their own choosing. And she was weak, her arms and shoulders burning with exhaustion. With a last desperate stroke, panting, coughing, she broke free of the hole.

Her boat went over the ledge. She boofed, wrenching up her legs and the bow of the kayak, paddling hard against the diagonal curler. In this huge flow the curler was a tube of water that tried to spin her sideways. She hit the bottom of the drop in a spray that drenched over her with icy water, burying the boat. She jerked her thighs up again, out of the tube, sliding to the surface. Instantly she maneuvered around rocks, through holes, paddling and coughing, her eyes blinded by spray. Another hole tried to drag her back and she leaned hard over the bow, using a variety of strokes, on instinct to keep the boat pointing downstream and moving forward. Rocks dodged up in front of her, invisible until the last instant, evil spirits from the deep, intent on her destruction.

A downed tree blocked the space between two boulders, creating a strainer dead ahead. Nell had a staggering vision of the strainer that had trapped her. Branches brown with death, interlaced, dragging in the water. She shoved the memory away and swept hard left, rotating her torso, guiding the boat obliquely against the current. The right side of the kayak slammed into the rock face and instantly the bow of the boat swirled around the pivot point. The boat shot hard river-right, right into another hole. At the last of her endurance, Nell gave a series of hard forward strokes and draw strokes. Pulled the Pyrahna into an eddy leading river-right. She compensated, braced and glided into still water.

She was coughing violently, fighting to paddle straight, to find the shore. The river bottom rose up, long and shallow, to a bank, and she thrust hard twice, to send the boat up the shore, beaching it firmly. Popping the skirt, she rolled the boat to the side and shimmied out. She lay on the rock-and-sand beach, coughing, the raw, wet sounds louder than the water.

Long minutes passed. Nell lay still, letting her body recover. Her head pounded, dizzy with the exertion. Her clothes were drenched to the skin and shivers shook her hard, even with the rashguard and polyester shirt she was wearing. At least she wasn't wearing cotton. There was an old saying, Kotton Killz; the water-absorbing natural fiber would have left her dangerously hypothermic already. As it was, she deeply regretted the loss of the dry suit to keep her dry and warm.

She was sure her fever was higher. Did being wet and chilled to the bone counter the fever? She didn't know, couldn't remember if she ever knew.

Every muscle in her body ached. Every breath ached. Every heartbeat, cough, sigh, swallow and pulse of blood ached. The sun came out from behind a cloud and found her, bathing her in faint heat. She spread her fingers into the light. Shifted slightly until her legs were in the sun. Slowly, some of the pain began to seep away.

Without warning, Nell fell asleep.

When she woke, it was to a whirling world and a fleeting loss of memory, a disorienting series of sun-washed seconds, during which pain pulsed through her with the beat of her heart. Her eyes focused. She recognized the pattern of rocks in front of her nose. Gingerly, she rotated to face the sky, the helmet kinking her neck at an uncomfortable angle. Nausea roiled in her like gnarly water.

She was sick. Flu or pneumonia, or both. Could you have both? Shoving with her elbows, Nell rolled over and struggled upright to survey the landscape around her. She had survived the El. She was on the shore of the Long Pool. Tossed by the current, she was river-right, a convenience term used by river sports enthusiasts. In a world with boundaries composed only by the movement of water, right and left were always determined when facing downstream, so that river-right and river-left always meant the same thing. She looked around. No Joe. No emergency X on a shore. No beached boat, bright red in the sunlight.

On the far side of the pool was another level shoreline, longer and deeper than this one. That was where the emergency access trail was, arduous and steep. On this side of the pool there was an old railroad bed, stripped of wood and rails, a path now used by horseback riders and hikers and the occasional four-wheel-drive park rangers' vehicle. It was possible that she could make it up to the gravel one-lane road and hike out. But it would take hours, longer than it would take to run the river.

She might get lucky and come across horseback riders who would give her a ride out. Or she could trudge for miles.

She studied the landscape. There was no sign of campers or hikers. No horse smell. Nell looked at her watch, gauging how much daylight she had left. She twisted to her feet with a groan that echoed over the rush of water.

She could ferry across to the other side of the pool. It wasn't even hard to do in the Long Pool, the current was so slight. But the trail out on that side of the river was a strenuous climb, hard uphill to a jut of land called the Honey Creek Overlook. Then another hard, miles-long walk on secondary roads to Burnt Mill Bridge, the input where she and Joe had started out. Again, she might get lucky and meet another hiker. Or she might not.

Nell lifted a leg and waggled her foot. She was in thin-soled river shoes, not hiking boots. She was hurt. Had all the breath of a…a dying moose, as Joe would say. Yeah. Hiking was out. Paddling was faster.

On the other hand, if she stayed on the water, she had to face the half mile of the Rions Eddy, followed by the steepest gradient of the trip, a drop of forty feet per mile with almost continuous class IIIs, including Jake's Hole, where the river took a 180-degree turn between cliffs of 300 to 400 feet. The Narrows. And her paddling wasn't exactly up to par. Nell looked at the sky, checking the weather. It was clear. The sun was warm. She had dried out considerably. She scanned the far shore again, hoping to see a hiker, signs of a campfire, anything. The hills and forest were quiet and empty.

She looked back at the water. A little more than three miles ahead was the old O & W Railway trestle bridge. There might be boaters taking a break there. Or campers. Or she might spot help before she even got there. But that meant she had to paddle the energy-draining, challenging water… She was between the devil and a deep blue crapid.

The deciding factor was Joe. If she stayed on the river, she might find him and be able to help. If she took the trail, another twelve to eighteen hours would pass before help would hit the water. So. Decision made. The river it was.

But she had to stay alert. If Joe had been standing on a rock in the middle of the river, waving his paddle and beating a drum, she might—*might*—have seen him in the last half mile. But she wouldn't bet on it.

Nell knelt at her boat and pulled out the last Backpacker meal. She should have heated it with the other batch. Stupid. For now, she opened the packet and poured a bit of water into it. In an hour or so, she might be able to eat it. Instead of a real meal, she ate more trail mix, finishing off half the bag while she stretched. She should have started out with a good stretch before she hit the water. Stupid again. She hadn't been thinking. She touched the bruised knot over her temple. It was marginally less painful. The cold, which was debilitating in every other way, had been good for the bruise.

Standing on the bank of the Long Pool, Nell pulled against muscles that were stiff and bruised, and wished for a bottle of Tylenol or ibuprofen. Of course, if she were wishing for something, it would be smarter to wish for Joe to appear, his red Pyrahna Riot play-boat cutting through the still water. But Joe didn't materialize, and neither did a bottle of painkillers.

Feeling a bit better, she drank ten ounces of water and climbed back into her boat, strong enough this time to put the skirt on without huffing. She had to hurry. Time was passing fast. Sundown was three hours away. She had no intention of spending another night on the river.

She looked around one last time. Evidence of high water was everywhere. Strainers were piled at the shorelines, stacked against rocks in jagged knives of detritus. The water snarled and growled like a wild animal. Nature howling at the moon. Hungry.

Shoving off into the Long Pool, Nell paddled through still water, angling downstream, watching the current to the side. The eddy line was a diagonal ripple at an angle she didn't remember from her last trip down the gorge. It flowed across the bottom of the pool and took a hard angular turn, a zig followed by a zag, as if something on the bottom was obstructing the flow of water.

She did a sweep upstream, followed by two forward strokes to approach the eddy line, then a quick peel-out just above the zigzag. She leaned downstream and braced through the current change. It was an effortless maneuver and Nell took a deep breath that, for the first time today, didn't ache. She set up for the class IIs and IIIs of Rions Eddy ahead. The next half mile of rapids were squirrelly but not exactly MacGyver water. She told herself that she could make it. She could do this. She was able to both work the rapids and watch for signs of Joe. She put paddle to water, passing a low boulder that had dried in the sun. Two black snakes lay in the feeble heat, warming on sun-heated stone.

The boat took the first quarter mile of the class IIIs like a knife cutting through water. Clean and smooth, not a wobble or bobble. The bow of the boat slid beneath the rapids and Nell compensated, using hips, thighs and feet to reposition the kayak and prepare it for the next drop. Watching for Joe.

As always, the river was deceptive. By comparison to some western rivers, the gradient drop wasn't much. But the water flowed around huge, vision-obscuring boulders, where short stretches of nearly flat but fast-moving water were followed by surprising drops and ledges. Unpredictable, capricious current changes and hundreds of undercut rocks, where water flowed beneath the visible part of the rock, tried to suck down any paddler who happened too near.

Between each drop, Nell scanned left and right, watching

for a man or an emergency signal. Or a red boat. She was looking left when she should have been looking right. The water dropped out from under her and the kayak pivoted hard right and down. The short dive left her leaning upstream. She turtled over. Her helmet banged against stone. Nell saw stars. Her head pounded with a vengeance. Icy water rushed up her nose and filled her ears. Freezing her. Cold shocked her like a frozen spear to the brain.

She was in a hole between two rocks and she was stuck underwater. The current knocked her boat against rock with the hollow drum of doom. Fear billowed as the instinct to breathe fought with the presence of water.

But she still had her paddle. And she hadn't been knocked out. *Thank God.*

With her left hand, she shoved at the upstream rock, then the downstream rock. Back and forth between them, working her boat out of the declivity. The water swirled her back in. Her lungs burned. She needed air. She needed—

The current caught her and bobbed her out.

But she was still underwater. Nell pulled the paddle under her. Gripped it in both hands. Twisted her torso forward for a sweep-style Eskimo roll. The water pitched her against another rock, banging her head and left shoulder underwater. Nell reacted without thought and twisted into a classic C-to-C roll. She didn't like the C-to-C, but it worked.

And she was upright. Light blinded her. Nell sucked in a breath that was half water and leaned into the current just as she went over another ledge.

4

A glimpse of twisted limbs, wet and black. A strainer—a full grown oak, half submerged, its branches tipped with yellowing leaves and its trunk wedged between two boulders—was just ahead. Blocking her course. A swirl of water opened out river-left.

Nell slammed her hips hard left and dug in, ferrying across the strongest part of the current. Paddling with all her might. She banged against the left bolder trapping the tree and let go of the paddle with one hand. Using her palm, she shoved herself into the smaller, weaker current to the side, a cheat created by the strainer debris. She caught a glimpse of a dead animal pinned in the oak, gray and waterlogged, fur dragged by the water. And a second glimpse, an instant still-shot of her palm pulling away, leaving a trace of a bloody handprint on the branch.

And she was around, into the cheat, bashing her boat bottom in the trickle of water. She allowed the kayak to bump onto a low rock and sat in the sun, unmoving, breathing hard. Shuddering. The roar of water was partially muted, an odd trick of acoustics stifling the sound. It was like she'd been shoved into a different world. Still and quiet and safe, full of shadow.

Her breath had a definite wheeze now. Her head throbbed almost as loudly as the water had only moments ago. Nell blew the river water out of her nose and sinuses, and leaned forward to rest her head on one hand. Her ring and the cold flesh beneath were icy on her hot face.

A tickle started in her chest. Nell coughed, the coarse ratcheting sound echoing along the rock channel. She coughed and coughed, her ribs spasming. Her abdominals clenched painfully and she coughed up a gob of…stuff.

She spat into the water where it was caught in a tiny whirlpool and swirled out of sight. The coughing stopped and she breathed. The wheeze was softer, less pronounced.

That dead animal… Not Joe. She knew it wasn't Joe. But still she wanted to find a way back upstream, just to check. Just to be absolutely sure. But it wasn't possible. No way. There had been no sign of Joe anywhere.

Her head demanded attention, its throbbing increasing in volume and intensity. She cradled her skull in both icy hands. The pain seemed to swell like a wave washing over her.

"I can't do this," she whispered. "I can't. I'm not gonna make it. Not alone." A single salty tear slid down her nose. For the first time since she was a little girl, Nell cried. Covering her sobs in the embrace of her own arms.

Caught in the shadows, in the narrow lee of rock, she thought about prayer.

She hadn't been to church since her father died. The car crash had killed both him and the wife of a church elder, with whom he had been having an affair. She had been twelve. And she had blamed God. Even though she realized that her father made his own choices and his own mistakes, and that God had nothing to do with either her father's infidelity or his death, she still blamed God. Because she knew that God, if he wanted to, if he really loved her, could have made her father love her mother. He could have kept her father alive. He could have. And he didn't.

And she hadn't prayed since.

But perched on a rock, in a trickle of water, near where Pine Creek entered the South Fork of the Cumberland, after facing her own death twice in as many heartbeats, with the worst of the rapids—the Narrows and the Hole—yet to come and her husband missing, Nell thought about prayer. She raised her head and looked up. The canyon walls were closing in, a narrow channel of foamy water and sandstone in browns and yellows, and gray-coal-stained river boulders. There was a patch of blue and glaring sunlight visible in the westward-facing cleft of boulders. She wiped her face, the chapped skin burning. Pale, thin blood dribbled from her fingers. This cold, the blood flow should have been constricted by the temperatures. But with a fever, her body was acting weird. She clenched her fists. Out of options, Nell talked to God.

"Get me out of this, okay?" Her voice was rough, pitched lower with sickness. Her words grated along her throat painfully. She massaged it with one hand and kept talking. "Get me out of this, help me find Joe, and…and we'll talk about us later. Okay? Just…don't let me die. And don't let Joe—" She stopped, the words strangled in her throat. Unable to finish the sentence. The thought.

Instead, she popped the skirt and finished the water in the third bottle, tucking the empty into the hull of the boat. That left her twenty ounces of water. She resecured the skirt and pushed off the rock, downstream, into the still pool. The roaring of the rapids ahead was louder than anything she had heard before today. In front of her, the river disappeared, crooking around and behind a massive boulder. In an instant she was back in the maelstrom. Heading toward the Narrows and Jakes Hole, watching for Joe. For any sign of Joe. Anywhere.

Canyon walls rose above the tree line around her, boulders blocked both water and her way. Water spirits, cruelly playful, knocked against the boat, tipping and redirecting and spinning it, trying to capsize her, tricking her with foamy, hidden dangers. Her boat was underwater as often as it rode atop it. She braced and stroked and pulled with the current, reading it, working with the flow to power her small boat. She swept past a flat-topped boulder capped with a series of altars. Guides often found places on rivers to leave stacks of the rounded, pancake-shaped rocks, each successively smaller rock balanced on the larger one beneath. It was half play, half superstition. Nell tipped her paddle at the formations in salute.

She whipped around a strainer that appeared out of nowhere. An image of the strainer that had trapped her flashed before her again, then vanished. But it left behind a hard ball of fear and desperation in her chest. She took the next series of wave trains too tight, too stiff, and was pulled out of position, making an ungainly inflexible run.

Just before the Narrows, she pivoted the boat into a tiny patch of still water river-right, between two boulders that didn't appear to be undercut, with no current that could pull her under. In the cleft they formed, she sat. Her breath heaved. Nausea stirred. Dehydration was raising its ugly head, but it was to soon too break open the last bottle of water. Way too soon.

Coming up was the meanest, most gnarly piece of MacGyver water on the run. A long, squirrelly, hairy-hard, impossible crapid to the max. She had taken it before, several times, but it was a dangerous stretch. The last time she ran it, one of the men in her party got dumped. He had to swim the hole and came out with a broken arm, dislocated shoulder and compound fracture of his right leg. Getting him to help had taken the entire five-man crew the rest of the day. It had been a hairy, scary afternoon. Randy, an old paddling buddy, hadn't been on the water since. And now she was running the hole alone. She searched around, up the canyon walls, between the rocks upstream and down. No Joe. But if he'd been tossed and made it to the shore-side of a boulder, he would be out of sight. He could be ten feet away and she would never know.

Nell popped the skirt and drank water, knowing that she had now taken in eighty ounces of water and hadn't yet needed to answer the call of nature. She dropped the bottle back in the boat and resealed the skirt. Checked her palms. The flesh was white and bloodless now, nails slightly blue gray with cold. A callus was torn and should be bleeding, should be hurting, but her hands were too cold to bleed and her adrenaline was pumping. She'd bleed and hurt later, when Joe was safe. When Joe was safe…

Chest muscles tight, she peeled into the current. The roar of water increased as the canyon walls climbed. Three and four hundred feet, they soared above her. After a glimpse around for her husband, Nell paddled hard, choosing a position midcenter of the Narrows. With a series of quick strokes, she helped the water take her.

The boat disappeared and reappeared under the water, bouncing over it. Spray slapped her in the face. She maneuvered the tiny craft through the growling snarl of water. Jakes Hole was just below her. The current to the inside of the turn swept under and vanished, taking with it anything it could grab. Water on the outside of the turn curled up, ripping against the rock face of the boulders and the base of the canyon. At the bottom of the turn, the water curled continuously, like an ocean wave breaking without ceasing, a trap for the unwary. The river plunged down and down, a powerful churn of white water.

Nell took the turn in perfect position, her body guiding the boat with ease, as if the water spirits had decided to lend a hand. She swept with the current, taking the crest high.

Around the turn, and down, she paddled with all the energy and might she had, letting the water carry her downstream, building momentum. She took a hard drop. Into another hole.

The kayak seemed to stop. Water sucked at the boat, pulling it back.

Leaning forward hard, Nell paddled, her whole body working to breach Jakes Hole.

She fought, reaching the curl and pillow of water that marked the lower boundary of the hole. Water shot at her face. Suction dragged her back and down. Her arms felt on fire. Weighted. Her wet sleeves dragged at her. And she broke through.

The small boat rose up and over and out in a sudden swoosh of movement and texture, the water beating at the hull. If she'd had breath, she would have whooped with success. Ahead were IIs and IIIs. Easy-peasy by comparison to the hole. She was laughing softly under her breath, but the movement of air in her throat was raw and aching. After he finished beating her butt for boating alone, Joe would be so impressed. She thrashed down the soft, panicked *"what if…"* that threatened to rise.

A quarter mile later, Nell spotted a patch of color. Her heart stopped. Breath froze. Her eyes glued to the patch of red. Red, hard plastic. Molded and rounded. Pressed between a rock and the base of the canyon wall.

She didn't remember ferrying across to the boat. Didn't think or breathe or hope. Until her small boat bumped into the patch of red. It was a kayak. Swamped. Upside down.

She touched it with a cold hand. Knowing. Knowing it was Joe's boat before she even turned it. One hand holding her paddle, one hand free, she slid fingers along the curve of hull, underwater, to the open cockpit. There was no skirt over it. No body inside, dead and drowned. She braced the hand gripping her paddle against the boulder and wrenched with her free hand to turn the boat up over her bow, hip-snapping to stay upright. Filled with water, the flooded boat was graceless, weighing easily four hundred pounds.

It rolled through the swirling river current like a dead animal. Upright. It was Joe's boat. Battered and beaten. New scratches and a hard dent in the point of the prow. But no Joe. No Joe.

No Joe.

She screamed his name, the sound lost in the continuous roar. Screamed and screamed, the name echoing with the water. Screamed until her throat was raw and only scratchy sobs came from it. Shudders trembled through her as she searched the rocks nearby for any sight of him. Fear and hope raged through her. She looked for a man holding a paddle high, waving to attract attention. Looked for rocks piled in an X. Driftwood in a rescue emergency position, tied in an X. Looked for a body. Looked for Joe standing on a rock, patting the top of his head in the "I'm okay" signal. There was nothing.

No sign of Joe beyond the battered boat. No indication that Joe had ever been here.

The small rational part of her knew that he *hadn't* been there. He had come out of his boat upstream somewhere. Hope believed—*knew*—that he had swum to a rock and climbed up high. She had missed his emergency signal. Had missed sight of him. And now he was behind her, alone and injured. Surely injured. Hope tumbled with despair.

Or perhaps he had come out of the boat just upstream, and had swum the Hole. Perhaps he was yet below her. Needing help.

Her fingers slid along the kayak as if petting it, numb with cold. The red of the boat filled her vision, obscuring the image of anything, everything else.

Blind with the bloody color of the boat, acting on instinct alone, by touch and feel, Nell popped her skirt and pulled out rescue supplies, rope and flex, and secured the boat to a slender rock upthrust in the river. The water-filled boat bobbled in the current.

Watching the boat, the roar of water seeped into her consciousness. The color of red bled away.

She had to get to the next takeout. Had to get help. Get a search party started. She had to get help for Joe. Leaving the boat tethered to the rock, Nell resecured her skirt. It took her three tries to get the skirt over the cockpit hole. Exhausted, she pushed into the current, heading for the takeout at the O & W Railway Bridge.

If she didn't get help there, then she would push on to the final takeout, Leatherwood Ford Bridge, at the Bandy Creek Campground. Leatherwood and Bandy Creek were smack in the middle of a national park, the Big South Fork National River and Recreation Area. If she saw no one on the way to ask for help, at least there would be qualified people at Leatherwood. Boaters, hikers, park service officers. Help in abundance for Joe.

She had covered three miles of rapids. There were three more miles to go.

Nell read the water and moved into it, an automaton.

She didn't think during the run, seeing it only as a series of still-shots. The water slamming upward in a column of spray. An altar of rocks seven stones high. A dangerous curl of water that wanted to pull her down. Buzzards pulling at a fish, its bones pale and thin. The glare of setting sun on the top of an oak. The image of a dead hemlock, branches feathered as if reaching for help. The feel of the rigid boat encasing her. The cold of the water on her chest and arms. The wet shirts holding little heat, leaching her meager body warmth away. Her paddle blade, entering the water in a clean stroke. The sight of an osprey overhead, wings extended. The inhuman beauty of the gorge, a palette of fall foliage against the sepia browns and muted grays of sandstone and granite walls. The rush of foam across her yellow and orange boat. Black, water-wet stone. Rushing water everywhere, a deafening roar. No Joe. No Joe.

No Joe.

The O & W bridge came into view at last, and Nell's eyes swept the spaces where boaters would often rest after the long stretch of rapids. The takeout was empty, the water so high the sandy beach drowned beneath it. There were no hikers climbing to the trestle. No hikers walking along the bridge. No beached boats or rafts. No smell or sign of campfire. But just in case someone was there and not visible from the water, Nell boofed her boat atop a rock and unskirted. On trembling legs, she rock-walked to land and made her way up the steep hillside and concrete platform to the stairs the park kept in good repair.

At the top of the sixty-foot climb, breathless, she surveyed the bridge and nearby camping area. The O & W railroad no longer ran, and its rails and ties had long been removed, leaving a nearly level, winding, one-lane gravel road that traveled along the gorge. Hikers and horse lovers and vehicles used it, but not today. There was only a scattering of dry horse manure to indicate anyone had been through in days.

Nell cupped her hands, found her breath and shouted. "Anyone here? Help!" She listened, hearing only the roar of water. Using the height, she scanned the rocks below for signs of anyone, but mostly for Joe. She saw no one. She was alone.

Fighting tears, she retraced her steps down to the river rock and pulled her body back into her boat.

Shoulders burning, muscles stretching painfully across her spine and ribs, Nell seal-launched off the rock, into the water, and paddled past the bridge. Took the last of the big IIIs. She was a machine, unfeeling, unthinking. Her paddle blades moved with eerie regularity, in and out of the water, side to side. Heading for help.

By the time Nell crossed under the bridge at the Bandy Creek Campground and cut the placid water to the Leatherwood takeout, the sun was setting. The river looked black and still, no longer a hungry predator. No longer interested in pulling her down. Bored with her. Moving on to other concerns, other prey.

Shivering uncontrollably, teeth chattering, she beached the boat, the hull skidding across the sand and pebbles with a harsh swear of sound. She smelled campfires. Saw lights far up in the hills near RVs and tents. Caught a whiff of grilling steak. At first she saw no one, and then, as the wind changed direction, she smelled a campfire close by—the heady scent of cooking beef and burning hickory riding along the breeze. She tried to call out, but her throat made only a faint croak of sound. Pain scratched along with the broken note.

Sitting in her boat on the beach, cold, so exhausted she could hardly move, it took Nell two tries to unskirt herself. She had to twist and roll to her side. Push herself from the cockpit to the sand. Wriggling one hip and then the other from the opening. Breathing hard, she lay on solid ground, her feet still tangled in the boat with her dislodged supplies.

She kicked her way free and made it to her knees, then her feet. Drunkenly, she moved through the dusk upwind, following the scent to the day-picnic area and parking lot.

The campfire was a brazier attached to the side of a beat-up RV. The scent of marijuana and beer rode the air now, tangled with the smell of burgers.

Laughter. Music. A guitar. She stumbled into the camp. Three men and two women. Images of them standing, turning, open mouths round in shock. And the sight of the ground rising at her, telescoped by blackness all around.

Nell's next coherent thought was of warmth and earthquake. Light. Water being dribbled into her mouth. The dark eyes of a woman, her face rosy in firelight. Cradling her as if she were a child. "Drink. Come on. Swallow. That's a girl." Nell swallowed. The water hurt going down as if her tissues had been abraded by claws. The tremors were her body, shaken by sickness or shock.

"We've called an ambulance," the woman said. "And the park service."

"Joe," Nell said, her voice less than a whisper. "My husband, Joe. He's lost on the river. Help him."

"Shit." The woman called over her shoulder, "There's another one still on the water." To Nell she said, "Where? Where did he go in?"

"Somewhere after the Double Falls," Nell whispered. "I got caught in a strainer. Had a concussion. He left me to go get help. He didn't come back." The enormity of the last four words hit her. Joe didn't come back. She closed her eyes and slid into darkness.

5

The sheets were scratchy and coarse. The scent of harsh cleansers and the faint smell of floor wax brushed her senses. She struggled to open her eyes to a slit of light. Bright. The ruthless dazzle of fluorescent bulbs overhead, the glare stabbing steel blades through her brain.

Pain caught her up, pounding in her head, spasms in her chest with each breath. Muscles so stiff they creaked like old rubber when she shifted her head. The steady beat of agony on her brain. Lids so heavy she fluttered them but they stayed closed. Hot blankets encasing her, a little bit of heaven in a sea of misery. Hospital, for sure.

As if the lights knew what was wrong, the bulbs overhead went dark. A small light to her side came on. She sighed, and the pain softened into rubber blades stabbing her, instead of steel.

Finally, Nell opened her eyes. She was in a hospital bed. Window on her right. Door and sink on her left. Another door was at the foot of the bed, a shadowed toilet within. A man sat in a chair near her. An older guy, hair more gray than brown, suit rumpled. His eyes were on her. She frowned. Something was wrong...

"*Joe.*" She wrenched upright and the pain exploded again. She groaned, catching her head in her free hand, an IV yanking at her other one. She dropped back to the mattress, aware in some fragile part of her mind that she was not making sounds out loud.

"They said to stay flat," a voice said. Cool. Conversational.

The man in the chair. Not a doctor. Not wearing the right clothes. Face too unemotional. Nell eased her hands away from her head and opened her eyes more slowly. Carefully, she turned and looked at him.

He leaned slowly forward and touched the fingertips of one hand to the tips of the others, dangling them between his knees, as if to create a sort of intimacy between them. Nell was pretty sure she hadn't seen him before, didn't know him, and didn't want to be close to the guy. He smelled of old coffee and even older cigarettes. He said, "What's your name?"

Nell considered. Not an unreasonable question. Just not one she was interested in. To save some pain, she whispered, "Have they found Joe?"

"The man you say is still on the water?"

She nodded slightly. It made her head pound harder, but it hurt less than her throat.

"River rescue is being coordinated right now. What's your name?"

She moved her eyes to the window, her thoughts mushy and slow. It was black outside. It was the same day, then. Or same night. "Who's in charge?"

"Park officials. What's your name?" Steel in the tone now. The guy was persistent.

"Nell Crawford Stevens." It came out a hard cee and sibilant esses in the whisper. "What's yours?"

"Do you know where you are?"

Nell had been dealing with negotiator types all her life. Nobody was better at negotiation than her PawPaw Gruber. "Army, The Nam. Quartermaster," as he always said. So Nell said, as distinctly as she could whisper, "What's yours?"

"Detective Nolan Orson Lennox, Sr., investigator with the Scott County Sheriff's Department."

Nothing more, nothing less. Oh, yeah. Just like PawPaw. Nell saw some buttons, each with a small picture of a bed in a different position. She pushed the one with the head of the bed upright. In her mind she heard PawPaw as the bed rose. *You want something? Always find a way to improve your negotiating position. Physical, mental, emotional. Next, offer something, so they have to offer something back.* "I'm in a hospital," she volunteered, feeling stronger now that she was more upright. "Who have they called to coordinate?"

"Your mother is on her way."

Nell looked at the cop in surprise. "My mother couldn't coordinate her way out of a paper bag."

Amusement lit his eyes, and Nell was pretty sure he had spoken to her mother personally. He hadn't understood her question. She couldn't care less who was coming to help *her*. She spotted an ugly, squat pitcher, beaded with condensation and pointed at it, asking for something, requiring the other party to the negotiation to do her a favor. PawPaw would be tickled when she told him. "Water?"

The cop—she had already forgotten his name—stood and poured her a glass of water. "Can you tell me what happened?" he asked. He handed her the cup and helped her to steady it when her grip was too weak to hold it without spilling.

She studied him over the rim of the cup and sipped through the straw. The water tasted wonderful. When she had enough and her mouth felt less like it was covered with river mold, she dropped her head back and said, "I mean, who have they called to coordinate the river search?"

The cop put the pitcher down. He looked her over, examining her as carefully as she did him, letting the silence build. "The parks people have called in a team. After all the rain, the gorge is treacherous enough to warrant only the most experienced, though, so the team'll be small. Maybe ten on the water. I understand that a few guides and rescue people from the Pigeon will be part of it." When she waited, he added, "A guy named Mike Kren called about three hours ago. He's leading them up. Some others were already closer in, rafting or kayaking. Most of them got here within the last hour."

Nell nodded, feeling her eyes water, the sensation painful on her raw eyeballs. Unfamiliar. She did *not* cry. She rolled her head to the dark window, moving slowly, and started to talk, well, whisper. She told him everything she remembered, as close in sequence as she could. When she mentioned the letter Joe had left her, the cop said, "This one?"

She looked at him, and he was holding the double-bagged letter. Nell extended her hand, and he placed it in her palm. She saw him looking at her hands, at the blood-crusted wounds, but she had eyes only for the single piece of paper in the baggies.

How come she felt that it was the last thing she would ever have of Joe's? How come she felt so…empty? *No. I refuse to think that way. Joe is still out there. All I have to do is find him.*

She smoothed the letter over her heart. Holding tight, so the cop couldn't get it back without getting personal, she took a breath that quivered through her. The bandages on her chest were small lumps beneath her hands, beneath the hospital gown she wore. She went on with her story. Everything she could remember.

She had reached the part about finding Joe's boat, when the door opened. Mike Kren strode into the room. It was like a small hurricane entered. "Hey girl," he boomed.

The tears that had been swimming in her eyes fell as she held out her arms to her best friend in the world. Her tears caught the lights and haloed him, bright glints on the silver in his hair. As if he were her own personal avenging angel.

Mike would have laughed at the thought of being compared to an angel.

He lowered the bedrail and sat beside her, his wiry body blocking her from the cop, and gathered her up in his arms. She sobbed into his chest, the familiar scent of the man surrounding her. She crumpled Joe's letter at him, indicating he should take it surreptitiously.

He tucked it into his own shirt before speaking. When the baggies were safe, he said, "Hey. What's this?" He turned her face up and touched her cheek, his finger coming away wet. "I never saw this before. Nell Stevens, crying? Tears? Devil must be draggin' out his long johns, 'cause it's cold in hell right about now."

"I lost Joe," she sobbed. "He's lost on the river and he's got to be hurt, and I couldn't find him—"

"Hey, hey, hey." He snugged her face against his shoulder, stroking her short hair. He lowered his voice. "I'm making you a promise. Okay? Right now. If he's findable, I'll find him." He tilted her face to him again. "You know that. I'd never leave somebody on the river in trouble. Specially not Joe."

But the words resonated inside her. *If he's findable...*

Nell stopped crying. Stopped breathing. She focused on Mike's river-brown eyes, steady and serene. If Joe wasn't findable, it was because he was stuck beneath an undercut rock or tangled in an underwater strainer. Or washed so far downstream he might not be found until low water in the next drought. It he wasn't findable, it was because he was dead.

The thought opened something up within her, a deep, dark chasm, empty and howling with icy wind. A chasm she had been ignoring, denying. A shot of something bitter and frozen rushed through her veins like ice crystals. She clenched Mike's shirt, the flannel and long-john shirt beneath bunching. "You find him," she whispered fiercely, her eyes demanding. "You find him and you bring him back."

He read her face, her demand, her desperation. Gently, Mike peeled her hands from his shirt and held them in his, like a promise. Or a benediction. He kissed her forehead, his lips cold and dry. "I won't lie to you. But you know I'll do what I can."

It wasn't what she wanted. It wasn't a promise to make it all right. But the chasm that had opened beneath her moved away a bit, to the side. Mike had never lied to her. He never would. No matter what. Not even to save her sanity. But if a mountain could be moved, Mike Kren was the man to do it.

He squeezed her fingers and let go, set his craggy, lined face in a confrontational expression, and turned to the cop. "Mike Kren."

"Jedi Mike? Old-Man-of-the-River-Mike?"

Mike blocked her and Nell could see neither man's face, but she knew they were taking each other's measure. Mike wasn't fond of cops. Nell rather suspected that the cop would pick up on that. And Mike was well known in the river-guide community as a pacifist anarchist. If the cop had done any research at all into river rats, he had to know that.

"Some people call me that," Mike acknowledged. He angled back to Nell before the cop could introduce himself, his weathered face creased in the soft light. "Tell me everything."

Nell whispered, pushing her broken voice, starting over with waking in the campsite. Mike asked questions as she talked, questions about water volume, wind and weather conditions, other boats on the river, the kind of supplies they had carried with them on the overnight trip. He asked about certain rocks, places where boaters could go missing for weeks or months. Questions about the cheat and what she remembered about the strainer. They were questions of an experienced river guide, and Mike's thirty years on the rivers in the Southeast U.S. showed in each. He concentrated on current changes, taking in her description of the big water, the tube that should have been only a curl at the El, listening with intensity about the zigzag current at the end of the Long Pool, nodding when she described the Narrows, tilting his head, his gaze far away, as if seeing it all in his mind.

Mike had been on rivers for longer than Nell had been alive and having him here improved Joe's chances more than anything. When she reached the end of her tale, Mike sat silent, rubbing her fingers with his thumbs, thinking.

"Okay. Gotta go, girl. Got supplies to get together. I shut the shop, put a note on the door for any drop-ins to head over to Amos's. He can have that church group coming in on Saturday, too, if we don't get back in. We'll lose money but it won't kill us like it would have before Labor Day. Later, girl."

He patted her shoulder, a single pat, like the promise he hadn't been willing or able to give. Mike pointed his finger at the cop, a gun gesture, and blew through the door like a strong wind, taking Joe's letter with him. The cop didn't know that. Yet.

Nell lay back on the inclined bed and closed her eyes, fighting for composure. When she could control the tears, she asked the cop what else he wanted to know. And wondered if she cared enough to ask him his name again.

The cop was silent for a moment and said, "You're a member of the river search-and-rescue team for the Pigeon River." It wasn't a question. Nell nodded. "You're certified in river rescue?"

"River rescue, swift-water rescue, first responder, wilderness first aid, a few others, all through the New River

Rescue Center." Her throat ached with the tears building behind her lids.

"Mighty young to be certified in all that."

Stupid questions, stupid comments. They needed to be talking about where Joe might be on the river. But he was a cop, and Nell had never once known cops to be useful on an SAR. They just got in the way. "I'm twenty-one. I took all the courses this past winter and early spring."

"With your new husband."

Pain sliced through her. His tone said, *Your new dead husband.* She nodded as the tears took over and leaked down her face. "It's where I first saw him."

The memory was a stabbing shaft, bringing her skin to chill bumps. She had been on the bank of the Nantahala River, putting together a Z-drag system to save an "endangered" swimmer in the water, a certification instructor at her shoulder. She had glanced up at the water. At a boater shooting past. Looking right at her with his daredevil smile, his intense eyes, so blue they might have been lasers. The connection so immediate it took her breath away still. And he was gone, his boat downstream so fast she couldn't follow. She had lost him. Until he showed up on the Pigeon River two weeks later. He'd been looking for her. And he'd found her. And now she had lost him again.

"Joseph Griffon Stevens."

She nodded. *I lost him.* The breath she took ached, as if it tore its way through to her lungs.

"You took all those courses so you could start up a new business." Nod. "A business that had to require a lot of up-front, start-up money." Nod. "And where did all the up-front money come from?"

"Joe got a loan," she whispered.

"A loan," he said, his tone odd.

Nell opened her eyes, seeing a halo now around the cop,

but if he was an angel, he was an angel of the devil. His tone was too guarded, suspicious and Nell didn't know why. She blinked and he wavered in the watery mix. Tears leaking down her face burned fresh trails in chapped skin. Her head was thumping like a jackhammer.

The words clawing down her throat, she whispered, "If you think I did something to my husband, you are stark raving crazy. Now go away." It wasn't the best thing to say in a negotiation with a cop—and everything was a negotiation, when it came to cops—but she just didn't care anymore.

The cop studied her, his gaze taking in her bruised and lacerated hands, her face, lingering on the bump in her hairline. "I'd like the letter back, please. Until the investigation is over with. Or they find your husband. I'll give you a receipt for it."

"No."

His brows rose. It was real surprise on his face, not some kind of fake cop look. But Nell had been raised with PawPaw and with Mike. She knew her rights, and like her independent mountain forebearers, she had little regard for keepers of the law. Nell just wanted them to get the heck out of her way and let her do her job.

"I won't sign a receipt. You get a subpoena," she whispered, "you can have anything I have. Till then, no. Besides, I don't have any letter."

The cop slid his eyes to the door. "I'll be damned. He took it, didn't he?" When Nell didn't reply, his mouth turned up on one side in a knowing half grin and he looked back at her. "We'll be talking."

"Whoopie."

The cop laughed, a single harsh bark of sound, and left the room, letting the door close noiselessly behind him.

Nell stared at the ceiling, silent tears dripping onto the flat pillow beneath her head.

* * *

Orson Lennox checked the phone's display. His dad. It was 5:00 a.m., but it was also his first day on the job with the Knoxville PD. The old man had known he would be up. "Yo. You still up, old man?"

"Cop hours," Nolan said. "And I can still whip your butt."

"No question about it. What's up?" Orson said, tying his spit-shined black shoes.

"You run rivers. Could a tiny little female with a concussion run the South Fork of the Cumberland alone? After a lot of rain?"

"You always run a river alone, Pop, no matter how many people are with you. But—" He thought a moment, trying to balance thinking like a paddler against thinking like a cop. "With a concussion? Only if she was real determined or real stupid."

"How 'bout if her husband went missing on the river and she was going for help."

"Possible. Any chance she did him in and tried to make it look bad? That'd make her pretty determined. He have money?"

"Friggin' loads. And it looks like he mighta beat her up first, so maybe she can plead self-defense. Thanks. And good luck today, okay?"

"Nine tenths preparation, one tenths timing," Orson said, quoting his father. He heard Nolan laugh at hearing his own words about the existence of luck quoted back to him. The call ended. Orson closed the cell, wondering about a paddler and her dead husband on the South Fork of the Cumberland. It was a perfect place to commit a murder and make it look like an accident.

6

"I'm fine, Claire. Really. And I'm leaving," Nell said as she pulled a second long-sleeved T-shirt over her head. One was white and the other matched her jeans. Her mother had color coordinated her wardrobe, which made Nell smile while hidden by the knit of the second shirt. She smoothed down her flyaway hair and checked the site of the IV, pressing on the bandage the nurse had applied after Nell pulled the tubing out. It had made a big, bloody mess. The nurse had tsked and said something about blood work indicating signs of dehydration.

Well, duh. You think?

Nell didn't remember anyone taking blood, but she had several bruised needle marks in both of her elbows. None of them looked like they were going to bleed again. Her butt, however was sore on both sides. She had taken two antibiotic shots, one in each cheek. They hurt when she sat.

"You look like you got beat up by a trucker," Claire said.

Not hit by a truck. That would have been too close to what had happened to her husband, Nell's father. But beat up by a trucker, that was okay. Even though truckers everywhere would take issue with her comment.

Nell bent over and stepped into her jeans, watching her mother through the wisps of her short hair. "I'm alive. What I look like isn't important. I'm going to the put-in. Mike will need someone to handle the radios."

"You have a concussion."

Nell bargained with a lie. "Once I get to water, where I can keep an eye on the SAR, I'll put on lipstick."

Claire hesitated, tapping her manicured fingers on the bedrail while Nell pulled on socks. Her mother bargained back. "And you'll stay in the RV. And not go on the river. At all. Promise."

"Off the river for twenty-four hours." When Claire didn't answer Nell said, "Take it or leave it. I'm twenty-one years old, so I can sign myself out of the hospital anyway. I know. I asked the nurse."

"Deal." Claire frowned at her. "You remind me more 'n more of my father, you know. More and more."

"PawPaw's good people, even if he is the biggest hillbilly in the state. So, thanks." Nell slid on laceless running shoes. "He didn't want to come?" she asked in a smaller voice.

"You know my daddy. He ain't leaving his mountain, his house or his dogs. Or that still he claims he don't have. But he sends his love."

Nell nodded and stood. Her grandfather and his shotgun would have been mighty handy against the cops, but beggars couldn't be choosers. "Gotta go."

While she talked to the nurse, Claire tight-lipped with disapproval at her side, Nell was careful to breathe shallowly, so that neither of them could hear her wheeze and somehow force her back to bed. Besides, she *was* breathing easier, and her fever was gone. Mostly. Nell could tell a difference in her body already, just since the shots. She wasn't well, but the pneumonia wasn't going to take over and put her back in bed.

The nurses called it "signing out against medical advice," or AMA, and it took half an hour. They gave her a sheet of paper about what to watch out for with the concussion and another about the infection in her lungs, then handed her a bag that contained her helmet, her river shoes and her river-wet underclothes. They had been cut from her body and were still dripping. Nell wondered why the cop hadn't taken them. Her PFD was gone. And she had no idea what had happened to her seven-hundred-dollar boat and the three-hundred-dollar carbon-fiber paddle.

Then she was in the parking lot in the soft morning sunlight. She spotted the RV. It was a one-year-old twenty-five-footer, bought from a foreclosure place off of I-40. Joe had bought it for them to live in, in Hartford, during the paddling season. They had left it in the Bandy Creek campground and she hadn't thought about it since. Seeing it warmed her almost as much as seeing Mike had.

She headed to the RV, trailed by Claire, who continued to chatter all the while about how she looked like she'd been beaten up, and why didn't she wear makeup at least for special occasions. When she could get a word in, Nell asked, "Who brought the RV in?"

"Mike, of course. You don't think I drove that monster. 'Sides, where do you think I got your clothes? I called Mike when I got close to Oneida and he met me in it. I followed him in. There's my car, see?" She pointed to the parking space behind the RV, the bright red two-door Mazda parked between the lines.

"You need makeup on," Claire said. Nell shrugged. "For the TV lady."

The words brought Nell up short. "What TV lady?"

Claire flushed slightly under her makeup, looking just a tad discomfited. Which meant it had to be something really awful. Claire could rearrange God's calendar and social life without batting an eye. If she was uncomfortable, then it was a doozy. "The one who wants to do an interview. Right over there."

Claire pointed and Nell saw a white news van with a satellite dish on top heading their way. Nell turned furious eyes on her mother.

"Don't you go looking at me in that tone of voice," Claire said, pouting and sliding into the dialect of the Tennessee mountains. "'Sides. They can help get the word out. Get more people to help look for Joe."

"We have all the help we need, Claire. Only trained and certified rescue people need to be on the Cumberland. It's too dangerous."

"You were on it," Claire said, as if that lessened the classification of the river's rapids. And in Claire's mind, it likely did. As if she just had a new thought, her mother held her big baby blues wide, heavily mascaraed lashes batting once. "And it'll be great publicity for the business when they find and rescue Joe, your names all over the TV airwaves."

Nell bent to one of the storage compartments that lined the base of the RV and found the spare key where Mike had left it. Joe had the original. Her heart stuttered at the thought. She slammed the storage door shut with unnecessary force and unlocked the door to the RV, closing it on her mother's face and the TV reporter, who was climbing out of the news van. Before the driver could think to block her in, Nell started the engine and pulled out of the parking lot, leaving her mother and the reporter blinking in the sunlight.

Nell didn't like surprises. Claire knew that. And she had better things to do than…than… Nell bashed the steering wheel with her fist and dashed tears from her eyes as she made a turn. She and her mom hadn't had a real conversation since her dad died, but surely…surely Claire knew she wouldn't want to talk to a reporter. Didn't her own mother know her better than that? A soft voice whispered in the back of her mind, accusing that she hadn't given Claire a chance to know her better. Not since the accident that claimed her father and the woman he was sleeping with. Nell shoved that thought away for later. Right now she had to find Joe.

By the time she reached the put-in at Burnt Mille Bridge and parked, Nell was exhausted. Her headache had grown from a soft rattle of padded drumsticks on her skull to a big bass drum of misery. She popped two ibuprofen, forced down a bowl of cereal and drank a liter of water. Then she flipped supply switches, making sure the RV had plenty of propane, water and space in the waste-storage tanks. Habit. She knew exactly what was left, because neither she nor Joe had used much of anything on the trip.

She gargled with warm saltwater to help her throat, found an old pair of Joe's sunglasses and slipped them on, then added a sun visor, one that went all the way around her head instead of clamping on the sides of her skull. Her injured cranium couldn't handle the pressure. She pulled on a sleeveless, insulated vest over the tees, still feeling the cold of the river. Hypothermia could hang around, especially after a lot of stress; Nell figured the trip down the river qualified as a lot of stress. Satisfied, she stepped into the October sunshine.

The put-in at Burnt Mill Bridge on the Clear Fork River was a place with a whole lotta nothing. No fast food, no gas, no hotel, no camping, no amenities at all. It was not much more than a double loop of gravel off a secondary road, a tiered grassy area in the trees with picnic tables, a few park trails and the old, blocked-off, one-lane trestle bridge. The bridge looked like a rusted derelict against the brand-spanking-new one.

The site was the midway point on a run that started ten miles upstream on the Clear Fork River and ended seven miles downstream at the Leatherwood takeout, and any river runner who had once been there could find it. However, if Claire tried to find the put-in, Nell's mother would end up lost in the middle of nowhere. Nell felt a bit guilty about leaving her mother in the hospital parking lot. As soon as she could borrow a cell phone she'd call her. For now, it was too late to do anything about her mother's whereabouts.

In the Burnt Mill parking area, there were five trucks, two vans and Mike's huge SUV. More vehicles turned in to the parking area as she watched. Equipment and people were scattered across the gravel and grass in a mass of organized chaos. Kayaks, paddles, helmets and PFDs rested untouched on the slip of sandy bank that showed above the high water. Rescue ropes, flex, biners and other equipment were being tested and inspected by a couple dozen men and women, some wearing wet suits, dry suits and river shoes, others in hiker's gear and boots.

A park ranger in his brown uniform looked rumpled and unshaven, and was almost twanging with energy. He stood with Mike and a group of boaters and hikers, each with a radio, checking equipment. There was a Cumberland County Rescue Squad van, the volunteers dressed in matching red T-shirts over warmer clothes in the cool morning air.

In the center of the throng was one full-size, self-bailing, Maravia Ranger river raft. It was Joe's and hers—the shop name painted on its bright blue side—and was fully inflated and ready to go. Clearly Mike hadn't transported it from the shop filled with air. He must have brought an air compressor with him in his truck. Organized as always.

Mike raised his paddle above his head, calling her over. Nell pocketed the RV keys and headed across the lot. There were familiar faces from Pigeon River in the crowd. Besides Mike, there was Harvey, RiverAnn, Turtle Tom, Hamp and Stewart, all guides she had worked with during her summers on the river, before she and Joe dreamed up Rocking River, the mom-and-pop river-guide, white-water-rafting and kayak-instruction shop they had opened the previous May. Seeing them so far from home, obviously here to help, brought tears to her eyes and Nell was glad she was hiding behind the dark lenses.

She stopped and greeted each of the guides, pulling on Harvey's new beard, touching Turtle Tom's newest tattoo, a huge-busted naked woman sitting on a rock beside an altar of river stones. He wore a sleeveless T-shirt to show it off. She flicked Hamp's hat, a brown one with the initials of his school on it, Furman University, and kissed Stewart's cheek. Stew wasn't very bright, but he was a sweet guy, and he had no idea he was so gorgeous. He didn't talk much, and he ducked his head, letting curly black hair cover his face.

Nell carefully didn't comment on RiverAnn's latest weight gain, just lifted a hand in salute. The girl gained and lost the same fifty pounds every year and seemed to be ending this season heavy. Still in high school, RiverAnn had hung around paddlers ever since she could drive, working as a waitress in a small restaurant that serviced the truckers who frequented I-40 and the few river people who stayed through the off-season, and working as a river guide in summers.

Nell had seen her a few times throughout the previous river-rafting season because she worked for Amos, the owner of the competition rafting company next door. But the girl stayed pretty much to herself and whatever river guide, climber or snow-patrol dude she happened to be with that season. RiverAnn laid her head on Harvey's shoulder and Nell didn't persist in trying to catch her eye. It seemed that she had picked out her winter beau already, and had eyes only for him.

Mike gave Nell a one-armed hug and handed her a high-power, multifrequency, two-way radio, a fancy walkie-talkie. She pressed the transmit button to hear the squelch sound, making sure it was working properly, and noted the channel the searchers were using. Cell phones didn't work in the bottom of the gorge, and were carried only for emergencies where a paddler might have to climb out and call for help. The radios, while line-of-sight, were better than nothing, and radios could be used to pass messages up and down the gorge. Nell slid it into her vest pocket.

Mike said, "We're ready to hit the water. Two of the hiking crews already left. We'll have radio support all along the river, with hikers situated on the crests of the canyon walls, on the O & W road and the bridge. A couple of the most experienced guys are ready to rappel down to the canyon gorge." When she raised her brows in surprise, he added, "They have climbing gear and experience, and I want to be able to throw a rope to shore and have it secured to a rock if we need it, or have them climb down to check out something we see up higher."

Nell nodded, understanding and agreeing with his strategy. In swift water rescue, ropes were usually tied off to trees onshore, but parts of the gorge had few trees near the water. It was the closest thing to a western river gorge east of the Mississippi. Rock, rock and more rock close to the river, lots of white water and not much of anything else.

"We got three in the raft with me, and seven in kayaks. There's another small team starting out from the put-in at the confluence of the Clear and the New Rivers at 10:00 a.m. We'll meet them and work it from there."

To Nell, Mike asked, "You met the team leader yet?"

"I thought that would be you." Nell said, surprised. She was gratified to hear some life and volume in her voice. The hoarseness was fading.

"I'm taking up the rear in the raft." He boomed out, "Elton. This is Nell."

A slender man, not much taller than she was, handed a rescue rope to a woman beside him, raised his hand and walked over. He was blond, blue-eyed and all muscle, with the prematurely weathered skin and all-year tan of a river rat, ski patrol, mountain biker, hiker dude. A typical outdoor-loving mountain boy. Encased in the wet suit, he had the sinewy body of a black snake, a rolling, confident gait and not an ounce of body fat. He looked her over, seeing beyond the black eyes and bruises. "Hit a rock?" Elton asked, his voice soft, his words efficient.

"Concussion," Nell said.

"Walk me through it."

Once again Nell told her story and as she spoke, the crowd gathered around her. It was the first time they had heard the tale and she saw nods and shaken heads. When she reached the part about finding Joe's boat, their eyes slid past her. Eyes that were filled with sympathy. Eyes that said her husband was dead. Stewart's eyes filled with tears and he turned away. Harvey looked down, shaken. RiverAnn took his hand and squeezed. Turtle Tom reached out a hand and gripped Nell's shoulder. "We're here for you, Nell. Hang tough."

Her throat closed up and Nell patted his hand, fighting for a breath, finishing with tears in her own eyes, tears that were becoming habitual and unwelcome. Her Tennessee dialect strong in half-whispered words, she shook off his hand, took off her sunglasses, claimed the eyes around her and said, "Joe's out there. In trouble. With no one but youns to help him. Please. Find him and bring him home."

Mike looked at Elton, who gave him a single nod. "Let's do it, people," Elton said.

As the group began to disperse, each person to his or her assigned job, Nell went to every single one, clasping a hand or giving a hug, depending how well she knew each. Saying the same thing over and over. "Thank you. Thank you so much." The once-alien tears no longer felt so foreign, and Nell didn't try to keep them from falling, even though they burned, even though they made some of the searchers uncomfortable.

To the guides from the Pigeon, she added an extra word or two. "Thank youns for being such good friends. Thank youns for coming all this way for Joe."

Each of them seemed awkward, embarrassed with the extra attention, and Turtle Tom shook his head, hugging her. "I just wish it hadn't happened. You know?" he said, his big brown eyes staring at the trees on the far shore rather than at her tears.

"I know," Nell said, feeling the guilt well up in her. Joe was lost. And if she hadn't gotten stuck in a strainer, he would be fine. It was her fault. All her fault.

7

A swift-water search and rescue was a risky business. Nell had seen a simple training run turn dangerous with a foot entrapment in two feet of water, or as a submerged strainer trapped an unwary swimmer. No team leader wanted to evac out a hiker with a broken leg or be forced to rescue one of the rescuers, but it happened, and a good team leader was prepared for it.

Nell watched Elton give instructions, making sure that each radio was on the same channel and assigning other channels for nonemergency chatter. He liaised with the sheriff's deputy who drove through the lot. He chatted with the park rangers, two of whom drove up just before they hit the water, and the hyper guy who was leading one of the canyon wall hiking teams. Some of the hikers left by van and Jeep to start out from the takeout and work their way upstream. Three kayakers were on the water early, practicing rolls. It was bedlam, but it was structured bedlam.

Then Elton blew a piercing whistle and shouted, "We do a complete river run this morning, from put-in to takeout. We'll be meeting up with Argonaut at the confluence of the Clear and the New, and taking the last rapids down together." The teams nodded, recognizing the moniker. Argonaut was Jason Adams, river-named after the historical sailor. "Everybody keep an eye out for emergency signals, branches or rocks in an X shape, fire, equipment, even a person lying on a bank or rock.

"Remember to check clefts that might have been available to a boat in bigger water. Today it's running at fifteen hundred. It was up to twenty-five hundred CFS earlier, so we're looking at two feet of river we don't have today. I want the kayakers to scout the shore as often as possible, but don't get left behind. Stay with the group. I want to be down the river by 2:00 p.m. Hikers, take the paths. Watch for signs.

"In places where line-of-sight radio communication is impossible, three long whistle bursts means we found him. Everyone who hears the whistle, pass the word where we are, and move into place to get him out. Anyone not close enough to be of immediate assistance, get your butt back to a put-in or a takeout.

"Anyone who gets injured on the river but can paddle to a support site alone, get off the water. We'll have support in four places. At Leatherwood takeout, of course—" Elton held up a finger "—at the confluence of the Clear and New Rivers above the Double Falls." He held up a second finger and then a third. "At the start of the Narrows, but that one'll mean a hike up to the old railroad road and no parking to speak of, so try not to get hurt there so we don't have to stop and drag you up the mountain." Everyone laughed and Elton held up a fourth finger. "And at the O & W bridge. Paddle to whichever support site is closest. Questions?" Everyone here knew the river and no one raised a hand.

Elton said, "The support teams will have food and water for anyone who needs it, and trucks to cart you out. We'll have support people at each site by noon, but unless you get hurt, you'll be carting your own boat and gear to the trucks. No princess rides today." That got another laugh. Princess rides were raft trips with a pretty girl as one of the paddlers.

She usually got to sit and look at scenery while the other rafters did all the work and the male guides ogled her.

"In the event that we don't find Joe by two, we start a slower, more methodical search downstream from the confluence above the Double. The paddlers will rendezvous at Leatherwood at 6:00 p.m. There'll be trucks at the takeout to haul your boats from the river upstream to the campsite at the confluence or back here to get your vehicles. We have permission to camp at the confluence for those interested.

"Hikers will meet up with a support team at 6:00 p.m. Same thing with regard to transportation."

He looked around the gathered, meeting eyes. Making his most important point. "No fun and games today, people. No playing. Not until after Joe Stevens is found. Got it?"

A chorus of yips followed his question, and several boaters gave the Hawaiian "okay" sign of thumb and little finger in the air, the other fingers curled under, hand waggling. The hikers took off with long strides. The Ranger raft pushed off, into the sluggish current. The hardboat paddlers went to their kayaks and began the serious business of getting on the water. Those still onshore skirted themselves into their boats and slid into the water and under the old and new bridges.

Nell watched as they moved down the river and slowly out of sight. When they were gone, she surveyed the nearly empty lot. One of the two park guys pulled out, spinning gravel; the other one strode up to the second tier of parking.

Soon the rescue squad auxiliary organization would be bringing food for the searchers and organizing ways to make sure each hiker and boater had ample supplies of water and food. There would be coffee, doughnuts, trail mix, sandwiches, maybe some soup to ward off the chill at each support station. People who were willing to run errands. Medical personnel. News vans. But little of that would take place here. Most of it would be at Leatherwood at the bottom of the run, and at the two put-ins midway down.

Nell knew she would have to move soon to keep up with the search, and wondered if the RV could make it down the one-lane, steeply graded, sorta-maybe-could-be-a-road to the parking above the confluence near the Double Falls, or if it would be better to park at the top of the hill above the Narrows. Turning the RV around on any of the one-lane roads would be a bugger. The O & W would allow a turn-around, but if she met anyone coming, she would have to figure out how to back up. Maybe for a long way. She didn't want to have to. That left Leatherwood or the confluence for her day camping.

The news van she had run from pulled into the lot and headed for the lone park ranger. *And then there'll be the press,* she thought. Nell escaped to the RV and headed out.

Nell was parked at Leatherwood near two groups of day campers with rowdy preschoolers, and bored high schoolers and the lone support vehicle to arrive so far, a beat-up pickup truck. The truck bed contained extra paddles, rescue ropes, and a rescue stretcher, the kind shaped like a canoe, with flex security straps and tie-offs for hauling a wounded victim up a steep hill. An old man was sleeping in the cab, his head tilted back, mouth hanging open, hogwashers and a threadbare white T-shirt the only parts of him visible.

She turned to the water. The river was still high, rushing over the low bridge kept open by the park rangers to show campers and tourists where the original Leatherwood Ford used by colonists and by the Indians before them was. Cars and trucks no longer used the low bridge, not since the construction of a steel and concrete bridge. The newer bridge was normally some twenty-five feet above the river flow, but the distance was less today, with fresh, dark high-water marks two feet higher.

The storm that had turned the river into a raging torrent had come out of nowhere. In forty-eight hours the high water would all be gone. But for now, it was a foamy blur in her tears. Nell wanted to be out there with them, on the water, helping with the SAR, but she knew that with her head pounding and her vision not quite steady, she would become a liability to the water team. It was the first time since she was sixteen that she hadn't been on the water during an S and R.

She sat at the small dining table, staring across at the seat Joe should have occupied. Like most married couples, they had each chosen a seat and stayed in it for meals. Joe sat with his back to the driver's seat. Nell faced him. Now his seat was empty, but there was evidence of Joe everywhere. His map of the river was unfolded on the dinette seat, next to his beat-up copy of *Southeastern White Water*, the out-of-print kayakers' bible. His second-best sunglasses were open on the dash, but had slid into the angle between windshield and dash. She hadn't noticed them when she drove to the put-in.

Joe collected sunglasses like some people collected dishes or furniture. He owned several pair of the kind with yellow lenses that claim to give the wearer the sight of eagles, several more that were polarized, others that were cheap dollar-store glasses he didn't mind losing. His current favorite pair was with him, wherever he was.

A John Deere hat hung from the hook over the door. His Jeep keys dangled from the key hook. A T-shirt drooped from the hook in the hallway. The sheet draped out from beneath the bed's comforter, left there when she had made the bed, the morning they took to the water.

She looked at the radio, sitting on the table. Silent. Nothing was happening on the water. By way of the radio relay, Nell had learned that the boaters had made it over the Double Falls, and Elton and Mike had sent the faster kayakers out to the shorelines around the pool at its base. Elton had inspected the campsite where Nell had woken. Mike and his crew had tied off above the drop and were checking for signs of passage.

At loose ends, Nell stood and walked through the RV, their new "summer home," occupied by them exactly three times before this trip. She studied the small space. Touched the towel hanging off the tiny oven. Lifted Joe's T-shirt hanging on a hook in the hall and held it to her nose, then she wrapped the shirt around her neck for comfort. Tucked the sheet under the mattress. Smoothed Joe's pillow.

The RV was too small and compact for a large family, but it was just right for them. The queen bed was in the back, with storage hidden behind tension doors that thumped shut like cupboards on an oceangoing boat, keeping the contents inside during rolls and pitches on the road. The special cabinets lined the walls at the ceiling all around, along the walls, and even under the bed and beneath the dinette couches.

There was a tiny kitchenette and a bathroom with a shower so small that Joe bumped his elbows when he washed his hair, thumping and banging like a bass drummer. The miniscule bathroom sink and formed-plastic toilet looked like something from a dollhouse.

The dinette was situated across from the efficiency-size appliances, a narrow table between two bench seats. Because she would be here awhile, Nell leveled the vehicle with the automatic levelers and activated the slide that extended the dinette section of the RV out nearly three feet, giving her floor space. If she wanted, she could move things around and make the dinette into a couch or turn it into an extra bed. She swiveled the driver's and passenger's seats around to face back, making a place for seating. Nell wanted the "after-search decompression" to take place here.

And if Joe needed medical attention, the floor space

would let medics work on him if there was a delay with the ambulance from Oneida. The vision of Joe lying on the floor, bleeding, a compound arm fracture needing attention, was so strong she had to blink it away. The image was replaced with an image of her husband lying dead on the carpet, pale and bloodless and blue. Acid rose in her throat.

She made it to the bathroom and threw up the cereal she had managed to get down. Curled on the small floor of the bath, she gave in to a hard cry, the sound of her sobs louder than the screams of the preschoolers only feet away. When the emotional storm passed, she crawled to her knees and flushed, pushed to her feet and brushed her teeth. Wiping her chapped face, she stood in the center of their summer home, alone and with nothing to do.

She was frighteningly grateful when a knock on the door interrupted her. So grateful that when it was Claire, with the reporter just behind, Nell didn't even care. She threw herself into her mother's arms and held on for life. For once, Claire didn't babble or berate, or even rebuke her for taking off and leaving her in the hospital parking lot. She seemed to recognize her daughter's anguish and so she stood there on the gravel lot above the Leatherwood takeout and rocked her, stroking her hair. Saying nothing at all.

Orson stood beside Nolan and the unmarked car, watching. The girl was pretty torn up, all right. But her black eyes and beat-up hands, and the wounds on her chest that his dad had managed to find out about from a gossipy contact at the hospital, made them both think about domestic abuse and murder. And about the money. There weren't many people who wouldn't kill for that much money. Self-defense? Greed for sure.

"I'll talk to the blonde," Nolan said. "See what I can learn from Nell Stevens's little pal."

"You've always said that sometimes there are benefits to the job," Orson murmured. "And the cute friend looks like one of them."

Nell and Claire sat in the RV together, listening to the reports that were passed up and down the gorge on the radio. Claire had forced her to eat, and when the meal wouldn't stay down, had fixed her a cup of tea and held her hand while she drank. Her mother didn't nag or push her own agenda, as Joe would have said. Not exactly. But her few quiet comments eventually wore Nell down and she consented to talk to the reporter, agreeing to issue a statement. *Issue a statement.* Joe's kinda talk, not hers. But Claire played on Nell's burgeoning worry and guilt to get her on camera, saying she should be thanking the searchers and all the auxiliary helpers, which might not have worked had Nell not been on SARs herself and known how much a simple thank-you meant.

Just before two in the afternoon, in time for the news update on local TV, just before the boaters reached the takeout, Nell, wearing her mother's makeup to cover some of the bruises, emerged from the RV and let the production guy hook her up to a clip-on microphone while standing in front of the RV. It wasn't the on-camera interview that the reporter wanted, but it was all Nell would agree to.

Fidgeting, uncomfortable with the idea of the mic clipped under her shirt, and still unable to speak in more than a whisper, Nell looked at the reporter, Bailey Barnett, with her perfect, bobbed brown hair and her false expression of concern and said, "I appreciate all the help of the volunteer searchers who are giving up their free time. And the park service and the sheriff's deputies and the rescue-squad auxiliary members who are providing food.

"My husband, Joe, tried to rescue me when I was hurt." The tears she had not wanted to spill while on TV fell over her cheeks, burning. Joe was going to tease her unmercifully about that. "And now the good people of several counties are helping to rescue *him*. Thank you." Fingers fumbling, she unclipped the mic, handing it back to Bailey while the reporter was asking her questions she simply couldn't answer.

Waving away the attention, trying not to sob, Nell once again vanished into the RV and the anonymity and safety it offered. Claire made her another cup of tea and Nell stared at the river. Waiting.

From the open doorway, Orson watched his dad. The older cop leaned against the file cabinet in his office and watched the news. The little wife wasn't holding up very well. Her black eyes, even under the makeup, were looking more purple, evidence that the bruises were a couple days old at least, though a doctor he knew had confirmed that the cool weather and cold river water might have slowed the speed of healing.

A little blonde stood behind Nell Stevens. Her mother. Orson had expected an older woman. She must have had Nell when she was ten, because she looked all of thirty.

Without turning around or giving an indication he knew Orson was there, Nolan said, "I'm getting old, Junior. The mother of a twenty-one-year-old looks good to me." He swiveled his head and met Orson's eyes. "You gonna stand in the hall all day?"

"No." But the blonde did look good. All perky and bubbly and full of life. The kind of woman his father favored, a woman not unlike his own mother, who had died shortly after he was born.

"Claire Bartwell answered all my questions without a qualm when I approached her at the Leatherwood Ford. Unlike the wife," Nolan said. "'Course, the mother didn't know I was a cop at the time."

Orson had heard all about that interview on the way up,

and didn't know whether to applaud the girl or convict her. Either way, she was good. "This what you called me off patrol and made me drive two hours for?"

"Yeah, come on in, Junior." Nolan said. "Take a look at all this river crap."

Squatting in front of the desk, he watched as his father laid out the dry suit Nell Stevens had worn, or claimed to be wearing, when she was caught in the strainer.

"It took some doing, but I tracked down the boat, paddle and some of the gear she had on when she made it to shore," Nolan said. "Sorry about taking you away from your first day on patrol, Junior."

Orson half grinned at his father's insincere apology and dropped down, resting his weight on one foot, an elbow on the other knee, his spit-shined black patrol shoes grinding on the grimy office floor. "You're not sorry."

"Nope. I'm not. I need an expert and you're the closest thing to it. What can you tell me about this equipment?"

Orson flicked the dry suit to him and studied the punctures. "These are consistent with being caught in a strainer." He turned the water-repellent kayak skirt over and pulled off several of the upper layers of duct tape so he could examine it too. He lined the skirt up around the dry suit.

"Huh. The skirt fits up that high?" Nolan asked.

"Yeah. These repaired puncture sites in the skirt match up with two in the dry suit. This other one in the dry suit is higher up, in an area of the chest that would have been protected by the PFD. But notice the angle of the tears." Orson stuck a finger through the dry suit. "All at an angle, up, as if a branch wedged up under her vest and caught her chest. She got wounds consistent with that?"

"E.R. doctor says yeah."

"Crap," Orson said. "You check the underside of the tape for fingerprints? If not, you'll have to run them against mine." His dad grunted, unconcerned. Orson pulled the PFD to him and examined the inside of the bright orange Kitty vest, a vest made for women, specially shaped to allow room for the extra padding God gave most females. He pointed. "Scratches are consistent with branches." He pulled the rescue knife from its sheath in the front of the PFD. "You checked it for blood?"

"Clean."

"It's a Gerber. They make several styles of rescue knives." Orson held the blade to the slashes that had opened the dry suit's limbs and torso. "Whatever cut the dry suit looks like it had a few serrations on the blade, maybe up near the haft. See?" He offered the suit and Nolan fingered the ragged spot on the fabric. "This knife's straight. No serrations. So unless she had another knife, she didn't cut up her own suit, except for here. Looks like she cut a strop off. I wonder why." He inspected the vest. "Someone cut the bottom strap. Maybe to get her out of it."

Nolan stood, sat his butt against the desk and gestured to the other equipment. "What else can you tell me?"

Junior looked at the boat. It was a bright yellow and orange Pyrahna 230 Micro Bat. Not new but not beat all to heck either. He turned it over and a dribble of river water ran out. "Scratches indicate it's seen a lot of use, but it's not ready for retirement yet. It's a fast, responsive creek-boat. It can take anything up through a class V if the paddler is any good. It's too small for my tastes, but I like a more stable boat. It'll roll easily, but if a small paddler gets into squir-relly water it'll toss him around like a cork."

"I could carry the wife around under my arm all day and not get tired."

"Sounds painful for her," Orson said. His dad snorted softly. Orson removed the rescue bag and went through the equipment. "Whoever packed the equipment was thorough."

He held the duct tape from the emergency kit up to the light, comparing it to the tape that repaired the holes in the skirt. "Seems to match. You sending it off for comparison?"

"Yeah. If we find a body. Or if we find reason to charge her."

Orson rubbed fingerprint dust off the roll of tape and looked the question at his father. Nolan shrugged. "Collected. Not run. I'll send them in if I need to. Later."

Orson looked at the kayak seat and found a section of hip pad was missing. In its place was a rolled-up section of dry suit. "Here's the missing dry-suit parts." He removed it and compared the knife cuts on that portion to the knife cuts on the dry suit where the girl had cut it. "Definitely two different knives." He found a meal pouch and opened the Ziploc bag, sniffed and quickly closed it. "Looks like she prepared a cold meal and never got a chance to eat it."

"Cold meal?"

"Yeah. Dehydrated food is intended to be prepared with hot water and eaten fresh, but you can eat it cold—it just tastes like crap. Survivalists will put a little water in a meal packet and let it sit to make it soft enough to eat. This one's gone sour. It won't stink a lot but you might want to double bag it."

Orson pulled the sleeping bags out of the boat. They were packed one inside the other, tightly rolled, stuffed into a waterproof bag and tied with bungee cords. He opened the waterproof bag and spread the sleeping bags out on the floor. "If she was caught in a strainer, injured and shocky, her husband might have put one bag inside the other like this and gotten in with her to keep her warm."

"Matches her story," Nolan conceded.

"Or indicates she's very well organized and planned ahead."

Nolan grinned. "Junior, the girl I talked to in the hospital?

Even beat all to heck, she kept her head together. Emotional, but not to the point of hysteria or even confusion. She was sequential with her story, not jumping from event to event, like most people I interview. She's organized. Too organized. Knows her rights. If I get a reason to use county money, I'll send all this to the lab. For now, it's just conjecture."

Orson stood, and his father stood with him. "So, you think maybe she's been planning it, waiting for the right opportunity. The river trip gave it to her." Orson shrugged. "Bust her ass, Pop."

Nolan shook his head. "Not yet. Waiting to see what the SAR turns up. But I didn't call you back just to look at this river crap. I have a job for you, Junior."

Orson didn't like the gleam in his father's eyes. Not one bit.

8

Listening to the searchers' comments on the radio as they were relayed up and down the river, Nell fought tears and lost when they found Joe's kayak and removed it from its securing lines. Her head in her arms at the kitchen table, she heard each report. Waiting. Waiting for any good news. Waiting for them to find Joe. What she heard was information she already knew. The kayak was empty. No supplies. And no Joe nearby, on a rock waiting for help, trapped in a strainer.

No Joe. Not anywhere, alive or...or dead.

One kayaker was assigned to bring the boat in to the takeout, and the team started down the last stretch of the river. It would take a few hours to do a cursory search. There wasn't time to do a full, in-depth search before sunset.

Nell's tears splattered on the kitchen table with tiny taps of sound to form a pool. Her breath shuddered along her throat as if claws ripped at it. She silently begged God, begged him, to let her husband be alive. She knew, in some miniscule rational part of her mind, that she was out of control. She, who never cried. Never prayed. "Please," she whispered. "Please."

Nell felt Claire's cool palm on the back of her neck, stroking and soothing. "It's okay, honey. They'll find him."

Though she heard the lie in her mother's voice, Nell

swiveled in her seat and wrapped her arms around Claire's waist. Her face buried in Claire's stomach, her mother's jeans rough on her tender skin, she wept.

Claire massaged her back and neck as the dammed-up emotions flooded out and away. Her mother murmured softly, "It's okay. You just cry it all out. I'm here, honey. I'm here."

"I can't do this," Nell whispered brokenly. "I can't do it. I *need* Joe back. I need him. I'm not strong like you. I can't do this." She rocked her forehead against her mother. "I can't do it."

Claire's stroking hand slowed and stopped. "I wasn't strong when your father died. I was a mess."

Nell looked up into her mother's face. "You never cried."

"I cried. I cried and cussed and threw things and cried and cussed some more. And I hated him for the longest time." Her pink-lipsticked mouth curled in a sad smile and she brushed Nell's stiff hair back behind an ear. "And even after all that, even after all these years, I still miss the cheatin' son of a gun. Can you believe it?"

Nell laughed, a hiccup of surprise. "No."

Claire waved a hand in the air as if to rub away the negative. "I do. Still. But it was pure torture to live through, him running off with that woman, the church elder's wife, and them getting killed together. All the gossip at church and in town. The whisperin'. The way the newspaper kept on and on with the story and brought it up over and over during that trucker's trial for drunk driving and resisting arrest. It was all I could do to get through each day."

"I didn't know," Nell said, the words hoarse.

"'Course not. I had to protect you. You were mine, all I had left to love and provide for. So I survived. And now you have me to survive for. 'Cause I don't know what I'd do without you." She wiped Nell's face with the pads of her thumbs. "Come on. Lie down a while. You need to rest."

"I can't sleep." Fresh tears ran down her face, stinging like salt in wounds. "I can't. Not until they find Joe."

"I didn't say anything about sleep. I said you should rest. I'll sit with you. And I'll listen to the radio. And if you doze off, I promise to wake you if they find anything. Anything at all. Come on." Claire pulled Nell up. Docile, she followed her mother to the bed. Like a child, she lay down when her mother folded back the sheets and held them for her. They were fresh and cool and smelled of Joe. Instantly, she was asleep.

Orson watched from the shadows as Nolan reached to knock at the door of the motor home. It flung open and the old man stepped back, jerking his hand from the swinging door. He looked up to see those blue eyes. Nell Stevens's mother. Claire. His dad's mouth opened, but no words came out. Orson hid a smile.

The woman stared down from three steps up, sparks flashing. She came down the steps at him, her face flushing red with anger. His dad, who had faced down moonshiners and pot growers and backcountry mountaineers carrying shotguns and a total disregard for the law, stepped back. She walked up to him, shoulders rigid and fire in her eyes, backing him another two steps before he was able to stop his backpedaling progress.

She leaned into him, her chest a fraction of an inch from his, her chin outthrust, her finger pointing. Pale pink nail polish, Orson saw, that matched her lipstick.

"If you think you're gonna wake my daughter, you have another think coming. My girl is asleep, after crying her eyes out. You can just wait. You hear me?"

"I wouldn't think about—I just need to ask—"

"You need to ask nothin'. I know how you cops work." She put her hands on her hips. Orson saw his dad looking at her mouth. "You start out all sweet and nice and asking simple questions and then you lower the boom with some other awful question that says you think somebody's guilty of something. It's a sneak attack, is what it is. Jist like that sneaky way you questioned me about it all without telling me you was a cop. And my Nell is too broke up over Joe to be hurt like that."

"Miz Bartwell, I—"

"I know you got a job to do. I know somebody's gotta ask the hard questions and look for guilt. I know somebody's gotta interrogate, and investigate, and stick his nose into other people's business. Like assuming my girl is guilty of killing her husband and hiding the body. Right?" she demanded. She shoved her chin closer, nearly touching the old man's chest. "Right? That's what you gotta ask?"

Orson was pretty sure his dad had started to sweat. He nodded like he couldn't help himself. He'd probably have agreed that the sky was green if she told him to. Twenty-five years as an investigator questioning the biggest and baddest the streets had to offer, and this little bitty woman... Orson laughed silently. She scared the hell outta him.

"I understand that," she said. "But you gotta understand that I gotta job to do too. And my job is to protect my baby. And if you try to hurt her, if you try asking mean questions jist to see her cry, if you try to make her feel worse than she does now for gettin' hurt and makin' her husband go down a dangerous river alone to get her help, and then not come back from it, I'll scratch out your blasted eyes. I'll cut out your innards and leave your bloody, dead body where only the maggots can find it. And then I'll pray over your dead, bleeding body that the Lord will somehow save your immortal soul, if you really have one. Are we clear?"

"Pretty clear, ma'am."

"Come back later." Claire stomped back up the steps and closed the door in his face.

"Did that little woman just threaten you with blinding, death and maggots?" Orson asked from the shadows. "Isn't it against the law to threaten an officer of the court?"

Nolan looked over at Orson, leaning a shoulder against the side of the RV, arms crossed over his wet suit, ankles crossed. Amused as hell and not hiding it. Nolan shook his head. "Yeah. I think I'm in love."

Orson snorted. "She'd eat you up and spit you out, old man."

"Like I said. I think I'm in love."

"One 'a these days your love of bitchy women is going to get you killed."

"Feisty. Not bitchy."

"You say potato, I say bitchy. But I did notice that she didn't use a single cussword in all that tirade."

"And she did offer to pray for me." Nolan laughed and nodded his head at the river; the two men walked toward the slow-moving water. "You ready to go undercover?"

"I'm ready. But you know for a fact that the more experienced men will say I got this job on your coattails."

"I asked who had river experience. You were the only one, Junior. Get in there and make nice with the kayak search crew. And don't screw up, son."

"Thanks for the vote of confidence," he said wryly.

"You want a pat on the butt, play football." Nolan Lennox turned and walked back to his unmarked car, leaving Orson to join the search team and find out who knew what about Joe Stevens. As lead investigator on the Joseph Stevens case, his dad had bigger fish to fry.

As the shadows lengthened along the Leatherwood Ford Bridge, in the extended dusk that steep valleys and rivers always experience, Nell stood on the shore, hiding beneath a wide-brimmed hat and sunglasses, waiting. Her mother was at her side, with one arm around her waist, body heat a comfort at her back. She wanted to be there when the boaters brought Joe's boat in.

There were four news vans behind them, all with cameras trained on her, one van for each of the competing networks working out of Knoxville, the closest city big enough to have its own TV stations. NBC, CBS, ABC and the local cable van were all present. Nell had seen her own interview on the air before shutting the TV off. She knew how unlikely it was for reporters to get the details right this early in the search, before they found someone—an unnamed source— to give them the skinny. She wasn't interested in hearing their on-air misconceptions and mistakes or their take on the search.

Joe's disappearance had made state news, and some pundits were implying that she had done away with Joe, an implication that should have made Nell furious, but only left her exhausted and more determined than ever not to grant interviews to predatory reporters. After hearing the insinuations on local talk radio, Claire had agreed that they were vultures. She had stepped in to protect her daughter's privacy, telling reporters to stay back or she would shoot them herself, not that Claire owned a gun. Nell leaned in to her mother's body as she stared at the empty water, the current only a ripple.

Near 4:00 p.m., the first kayak came into view, followed by the rest of the small craft and then by the Maravia Ranger raft, Mike sitting up high on the stern of the boat. Nell saw them all, but her eyes were on the red playboat being towed by the kayaker in the middle of the pack. It moved in erratic patterns behind the towboat, the lack of weight making it skitter across the surface of the quiet pool like a water spider.

Playboats were used by extreme kayakers who wanted to take class V rapids, and then do tricks and stunts in them. The responsive little boats required the weight and experience of a skillful paddler inside to track smoothly. Empty, Joe's boat had no grace or style or spirit. Nell had an instant of memory—Joe in the boat, practicing a backflip, his body and boat in the air, upside down, churning water below him, his paddle spinning, a wide grin on his face.

She quivered with reaction. Her husband wasn't dead. He was alive. He had to be. He was too vital, too vibrant to be… to be dead. Tears started to fall again.

Wavering in her tears, the boats scraped onto the shore, hulls rubbing on sand and rounded river rocks. Nell blinked hard and focused solely on her husband's boat. She moved into the shallow water and knelt, one hand out to pull the forty-pound boat close to her. It ground across the surface of the shore, the empty hull hollow-sounding, magnifying the noise like a drum. She ran her hand across the boat.

It was battered, with long scratches along the sides, new gouges where it had impacted rock. Some parts of the top-of-the-line outfitting—the hip pads, and knee braces that Joe had duct taped in for a permanent fit—were missing, leaving only the seat, structured metal bracing and hard plastic.

Nell had seen a lot of boats in her time, many that had taken rapids without a boater. A lot of them had looked like this, the insides partially missing. Wherever Joe had come out, it hadn't been just before the location where she found the small craft. It had happened upriver of the rock that had snagged his boat. Maybe at the top of the El. The boat had taken several drops or been caught in a hole to look this banged up.

Blinking hard, Nell wiped her nose and stood. Silently, she touched the shoulder of the kayaker who had brought the boat in. It was Harvey, one of the guides who had made the trip up from the Pigeon to help in the search. His beard was beaded with river water, his hazel-gray eyes not meeting hers. His shoulder was cold through the dry suit he wore.

"Thank you for bringing Joe's boat in, Harvey."

He shook his head, staring across the river. "Shouldn't 'a happened," he mumbled.

Nell laughed, a bleep of pain that she quickly smothered in the crook of her elbow, covering her mouth and chin. Her hand tightened on his arm as Joe's image fluttered in her grief. "No. It shouldn't have. If I'd seen the strainer in time, Joe wouldn't be hurt somewhere on the river. He'd be here right now."

Harvey slanted his eyes at her, his expression guarded and grieving. Nell stepped back. Realized that he believed Joe was dead. He believed it completely. In his mind there was no hope for Joe. None at all.

Nell dropped her hand as if his touch burned her.

Picking up his boat and equipment as if the forty-pound kayak weighed nothing, Harvey walked off. Horrified, Nell watched him walk away.

His helmet beneath one elbow, paddle to the side, Mike approached and hugged her, seeming not to notice her unyielding body or the tremors that coursed through her. He said, "We're going back out soon as we can get up to the confluence put-in. We've got enough time to do a good search above and along the shores of the Long Pool. I'll drive your RV and you ride with Claire."

A freckled, redheaded reporter jammed a microphone beneath Mike's chin. "Are you Jedi Mike?" he asked, youthful exuberance in his tone.

Another reporter, a petite brunette, shoved a mic in close as well and said, "Do you think the missing kayaker is still alive?"

Claire pulled Nell away from the gathering throng of

cameras and reporters. It was obvious that this new group didn't know who Nell was. Not yet. The bob-haired reporter from the morning, Bailey something, was not with this crew.

A third reporter elbowed past them and jogged to Mike, asking, "What are the feelings of the searchers? Are you any closer to finding the missing man?"

Contempt on his face, Mike picked up Joe's boat and angled away, leaving the path open for Nell and Claire to escape. He caught Nell's eyes and jerked his head at Claire's car, a clear order to get inside. Turning to the water, he shouted, "Elton! Let's get the boats loaded up. Daylight's wasting."

Walking backward, Nell saw the first reporter pivot in front of Mike, blocking his way. "Can you tell us what's going on, out on the water?" the guy asked. "Have you seen any evidence of the missing boater?"

Mike rounded on the hapless reporters and fixed them all with a furious glare. "We're busting our humps, is what's going on out on the river. Why don't you get your lazy asses out there and help the hikers instead of getting in the way and asking damn-fool questions?" The reporters seemed to skitter into a group, as if seeking safety in numbers from the irate man.

Elton stepped in and softly said, "Maybe I can help?" The reporters ganged up around him and threw questions at him fast and furiously while Mike and the other searchers and on-lookers loaded up the boats. Still walking backward, Nell watched as Mike loaded Joe's boat with the others and tied it down with twine in a complicated naval knot. She wanted the boat with her. But she knew Mike would take care of it.

Nell slid into the passenger seat, and Claire started the little red car, pulling out while they were still buckling their seat belts. Silent, they drove from the takeout. Claire shot her a glance once the car reached the secondary road and said,

"You're still mad at me for getting that reporter to come by this morning, aren't you?"

Nell sighed and rubbed the bruised spot on her temple. It wasn't as painful as it had been, the headache kept at bay by constant use of Tylenol and ibuprofen. "Not mad, Claire. It's just that I've seen reporters on a bad SAR. I know how they get. They'll give me until tomorrow before the innuendos turn into bald accusations." She laid her head against the molded headrest.

"They're gonna accuse you of killing Joe and dumping him in the river. That what you're saying?"

Nell laughed, the tone desolate. "Yeah, Mama. That's what I'm saying."

As if Nell's use of the word *Mama* had been a shock to her, Claire fell silent and concentrated on driving. If Nell'd had the energy, she'd have worried about the look of concentration on her mother's face. It always presaged trouble ahead or guilt for something already done.

The radio squelched all afternoon, comments and orders and reports passed up and down the river. The hikers were in constant communication with the kayakers, checking around each boulder, inspecting downed trees with limbs in water and roots on land. In the current, the most experienced rescue volunteers checked out eddies that looked wrong. Eddies that might have been caused by a body in the water.

Mike and his paddlers stabilized the Ranger raft with ropes attached to trees onshore, securing it over the zigzag current at the base of the Long Pool. Held in place, they dragged the bottom with a grappling hook, trying to snag whatever was down there, affecting the current. Nell, sitting in the RV, was so tense her stomach was in knots, a hot pain just below her breastbone. The thought of food still made her

sick to the stomach and she turned down the offer of a bowl
of soup from her mother and hot dogs from the rescue
squad's family members who kept the hospitality wagon
open and running.

By 6:00 p.m., the searchers had checked every rock and
bit of shoreline upstream of the Long Pool and around it.
Every strainer had been pulled from the river. Every eddy
that looked wrong had been dredged. All were caused by
trees or rocks that had shifted. Not by a body. They had me-
thodically searched every possible location for Joe. And for
his body.

The shorelines farther downstream, in the deepest part of
the canyon, would take another twelve hours or more to
search as thoroughly. The call came over the radio to head
in. It was impossible to make it back upstream. Most of the
kayakers had brought overnight gear, but it wasn't with them
on the river where they could camp overnight; they had to
make it to the takeout or the next support site at the O & W
Bridge by sunset, get carted back to their gear and set up
camp before total dark. They had less than two hours.

Nell waited for the searchers at the put-in of the confluence of Clear Creek and the New River, sitting in the passenger chair of the RV cab, which Mike had brought in
before he hit the water again. She watched the activity
between the cracks of the closed RV curtains, kneading her
fingers in anxiety.

The put-in here, midway down the gorge, was a rough,
unsophisticated version of the Burnt Mill Bridge put-in. It
sported a bumpy, one-lane road that curled midway down
from the plateau at the top, to the footpath that led the rest
of the way down to the river. The so-called camping area was
a gravel loop of the road. No picnic tables. No Port-a-Potties.
Nothing but a ring of trees and several fire pits. The walk to

the river was a steep, winding, downhill path on loose gravel, sandstone rock and trail-hard dirt.

The press vans came and went, but only one or two reporters and cameramen took the long walk down to the water for footage. The auxiliary rescue squad showed up about six and parked their van on the highest ground at the top of the circle. One woman lit a camp stove and started coffee. Another began to open buckets of donated Kentucky Fried Chicken. Together they set out coolers full of drinks and heated all the fixin's. The smell of chicken laced the air like a greasy but delicious perfume.

The hikers dribbled in by twos and threes, rubbing aching calves and stretching, some trekking to the river to soak tired feet in the cold water and take sponge baths. Others grabbed a chicken leg and took off for home, eating while driving away. From here, the sun was a brilliant globe dropping below the western hills, throwing long shadows across the campsite.

There was a gold glow to the evening air when the kayakers roared up in Mike's big SUV, the boats bouncing behind on his trailer. At the sight, the chief auxiliary lady rang a big bell and started dishing up food. Nell watched from the cab, unmoving.

"You should go eat with the searchers," Claire said at her shoulder. Her mother had been appearing there often, not touching, not saying much, just being there. Outside, more cars and trucks pulled up as searchers returned to the nearest support site for dinner.

"Nah," Nell said, leaning toward the curtain cracks. "I'm fine."

"You should go eat with the searchers," Claire said, an unaccustomed resolve in her voice. "Not for you. For them."

Nell looked at her mother. Claire wasn't usually the "buck up and smile" kind of woman, but Nell knew she was right, and by the glint in her eyes, she wasn't taking no for an answer. Fingers like steel, she tugged Nell to her feet and pushed her out the RV door toward the rescue food van. "Go. Tell them you appreciate all the work and the food and the help. Sit with them. Eat with them. It's only right."

Nell tucked her hands into her jeans pockets and stopped in a shadow, watching. There were no showers at the put-in. No running water. For toilets, the hikers and boaters made do with shovels and trips into the forest, and since everyone stank of sweat and river, who cared? The smells of body odor and chicken and coffee filled the evening air. In the center of the circle, someone lit a bonfire of deadwood from the nearby woods, and the sting of smoke and kerosene added to the miasma. Someone else brought out a keg of beer to massed whoops and cheers and applause. The air chilled quickly now that the sun was down, and Nell wished she had pulled on a sweatshirt or sweater. A cool breeze played with the unprotected skin of her neck and face. An owl called, seven notes of rhythmic hooting, claiming territory.

The scene was powerful. Every smell, every sound, every sight was intense, jarring, as if her mind was on overdrive, glaring with intensity.

Mike spotted her in the shadows and handed Nell a plate of food and a huge foam cup of sweet tea. "Sit and eat. You look like shit," he said.

Nell choked in laughter with the same despairing tone her voice had held all day. She knew she sounded broken. Shattered. And that wasn't fair to the people around her. They were fighting for Joe. If they found him, injured, in the most dangerous place possible, they would risk life and limb to save him. She owed it to them to be there for them tonight.

She took a deep, steadying breath and drank a long draft of tea. It fell down her esophagus, cold and sweet. Hunger stirred, and her mouth watered at the scent of KFC. She took another breath, feeling it fill her lungs. The way she filled her lungs before a challenging run on a class IV and V river. Tears wanted to fall and she forced them down. Not tonight. Not in front of these people, her friends.

Claire brought her a folding chair from storage in the RV undercarriage, and Mike placed it upwind of the fire. Turtle Tom put a log beside her and sat close, silent, eating. Harvey and RiverAnn sat across the fire, touching often. Stewart and Hamp, his Furman U. hat glowing in the firelight, sat near the keg. Natch.

Someone brought out a guitar and several people started setting up tents. As on many such SARs, they were going to spend the night on the river.

A woman Nell didn't know brought her a sliver of coated, waterproofed neoprene. "It's from your strainer," she said, putting the two inch by quarter inch strip into Nell's palm. Nell recognized the scrap from her dry suit and closed her fingers on it. She thanked the woman, blinking away tears. The guitarist started playing an old Doobie Brothers song. The smell of beer wafted on the air. In the background, the auxiliary-support women cleaned up the KFC boxes and closed the van, the doors loud in the night. The engine started and the van pulled out, lights bouncing into the trees, crawling the treacherous hill up out of the river gorge.

Dark night fell and bright stars filled the sky between trees overhead. Two owls hooted back and forth. Sporadic conversation around the fire hit on politics and religion without creating a ruckus, then moved on to a fantasy series someone was reading. Eventually the talk turned to the searchers' day, of what went wrong, of who had to swim because they couldn't do an Eskimo roll, of the big water and the difficulty in taking the gnarly drops, of who built an altar of stones in Joe's honor, of who had a new boat and how it reacted to the water. Of…of everything. The voices ran together in a smoky haze. Nell smelled marijuana, cigarettes, beer and chicken, and heard laughter and the occasional song and the rarer sound of two lovers in the night.

"It was rad, man. Totally rad. I did a gainer without thinking about it."

"Not today, I hope," Elton said, taking the moment to remind everyone, "No playing on the river during the search."

"Not today. On the Green, Elton. Relax, man."

"I did a mobius in that boat, but it was hell on the toes. I traded it in on an old school. A Perception Arc-ProLine."

"I heard Perceptions started using cheap plastic."

"That's why I went with a nineties version. Got it on eBay, cheap. Beat all to heck, but worth it to protect my feet. They were getting boogered up in the playboat. If you know what you're doing you can stand a ProLine straight up on its tail."

"I got a ProLine. Haven't used it in years. Maybe I'll try it tomorrow."

"Sammy got a new tat. A lion across her shoulder, with the claws up under her boob."

"Wanna see it?" Sammy asked to a chorus of wolf whistles. Pulling up her shirt, she showed the lion on her back. When the guys wanted to see the tail she shook her finger at them and said, "That's for my soon-to-be-hubby and for him alone."

"Marry me, baby," a voice shouted. Everyone laughed.

"You see that tree they pulled outta the Long Pool? Looked like something prehistoric."

"I did a fakie once. Busted my head on a rock. Took twenty stitches."

"I knocked out my front teeth doing that, dude. Got a mouthful a porcelain, playing on the Gauley."

"I busted my arm and collarbone on that river. See this lump?"

"You see that dead deer they pulled outta the strainer at the Hole? Musta been a hunnerd and ninety pounds. 'Course it was bloated up pretty bad."

"I ran the Upper Pigeon after Ivan."

"You're shittin' me."

"Some dude got a video of it up on YouTube. I'm taking a class III that had so much water it was a class V. It was totally radical, man, I'm telling ya."

"You're crazy dude. I saw what that water did to the riverbank. Took it right out up to thirty feet high."

"I busted a good boat on the Ocoee after Ivan. A nine-hundred-dollar Hoss. Opened it up on a rock like a can o' sardines. Had to swim nearly a mile midway after dam three. Lost a good paddle too."

"Fish story!" someone shouted.

"A mile, my ass! You barely went over a two-ledge."

"Busted my leg."

"Getting out of your boat. 'Cause you couldn't roll in fast water."

Nell began to relax. River talk. BS from the word go. You could believe one in three claims, and then only half of that one. It was home. She slumped down in her folding chair and relaxed. The guitar player started on old Negro spirituals. "Swing Low, Sweet Chariot" segued into "Sweet Little Jesus Boy." Nell ate chicken and kept it down, and drank tea and sang along when the guitarist played "Rocky Raccoon." She wiped away tears, because Joe wasn't with her. And she had a bad feeling that he never would be again.

9

Claire had turned on the water heater, and made Nell shower and wash her hair, claiming she stank as badly as the searchers. Since she hadn't showered at the hospital, her mother was probably right. RVs didn't carry a lot of water, and the waste tanks were small, but every shower head came with a little slide-switch that cut off the water temporarily, like a garden-hose head. Then, with a flip of the switch, the water would flow again at the set temperature. A camper could wet down, stop the water, soap and shampoo, flip on the water and rinse with minimal water use. Nell felt better after washing away the river, sweat and hours of worry-stink.

There wasn't enough water to offer all the searchers a shower, which made Nell feel guilty. Again. She wondered how much money she had in her account and if she could afford to pay for a hotel room where all the out-of-towners could get clean once a day. But she didn't know where the closest hotel was. Something to worry about tomorrow.

When Nell stepped out of the shower, Claire had made the dinette into a bed and spread the extra sheets and a blanket over the lumps of the cushions. It looked like her mother was staying in the RV tonight. It looked like a miserable way to sleep. Nell raised the queen mattress of the bed in back, revealing the storage beneath, and pulled out an inflatable mattress topper.

"Hallelujah," Claire said, stripping the sheets back off and plugging in the mattress pump's power cord. "I was seeing a month in the chiropractor's office and bills up the wazzoo."

"Who's keeping the shop while you're here?" Nell asked, belatedly remembering Cuts in Style, her mother's three-person hair and nail salon. "And Butchie," she added, asking about her mother's ferocious, six-pound yapper-dog.

"Butchie's staying at the shop. The girls are feeding him, and the doggie door lets him go out when he needs to." Claire unrolled the mattress and turned on the air pump. The small motor chugged and she raised her voice to be heard over both it and the generator. "Betha and Ronnie can hold down the shop for a few days while I take care of my baby." Betha and Ronnie were the other stylist and the nail tech at the shop, and Claire's best gal pals.

"Thank God for the cell signal out on the secondary road," Claire said. "I called and rearranged my appointments for the next couple days, moving 'em into Saturday and next week. I'll bust my butt gettin' it all done, but my clients understand. Family comes first."

Nell touched her mother's shoulder, uncertain, feeling confused. Claire looked at her, nearly eye to eye. It was an unaccustomed angle, and Nell realized she hadn't stood close to her mother and really looked at her in years. Not since her father… Nell watched, seeming to stand outside herself, as her mother read her confusion, her hesitation. Claire dropped the mattress and reached out her arms.

Nell stepped into her mother's embrace, remembering all the times today that Claire had been there, comforting, hugging, offering a kind word. When did her mother become so…nice? Or maybe she had always been nice and Nell had held her at arm's length.

Blaming her for her father's betrayal. Oh, yeah. Blame. Nell held her mother, feeling the sturdy bones and the strong muscles of the tiny woman. Knowing that she was built like this too. She had gotten her height and shape and strength from her mother and not much of anything but heartache from her charming, outgoing, lying, cheating father, the man she loved more than life itself, and who had gone off and gotten himself killed.

It wasn't her mother's fault he left his wife and child and slipped away to sleep with another woman. It wasn't her fault their car was T-boned by an eighteen-wheeler pulling across the highway from a beer joint to a truck stop to allow the driver to sleep off a drunk. Not Claire's fault. And not her own fault, either.

Nell laid her head on her mother's shoulder. "Thank you."

Claire patted her back and eased away. "Thank you for letting me be here."

"I've been a bitch, haven't I? Since Dad died." Nell felt her mother inhale, could almost feel her think about her answer.

"You were hurt. I understood. Now. Help me get this mattress inflated so my poor ol' back can survive the night. And if you got an extra pillow, I'd appreciate it."

"You can have mine. I'll sleep on Joe's."

"Of course you will, Nellie baby. Of course you will."

Orson watched the RV until the generator was turned off and the lights went out, then zipped the tent flap closed and curled on his side. The October night held a sting of cold and he cupped a hand around his nose to warm the air. He considered what he had seen of the girl during the evening.

Little-bitty thing. All muscle, not much in the way of curves. Crying a lot. Strong willed. Stubborn and opinionated—he knew that from his old man, and saw evidence of it when she carried her foam cup to the garbage can, refusing to let someone else do it. Knew it from the look she gave a hiker she saw drop a KFC box on the ground. The guy was twice her size and yet he mumbled his apologies and picked up the box, took it to the fire and burned it with the others. She was a greenie, but most people who lived on the river were environmentally conscious. Didn't mean she wasn't a killer, too.

But when she spoke of Joe, she spoke in the present tense. As if he were alive, hurt somewhere. Killers often slipped and used past tense, because they knew the victim was dead. He had started out thinking she had probably killed Joseph Stevens. Now he wasn't so sure. He had seen photos of Joe. He was a big guy, a little over six feet, maybe one-ninety. If she'd killed him, it was either a crime of passion or she had surprised him. He'd have to ask the old man if she owned a weapon. Tomorrow, he'd keep close to her on the water. Word from Jedi was, she might be joining the searchers on the dangerous lower section of the river. Jake's Hole. He'd see then what she was capable of.

A faint gray light of dawn was tiptoeing through the window blinds when Nell stretched hard and rotated her body out of bed. Guilt sat on her like a river rock, guilt that she had slept a few hours in a comfortable bed while Joe was out there, hurt, sleeping on the shore or on a rock. Unconscious. Bleeding. She had pushed the fears of him being dead deep inside during the wakeful hours of the night. He was alive. She knew it. He had to be. She couldn't live any other way, not without him.

Nell rose and washed at the bathroom sink, using the tepid water left over in the hot-water tank from the night before, moving quietly. Claire slept like a rock and she wouldn't wake without a good shaking, but Nell wasn't taking chances. Her mother would surely try to keep her off the water today, and Nell couldn't survive another day of inaction.

Her dry suit gone, she pulled on a wet suit, smeared 40 SPF sunscreen on all her exposed flesh, and made coffee for Claire. Nell was halfway out the door before she remembered she didn't have a boat, a PFD, a skirt or a paddle.

She looked out over the sleeping camp in dismay. Tents and kayaks were in haphazard spots. Coolers locked against bears were scattered all over. Several campers were up already, making their way to the bushes and back, scratching, checking over boats and equipment, yawing, turning on camp stoves for coffee or tea. Others were struggling out of tents. Others were still snoring. Smoke from the ashes of the bonfire wafted across the camp. Birds called, filling the air with morning song.

Nell quietly shut the door to the RV, walked across to Mike's SUV and tapped on the window. A moment later Mike rolled it down and yawned at her, his sleep-creased, sun-furrowed skin pulling, blinking blearily. "Morning, babe. You got coffee?"

"I started a pot in the RV. You got a boat and equipment I can borrow today?"

Mike opened the door and crawled from the vehicle. Nell spotted the bed he had made in the back, an inflatable mattress big enough for two. Another form moved weakly on it and groaned. Mike was between wife number two and three. Looked like someone might be aiming to fill the breach; whoever she was, she pulled a blanket over her head before Nell could identify her.

Standing barefoot on the gravel, Mike stretched and yawned again, taking in the sky and the river nearby. "I got an extra PFD we can make work, but no boat or skirt. You'll have to ride in the raft with me."

"I want a kayak."

"I want to win the lottery but I ain't seen no flying horses lately. But—" he pointed away from the water at the entrance of the put-in "—that might help." A pickup truck was grinding its way down the steep slope with a bright yellow and orange kayak sticking out of the back. Nell's boat. Even in the dim light, she recognized the cop who had questioned her in the hospital. She couldn't help but be surprised, not at seeing him but at seeing her boat. It was evidence, wasn't it? Evidence of her killing Joe? The early-morning chill worked its way beneath her wet suit. She took a breath to calm her skittery nerves.

Mike striding behind her, Nell paced over to the pickup. "Detective." She nodded at him.

"Miz Stevens. Jedi Mike." He rested an arm along the window opening. "I brought your boat back."

"Why?" Mike asked. "You got a missing husband, no body, lots of possibilities for foul play." Nell flinched, her false calm vanishing. Mike put a hand on her shoulder. Nell sucked air hard, the sound labored in the cold, and tried to find her composure. The cop watched her, eyes squinting in the sunrise. "So, why are you giving her back the boat?" Mike finished.

"I heard she wanted to go on the water today. Thought if she had the boat and her paddle, it might make it easier. Though I'm keeping the skirt, the emergency equipment, and the lifejacket."

"You got a spy in the searchers?" Mike asked, tone accusing.

The detective tilted his head, amused. "There's concerned citizens everywhere."

"And you think if you made it easier for her to go on the water, she'd take you right to the body."

Nell jerked again in reaction and wrenched out from beneath Mike's hand, rounding on him fast. "If you think Joe's dead, maybe you should just stay onshore with the auxiliary." She stepped to the back of the pickup and dropped the tailgate. The heavy metal and the boat bounced, the clangs and thuds echoing. One-handed, she lifted the forty-pound boat and slung it high, propping the cockpit over a shoulder. She grabbed her paddle with the other hand and raised a knee to slam the tailgate.

"Hey, people," she shouted over the camp. "Get your butts in gear and get on the water. Time's wasting!" Behind her, she heard Mike sigh, a long-suffering sound. She ignored it and shouted again. "And while you're at it, I need a small-size tunnel skirt. Anybody got extra?"

"Feisty, ain't she?" Nell heard the cop ask.

"You got no idea. She's good people. She didn't hurt her husband," Mike said, defending her.

Nell warmed and felt some of her anger leech away.

"Good people can kill in a moment of passion," the cop said.

Nell hunched her shoulders, though with the boat and paddle, no one could tell.

"RiverAnn's got a skirt," Turtle Tom shouted, sticking his head out of his tent. "But I'm not going on the water till I've had breakfast."

"Wimp!" someone shouted from the woods. Other searchers laughed and Tom laughed with them.

"Cold cereal and fruit are ready now," a woman shouted, "and Hardee's has offered to bring hot breakfast for every-body. But it'll be another half hour."

Nell looked around for RiverAnn. Instead, she saw Hamp, carrying a skirt across the lot, walking gingerly on the gravel, his bare feet pale and gangly. He shivered in the morning chill, wearing only a pair of baggy shorts and T-shirt. "She said you can use her old one," he said, holding the skirt out.

Nell took the river gear and scanned the area for RiverAnn. When she saw the girl standing near a tent she waved. "Thanks," she shouted.

Ann waved back. "Anytime. I'm too fat to wear my small stuff right now anywho."

Nell didn't quite know how to reply and settled on repeating her original thanks. Back at Mike's SUV, she opened the door to find the vehicle empty. Mike's nighttime cohort was gone. Nell picked up his extra vest and tried it on. It wasn't perfect, but it would do in a pinch. A quick glance at the elastic, neoprene skirt showed it was a fit for the boat and her waistline. "I'm good to go," Nell said to no one.

To make up to Mike for her quick tongue, Nell went to the RV and poured an insulated mug of coffee. She shook Claire awake and put a cup in her hand too, leaving only after her mother actually opened her eyes and sipped. Claire pointed to a brown paper sack near the door, which Nell stuck under her arm, unopened. Back outside, Mike was staring at the cop's pickup as it bumped into the road. "Sorry," she said, handing him the mug.

"Coffee cures a lotta insults," he said.

He looked her over before gazing out across the campsite. There was significant activity around the clearing. Tents coming down, someone taking a leak on the smoking coals. Nell heard Mike sigh again and she managed a smile. "River rats," he complained.

"They gotta put out the fire somehow," she said.

"When your mom comes out, at least pretend to be horrified, okay? She already hates my guts for teaching you to kayak and turning you into a tomboy. If she discovers I've exposed you—pardon the play on words—" he gestured to the dribbler "—to such immoral activity she'll never forgive me."

"Sorry." Nell made a fist and socked his arm gently. "I suck at pretending."

"Yeah. I know. It's one reason why I like you so much." Mike looked her up and down, considering. "You know we probably got a spy for the cops in the group, don't you?"

Nell faced him solidly. "I didn't kill Joe. Which is what the spy will find out when we find Joe alive. So it doesn't matter."

Mike sipped his coffee, watching her over the rim, steam billowing up into his eyes. "Good point," he said at last. "Breakfast is here early." He nodded at the van bumping down the access lane. "Eat, pack plenty of water and snacks, and get your boat loaded up on the trailer. I got an ATV coming to tote the boats down to the river. Save us the risk of someone twisting an ankle."

"Smart," Nell said.

Mike ruffled her hair. "Suck-up."

Nell ducked her head to hide a smile. "Trying to make up for being a bitch."

"Nothing to make up for. You take care of yourself out on the water today. It's gonna be hard, dangerous and long."

Nell nodded, dropped the sack Claire had pointed at into her boat and went to help with the food. Today was the day they would find Joe.

An hour later, Nell was standing at the bottom of the gorge at the confluence of Clear Creek and New River. Though not as high as the day she and Joe had barreled through it from the easy-peasy section of the Clear, the water was still big, as creeks upstream poured storm runoff into the chasm. The eddy where the two streams met was nearly a foot high, a twenty-foot-long churn of white water. A whirlpool swirled with flotsam at the put-in. And the bus-size rocks along shore were wet at least twenty-four inches higher, evidence of the recent bigger flow.

"You ran this when it was two feet higher?"

Nell turned and saw Turtle Tom, his tattoos bright and fresh looking, the buxom girl on his biceps looking perky. She gave him a one-armed hug and said, "Yeah. You know

Joe. A certifiable creek-running nut. He's decided to run every creek and river in the plateau."

Tom snorted and looked away, his long eyelashes catching the rays of the rising sun. "Guy's one of a kind, all right." But his tone was guarded, as if he really wanted to speak in the past tense.

Before the silence stretched into an uncomfortable length, an ATV toting a trailer bounced down from the foot trail, loaded with supplies. They both turned and looked, not watching each other. "Amazing, though, what you don't know about a person," Tom said, his voice ruminating. "Even after you been with 'em a while." The ATV skidded to a stop, and paddlers from all over trotted over to it. "Bet all the stuff on the news was a shocker," Turtle Tom said.

"I don't listen to the news."

"Smart. Bunch a crap, most of it."

Nell looked up, suddenly hearing Tom's comment. "Shocker?"

A whistle blew, sharp and piercing, Elton calling them together. Turtle Tom lifted two fingers in a casual wave and trotted off without answering. Briefly, Nell thought about returning to the RV to listen to the radio, but Elton raised his arm and, with a sweep, gathered them all close for instructions.

Feeling a new stirring of unease, Nell joined the small crowd.

10

Hanging back, Nell watched as the first kayaks took the Double Falls, the roar so intense that they used hand and paddle signals to indicate who was going where and when. The rapid was composed of a complex boulder field that hid the river from view, not allowing a boater to see the water ahead or to gauge the drops in advance. From upriver, the boulders made any paddlers downstream disappear from view.

Elton had positioned rescue guides on top of boulders with throw ropes, should someone have to swim. If a boater had to do a wet exit on the Double, they might need a hand to avoid the undercut rocks wanting to pull them under.

The two lead paddlers fanned out above the falls, searching the banks, studying each ledge and undercut rock, looking for places where Joe might have holed up if injured, or washed up if unconscious, or where a body could be hidden. Two other kayakers took the cheat, their creek boats and small body weight allowing them to make it through the trickle of water left from the storm. Nell recognized the woman who had given her the sliver of dry suit and lifted her paddle in greeting. The woman waved back just before she disappeared behind rock. Nell didn't want to see the cheat—the place where she had condemned her husband to injury and…and going missing.

A minute after the first four kayaks vanished from view, the next two boaters took the Double, automatically keeping a reasonable space between each boat and an eye on each other for safety. And then it was boat number seven's turn. Nell took the center line of the falls, keeping one blade or the other of her paddle in the water, bracing often as the churn banged her boat against rocks before the river was drawn together in a rush, deepening between the narrowing riverbanks and the house-size rocks that marked the start of the Double. The snarl of water was a physical vibration through her boat. She hit the first big drop. The water swirled tightly, sliding down hard over a long drop. Still running big water, it was a slamming run, but she handled the white water efficiently, guiding the yellow and orange boat with her lower body.

She hit the curling wave at the bottom, her boat cutting through the splash, disappearing totally and resurfacing after a sharp upward thrust of her knees, water in her eyes and up under her unfamiliar helmet. She hit the bottom of the second drop, compensating with a hard brace as her boat flipped halfway over, and she was past the Double.

The sun, pallid and weak, nested in the treetops just above the eastern horizon, teasing with undelivered heat. In the wet suit, Nell was drenched to the skin, the cold stabbing like knives. The skin of her hands whitened and puckered on the lightweight paddle. She was breathing deeply with exertion, and felt a measure of the familiar fear return. Joe was somewhere ahead. And, likely, a dangerous rescue.

She was tiring faster than expected, her energy draining as she maneuvered her boat out of the current, into an eddy and still water. A concussion took a lot out of a person. That and the lack of sleep, lack of food, dehydration and worry. Safe, at the bottom of the falls, watching the other kayakers appear from the rapid, she popped her skirt and drank half a bottle of water, sitting in the sun for its weak heat.

Drinking, breathing deeply, Nell made herself turn and look up the bank at the small area where Joe had left her, noting that she couldn't see atop the flat place where she had awakened. Alone.

Elton bumped her boat with his. "This where he left you?" he asked over the sound of the water.

Without looking at him she nodded and pointed. "That flat area there."

Elton drew his boat to the shallows and popped his skirt, pulling the kayak up the shore after him. One of the Perception Arcs followed, the paddler beaching his boat and climbing up the rocks. They were looking for any clue to Joe's whereabouts.

Elton put his head close to the other man's and they nodded, gestured at the bluff rising from the river and walked the small space itself. They squatted and all but the tops of their heads disappeared. Nell turned her boat away from the men and stared upstream, over the Double.

Turtle Tom guided his mustard-yellow Liquid Logic kayak close and looked Nell over. "You okay?" he asked, voice pitched to rise above the falls.

Nell nodded, knowing her expression was giving away more than she wanted.

"You need anything, you holler. I'm here for you." When she nodded again, Tom swept and changed direction. As he moved, the sunlight caught the brown of his eyes and added a blue note. Tom was a pretty man, even with all the tats, and Nell knew he was much more than the poor, undereducated river guide he appeared. Tom came from money, enough that he could live anywhere and any way he wanted. Trust-fund money. House-in-the-Hamptons money. Ivy-League-schools-and-trips-abroad money. Not a fact he shared with the other guides, but one he had told Joe and her when they opened the shop.

"Thanks," Nell said to his back, feeling a bit of her unacknowledged loneliness fade. Waiting in the still water at the side of the small pool, she watched the kayakers paddle around, searching the banks. There were more of them today, eleven in all. The initial plan was for some of the paddlers to stay on the upper section of the run, especially at the Long Pool, checking again in areas that had been dredged yesterday, while the larger group went on downriver to the Narrows. Earlier she had overheard a kayaker say that they were there to "see if anything interesting floated to the surface."

Mike had shot the guy a nasty look, which Nell appreciated on one level, but if the searchers had to watch their mouths because of her, it would make for a long day. Mike had backed off when she shook her head at him, but she knew his protective instincts were likely to pop up again.

The Ranger raft, with the same four people in it as yesterday, came over the Double Falls, last craft in the search, drenching everyone in the raft and eliciting a few yodeling yells. Mike steered the craft toward her and bumped it against a small rock to stop its motion. The little pool was only a few yards long and the current through the middle was swift. With a draw stroke, Nell eased into a cleft between rocks, making room for the raft.

"Joe isn't here," Nell shouted to Mike over the water's roar as the raft drifted closer. "He had to come out after the Double."

Mike nodded and hollered back, "I know. But it's smart to check everywhere, and Elton isn't going to let us miss anything." The raft bumped against her kayak. "You okay?" he asked now that he was closer. "Headache?"

The other three in the raft looked at her with concern. "I'm fine," Nell said, hearing the impatience in her voice.

"You better be," he said. "Your mother chased me down

before we left and tried to tear me a new one for letting you on the river." He touched his helmet in a salute and steered the raft in a half circle, watching the boaters.

When the kayakers completed a thorough search of the small pool, Elton whistled to let them know it was time for the Washing Machine and the El. Watching the six boaters in front of her start the run, Nell screwed the top back on the water bottle before resecuring it in the boat. She bent forward, stretching RiverAnn's skirt back in place.

There was a lot of give-and-take on the water in a paddling group, even in a search and rescue operation. Everyone tended to change position a bit, all but the team leader who stayed at point, in front, and Mike in the rear. Between them, Elton and Mike kept track of every boat. Nell watched the sixth paddler in front of her disappear and took her turn.

With a draw and sweep stroke of her paddle, she turned upstream, reading the water. Deftly, she stroked into the eddy, leaning downstream as the current caught her and whipped her boat around. Using powerful forward strokes, she headed toward the Washing Machine, positioning herself among the other kayaks so they didn't get in each other's way.

The initial drop was turbulent, the river roiling and dipping like a living thing. The water level was lower today, making the long line of class IIs sharper and tighter. There was less recoil, less big water, but it was still bigger water than most of the paddlers had ever taken here. Unlike dam-fed rivers, which maintained the river flow at each release to make power, rain-fed rivers give a different ride every day. A boater could run the same river over and over again and still have things to learn about it.

Nell's little boat took the rapids with a steady hard bounce, jarring her, making her glad she had popped two ibuprofen at breakfast and tucked another two in a Ziploc baggie for later. The headache she had nursed was still a shadow on her brain, reminding her she had been injured, that her she really shouldn't be on the water today. Reminders she steadfastly pushed into the back of her brain with all the other stuff she could think about later, after they found Joe.

There wasn't much in the way of a resting spot after the Washing Machine, but kayakers ferried through the current and checked banks and around the bigger rocks. One guy secured his boat, got out and looked into a narrow cleft that was currently above the waterline. Nell searched the shores with her eyes, probing for any sign of Joe or his equipment. She didn't search below the water. He wasn't there. He couldn't be.

The water felt even colder than it had when she was feverish, only two days past, and Nell shivered, backpaddling to keep in place in the mass of boaters stretched out along the river. Several times she felt she was being watched and looked around, but no one was looking at her. Above her, on rocks, two paddlers with rescue ropes were scrambling up the rocks, just in case, their boats secured and bobbing in the eddy.

At Elton's whistle, the six boaters in front of her sped toward the El. One at a time, their kayaks swept forward and were seized by the current, then plummeted and sluiced through the difficult run.

From behind, she saw each paddler study the shoreline and rocks as they sped past. One boater did a hard river-right turn, running his boat totally out of the rapid and up onto a flat rock to inspect a bit of shore not visible from the water.

Her heart squeezed painfully, waiting as he poked something with his paddle, her breath tight with hope. And tumbled hard when he thrust a hand against the stone, pushing back into the river, tears of disappointment gathering, and she forced them down, blinking and swallowing. Not now. Later. She could cry later.

Hamp tapped her boat with a paddle, and gave her a thumbs-up. Though Nell couldn't hear him, she read the guy's lips through his wispy beard. "We'll find him." Nell nodded, and he added, "Sweet run, girl." But a pain was growing in her chest, so tight she thought she might explode.

When Hamp dropped from sight over the ledge, Nell drove her small boat into position in the current. Busy watching the search, she was slightly out of place. Unexpectedly, the water snatched her kayak and pulled her forward. It was nearly impossible to refuse the river when it was ready for you to move.

She was only a little early, and rather than fight the current, Nell let the river capture her. She inhaled and exhaled deeply, relaxing for the rapid. She headed for the El alone, her place in the line of boaters out of sequence but not dangerously so, getting a glimpse of the paddlers behind her jockeying for new positions.

The water was wicked squirrelly on the approach to the El, and she braced more than she paddled, working herself into position. The hole seemed more determined today, sucking at her boat, slowing her momentum. Nell dug in, leaning forward hard with each strong stroke, willing herself downstream, still darting her eyes left and right, looking for Joe. The hole released her and she shot forward, straight at the ledge.

The El was riotous, a rodeo-bull ride where the kayak rode the crest of the water one instant and pitched beneath it in the next. The river curved up, over the ledge, with a hard jounce. She rocked a hip up and pushed with her foot as she took the drop. As always, the nasty diagonal curler gave her boat a come-hither tug, trying to dump her over. But it wasn't as big today as the last time she took it, and Nell made the drop smoothly, plunging into the lower water with two vigorous thigh lifts.

She glided into the Long Pool. With a series of strokes, she pulled out of the current river-right, spotting Hamp, RiverAnn, Harvey and Stewart river-left. She waved and Hamp lifted a paddle in response. The boaters behind her arrived more or less in sequence, but the last two kayakers taking the ledge were too close together, and one of the boats, a yellow creek boat, hung a moment too long on the ledge. The other boat careened toward it, a purple-and-green blur, the boater trying to maneuver hard left, a look of restrained alarm on his face. He jerked his right hip up hard, revealing the hull, all but lying down on the water, bracing so hard his shoulders pivoted behind him. He made it. But the water was feeling malevolent. It picked up his boat and tossed it.

Nell watched in horror as the small crafts collided.

11

The purple-and-green kayak and the yellow creek boat hit with a dull thump that rose above the roar of the falls. The creek boat overcompensated and spun hard right, down into the curl. It went over the ledge on its side. The purple-and-green kayaker wrenched his boat back under him with a powerful hip snap and somehow hit the bottom of the fall nose down, a foot to the side of the creek boat. Horrified, Nell expected him to end up in a vertical pin, but he pivoted his entire body and the boat back under him. It was a beautiful, athletic move.

She had her rescue rope ready, having popped her skirt and pulled it out without thought. Tension zinged through her, heating her body in a flush. The purple-and-green wobbled, then made it out of the foamy trough in a flash of color. The yellow creek boat came up empty.

"Swimmer!" Nell shouted as others took up the call. The boaters standing on rocks searched the water with their eyes, holding throw ropes, but the swimmer didn't surface. Closest to the falls, Nell reset her skirt and paddled hard toward the bottom of the El. Peripherally, she saw the other kayakers stroking upstream or ferrying across current. And the next boat was coming over the ledge.

"Crap!" the purple-and-green boater shouted. Nell skimmed past him. His rope was in his hands, his skirt undone. The swimmer came up feetfirst, one foot and knee, then the other foot. Not the reemergence of a conscious boater. Time did a funny little shift, slowing down. The light hit the water in a shimmer. The roar of the falls diminished. The swimmer's body slowly rotated to the surface, face up, almost balletic, caught in the flow. His mouth and eyes were open, full of water.

Nell reached him, grazing his knee with her boat. The current revolved his body over, facedown in the water. Presenting the back of his head. She gripped her paddle and rope in her left hand and shifted in the bottom of her boat, preparing to take on weight. One-handed, she grabbed the back of his PFD. Hauled his head out of the water. Blood poured down his face. Rivulets of bright red. For an instant, just a moment of time, Nell again thought, *Joe*... But he wasn't Joe. She knew that. He blinked, gagged, and time fell back in place with a deafening growl of white water.

The purple-and-green Arc-ProLine scudded up close, back paddling. He rafted his boat to hers on her left, running a piece of flex through the boat's handholds with a quick jerk, pulling her kayak against his, restraining her craft, giving her security. He took her rope and paddle, freeing both of her hands. Nell shot him a quick look and saw black brows. Greenish eyes. A flash of sunburn, as he tucked her paddle and rope into the open cockpit of his boat.

She turned back to the swimmer. Nell caught a look at his face and recognized Scooter, a river guide who had worked the Pigeon a couple of summers when she was a teenager.

A kayak came over the ledge, sighted them, dodged right and boofed, hitting the water flat with an echoing splat. ProLiner didn't bother with words. He started pulling through the water with draw strokes, snapping his hip, using his entire body to move the boats.

The swimmer Nell was holding vomited, twisting his hips

up with the spasm, pulling his head down, into the water. Nell let her body follow him, stretching her arms and torso, knowing that, if not for the expert rafting of the ProLiner, she would have been forced to let go or be pulled under. Using her hip, she pulled the swimmer's face back to the surface. But it wasn't enough. She had to get him out of the river.

"Can you get him on the front of your boat? Or do you need me in the water?" ProLiner asked.

"I got him. Ready," she said, not quite a question, more a warning. Not waiting for an answer, she hauled hard, kicked with her hip to counterbalance the weight, and rotated the swimmer to her, draping his body over the front of her boat, up across the cockpit. Her kayak lunged, threatened to roll and dump with the maneuver, but the rafting to the other kayak held. The swimmer's hands fluttered weakly. He took a breath, chest moving in her arms.

"He's conscious. Sorta," she said over the sound of the El. "But we need to get away from the ledge. The raft will be over in about—" Nell looked up. Spotted the top of Mike's head from his perch, sitting up high on the back of the raft. The Ranger was still upstream, but committed to the rapid, too late to turn back. "—now!"

ProLiner looked up at the El. Swore viciously. The rescue guides on top of the rocks should have warned the raft off and hadn't. Both men were shouting and waving paddles, but it was way too late.

The Maravia Ranger raft came down the falls straight at them.

Mike spotted her. His eyes widened. His mouth moved in a curse and he shouted instructions to the crew. Expert paddlers, they spun the raft the instant they hit the trough, using its momentum to whip the ungainly craft. It went around in a dizzying swirl and past them. Around her, the kayakers cheered and clapped, the sounds of triumph and relief bouncing off the water behind them.

Nell swallowed hard and let out a breath she hadn't known she held. Holding the swimmer, she lifted his head and made sure his airway was open. She could hear his breathing, a wet, gurgling sound. ProLiner guided the boats beyond the eddy line and into the still water. Nell cradled the swimmer.

Looking around, she counted boats, noting that Mike and Elton were doing the same. Stoned Stewart, moving with the lethargic motions of a heavy marijuana smoker, had reached the swimmer's empty boat and tied it off behind his kayak. Hamp had found a paddle. Two other boats were picking up flotsam, stuff that had come out of the overturned kayak. Everyone converged on the swimmer, reaching their joined boats just as the ProLiner and she bumped shore. The Ranger raft spun in next, using the speed of the falls to beach quickly, grinding on the narrow lip of sand.

After that it was havoc, as ProLiner and Mike dragged the swimmer onto shore, and Elton and Mike took over lifesaving. Everyone on the run was certified in emergency swift-water rescue and basic life support, but Elton and Mike were the most experienced in advanced life support, or ALS, protocols. Both carried mouthpieces used to give artificial respiration and Elton even had a tiny bag of advanced medical supplies.

Nell sat in her boat, shivering with reaction. Her kayak was half in the water, half onshore, still rafted to the old-school Precision Arc-ProLine. The purple-and-green kayak had a lot of wear on it. Not a playboat, but a good boat to use in a search and rescue—stable and easy to maneuver.

Someone had talked about ProLiners at the campfire last night, and she wondered if the kayaker who had helped her was the same guy. But then she saw another ProLine, different year, different color scheme, a bit shorter in length.

She realized her thoughts were drifting. Seeking distraction. Needing diversion to keep her thoughts off of Joe. Joe, who had come out of his boat, just like this guy had. Somewhere on this river. With no one to help him.

She had to blink away an image of her husband floating facedown along the river, caught so that the current held him that way, not allowing the PFD to do its job and flip him faceup. Joe, drowning. Alone.

To occupy her mind and throw off the vision, she worked at the knot in the flex that rafted her boat to the ProLine kayak. But her fingers were cold and stiff, and the simple knot didn't want to come free. She couldn't see it for the tears in her eyes.

"Here. I'll get it." The voice from the river. His hands moved over hers, pushing her fingers away, as he proficiently untied the knot. "You did good out there," he said.

Nell took a breath that pulled against her throat, a soft shudder sounding like a sob. She batted the tears away and managed a smile. "Thanks. But if you hadn't gotten us those few feet over, we'd have been staring at the bottom of the Ranger. So, back at you. Nice job."

He was down on one knee, kneeling on the bank, as he pulled off his helmet and shook his hair. It was still mostly dry. "Junior," he said, tucking the helmet under an arm and extending his hand.

Nell took it. "Nell Stevens."

"Yeah. I know." She looked the question at him. "Wife of the boater we're looking for? I was at the put-in overnight. Saw you at the fire."

Nell eased her hand from his. "Thank you," she said. "For being here. For helping…" Her heart squeezed shut. The sentence trailed off. *Joe in the water. Dead.* The picture wouldn't go away. She closed her eyes.

"Glad to be able to help," Junior said. He touched her

hand and she met his eyes, greenish and intense. He extended her paddle and rescue bag that he had tucked inside his boat. Before she could respond, someone called his name and he stepped over people and boats, his back to her.

Nell climbed out, removed her helmet and ran fingers through her damp hair. Stretched. She pulled her boat and the ProLine up onshore.

In the middle of the small group of ALS workers and on-lookers, the swimmer coughed.

A few minutes later, with Scooter stabilized as well as they could get him on the river, Mike and Elton began planning the arduous process of getting an injured boater up out of the river gorge and to a hospital. They split the paddlers into two groups, one group to cart Scooter up the gorge to the gravel access road and the rescue crew, the rest to search the Long Pool. "Junior," Elton called. "You take team leader for the dredging."

Junior looked like he might argue, but Elton turned away, not giving him a chance to speak. Nell hid a grin. There were drawbacks to doing a good job. Like promotion.

She dug around in her beached boat and pulled out the brown paper sack Claire had packed for her. Her mother hadn't fixed her lunch since grade school, and had never prepared a kit for the hard work of paddling SAR. Claire had always felt she shouldn't encourage her tomboy daughter's addiction to rivers by being helpful. Nell hadn't expected her mother to offer assistance even today.

Claire had surprised her. The contents of the paper bag were also a surprise: two Snickers bars, a big baggie of trail mix, a Coke for the energy boost and an apple—a Haralson, one of her favorites. Taken together, they were the perfect river snack, high in carbs, fiber and fats, a little protein, and a sugar and caffeine kick.

Claire didn't like trail mix or apples, which proved

that, although her mother had been against Nell's love of swift water, she had been listening when her daughter's friends and she gabbed about river trips. The packed snack was a gesture of affection, an emotion that had been strained between them for years. Nell's fault. She knew it. Just as it was her fault that had sent Joe onto the river to save her.

Guilt sat like a devil on her shoulder, digging his pitchfork into her heart. She guessed she needed to talk to Claire. About a lot of stuff. And soon. They hadn't talked—really talked—since her father died. The old sorrow at his death raised up and pierced her, painful and sharp, sliding in beneath the new pain of Joe being lost on the river. Nell took a deep breath against tears. She was inordinately weepy, and accepted that she would be until they found Joe.

She crunched into the apple. Haralsons were tart and crisp, though it could just as well have been ashes as she ate. Miserable, Nell shoved the last chunk into her mouth and tossed the core into the woods, the biodegradable pulp and seeds good for the environment. Maybe next spring an apple tree would sprout here.

"Litterbug."

Nell looked around and saw Turtle Tom, Harvey and RiverAnn behind him, Harvey's beard wet with river spray, RiverAnn sitting heavy in her boat. "Apple," Nell defended, hiding her full mouth and her tears behind a hand. Tom was slender and muscular, with long, curling dark hair. Despite being so wealthy, his river gear was beat up and battered. Most rich hair-heads had the newest equipment and all the girls. Today, Tom was alone, unlike Harvey, who cast longing and miserable glances at RiverAnn. Trouble in paradise, it seemed. RiverAnn was a river-rat magnet, but it looked like her affections were currently bringing something less than joy.

When she had swallowed, Nell said to Tom, "Want to partner up?"

"Sure." He was a man of few words, which Nell had always appreciated. She finished off the first water bottle and tucked it away.

Moments later, the paddlers all paired up—Elton and RiverAnn, who was shooting evil glances at Harvey; Junior with Hamp; and Nell with Turtle Tom. The others were climbing the gorge with the injured Scooter. That left only Harvey alone.

Harvey grumbled, "I'm odd man out. Junior, Hamp, I'll make it a threesome."

"Fine by me," Hamp said, "but no tongue." Everyone laughed dutifully at the old joke.

Nell and her new partner glanced at each other and, with the near-psychic communication of experienced paddlers, got in their boats, set their skirts and pushed off. Nell feathered her paddle until she had enough speed to make her boat track straight. Creek boats like hers were notoriously hard to paddle in still or slow-moving water, needing swift water and rapids to display their design characteristics. Tom's longer, sleeker boat was better suited to the SAR, and he opened up a wide space between them at first.

As soon as she had a good rhythm and decent speed going, Nell followed Tom around the upstream shoreline of the Long Pool. The sun was overhead, growing hot in a cloudless sky. The air, so chilly earlier, warmed through her wet suit. Shadows dappled the surface of the water. Leaves fell and floated on the current.

Overnight, fall had come. Dogwood and sourwood trees had taken on color. If Nell hadn't been grieving and fighting desperation, she would have enjoyed the day. Instead, it seemed like a mockery from God—a day so perfect and yet so full of fear and heartache.

Half an hour into the shore search, someone blew a whistle, a single piercing blast. Nell whipped her boat around, finding the paddler who had given the alert. It was Elton, standing onshore, paddle in hand. He pulled something from a clump of debris. Even across the pool, Nell could tell it was red. She dug in with hard forward strokes and reached the far shore. He was holding a PFD.

"Joe?" Nell called out, breathless, searching the shore with her eyes. "Is it Joe's?" She eddied out, her boat bumping Elton's.

Elton handed the PFD to her. "Check the shoreline," he instructed the other paddlers. But Elton himself stayed with her, his blue eyes steady but empty, watching. Nell, hands shaking, turned the vest, inspecting the equipment, recognizing Joe's extra nose plug and his whistle. "It's Joe's," she whispered. Tears filled her eyes. "His knife is missing, but it's his vest."

Elton took the PFD from her. Nell felt something small but vital snap inside her. She reached for the PFD. "I want—"

"The cops will need it, Nell," he said softly.

"Cops? Why—"

"The straps are all still in place. So is the zipper. It was cut off," he said gently. "And there's blood on the flex."

"Blood?"

She curled her fingers under, her paddle cold in her hands. She met Elton's eyes, then Turtle Tom's. "Blood?" she said again, feeling as if she had never heard the word before. The world tilted and swirled like a slow, falling current. Silent, Turtle Tom unskirted and stepped from his kayak. Stepped into the brush to join the land search. He looked back once, his eyes full of questions. And what might have been accusation.

12

Joe had come out of his boat here. Or maybe even above the El, his gear floating downstream. Perhaps he had been caught in a strainer, PFD hung on the limbs of a tree, drowning, and cut himself free. Or he had been cut from it. That was the look Turtle Tom and thrown her way. Suspicion. Condemnation. Nell shuddered.

They searched the Long Pool thoroughly, Junior and his partner tying off with joined rescue ropes to a tree onshore, again dredging the bottom of the zigzag current with a grappling hook. Again they found nothing. Tom skirted the shore, getting out several times to inspect likely-looking sites where a swimmer might have washed up or taken refuge in high water. Elton and RiverAnn took the opposite shore and then they crisscrossed, each team inspecting the shore just searched by the other team, just in case a different pair of eyes might spot something. In two spots, RiverAnn worked her way up the hill, into the brush and back. She never once looked Nell's way and Nell felt the accusation and condemnation in the girl's stance. Then they moved downstream, trading off from river-left to river-right midway through. But there was nothing. No sign of Joe.

Nell, frozen in shock, sat unmoving in her boat in shallow water, trying to envision how a swimmer would survive through the rapids they had already run, if he had come out of his boat *and* his flotation vest. If he wasn't on the banks of the Long Pool, and if the water had carried him farther downstream... If... The world closed in, cold and brittle as ice.

She swallowed down her desperation, remembering the section of river coming up next, the run that dropped between canyon walls. There were hundreds of places where Joe could be if he cut himself from his vest and swam on, caught in the current. Fighting to keep her heart from racing out of control and her breathing steady, Nell held on to the hope that Joe was just ahead, waiting for her. But the hope had grown much fainter, more amorphous. Like mist, the hope gave no purchase for her desolate heart and hands.

A helicopter dropped into the gorge, fighting downdrafts and thermals, malevolent air currents that tried to crash the craft. But the pilot was either very good or very lucky, jockeying across the currents as if he could see them swirl. Nell stared at the craft, hope writhing in a frenzy, as he made two passes along the river. But the pilot gave no indication that he had seen anything interesting before he moved on downstream to continue his search. Nell blinked back tears, fear crushing her heart in merciless claws.

An hour later, the paddlers returned from their rescue hike with the report that Scooter was breathing fine, and got back on the water. But Nell was aware of the whispered conversations and the furtive glances of her cosearchers. Their expressions were pitying and speculative, thinking— believing—that Joe was dead, and that she perhaps killed him. Nell dragged in a breath, wanting to scream, and looked away, unable to meet their eyes. She watched, silent, as Elton handed the damaged vest over and Junior stored it in his boat.

She was grateful when the entire crew skirted up or secured gear in the Ranger raft. No matter what they privately—or not so privately—believed about Joe, they pushed off into the water, ready to search. Their suspicion made Nell dig in with her paddle and work harder, willing them to believe with her that Joe was still alive. Willing that they not give up. Demonstrating to them with her body language, her tears and her determination that she loved her husband, and that there was still hope.

The water level had continued to drop during the day, and the sun was warm on her shoulders as she swept into the current. Tom stayed with her, his boat just behind hers through the class IIIs that came up next, and his presence was a balm. Patiently, he followed her when she ferried river-right across the current and beached her boat to check a clump of detritus, and again two minutes later, when she ferried river-left to look into a crevice between boulders. He unskirted his own boat a half-dozen times to check narrow passages and undercut rock. When she began to grow tired, her arm muscles giving out, and she was unable to reskirt after scrambling across boulders, he gave her a hand, pulling RiverAnn's neoprene skirt back over her own cockpit rim, not saying a word about her energy levels or lack of stamina. Slowly, as the hours passed, the accusation and speculation in his eyes waned. He became, again, her old paddling buddy.

The search party pulled strainers out of the water, walked the meager shorelines, crawled around on boulders piled like blocks left behind by a giant's child, their bodies dwarfed by the massive behemoths.

As the gorge walls rose for the Narrows and the paddlers worked their way downstream, the river rats paired up with the hiking teams who were covering both sides of the canyon with binoculars and radios. When the class IIIs were declared clean, they took Rions Eddy and Jakes Hole, the water so swift and loud it was impossible to hear speech or whistles and they communicated by hand and paddle signals.

Elton and Mike ran lines to hold boats secure so they could check boulders and high-water holes and clefts in rock. It was painstaking, dangerous and agonizing work. Nell paddled until her hands had blisters alongside the old calluses, knowing that the others were surely suffering the same wear and tear. Each time she was close enough, she thanked a paddler, or gave a thumbs-up to those too far across the river's growl to hear.

And then came the word. The hikers on the gorge wall, three hundred feet above them, spotted something. The leader waved hard, his—her?—arm doing a full arm wave and pointing down. Something had been spotted where nothing was supposed to be. Nell's heart, so jittery it felt like she was attached to an electric socket, sped up even more. She pulled her rescue kit, lashed herself to a rock and waited, her eyes on the top of the gorge and the hiker who had a radio to his ear.

A flash of color drew her attention and she turned to see Elton. He shouted above the sound of the river, "What color wet suit did Joe wear?"

Nell shouted back as their boats bumped in the churning water. She changed the tense and stressed the verb, holding his blue-eyed gaze intensely. "Joe *wears* a black, sleeveless one-piece with red insets under the arms and along the sides of the legs. *Why?*"

"Hiker spotted something red between the river and the wall, caught on a strainer, up high enough that we can't get to it from the water, but under a downed tree so he can't get a good look at it. He's got climbing experience and mountain gear with him, and he's willing to rappel down, but not if it's a waste of time." He put the radio to his ear, shouting to the hiker to take a look, while Nell rafted their boats together with flex from her kit, her hands shaking so hard she felt like she'd been hit by lightning and still had wild electricity flooding her nervous system. Tom rafted his boat to hers on the other side and put his hand on her shoulder.

Held in place as wild water bumped their boats together and against the rock, the three watched as the hiker secured himself to something on the cavern heights, taking so long Nell wanted to weep. Her hands gripped and relaxed on her paddle in frantic worry.

Finally, he came to the edge and eased down until his feet were on the vertical wall, his rope and gear holding him in a semisitting position. With a small leap, he thrust out from the rock and dropped to hit feetfirst against the wall and jump away. Graceful as a spider, he rappelled down the gorge.

Her heart ached with each beat as her eyes followed the man down the wall. She didn't breathe, didn't blink, hope so tight in her chest she thought her heart would burst this time. Three hundred feet below, he vanished from sight behind a rock so big Nell hadn't realized it was a boulder separate from the wall itself. Lost from sight, she heard radio traffic on the radio held to Elton's ear, but she had no idea if he was shouting with joy or giving bad news.

After far too long, Elton turned to her, his face giving nothing away. "The rappeller radioed in that the red was a shirt, not a wet suit. Not Joe."

Tom, his kayak bumping next to hers, squeezed her shoulder. Her gorge rose, hot and burning. She heaved. Her stomach emptied into the water and across her boat. Dry heaves followed, and she heard her sobs, coarse and half screaming, like the sound of an angry river in her mind. She raged, hitting the boat with her fists, dropping the paddle. Beating. Beating. The noise a hollow thump of grief and misery.

When she was empty, her anger spent, Nell lay over the bow of her boat. Tears still fell, burning across her chapped and sunburned cheeks, her skin against RiverAnn's kayak skirt. Tears dripped onto the wet weave, forming a puddle separate from the wet of river water.

Joe was gone. Joe was…dead.

Long minutes later, Turtle Tom gently pulled her upright. She sat in her boat, rocked by the water, nerveless, wrapped in horror. Tom washed the vomit off her boat, splashing its surface with river water. Slowly, she raised her head and met Elton's eyes, bluer and brighter than the noonday sky. They were filled with understanding and an awful, terrible *pity*.

He handed her one of his own water bottles. "Drink," he said above the sound of the white water. She did. It was like drinking vinegar and gall, bitter and rough. When she emptied the bottle, he took it back. "We aren't done yet. We still have a lot of river to search. Do you want to get out at the O & W bridge?"

"No," Nell whispered, tasting vomit on her breath. "Hell, no." She wiped her mouth and looked at him. She took a breath so cold and wet it was like the hand of death. And in that moment she accepted the possibility that Joe was gone. "If my husband is alive, we'll find him and I'll be there when we do. And if he's…" She took a second breath and her words rippled and quivered with pain. "If he's dead, I'll be there to recover his…body." The words resounded in her mind like a shot in an empty room. "But I'm not quitting."

Elton nodded. "You need calories. You got something to eat?"

Tom said, "She's got trail mix. The kind with yogurt-covered raisins in it. I'll make sure she eats when we stop for lunch."

Nell wanted to laugh at the unimportant worry about food, when Joe was gone, but her soul had bound up all her emotions in one huge, aching ball and tucked it under her breastbone where it sat, throbbing with painful pressure. "I'll eat," she said, knowing where the SAR team leader was going with his concern. "I'll keep it down. And I'll pull my weight and not be a hindrance on this search."

Elton ran his eyes over her bruises and glanced at Tom. "Make sure she keeps it down. If she has problems, let me know."

Tom nodded. "I'll look after her."

Nell looked at Tom, and saw that all his earlier suspicion had been replaced with something else. Something kinder—the same pity that Elton wore. The sight started her tears afresh. She clasped Tom's hand and once again popped her skirt. She removed the baggie of trail mix and unstrapped a bottle of water, then passed it to Elton to replace the one she had used and took another bottle for herself. She opened the bottle and drank, ignoring the call to relieve herself. She could take care of unimportant things later. She ate two handfuls of trail mix. She didn't gag.

Elton nodded, satisfied. He unrafted his kayak from hers and spun his paddle in the air, a signal to proceed downriver. While the rappeller worked his way back up the limestone canyon wall, the river portion of the search and rescue operation for Joe Stevens started again. Nell and Tom went into a narrow cleft between rocks and shoved paddles into undercuts to see if they hit anything soft. They didn't. And the paddlers moved on.

Dusk lasted a long time in the Narrows. For hours, the sun disappeared behind the gorge walls and reappeared. Gold rays lit the tops of the stone walls and the trees clinging to narrow ledges, in layers of ocher and sand and the reds of early fall.

Nell didn't notice the scenery. Her head was pounding, muscles in her shoulders and arms rigid with exhaustion and pain. The ripe scent of sourwood trees, so strong in autumn, reminded her of the smell of death and all things foul. Acid rose a half-dozen times in her throat, but she forced it down and kept up with the paddlers, doing more than her share, until it was nearly too dark to see and Elton called a halt. Exhausted, they paddled into Leatherwood takeout.

The day-camper parking lot was full of cars, trucks and news vans. The beach was full of people, family of the searchers, rescue-squad auxiliary members handing out coffee and water bottles, and the requisite locals out to rubberneck. And RiverAnn, who had reached the takeout early, standing hip deep in the river, craning her neck for Harvey. Near her was Claire, standing with her back to the park, knee deep in the river, her calf-long pants folded up and her arms crossed as if with chill. When Nell met her mother's gaze, Claire waved her over, her body taut and gestures urgent.

Nell paddled to her, the water plenty deep enough for her kayak. Claire caught the boat and steadied it, her eyes searching Nell's. "Any news?" she asked.

"No." Nell's eyes filled with tears. "No sign at all."

"Well, I wish I could say things were better for you, here but—"

Splashing sounded behind Claire, and her mother tottered as if she had been shoved. A microphone the size of a kid's football was shoved under Claire's arm. Oddly, it had a fuzzy sock on it.

"Are you Nell Stevens?" the well-dressed woman behind the mike asked, spattering through the low water, her dress pants folded up like Claire's. "What do you have to say about the accusations made by your in-laws in the disappearance of your husband?"

"In-laws?" Nell asked, surprised. *In-laws? What in-laws? Joe doesn't have a family.*

13

Nell hadn't realized that she had spoken the words aloud until she saw herself much later on the television in the RV. Clean, warm, dry, boneless with shock and fatigue, she sat at her dinette, her injured hands interlaced listlessly in front of her, and listened to the news. News about who Joe was. About the man she had married.

The reporter was one of those glowing, blond, pale-faced, elegant city women who wore clothes and makeup like a model. Her excitement was palpable even through the TV screen. "Joseph Stevens, heir to the Gregory Stevens textile fortune and recently believed to be one of New York's most eligible bachelors, is missing. Best known for his philanthropic work on literacy programs, he vanished in northern Tennessee on a white-water kayaking trip. Here is what his *new wife* said, coming off the water after today's search."

The scene flashed to a shot of Nell, sitting in her boat, looking pale and wan, eyes black and green, her helmet, skirt and boat hiding most of her. "In-laws? *In-laws?* What in-laws? Joe doesn't have a family." The picture flashed back to the reporter, her eyes glowing with gossip.

Claire cut off the TV, glancing uneasily at the cop sitting in the passenger seat. "You've seen it enough times already, Nellie baby."

"He lied to me," Nell said, staring at the black screen. "Our whole time together, he lied to me."

"Joe loved you. He wanted to protect you."

"Or he was ashamed of the little Appalachian girl he married," she said, hearing the scorn and loathing in her own voice and helpless to stop it. "With her broken nails and river-wet straggly hair and Tennessee accent. And he didn't want them to know about me."

"He never told you about his family?"

Nell twitched, hearing the cop's voice. When she turned her head, her neck muscles kneaded together like dry rubber; she had been sitting still so long, watching television, that her body had frozen in place. She focused on the man in his wrinkled suit. The cop from the hospital. Maybe fifty years old. His hair thinning. Slightly overweight. His chair was underneath the TV. Forgotten.

"Oh, yeah," she said. "The cop. The one who thinks I killed my husband." Nell rubbed her eyes, so dry they ached. "My *rich* husband. God. I even have a motive, don't I?" Nell turned and looked at her mother in horror. "He had money. And a family."

"You didn't sign a prenup?" the cop asked.

"A what?" Nell asked, bewildered.

"A prenuptial agreement. Limiting how much you get in the event of his death or of divorce," the cop said.

"No, I—" Nell rubbed her head, remembering the attorney and his fancy office in Knoxville. "Joe and I saw a lawyer. We made out wills. We signed the corporation papers for the shop. I guess there could have been—" She stopped, everything hitting her at once. Her mouth opened slowly. She stared at the cop. "I need a lawyer, don't I?"

When he shook his head and started to speak, she interrupted, "I don't even know your name." But she remembered the lawyer's name. L. P. Berhkolter, at Berhkolter, Smith,

Rector and Associates. Standing quickly, she held out her hand to Claire. "I need your phone." Without a word, Claire passed her the cell and Nell stepped out into the night, leaving the cop to Claire's untender mercies. She could hear Claire's tone through the RV walls and smiled into the dark, not feeling the least bit of remorse for the cop and his tongue-lashing.

She punched into the Internet and looked up L. P. Berhkolter's number. Fingers shaking, she dialed it. Listened to it ring.

The RV was parked above the Leatherwood takeout, Claire having handled all the details herself. Knowing what was coming, her mother had rented an RV site at Bandy Creek Park, shanghaied help from one of the auxiliary workers and taken both vehicles up the winding, sharply inclined roads. Always one to get things done, even if it meant asking for help, she had gotten another camper to show her how to hook up power, water and cable. All so she would have a place to take Nell. Nell had never been so grateful for her mother's take-charge personality.

She had stopped calling Claire 'mama' the day of her father's funeral. That day had dawned so bright, sunny and warm that it felt downright sprightly, a foul insult to the burial of her father. It should have rained and sleeted and winds should have howled down the mountain, giving voice to grief.

Daddy had been Nell's shining star, her hero, her greatest joy. They had done everything together in life, fishing, canoeing, hiking, school projects. And yet, he had died while driving back from a romantic assignation with a woman not his wife, and not her mother. His family hadn't been good enough for him, it seemed.

Nell didn't sleep for two days after he died, and when Claire came out of her room the day of the funeral, dressed in black, her face looking composed and serene, no evidence of sorrow, something had hardened inside Nell. Hardened and frozen. She had hated her mother with a sudden and total and complete hatred, thinking she had felt no grief, no pain. But maybe it hadn't been that. Maybe Claire had just been taking charge, doing what needed to be done, to survive through the next second, then the one after that. For her? Had Claire buried her own pain to be strong for her grieving daughter?

The phone was picked up by an answering machine, bringing Nell back to the present and her new pain, her new loss. She took a deep breath and forced calm, into her voice. After the message, Nell said, "This is Nell Stevens, Joseph Stevens's wife. I need you to call me right away. I have a cop in my RV and reporters telling me—" She stopped, putting a hand on her neck. Her fingers were quivering and her skin felt cold and dead. "I need information. And help. Okay? Call me." She gave Claire's cell number.

The RV park was not well lit. In fact, it wasn't lighted at all. Nell was wrapped in darkness, hidden in the night. To her left, the windows of a fifth-wheel travel home were bright. To her right, a horse trailer with live-in cab was illuminated by a lantern. Campfire smoke blew on the slow breeze. Overhead, the stars were so bright and numerous they were like a carpet, something no city person ever saw. Pollution and city lights hid most stars.

Joe had told her that. *Joe.* Her heart ached so badly she wanted to cry or scream. Joe, who was gone. Joe, who had lied to her.

And then she remembered a conversation they had shortly after they met. They had been paddling together in a group of kayakers, taking a break after a strenuous section of the Ocoee River. They had dinner plans for that night, the two of them. Third date. Already there were sparks between them. Had been from the moment they met.

"Would you date a rich man?" Joe asked.

"Nope." She had laughed at the thought and twirled her paddle.

"Why not?" He rested across the cockpit, his eyes on her. Only on her. He had always given her his total attention, as if he found her the most interesting thing on the face of the earth. As if he'd been entranced.

"First off, no rich guy would want to live on the river. He'd live in some big city close to his job. Maybe commute on weekends or something. Second, no rich guy would want a poor Appalachian American. That's what my granddaddy calls us. Not hillbillies. Appalachian Americans." She laughed and saluted him with her paddle. "Though PawPaw is pretty much the epitome of a hillbilly. A rich guy would cheat on someone like me in a heartbeat, try to change me and make me move. And he'd likely bore me to death."

"Ouch," Joe said, his eyes amused. She'd ached to touch the two-day beard he'd sported. It had been rough under her fingertips later that night when she'd given in to the impulse. And he'd caught her hand and kissed her fingertips, his eyes intense, their steak dinners forgotten. On their wedding night, he had told her he'd fallen in love with her that day, the day she told him she wouldn't date a rich man.

Is that why he had lied to her?

Nell closed her eyes on the tears. The phone rang, the trumpet ringtone Claire used for any unknown caller. Nell looked at the number, finding it watery. She touched her face. She was crying again. She sniffed and wiped her eyes, seeing the number she had just dialed. The lawyer. She answered. "Nell Stevens. Thanks for calling me back."

"Louis Berhkolter here. I was working late, Mrs. Stevens.

And actually I was waiting for your call. I've left several messages on your cell phone."

"The cell was ruined in the accident." Suddenly she didn't know what to say, and an awkward silence followed her statement.

"I suppose you have questions," Berhkolter said.

"You could say that."

"Are the police giving you a hard time?"

"Was Joe rich?" she countered.

The awkward pause was on Berhkolter's part this time. "He never told you," he said.

"No. He never told me." Nell could hear the bitterness in her voice, and knew Joe's lawyer had to hear it too. "He lied to me. All the way through. About everything."

"I suggested to him that you might not appreciate being kept in the dark."

"The cops think I killed him for his money. They asked if I signed a prenuptial agreement. Was that what I signed? In your office? The one that said if something happened between us or to him, then our kids, if any, got his estate? It wasn't important at the time, but I remember that one. Was that a prenup?"

"Of sorts," Berhkolter said gently. "But Joe left you well provided for."

"Joe can take his money and shove it where the sun don't shine," she said, turning to the RV and resting her forehead against the side, her arms curled up around her, the cell dangling from her fingers over her ear and cheek. "I don't want his money. I just want…" *Him…I just want Joe. But he isn't here. He never was, not really. Joe was a shadow. A myth. A lie.*

"Have the police questioned you in his disappearance?"

Nell laughed, her breath blowing back in her face. "Yes. Do I need a lawyer?"

"Tell the officer or detective that you will be happy to answer law-enforcement questions, but only with your attorney present. I don't handle criminal law, but Jacob Smith, with our firm, does. He's a very competent attorney. I'll pass your name and the circumstances along to him, and he can meet you at police—"

"I'm not going anywhere till Joe is found," Nell said, her tone aggressive. "That's what I'm telling you and that's what I'm telling the cop. And then you and me gotta have us a little chat about my *rich* husband and his *damn lies*." She pressed the little red button that ended the call.

Throwing open the door to the RV, Nell stormed up the three steps and slammed the door behind her. The atmosphere inside was charged and heated, as if she had interrupted an argument. The cop and Claire were glaring at each other, and her mother's fingers were curled into claws. The sight gave Nell a fierce satisfaction.

She looked at the cop. "What's your name?"

If he was surprised that she didn't remember his name, it didn't show on his face. "Detective Nolan Lennox, Sr."

"L. P. Berhkolter, at Berhkolter, Smith, Rector and Associates are Joe's lawyers. Jacob Smith is my criminal attorney." Nell's eyes filled with *tears. Oh, God. I have a criminal attorney. Who could think I killed Joe?* "When they find Joe, I'll come in for a talk. But for now, get out."

Lennox sat there, his steady gaze on her. "And if they don't find him?"

Don't find him? How could they not find him? Because he's stuck under an undercut. Dead, her mind answered instantly.

The world went black around the edges. Slowly, she shook her head. But the blackness grew, leaving only Detective Nolan Lennox, his face framed by the awful night. And then that too was gone.

* * *

Nell woke to a darkened room, the scent of herb tea soft on the air, that red tea Claire liked. There was no moment of uncertainty, no blissfully calm instant when she could relax, unaware that Joe was missing. She knew. She remembered. She rolled to her feet and walked out of her bedroom, down the short hallway to the dinette. Maybe eight feet. She wobbled all the way. Sat beside Claire. The TV went dark.

"I passed out."

"Yes. We noticed," Claire said, her voice emotionless.

"Lennox carried me to bed?"

Claire nodded. "You slept three hours. You're under a lot of stress. You need to eat better. Drink more water."

"I'll rest when we find Joe." Nell took a breath that made her bruised ribs creak. When she spoke, the words came out faint and hopeless. "*If* we find Joe," she said. "But I'm staying off the water tomorrow. I'm too much of a distraction. I'll join one of the auxiliary teams instead. Can I borrow your car? And can you stay on a couple more days if necessary?"

"Of course, to both questions." Claire poured a mug of tea and placed it in her hand. "I know you love kayaking, but I agree. This time, I think it's smart for you to stay off the river." She smoothed Nell's hair back, tucking the short ends behind her ears. Nell closed her eyes and leaned into her mother's hand. It was warm, her skin soft and scented with something sweet, papaya or melon or something, a new cream Claire sold at the shop. Nell drew in the scent and some of her anxiety slipped away.

"I don't know much about searches on a river," Claire said, her words tentative. She stroked Nell's face and Nell smiled, her eyes still closed. "Is it…likely that Joe is…still alive?"

Nell straightened, opened her eyes, her hands stiffening

on the mug. It was Joe's mug, federal blue with a red kayaker silhouetted on it, and the offbeat, suggestive phrase "Paddlers Go Down in Wild Water." Joe loved this mug. Her throat tightened and she dragged her fingertips across the porcelain as if it were an amulet, full of wisdom, a bottle holding a genie. "No," she whispered. "It isn't very likely."

The silence in the small RV was heavy, as if the air itself were weighted with pain. "Drink your tea, then go to bed," Claire said. "We'll talk in the morning."

For the second time in recent memory, Nell did what her mother ordered. She drained her mug, the red tea tangy and tart. Rising from the small sofa, she went back to bed.

The next morning, Nell was up before dawn, dressed for cooler temps, her lunch and hiking gear packed and her hiking boots laced up. She left the cell phone and a note for Claire on the coffeemaker.

Claire,
    Like I said, I'm staying off the water. I'll be with one of the auxiliary teams, probably at the O & W bridge. I packed a lunch. I'll gas up your car and pick up cereal and milk on the way back.
    Nell

Night still had dawn by the throat when she pulled out of the campground and headed to the O & W bridge. The railroad bed was close to Bandy Creek, as the crow flies, but a long drive on winding, gravel-surfaced, mountain roads. It was barely dawn when she reached the bridge, and far after dusk when the park ranger called for the day's search to end. Nell was bruised, blistered and exhausted with both the physical strain of the strenuous hike and the emotional strain of knowing that Joe was likely dead. Lost to her forever.

Silently, during the long dusk, through lengthening shadows and dropping temperatures, she hiked with her team back down to a little-used rough trail and two ATVs with short trailers that waited to take them back to their cars. By the time they rendezvoused with the auxiliary team, they were all layering clothes back on and stars were glowing in a cloudless blue-black sky. Still silent, she rode in the trailer, holding on to the short sides to protect her body against the rough ride, the jounces irritating her healing bruises all the way back to the O & W bridge.

Failure weakening her resolve, Nell dropped her gear into the backseat of Claire's car and started the engine, sitting in the driver's seat. Tears striped her face with raw tracks, but her sobs were hushed, crying for her loss, crying for Joe. Crying alone as she waited for the other SAR searchers who were not camping at the O & W bridge to head out. Drained, she appreciated the warmth of the car's heater on her grief-chilled body. Comfort and misery, tears and guilt warred within her.

In the dark, the cavalcade of cars and trucks left the bridge, traveling back through the long, meandering road, headlights once illuminating a lone black bear. It lumbered off without apparent fear, into the shadows. Full night fell before they reached Toomey Road and Nell was glad she could follow the taillights of the car in front, and even more glad when that same car stopped for groceries at a mom-and-pops style convenience store, reminding her that she needed a few supplies.

It was after eight when she pulled into the campsite and parked beside two strange cars, a black Lexus with a rental-agency sign on the bumper and a black Caddy with Tennessee plates. Worn and aching, she carried milk and a box of oatmeal to the door of the RV, the mingled scent of campfires and charred meat making her stomach rumble despite her tension and fear. All she wanted was a shower and her bed, but before she reached the door, she heard a raised voice from inside. Claire, angry, laying down the law. Or more than that. Claire had to have seen her car pull in. Her mother was giving her a warning. Someone else answered her back, more controlled in volume but still irritated.

Mutely thanking her mother for being a manipulative little Southern lady, Nell climbed the steps and opened the door, moving fast. Within, the voices shut off abruptly, but tension laced the air like electricity from a downed power line, the hazardous aftermath of a storm. She pulled the door closed behind her and scanned the small space.

Three strangers sat at the dinette, overdressed in city clothes: a woman whose perfume saturated the air, and two men, one young, maybe in his twenties, one older, maybe fifty. None of the unwelcome visitors looked like media. But they all looked like trouble.

Claire and Mike sat in the driver and passenger seats on their small raised platforms, the bucket-seat chairs swiveled around to face the rear. Part of the teaching that both Claire and Nell had absorbed at PawPaw's feet—take the high ground. Look down at your adversary if possible. If not, take the best chair and the best angle of light. Find a way to establish control.

"Nell," Claire said, a warning tone in her voice. "This is Yvette Stevens and her son Robert. They claim to be Joe's mother and brother. And this is Louis Berhkolter of Berhkolter, Smith, Rector and Associates. Louis is here to put out fires. The Stevenses have come here to talk about Joe and his money. And to meet you."

With all the years of confrontation-and-negotiation training from her grandfather under her belt, Nell measured the strangers and Louis, whom she recognized from the trip she and Joe took to his office when she signed the legal papers for the shop. The clothes and jewelry on the other two cost more than the RV, she was sure. Heck, their haircuts probably did too. Nell knew that Claire's last four words were put at the end of the statement on purpose. Meeting Nell was an afterthought on the Stevenses' part. There was no doubt that the pair were trouble at worst, a nuisance at best. The woman, with her pinch-mouthed moue—her mother-in-law, for heaven's sake—could have passed as the Wicked Witch of the West. The young man was a follower, and would take Mommy's lead. The lawyer was a different matter. He was holding his cards close, his face expressionless.

Before anyone could react, Nell dropped the groceries on the short counter, squared her shoulders and said, "I'm getting a shower. I see you've helped yourselves to my tea and coffee. You're welcome to join me for dinner, too, when I get clean. We're having oatmeal. Till then, frankly, you're uninvited and in the way." With that deliberately insulting statement, she turned and swept down the short hall, pulling the folding door shut behind her.

Behind her she heard Mike laugh. "That, boys and girls, is a gauntlet, just in case you missed it. Told you she could hold her own."

Nell had no idea who he was talking to, but the words warmed her. Mike and Claire were solidly in her corner. Against the family Joe had denied existed.

Nell showered and washed her hair. Shaved her legs. Smoothed her nails and put on some concealer, powder and lipstick from Claire's supplies spread across the tiny bathroom counter. She had been watching Claire make herself up all her life and though she would have rejected the claim that she knew how to use the stuff, Nell could figure out the basics okay. She dried her hair and put on fresh clothes. Added powdered deodorant to the toilet and flushed it into the holding tank to keep the stink down until she could dump the waste. Sprayed the shower with cleaner. By the time she was finished, the harsh scent of cleansers and chemicals filled the RV, overpowering the expensive perfume Mrs. Stevens wore. No, not Mrs. Stevens. *Yvette.* Nell grinned.

Having dawdled as long as she could, Nell turned on the exhaust fan in the steamy bath, stepped into the hallway and pulled the door shut behind her. She walked to the front of the RV, all of five steps, and took the driver's seat vacated by Claire. Her mother gave her a look as she sat, and Nell understood. *Us against them. Gotcha.* Claire held out a bowl.

"Thanks for fixing some oatmeal, Claire," Nell said, accepting the bowl from her mother. Nell was finicky about her hot cereal, wanting it stone-ground, high protein and not instant. She wanted it cooked only one way, with the water salted and the cereal added after the water reached a boil. Then the stove was turned off and the cereal stirred for thirty seconds before being placed into a bowl, cooked fast so it still had texture and bite. Four heaping teaspoons of sugar went on top and milk was added. Comfort food that couldn't be beat. Claire had taught her how to make oatmeal right, and even Nell couldn't quite duplicate Claire's touch at the stove. "Youns not eatin'?" she asked, deliberately drawing out her east Tennessee accent.

"Thank you, but no," the woman said, not able to hide a faint shudder.

Nell shrugged and dug in, studying her new in-laws, letting her mind roam through how she would handle this interview. Because that was what it was—an interview, not a family gathering. Her mother-in-law clearly looked down on everyone in the RV, especially Nell. The Stevens were too good for the likes of Appalachian Americans, too hoity-toity. Which ticked Nell off.

Halfway through the silent meal, she met Claire's protective glare, hoping to see if her mother understood what she was doing and why. Claire's lips twitched and she gave a miniscule nod, waiting for Nell to take the lead. Unless PawPaw Gruber was present, that was the way they had always done things when trouble came calling, Nell in the lead, Claire shortly behind. They had dealt with bill collectors and IRS people, school principals, difficult neighbors, and, once, a revenue man in the same way. Which, in the case of the revenuer, had turned out to be a smart response. PawPaw did like his liquor. And he didn't like revenuers.

When her bowl was empty, Nell handed it to Claire. "Thank you," she said. Then she looked at the Stevenses, her decision made. These people were here to cause problems. She would beat them to the punch. The gloves came off. "Joe said he didn't have family. I'm guessing he didn't like you much."

Mike barked with laughter. Yvette spluttered. The lawyer sharpened his attention on her, surprised. The younger man, Robert, looked amused, the way a cat looks amused at the mouse it has cornered. Nell smelled alcohol; the red rims around his eyes told her he'd had a few too many.

"Joe didn't tell us he got married," Robert said, waving a negligent hand. "But maybe it was because he knew the girl he married couldn't measure up to family standards."

Good. The city boy knew how to fight. Nell smiled, baring her teeth. "Joe knew I had no intention of moving into his life. I don't like rich people. They're two-faced and sly and you can't trust 'em. Joe felt the same way. Probably because of youns, or people like you.

"So I'll say this. Joe and his fancy lawyer here drew up papers that put the money I didn't know he had where he wanted it to go. I won't be fighting for Joe's money. Whatever he did with it is fine with me. So youns can get up, get outta here and deal with Mr. Berhkolter. I'll keep looking for Joe."

Robert flipped that hand again and stared at Nell's chest when he spoke. "According to the park rangers, Joe is probably dead."

Nell smothered a flinch and hammered down her tears at the bald statement. This kid fought dirty. She admired that on some level. She wondered if he wanted to take it outside, and figured she could beat the drunken sot with one hand tied behind her back.

As if he read her thoughts, "And they say it's possible they'll never find his body. What then?"

"My eyes are up here, Robbie," she said, pointing to her face. "Stop staring at my boobs. I'd 'a thought your mother woulda taught you better, you being a pure blood and all. But I guess breedin', and the lack of it, will tell."

Laughing softly, Mike said, "Nell's got a bit of a temper." It wasn't an apology. He sounded proud. Then his laughter died and he leaned in toward the guests to answer Robert's question for her. "Sometimes people don't get found. But no one on this SAR is ready to consider that right now. Everyone who knew him liked Joe."

"So go talk to Joe's fancy lawyer. I'm tired and I need to sleep." Nell stood and walked past them all to the back of the RV. She pulled the thin folding door shut and snapped it closed. Knowing she had just ticked off the new in-laws, and probably the lawyer too, Nell stood beside the door and waited until they left. The outside door closed and the cars pulled away. Through the plasticized door, Claire said, "Everybody's gone but me. You really want to tick off your in-laws before you know what they're doing here?"

Nell opened the folding door and walked to the refrigerator. From the freezer, she took a Hershey dark chocolate bar and broke off two of the rectangular pieces. On each, she smoothed a spoonful of extra-crunchy peanut butter, and gave Claire one. They both ate. When the treat was gone, Nell fixed them each a second piece. Usually she only allowed herself one, but she needed the taste, texture and consolation of the chocolate. Only when it, too, was gone did she answer her mother's question, ticking off the reasons on her fingers.

"I'm guessin' there's a good reason Joe didn't tell me about the Stevenses. I'm also guessin' the lawyer knows what that reason is. It don't take a rocket scientist to figure out that they're here after his money. If they had loved Joe, at least one of them would have been on the SAR today looking for him, hiking and sticking a nose into the search business. They looked too comfy and too rested to have been on the search or to have been grieving." Nell waved five fingers in the air. "Considering all that, would PawPaw have treated them any better?"

"That old coot woulda met 'em at the door with a shotgun. There's plenty 'a room out back for a few more graves."

Nell and her mother shared a grin. Family legend said that PawPaw's daddy had buried a couple of revenuers out back when they came calling during the dark days of the 1930s Depression and Prohibition. For decades, every kid in town had gone digging to discover the truth, but the graves, if they really existed, were deep. And PawPaw and his daddy had made sure that any possible and subsequent stills were hidden too far back in the gullies and woods to be discovered. PawPaw claimed he no longer made 'shine, but the crusty old man always had a jug of the blue-flame good stuff hidden somewhere close by.

"You gonna be okay?" Claire asked.

"Yeah. I'll be fine." Nell shrugged each shoulder hard, working out the kinks, knowing her reply wasn't true but was expected. "Thanks for the warning when I drove up."

"That's what mothers are for. Get some sleep."

Nell pulled the bedroom door closed and climbed into bed, hearing her mother move around as she made up and inflated the air mattress that fit on the dinette. The sounds were soothing, and she fell asleep knowing she was well protected.

Evil dreams woke her before dawn, images of Joe hanging from a branch, impaled just like a turkey she had seen on the hike, his entrails pulled from his body. Nausea assaulted her with gut-wrenching sickness. She made it to the bath, hugging the toilet, and emptied her stomach. Still she heaved, her ribs and stomach protesting with pain. She was so loud she woke Claire.

Her mother put an ice-cold wet rag on her neck and massaged her back. When the heaves lessened, Claire flushed the low-water toilet, flushed it again with clean water, and walked to the kitchen. She brought back two cups of thin red tea, then sat on the floor in the hall, her knees inches from Nell's, drinking from her own mug. When she could stand it, Nell took a sip and sighed. Her stomach settled instantly. "Thanks."

"You're welcome," her mother said. Her un-madeup face impassive, her gaze steady, Claire said, "This isn't the first time you tossed your cookies. You usually have a cast-iron stomach. Are you pregnant?"

Nell opened her mouth. But no sound came out. Not a word. Not even a squeak. *Pregnant?* She looked down at her stomach and stared. The scent of the red tea was sweet and tart, punctuating the moment. *Pregnant?*

"I'm on the Pill," she managed to say. She looked at her mother, horrified, but with some other emotion, some nebulous feeling she couldn't name, budding up within it. She wasn't quite sure she wanted to acknowledge that emotion. Not yet. Maybe not ever. She put her hand on her stomach. Flatter than a fritter.

"Uh-huh. Lotta get babies born to women on the Pill, ya know. And I bet you forgot a time or two."

Nell's mouth dropped slowly open as she tried to remember the last time she took a pill. The day they left for the trip? The day before that? "Oh…crap," she breathed as the unnamed feeling twisted inside her like water snakes.

Gently, tenderly, Claire smiled. "I never had me a single day 'a sickness with you, but some women do. I got one 'a them auxiliary ladies to pick up a few things in Newport when they went back yesterday. Day before yesterday, now. I told her I thought I was pregnant 'cause word of you being pregnant would be all over the TV if I didn't. But I swore her to secrecy anyway. She brought me a couple pregnancy test kits. You want to pee in a cup for me?"

Nell stuttered hard with what could have been laughter had it not sounded so desperate. "I'm not pregnant," she whispered. Claire shrugged as if she didn't care one way or the other, but Nell had seen her face. Claire cared. Claire *wanted* Nell to be… She took a breath of spicy tea steam. Claire wanted her to be *pregnant*.

She made it to her feet and opened the cabinet door over the toilet. She kept paper supplies there, including cups. She pulled one from the plastic sleeve. Nell looked down at her mother, sitting on the RV floor. *Pregnant?* No way. But she pulled the bathroom door shut and sat, holding her teacup in one hand and the paper cup in the other. Thinking. No. No way. Joe's baby? She smothered the thought and that tenuous, burgeoning emotion and collected a sample.

She opened the door and met Claire's eyes, then took both cups with her to stand in front of the small kitchen sink. The drapes were drawn, covering the huge windshield. The narrow blinds on the other windows were twisted closed. It was just Nell and her mother. And the small plastic kit on the countertop. Nell put the sample cup in Claire's hands.

Claire tore the box open and removed a white plastic kit that was shaped like a digital thermometer. Using a dropper, Claire added four drops of urine to a small, square depression on one end of the kit. Then she took her cup of tea and sat on her bed. Patted the spot beside her. Nell curled one leg under her and sat on the edge, tiny shocks of energy pelting through her. One toe tapped the floor, an irregular rhythm. She sipped the cooling tea. "How long?"

"Four minutes."

Nell closed her eyes. *Do I want this? Do I want to be pregnant?* She couldn't answer herself. She was afraid to answer. But that vague, jittery, expanding emotion seemed to sway and settle inside her.

The seconds ticked by. Long before the four minutes were up, a pink cross appeared on the wand. As if by magic, it grew darker, deeper. Nell turned to her mother. Questioning. Claire stroked Nell's hair back behind her ear.

"Congratulations, Nellie baby. You gonna be a mama."

The next morning, on the fourth day of the SAR for Joseph Stevens, a storm hit. The weather forecasters had said it would head miles east, dropping its rain on the North Carolina side of the mountains. It didn't. It pelted the plateau with four inches of rain. The water level on the river and in the creeks rose fast, trapping two hikers on a boulder in the middle of a raging river. While rescuing the hikers, the rescue raft overturned and sent the searchers roaring downstream straight at the El. A paddler was lost and feared dead, turning up hours later stranded in a tree. Because of the rising danger, the search and rescue for Joseph Stevens was called off. The police investigation was stalled due to lack of evidence.

Nell, not knowing what else to do, went home. So did the other searchers. And Claire. Nell's newfound in-laws went back to New York City. Weeks passed. Then months.

Joe Stevens's body wasn't found. Eventually, the talk died down, if not the suspicion. Nell understood that almost everyone she knew—with the exception of Jedi Mike, her family and maybe Turtle Tom—believed that she was somehow involved with the disappearance and probable death of her rich husband.

PART TWO

14

Nell shaded her eyes and stared upstream. Mike was team leader for the last five-raft-tour of the day, and JJ was with him. Her six-year-old son thought he could do anything on the water that Jedi could, and while he could read water better than most guides, and understood the nature of rapids and confluence and holes and wave trains, he was still just a little boy, one who played with light sabers and video games on rainy winter days. His small body mass made him the most likely person in the boat to get dumped into the river if things went wrong. The Upper Pigeon had no undercut rocks or terminal hydraulics, but a hole that an adult could float out of in moments could easily become a "keeper" for her son. She didn't want to hover—JJ hated that. But she worried every single moment he was on the water.

Of course, Mike would call her if there was a problem. The Pigeon, so close to I-40, had good cell coverage. But still. Nell swayed slightly, shifting her weight left and right, battling down familiar panic. JJ was okay. He was with Mike. He was fine.

The first bright blue Maravia Ranger Rocking River raft floated around the bend in the river and under the bridge, the guide calling instructions to the paying customers. "Paddle right, head river-right of the island. Good! See that stone barrier and the small **pool just** beyond it? That's the takeout. We want to beach all the way down at the bottom of the pool, to make room for the other rafts. See Miz Nell? Yeah, yeah. Right up to her!"

Nell raised her arm and waved, recognizing Hamp in his decal-laden helmet and by his customary "yeah, yeahs." Behind him floated the next raft, the guide shouting the same instructions. "Thank you, folks," Hamp said, his voice carrying as he bumped shore, "and remember, next time you're in the Tennessee mountains or plateau, look up Rocking River. We have locations on the Nantahala, the Ocoee, and, yeah, yeah, right here on the Pigeon. No rafting company takes better care of you than Rocking River guides."

Nell flashed him a smile. Mike and she had scripted the spiel the guides used on trips down the rivers, but the guides had added the advertising finale themselves. Nell couldn't help but be pleased, even when worry for JJ was dancing along her spine.

"Up the bank to the shop, ya'll," she called as the paying customers debarked. "Melissa will show you what to do with your helmets, vests and paddles." Behind her, she heard Melissa calling out instructions and starting her shtick about photographs taken on the run and ready to be viewed inside. Turning back to Hamp, Nell asked, "Everything go okay?"

Hamp grinned and shot a sly look at the raft that bumped shore beside him. "Yeah, yeah. But Harvey got caught on a rock and Mike had to bump him off."

"It was so cool," one of the customers said, a kid of maybe twelve, freckles across his nose and his clothes still wet from a swim. "We were rocking back and forth and we couldn't get off and the Jedi guy just slid right at us and

Wham!" He slapped his hands together hard, the slap echoing over the water. "We were off."

The kid looked behind him and laughed. "And Mama got dumped. You shoulda heard her screaming."

"It was cold," the woman said, but she was smiling. "It was great. Better than Carowinds and Six Flags Over Georgia put together. We'll be back."

Nell made the appropriate noises while helping an older woman out of the raft and up the bank. When she returned, rafts three and four were in sight. Mike's was still upstream.

"Harvey took a swim on that bump-off, though," Hamp said.

"I know," Harvey said, holding up a hand to forestall comments and shaking his head. "I got to buy the beer tonight. Can I get an advance?" he asked, his face woebegone above his tangled beard.

It was a tradition on the river. Any guide who got dumped off his own raft had to buy beer for the others. It used to be a case of beer. But with all the rafting businesses on the Pigeon River and the expansion of Rocking River, the numbers of guides had increased. The penalty now was two cases of beer. The traditionally broke guides often had to borrow money when dumped. While she usually only loaned money for necessities, the tradition of beer for a swim was sacrosanct. Nell thumbed toward the shop. "See Melissa. She'll get it from petty cash."

"Sweet. Thanks, boss," Harvey said. He stepped into the thigh-deep water at the back of his raft and pushed it onto the bank. He and Hamp lifted the heavy boat without apparent strain and carried it up for cleaning and maintenance, making room for the other rafts.

The last boat to round the bend was Mike's, as always taking up the rear in case of problems or to rescue any swimmers. JJ was sitting beside him, his helmet and vest the same blue of the rafts, marking him as a member of the team. He waved his paddle in the air and patted his head when he saw Nell, the traditional signal for "I'm okay." The panic that always tried to steal her breath slipped away and was forgotten. Until tomorrow when he joined the crew for his next trip down the river.

Because she knew better than to embarrass him in front of his pals, the river guides, by hovering until his boat came to a rest on land, Nell trudged back up the bank and into the shop, dodging rambunctious kids, their parents, guardians and friends. Melissa—thank God for Melissa—had them all corralled and had put Harvey and Hamp to work getting the guests to rinse PFDs, store paddles, and drag boats up to the shop. Inside, customers were buying colas, T-shirts, and towels, and paging through photos on the laptops looking for shots of themselves, and then screeching with embarrassment or delight. She could hear the showers in the back of the shop as customers took advantage of hot water before heading out in their cars. Someone was singing opera. At least she thought it was opera. The melody went up and down a lot and it wasn't in English.

Nell rang up purchases, gave directions for finding photos and helped one teenager out of his PFD when the zipper stuck. That one went into the corner with the other defective and damaged gear to be examined come fall, after the season ended and the shops all closed. The summer had been hotter and wetter than usual, resulting in a lot of damaged gear, but Nell wasn't complaining. This season was busier and more profitable than any since she had taken over the shop to run it single-handedly. Profit, however, meant expenses too. The pile of stuff that had to be replaced was twice the size of last year's, and it was only July.

Orson ignored his dad, who stood in the entryway, looking over the dirty apartment and his son, and not hiding the inspection. The scars on his chest itched under the scrutiny, even hidden under his T-shirt. They were ridged, an angry red, bright against his pale skin in the bathroom mirror. While he usually was browned by the sun, the months of convalescence had taken a toll on him. He had lost muscle mass, energy and the tan that river rats boasted on arms and face, despite copious amounts of sunscreen. The hair he had not bothered to cut hung around his face and down to his shoulders. According to his dad, the last time he came to visit, he looked like a hippie instead of a decorated cop on leave from the Tennessee Bureau of Investigation. Not that Orson cared.

Sitting in the recliner, a beer balanced on his belly, he turned up the TV's volume, a not-so-subtle hint that he wanted to be alone. A baseball game played, though he would be hard-pressed to guess which teams were playing. Orson never looked at his dad.

"You don't even like baseball," Nolan said. When Orson didn't reply he added, "That's a sign, you know. Ignoring everything. Sinking inside yourself. Getting depressed."

Orson continued to ignore the old man. He couldn't understand. He was still a cop. He'd never been shot. He hadn't lost everything that had any value to him.

"I've seen the signs in other cops who took a bullet."

The Knoxville Field Office had granted Orson leave to recuperate, but had sent notice that they were reassigning him to the Cold Case Unit when he came back. The high muckety-mucks were taking him off the streets, his injuries sidelining him to less physically demanding areas of law enforcement. Not what Orson wanted. No way near. He wanted to stay on as an active investigator, not be given a pity job. Morose about the reassignment, his slow recovery and the divorce that had followed his discharge from the hospital, he'd begun thinking about quitting the force. And every day that the pain continued, the desire to quit, to walk away, grew.

"I heard the rumors," Nolan said. "You're thinking about going into teaching or some such crap. But I know you. You'd be bored inside a week, dealing with spoiled-rotten high-school kids."

Orson said nothing, his gaze never wavering from the television screen. He bumped the sound up another notch.

"You could do a lot of good in cold cases if you'd let yourself, Junior. You'll never be happy doing anything except being a cop."

Orson hadn't been happy about much in the last year. Not since he killed that kid. Even being cleared of a wrongful shooting and having the death labeled "appropriate use of force" in the defense of a wounded and dying fellow cop hadn't eased the raging anger and guilt that plagued him. If the other cop had lived, it would have made a difference. But to Orson, everything since had looked futile. It was a cheater's way out, but he had given up. And he had no intention of letting his father drag him back into a life where he had killed a teenage boy and still couldn't save his friend. No intention whatever. Never again.

It took an hour for Rocking River to empty of customers, most of which were assisted by Melissa so Nell could hide away in the miniscule office. It took longer and longer each day to tally up the day's receipts, close down the cash register, check in with the managers of the other two shops and deal with problems. As the sun dropped toward the horizon, Mike kept the guides hard at work cleaning the rafts and equipment, and a guide took a hose to the bathrooms and showers once the customers vacated them. Nell had made shower cleanup part of the job on a rotating basis, with each guide taking one day of the week. They had complained, until the first one got his paycheck and saw the extra money. It wasn't much, but it was beer money, and to most guides that was enough to make cleaning showers and toilets worthwhile.

As a team, the guides stacked the rinsed boats in the equipment shed at the front of the shop. The Ranger rafts took up most of the space between the parking lot and the inner glass door of the shop, placing the expensive gear near the front where sheriff deputies could check on it without getting out of their cars, and making it difficult for prospective thieves, thugs or vandals to get from the outside of the shop to the stock inside the next door.

When they were finished, Mike came through, waved at her and said, "Later," and took off for supper and beer. As usual, the security lights had come on and the shop was silent when JJ stuck his head into the office. "I'm hungry, Mama. How much longer you gonna be?"

Seated at her makeshift desk, Nell looked up from the laptop and the IM message from Trophy at the Nantahala shop. Before she answered, she hit the enter key and logged off. "You're always hungry."

Taking that as a compliment, JJ sauntered from the equipment shed into the shop proper, his swagger an imitation of Mike's river walk. Shaggy hair framed his tanned face, baggy shorts and T-shirt hanging on his rangy, lithe frame. JJ was solid muscle and, when he wasn't pretending to be Jedi, Nell could see Joe in his walk, in the tilt of his head. He leaned against her, one elbow on her thigh, and patted his lean stomach. "I'm growing. Two inches since school let out." He added offhandedly, "Jedi said I could eat at the guides' house if you're gonna be too long."

Nell controlled a grin. Keeping JJ away from the guides when they got off the river was becoming more difficult every day. Nell had laid down strict house rules when JJ was around the guides' sleeping quarters, and since it was rent free, no one would gainsay her. While all the guides liked JJ, rules against drinking, smoking anything, including cigarettes, and carousing went a long way to lessening his appeal after hours. "Mike volunteered that, did he? All on his own?"

"Well…not exactly." JJ knew better than to be caught in a lie, but he had reached the age when he pushed his boundaries. "But he heard my stomach growling." He looked through his too-long bangs at her, nearly eye to eye with her sitting at the desk. "He said I sounded like a black bear and said I should eat. And I asked if I could eat with the guides."

"And he told you to ask me?"

"If I don't eat," he groaned the words and gripped his stomach with all the dramatic wiles he could muster, "I'll *die* of starvation. And then you'll cry, and Rocking River will close, and then you'll starve to death, too, and we'll *both* be *dead*."

Laughing, Nell hugged him, and because they were alone, JJ hugged her neck.

Hanging on to her, he thought a moment, seeking an argument that might sway her. "I gotta eat or I'll stop growing and then I can't run rivers." Nell had once made the mistake of telling JJ that his father had set a goal to run every river and creek in the Southeast, and was halfway there when he disappeared. The goal had instantly become JJ's own; her son was nothing if not competitive. A self-proclaimed river rat, JJ intended to run every creek and river in Tennessee before he turned twenty-five, and anything that might stand in his way was fiercely and swiftly eliminated.

Nell pushed his hair behind his ears, recognizing it as the same gesture her mother used on them both. "Not tonight, darlin'. Mama Claire has supper ready." When he opened his mouth to argue, Nell said, "You get to eat lunch every day with the guides, and when they invite you to supper, you can go. But not every night. They need time away from the bosses. Even Mike says so and stays away except by invitation."

The mention of Mike settled the argument, but JJ still had to bargain. "Then I get to lock up. Alone this time. Without you to help."

Nell pretended to ponder the request as she gathered up her things. She pointed to the keys on the nail behind the cash register. "Deal." Smug, JJ took the keys, set the alarm in the shop and led the way, locking the dead bolts on the office door, the three dead bolts on the equipment shed out front, the showers out back, and checked the doors to the vans and the big yellow school bus that carted customers to the put-in upstream. Nell just watched, tears in her eyes. JJ, playing the part of the man of the house.

Though it had been over six years since Joe disappeared, seeing his son always made Nell ache for what might have been, knowing that Joe would have adored JJ. She had a decision to make about Joe soon, and her feelings for JJ were making the decision harder. But the Stevens family would be down from New York at Thanksgiving for their yearly visit, and as always, they would demand that she go to the courts and have Joe declared dead. With the seven-year anniversary of his disappearance coming up—the time she could legally apply to the courts for his estate to be settled—Nell had little recourse in denying them.

Orson watched as Nolan stepped into the sunken living room, with its dusty floor and worn-out furniture. Dust bunnies scurried away as he walked. He dropped a police file on the coffee table in front of Orson's chair and wandered into the kitchen. He came back with a bag of chips and a Samuel Adams beer. His dad preferred Pabst but since he wasn't complaining about the brand, Orson guessed he had bigger fish to fry. He just wished his dad would go the hell away.

Nolan sat on the lumpy couch his ex had left when she took off with the good furniture and most of the money. He sat back as if he intended to stay awhile, drank a long draft and lifted his feet to the scarred coffee table. With his foot, he shoved the file closer to Orson. "Got something for you, Junior."

Orson looked from the TV to the file, a quick glance before his eyes returned to the screen. "Not interested." His voice was gravelly and coarse, still damaged from the length of time he had spent with tubes down his throat, on a ventilator, his vocal cords damaged and little used. It hurt to talk.

"I need you to be interested. So sit up and take a look. Or I'll take you out back and beat some sense into you like I did when you were a kid."

Orson's lips twitched in what had become his smile since the shooting, but his eyes never left the flickering screen. "You never took me out back and beat me. You never beat me at all."

"Maybe I should have. Maybe then you wouldn't be such a putz now."

Orson's eyes narrowed and he felt something strangely like amusement curl up from deep inside him. "Putz?"

"Yeah. A putz. A wuss. Maybe if I'd 'a beaten some sense into you when you were a kid you'd have the stamina and mental fortitude to face a little injury, a little pain, and get on with your life."

Orson's lips went up a bit more but his amusement tasted sour and bitter. He drank half his beer in a long pull. Stared at the bottle, one fingernail picking at the label. "Little?"

Nolan pushed the file closer. "They only took out half of one lung. You got a whole lung and a half left. You ain't dead and you ain't in a wheelchair and you ain't on a ventilator."

Orson's glance flashed to him and away. His dad actually looked pissed off, like he'd been needing to say something for a long time, had let it build and was now ready to let it come out. A vein pulsed in his forehead.

"Yeah," Nolan sneered. "Makes me sick to my stomach to say it. But you're a *quitter*."

Orson flinched. Only a faint twitch, but he knew his father saw it.

And that made Nolan push. Hard. "You're breathing on your own and walking and talking and pissing without a tube, so it's time to stop feeling sorry for your miserable, whiny little self and get on with your life. Yeah, your wife left you, but she played you from the minute you met her. All boobs and bottle-blond hair and baby-doll voice. She faked a pregnancy to get you to marry her."

Orson shifted his eyes to his dad, holding his gaze. Nolan said, "What? You think I didn't know? Hell, I had her checked out. But you were sotted with her."

"*Be*sotted," Orson ground out, feeling the first flush of heat.

"Whatever. She was doing that bartender before you were shot. Her leaving you didn't have anything to do with the shooting or the injury and you know it. She was a bad choice from day one and you know that too. And you're sulking and you know *that*."

"Sulking?" There was more force in Orson's broken voice. He knew his dad was playing him like a bow across fiddle strings. But he couldn't help his own reaction. His eyes went dark and cold and focused. A hot flush raced through him.

"Sulking. Like a kid who didn't get what he wanted for Christmas. Well, too damn bad." Nolan drained his beer and stood.

Orson's gaze followed him. He couldn't help himself. He

lowered the footrest and sat straight. His own body odor wafted and swirled around him. He stank. He scratched his chest at the juncture between his ribs, picking at the ugly puckered scars.

Nolan went on, using his words like a battering ram. "You got a chance to live a life and be a cop. If you got the guts to take it. And there's other fish in the sea for you to fall in love with. If you want. This time with a woman who loves you back. *If* you want to live and love and be a cop. *If* you decide to. If you decide not to be a putz and a wuss and a quitter. It's up to you, kid."

His dad jutted a chin at the file between them on the low table. "If you want the case, they'll take you back starting tomorrow, working the cold case, a case we both had when you were a rookie. A case we never solved. You can be a cop. *If* you got the balls to try." With that, Nolan set down his beer bottle and walked out. Leaving Orson in the dirty apartment with the cold case. The disappearance of Joseph Stevens.

15

Nell looked up from the laptop screen when the door opened. The man who walked in was winter pale with long, black hair and soft greenish-brown eyes. He looked sick, like a druggie. And she was alone. Nell pressed a knee into the counter-space wall to position herself for the baseball bat she kept there in case of trouble. The rounded bat end touched her knee, just to the side of the button for the silent alarm that sounded up the hill in PawPaw's house. She had never had to press it, but it was always handy to know it was there.

"Can I help you?" she said, her tone half challenge, just on the edge of civility.

"You Nell Stevens?" he asked in a whispery voice, like sandpaper on stone.

"That's me." She folded the laptop down so the screen was hidden. She had a problem in the Nantahala shop and the IMs were getting heated. She pushed the computer to the side and bent slightly, circling her hand round the bat. "You want to take a trip it'll have to wait till tomorrow. River's off on Fridays."

"I'm looking for work."

Her hand eased fractionally. "Guide?"

"Kayak instructor. Word at the BP station is you need one."

The BP station served fast food all day and breakfast all

night and river guides ate there when they had the cash. It made sense that her need for an instructor might be bandied about there. This guy looked vaguely familiar, but nothing like a paddler. He looked like he had been up since last week. Like a good stiff breeze would blow him away. Like he'd been sick for months. Black bruises circled his eyes, his skin was sallow. Yet, his hair was clean and his beard was trimmed. She didn't smell old alcohol on him or old body odor, so that was a plus. The lack of a tan said he wasn't what he claimed, however. She straightened, lifting the bat.

Carefully, she stepped back, the bat held low at her side. Letting him see it. "Pardon me for saying so," Nell said, "but you look like a prisoner just out of jail, not like a paddler."

His lips twitched just a fraction, amused. Somehow, that amusement eased her growing concern.

"I was a state cop. I got shot," he said. "I can't be an active investigator anymore."

Nell saw the horror hidden just below the surface of his skin when he said the word *shot,* the misery buried beneath the casual phrase that followed. The bitterness in his tone was muted by the whispering voice, but it was there, and Nell believed him. She canted her head, deliberate, thinking.

"I'm hoping to make a little cash while I decide what to do with the rest of my life," he said. "You have a job opening and I'm a certified kayak instructor. A match made in heaven."

"You got your certification with you? ID? References?"

Eyes shifting to the bat, he stepped carefully to the desk and laid a packet of papers on the glass top. Still moving with care, he backed away. "All there. With my contact e-mail and cell number."

Nell glanced down and saw the name. Orson Lennox.

Nell raised the bat and patted it into her free palm as she looked him over. "What do you paddle?"

"I have two boats, an old Perception Arc-ProLine and a 2006 LiquidLogic Hoss. And a playboat," he added, "but the playboat is for fun and the Hoss is better for teaching. More stability if I have to do a rescue."

"You got 'em with you?"

"Beg pardon?" he said, looking a bit bewildered.

"Your boats," she said, letting him see her own half smile. "You got 'em with you?"

"Strapped to the roof of my truck."

"Let's see your stuff," she said.

"My stuff?" His face went through a series of comical changes as he tried to figure out what she was talking about. Then he blushed.

Nell grinned. "Your paddlin' skill, river boy. Get your mind out of the gutter."

He blushed harder and Nell laughed. "Drive upstream to the bridge. The river isn't running, but the water's deep enough there for you to give me a lesson. Get into your gear and onto the water. I'll be there shortly. Let's see if you can teach me how to paddle."

His face cleared and he turned and left. Nell laughed softly and dialed home.

Orson pulled his boat into the still water near the bridge crossing the Pigeon. He felt stupid, remembering his blush, thinking she was making a pass at him. *Idiot.* Just a damn-fool mistake. But she had looked…pretty. Standing in the shop, the air conditioner blowing a few wisps of hair, the rest up in stiff spikes. She had been wearing something on her eyes, and maybe a bit of blush. She had looked totally different from the Nell Stevens of six years before, her eyes black, her face tear-burned, her expression lost and grieving.

This Nell Stevens had looked composed, in control and self-assured. The way a killer should look. Of course, it had been six years. Her grief would have waned. If she had grieved at all.

Orson had decided to go with his given name rather than the name he had gone by on the SAR, undercover, six years before. Using his own name and his real background story made it easier, somehow, this time. Besides, he wasn't undercover. Nor was he officially on the job. He had just agreed to take a look at things on the cold case while he recovered. His own name put him halfway between two worlds, halfway between a cop on a case, and a former cop looking for work, which his story permitted.

He pulled on his skirt and slid into the Hoss. Knuckle-walking over the stones at the shore, he pushed off into the water. The still, smooth surface reflected back the growth on the far shore, the smell of the sun on the bank was slightly sour, warming the silt brought down by the higher flow the day before. A bird called, sharp angry tweets, full of alarm. A squirrel chittered.

Orson felt himself relax. His shoulders dropped and his spine loosened. His hands eased their grip on the paddle. He feathered his way across the pool. And for the first time in a long time, Orson Lennox smiled.

Forty minutes later, Nell parked at the Pigeon River bridge, just above the takeout for the upper half and the put-in for the lower half. She had taken the time to scan his paperwork, make a few calls, and found out that Orson Lennox was what he purported to be. A decorated ex-cop looking for work. If the cop she talked to in Knoxville was to be believed, he was a mixture of Gandhi, General Patton, the archangel Michael and a superhero. Whether or not that pedigree made him an able kayak instructor was unknown. If JJ and she were satisfied with his teaching skills, he was hired, but he had to pass the test first. And Nell and JJ were ferocious about teachers.

She looked at her six-year-old son and brushed the hair out of his eyes. "You ready to see if the new guy can teach?"

"I can teach. You should let me," he said, that stubborn tone in his voice that reminded her of Joe.

"You can't get certified yet. And I'm not gonna argue with you."

He glared up at her. Nell forced her grin to stay out of sight. He would take it as laughing at him, not laughter because she loved him. He wasn't prickly about much, but paddling was special. She was pretty sure JJ had river water flowing in his veins, not blood. She dropped her hand and unhooked his seat belt, then hers, and let the grin out, just a smidgen. "But...I told Mike he can take you to the Ocoee."

JJ whooped and threw himself at her, his arms around her neck in a breath-stealing hug. Hugs were rarer these days as JJ grew up, aware that river guides watched him and thought him still a baby. As he fought to be judged an equal, he spent less time with little-boy stuff. Like hugs. She hugged him back, his body solid muscle and bone against her. He pushed away. "Let's go see if this dude can paddle or if he's just a diddler."

Nell followed him to the back of the truck and hefted her own equipment. Together, cockpits of their boats braced over their shoulders, PFDs, helmets and paddles in their free hands, they walked down the gravel road to the water. Orson Lennox was on the water, sitting in his Hoss, facing the shore, nose plugs hanging around his neck, sunglasses hiding his eyes. He was lean to the point of emaciation, his arms mostly bone. What skin was uncovered by his vest and skirt was pasty. The water was totally still around him. He'd been there a while. Unmoving. Too far away for her to make out his expression.

"Whatcha smell, JJ?" she asked. A ritual question. Nell was training him to take time to smell a river. "Every river has a story to tell and a lot of it is in the smell. Its health, its rate of flow, its river-soul," she said with a smile. The smile widened when her son pulled the scent in, closing his eyes.

"It's slow and warm and lazy today," he said. "The level is lower than yesterday, 'cause I can smell the stink of…of—" He opened his eyes and scrunched up his face. "That word you use. That means rotten."

"Decay."

"That one," he agreed. "Smells like decay stuff."

She put her equipment on the shore and canted a hip, sniffing too. The bouquet of the Pigeon was usually clean and slightly smoky, with a faint undertone of ozone. Now, it was indeed warm, with the smell of the sun on still water. Oddly, today, it smelled full of promise. And hope.

When she opened her eyes, they landed on Orson. He dipped a paddle into the water, feathering his stokes gently from side to side. His kayak came at them in a straight line, no deviation, which came from skill on the water. He could paddle, no doubt. Just watching him was like watching a dancer, all smooth fluid grace. Reaching shore, the bottom of his poppy-red Hoss scraped on river rocks.

JJ dropped his gear. "I'm JJ and I want to learn how to paddle. Walk us through it."

"How old are you?" the broken voice asked.

JJ bristled. "Old enough."

That faint smile touched Orson's lips, a quirk, a reflex, as if he'd nearly forgotten how. "Your guardian sign papers to let you on the water?"

JJ looked at Nell, warring emotions on his face—that prickly anger at being thought a kid, and some uncertainty that the question might be important.

Nell said, "I signed release papers at the shop. Your boss has them. We both want to learn and we're brand-new to it." Establishing what kind of lesson this was. Telling him where to start. At the very beginning. Newbies.

Orson pulled off his glasses. "There's five things you need to kayak," he began in his raspy, wispy voice. "I call them the Big Five." He walked them through a description of the minimum pieces of equipment required to swift-water kayak, and their uses—specially designed kayak, double-bladed paddle, personal flotation device, skirt and helmet. He walked them through how to put the gear on. While Nell and JJ geared up, skirted up, and pushed their kayaks into the water, he gave them a thorough safety lesson, all delivered from the water, where he looked at home, almost peaceful.

The lesson took an hour. And he was good. Never missed a beat or left out a safety point. He wasn't just certified to teach, he had taught before, his spiel polished. On the water, he made them go through a wet exit three times each, watching them carefully for signs of fear, explaining that the body's need for air often led to panic, but to survive on white water, one had to remain calm, focused, in command. No matter what.

Yeah. He was good. But something about the man still bothered Nell and she didn't know what it was, except perhaps part of his stillness, his lack of emotion. His… watchfulness. Cop watchfulness, maybe, and PawPaw had taught them all not to trust cops.

Orson demonstrated the proper paddle grip and the basic paddle strokes—forward, back, sweep and draw. He made them perform for him, made them prove they could use the double-blades. As he talked, his voice grew stronger, not more raspy, which Nell figured meant that he hadn't talked a lot recently. Then he talked them through how to do a peel-out, entering an eddy line at the proper angle, leaning downstream, sweeping into the current. He demonstrated the technique, and watched them as they tried one.

Deliberately, JJ leaned the wrong way and went over. When

he came up after a wet exit, he asked, "What'd I do wrong?" JJ had seen a hundred such lessons. He knew the shtick and the right questions to ask. Nell dipped her paddle in the river, letting water flow from the paddle blade and plink onto the surface.

Orson gave that not-quite-smile and said, "You leaned upriver. Eddy peels are counterintuitive. Downstream leaning. Do it again."

Happily, JJ dragged his boat to shore, beached it, drained it and reskirted for the next part of the session.

When he reached the end of the introductory lesson, Nell said, "Okay. You can teach the basics." She paddled closer. "What else you got?"

Orson, who seemed completely relaxed, calm and almost happy, gave a grin. A real grin. Almost a *flirty* grin.

Something heated its way down her spine and skittered though her skin. Something half remembered and alien. Nell felt her cheeks redden; her mind went blank.

JJ, on her right, looked back and forth between them, curiosity on his face at a lengthening, awkward silence. The sun was overhead and glimmered on the still surface, obscuring the rocky river bottom, its rays hot on her shoulders and arms. "Teach me how to roll," JJ said.

Grateful for the interruption, Nell drew a breath, forced her nervousness down inside, and said, "Scenario is, we've been down the lower Pigeon, class IIs and IIIs with you, and down the Upper at low water. Midintermediate level. You know we're ready. This is our third lesson. Roll-clinic time. Go."

For thirty minutes, Orson instructed, showing them how to right an overturned kayak in a classic C-to-C roll, getting out of his boat and standing beside each of them in the waist-deep water, placing their bodies in the proper position, patting the hull to show where knee pressure went, where the body rested. When he touched Nell's shoulder, she expected to feel uncomfortable, halfway expected to have to give him a brush-off, but his touch was strictly professional. Not flirtatious at all.

Maybe she was wrong about the look on his face during the uncomfortable silence. Had to be. Men didn't flirt with her. Ever. But now she was uncertain about hiring him. Something about him…

When Orson was satisfied, he stepped back and said. "Okay, you got the idea. Let's see you try without assistance."

Nell pushed away her discomfort for later consideration. They rolled.

Orson climbed back into his kayak, laid his paddle over his cockpit and rested his arms and body in the loose, slumping position of the longtime paddler. He didn't bother to reskirt, but studied them back and forth. When he spoke, he addressed his question to JJ. "Well? Do I get the job?"

"I think he knows his shit."

"JJ!"

JJ ducked his head and looked away fast. "Sorry, Mom," he mumbled, not meeting her gaze. "But people say it. I heard 'em."

"Not in front of their moms they don't," Orson said mildly. "And not in front of employees or customers or anyone they want to impress. Know why?"

JJ slanted eyes at him, mutinous.

"Because it makes them look undereducated, rude and unkind." Orson slid his sunglasses back on his face, as if hiding, maybe hiding amusement from them both. "And you were being unkind to your *mother.* Not cool, dude."

JJ set his mouth in a stubborn line.

"We don't talk that way, JJ," Nell said, knowing she was about to kick a hornet's nest. "And if you can't see that even the guides know their language is bad, then you aren't old enough to be around them."

"Mom!"

"Grounded for the rest of the week."

"No! It's not fair!" he shouted.

"Actually, it is," Orson said. "My mom grounded me for a month when I was your age and said a bad word. 'Course, it was a really, *really* bad word." He turned to Nell and changed the subject. "Do I get the job?"

"What word?" JJ demanded.

"We have two beginners signed up for private lessons tomorrow morning. Be on-site with gear at ten." Nell looked at her son. "And if JJ is behaving himself—" she dipped her paddle and swept away from the guys, toward the shore, throwing her words over her shoulder "—and if he apologizes to me for shouting at me, using cusswords, then acting stubborn, he can be your second on the lessons."

"Hope he's okay, then, because it's been a few years since I taught. I could use the backup," Orson said.

Nell warmed at the reply, not knowing if it was true or not, but happy to have the reassurance, and to have another man around for JJ, even if he made her slightly uncomfortable for reasons she couldn't yet perceive. Mike was good for her son, but he was old enough to be JJ's grandfather and his whole life was bound to rivers. Nell wanted her son to have more. Orson, having been a cop, had lived beyond the narrow confines of white water.

"It's not fair," JJ said, sulking.

"Maybe not. But your mom's okay. And she's the parent."

Nell scraped her boat onto shore, listening to the sound of paddles dipping as the guys followed.

"I'm hungry," Orson said. "Anywhere around here a man can get a sandwich and an ice-cream cone? I'll treat you and your mom."

Though she didn't usually socialize with guides or employees, Nell called out, "The Bean Trees has sandwiches and burgers, and The Smokehouse has great barbecue and cones."

"Pick one," Orson said. "Just let me get changed."

16

JJ rinsed off under the outside spigot while his new idol, who had totally cool scars, took a tepid shower in the men's shower room. Already beyond the tiff in the river and having forgotten being grounded, he pestered Nell while she cleaned up in the RV.

"But you gotta see 'em, Mom. They're gnarly."

Nell permitted herself a small smile as she finger-combed her short hair in the mirror and raked gel through the ends in an upward motion. Claire was right. The blond, spiked tips were demanding another bleaching. She smeared on sunscreen and powdered her nose. Added a hint of coral lipstick. While she was dressing, she asked, "JJ, are you turning into a Peeping Tom?"

"What's a Peeping Tom? Hurry up, Mom, I'm starving."

"A Peeping Tom is a bad, low-life dude who sneaks around and looks in people's windows."

"Nope. I was looking in the door. How'd he get 'em?"

"I don't—" Nell stopped herself. JJ was far more mature than other kids his age, simply because he hung around with adults all the time. And river guides, which wasn't necessarily the same thing. There were only three other children his age living near them. All were girls and none were river rats. JJ read at a third-grade level before he started first grade. He had known there wasn't a Santa Claus from age four. He had watched *The Unit* on TV with the river guides for three months before Nell found out he was being exposed to the violent life of a special forces soldier. He was chronologically six. Nearly seven. Mentally, he was somewhere closer to sixteen, and he always knew when she was telling a white lie. Nell stepped from the back of the RV to the kitchen and slid her feet into bright yellow river flip-flops. "He was a policeman, JJ. He was injured in the line of duty."

"Like Sergeant Hector in *The Unit*. 'Cept he lived. Right?"

"I suppose. But you can't ask him about his scars."

"Why not?" her son asked, the belligerent tone back in his voice.

"Because that's something that he has to volunteer to tell." She grabbed his chin and made him look at her. "He might not want to tell it, JJ. It might be something he's not ready to talk about. Like when Perkins died and you didn't want to talk about your parakeet. He was dead and buried four days before you told Jedi Mike."

JJ frowned. "I didn't want to cry."

"Right. And maybe Orson doesn't want to cry. You cannot ask him."

JJ heaved a sigh. "Yes, ma'am. Can we go now? Hey. Why're you wearing lipstick?" His gamin face took on a sly smile. "Oh, I know. You want to do the big nasty, right?"

"JJ! No, I do not want— Where did you hear that?"

He shrugged his bony shoulders up to his earlobes. "Why? What's it mean?"

"I'm gonna shoot me some river guides. And no, I am not gonna be doing the big nasty with anyone. Do not say that again. To anyone. Or I'll tell Orson the story about you trying to learn how to do a C-to-C."

JJ ducked his head. "I was only four."

And cute as a button, too. And nearly drowned. But Nell

said neither, gathering up her check card, cell and ten dollars in cash. "Remember. No scars. No big nasty."

"Yes, ma'am."

Orson watched for Nell and JJ from across the street at the Smokehouse. He'd taken control of a table for four, washed the plastic tablecloth, brushed crumbs off the picnic-bench seat, ordered French fries as an appetizer and found a full ketchup bottle. The restaurant sold both fast food and groceries, with a preponderance of high-fat canned goods, frozen treats, cola and beer—which couldn't be consumed on the premises with the owner's current liquor license. Which meant there were a lot of to-go orders.

Around him sat truckers, a table full of hungover river guides starting their day at noon with carbonated caffeine and BBQ, and a dejected family of six who had hoped to take the upper Pigeon in a raft. The power company guaranteed to run water Tuesday through Thursday, and on Saturday. Other days were a crapshoot. The power company would open the dam sluices if they could sell power or if local need required it, and today they hadn't seen fit to let water into the river outside of the schedule, spoiling the family's holiday. The guides had given directions to the Nantahala, which was running today, but the parents had to move on, making the Tennessee plateau by dark. The kids were whining and spoiled. A far cry from the spunk, determination and bullheaded intelligence he could see in JJ.

The door of the RV parked in the gravel lot outside of Rocking River opened; Nell and her son stepped down to the parking area. JJ was wearing baggy shorts and an oversize gym shirt, and walked with a carefully studied swagger he'd clearly copied from a hero. The gait brought a smile to Orson's lips. Nell… Nell was in a short denim skirt with yellow flip-flops and a chest-hugging blue top with spaghetti straps. River-rat clothes, but on her they became something else. A fashion statement all her own. Wet blond hair stuck up in tufts. Though she was short, her legs, arms, shoulders and face were lean, strong and tanned. Casual. Earthy.

She squinted at the restaurant and lifted a hand when she saw him through the windows. Orson felt something turn over inside, something broken and sharp-edged. Something painful. He lifted a hand in return. Nell looked both ways, a hand on JJ's shoulder, and guided them across the street.

Hartford was an intersection just off of I-40. The air was constantly filled with the roar of eighteen-wheelers, the smell of exhaust and tires. It had little going for it except the river, and that the little town was bereft of chain food stores, hotels and the other boring parts of reproducible Americana. It was its own little piece of reality, with family-owned restaurants, a couple of bed-and-breakfasts and family-owned campgrounds.

He had done his research and knew that many members of the town council and county council wanted to make it easier for chains to move in, calling it progress. But they were making a mistake, in his opinion. The town was a slice of disappearing America. They should capitalize on that instead. Not that he'd be around long enough to tell any of them that. But he liked it the way it was. Homey. Different. Like Nell Stevens.

Nell belonged here. With her son.

Had she killed her husband because he wanted to take her and their then-unborn baby to New York to live? Had Joseph Stevens lost control, beat her in a fit of rage, and she killed him in self-defense? Had she just wanted the money? Or had he gotten stuck in a strainer and cut off his PFD to get free, then never resurfaced? Was Nell the grieving widow she had appeared nearly seven years ago or a cold-blooded murderer? Or was someone else involved?

If so, who? And where was Joseph Stevens? Where was the body?

Or was he even dead? Had he just up and left, disappeared into a new life somewhere? It happened. It wasn't impossible. But if so, then the guy had taken off without his money. Not likely.

And then there was Robert Stevens. The guy had money enough to hire a hit. It happened more often than people imagined.

His reverie broke when the door opened and mother and son walked into the Smokehouse. Both took a deep breath of the smoky, hickory-flavored air. JJ, forgetting his strut, ran over. "You ordered yet? I'm starvin'. They got real good barbecued chicken and I always get the legs. Mama likes the sliced beef, and Mama Claire likes the pulled pork. Whatcha gettin'?"

One knee on a bench, Orson pivoted and looked at Nell, standing at the chin-high ordering counter, chatting with the cook, a grease-smeared man in a dirty white apron, river clothes beneath. "I'll have whatever your mom is having." He moved to stand behind her.

Nell said, "The usual, Bones. Sauce on the side, okay?"

"I remember, Nell. What about your friend?" There was a world of innuendo in his tone and the back of Nell's neck colored.

Orson said, "I'll have what she's having, with sides of slaw and onion rings." He held up a Coke with one hand to show he had his drink, and reached over the meat display case with his other. "Orson Lennox. I'm the new kayak instructor for Rocking River."

"Ah," he said, sounding disappointed, the tone of a deflated inveterate gossip. "So, I'll put his on the shop tab, too?" Bones asked Nell.

"I have cash," Orson said, handing over a ten. To Nell he added, "Tab?"

"Some of the guides have cash-flow problems," she said. "I keep a tab open here and guides can sign for food. Food only, groceries or meals, no beer unless they have to make a swim buy. And only on the day before payday unless you come to me first. If you run the tab, I take it out of your check."

"Mom? You want Fanta or Dr Pepper?" JJ asked.

"I'll have the peach Fanta today, JJ. And you can have whatever you want."

"Even if it's got caffeine?" he said, incredulous.

"Today only."

"Peach Fanta?" Orson said, pointing to the table he had taken. "Forgive me for saying so, but that sounds gross."

Nell grinned up at him, accepting a Fanta from JJ as she sat, sliding her legs around the end of the bench seat. "No worse than what you're drinking. And no caffeine."

"And you live without caffeine, how?"

Nell laughed, a lively, energetic sound. A real laugh, not the public laugh most women used, no polite titter. Nothing like Janine... He stopped cold, staring down at the tiny woman. God help him. Janine had tittered. How could he have been so stupid as to marry a titterer?

"I drink caffeine," Nell said. "But only when I'm on the river. I had to give it up when I was pregnant with JJ and never started back on it, except as an energy drug." She frowned. "What?"

"Nothing." Orson straddled the bench, facing her, and drank his Coke, his mouth strangely dry. He pushed the French fries to JJ, who sat across from them, arms akimbo on the tablecloth, his chin cradled in his hands.

The boy immediately stuck three fries into his mouth at one time and started chewing, his head bouncing up and down to accommodate the motion of his jaw. Two inches of fries stuck out of his mouth, the potatoes waggling with each chew. As he swallowed the fries, JJ raised up and popped the top of the Fanta, sliding it across to Nell before popping the top of his own drink, a Cherry Coke. Orson took a fry, dipped it in ketchup and ate it. Grease and carbs, two of the food groups of choice for river rats. "You go on the river?" he asked.

"I pull my share of rafting guide jobs," she said, and Orson wondered at the careful way she said it. "You ever work as a guide or just kayaking?" she asked him.

"I'll guide, but it isn't my favorite. I like hard boats."

"River rat. Like me," JJ said. After a swig of cola to wash down more fries, he said, "But I'm gonna do it all, soon as I'm big enough to get my certification. Rocking River always needs guides," he said, sounding as if he was quoting someone older. Nell? "Tips are good. You should do guide trips too. Jedi Mike can take you down the Upper and Lower and get you trained."

Orson glanced at Nell, who was smiling at her son. "I'll do that," he said. Changing the topic, he asked, "What's JJ stand for?" He knew the answer, but he wanted to see what the boy would say.

"Joseph Junior. My daddy disappeared before I was born and Mama named me after him. What kinda name is Orson, anyway? It's weird."

"JJ!"

Orson laughed, the sound raspy and soft compared to hers. "It's okay. I was named after my daddy. He still calls me Junior. So do some of my childhood friends." He leaned closer to the boy, across the table. "But JJ is way better than Junior. And frankly, so is Orson."

"If you say so," he said, clearly disbelieving. "Food's ready, Mom."

"I'll get it," Orson said. He stood, lifting his leg back across the bench. He carried a tray full of paper plates and napkins and small plastic bowls of sauce. The smell was unbelievably wonderful. "If this stuff tastes as good as it smells—"

"Better," JJ said. "It's the best stuff in the world. Even Uncle Robert and Grandmother Stevens like it, and they don't like anything."

"JJ," Nell said again, sounding long-suffering. Orson laughed softly and Nell's eyes flew to his face. He wondered why, but JJ continued.

"Mom doesn't like it when I say it, but it's true," he said between chewing French fries and chicken leg coated in baked-on sauce and drinking Cherry Coke. The can was quickly coated with sticky sauce. "They come for Thanksgiving and they complain about the food and the beds in the house and the bugs—which is why they don't come in summer anymore—but they like the Smokehouse, except for the smell." He licked his fingers, smearing barbecue sauce up above his mouth. "Grandmother Stevens says the smell gets in her hair and she can't get it out."

Nell hid her eyes and looked at Orson. "He does know table manners. I promise."

The boy took another bite of chicken leg, his face liberally coated from nose to chin and ear to ear. "They make me go up there to New York City, which is *boooooring*. No rivers. Don't ever go," he advised. "And I have to go to museums and look at pictures. No, not pictures. *Paintings*," he corrected. "And statues. Which isn't so bad 'cause some of them are naked." He ducked his head and looked pointedly at Orson. "Naked *women*. Showing boobs and everything." He looked at Orson's plate. "Your food's gonna get icky."

Orson made himself look away from the boy to the plate before him. He ate a couple of French fries, stacked the thick-sliced beef between two slices of bread and spooned on coleslaw and extra sauce. He took a bite and almost groaned. From the way JJ laughed, he must have looked moonstruck. Mouth full, he pointed at the sandwich. "Thish ish the bes' thin' I ever tasted."

"Told you. Even Grandmother Stevens likes it."

"Except for the smell in her hair," Orson said around the food. Nell just shook her head, hiding a grin. He chewed and swallowed. "Is your mama gonna get mad at me for talking with my mouth full?"

"Yep. But I'm grounded already and you just work for her, so she can't ground you."

"Good thing." He swallowed, looked at Nell and took another big bite. Halfway through chewing he said, "Some food is so good you can't use manners when you eat it. It's the law."

"And you used to be a cop," JJ said, imitating him by taking a big bite of chicken leg and talking around the meat. "Sho you know all 'bout it, riii?"

A peculiar feeling swept through Orson at the phrase. *Used to be a cop.* If he went back to the job after his recuperation, he'd be stuck in an office with piles of old evidence, ancient cold cases. Interviewing witnesses and suspects who had forgotten or imagined scenarios. Bored to death. Never again going undercover, as he had occasionally been called to do. Never again an asset loaned to different units as needed. Not on the streets. Not investigating active cases, where the action was.

JJ was looking at him with worry in his eyes. Orson didn't want to be the cause of anything dark in the kid's eyes. He forced a smile, the sensation feeling strange on his mouth. Unfamiliar. How long had it been since he smiled with ease? Really smiled, because the expression was called from within, not manufactured, required for social convention. Long before the shooting. "Yeah. I used to be cop, so I know the law." He took another bite, chewed and swallowed. "But now I'm a kayak instructor." And he licked his fingers, to JJ's delight.

Nell sighed and cut a dainty piece of sliced beef, tapped it into the sauce and held it before her. "I am surrounded by hooligans and barbarians."

"You like barbarians?" JJ asked. "We got this cool DVD of Conan the Barbarian, who became the governor of California and has to wear suits with ties now." He grabbed his neck as if choking. "Yuck. He's got a cool sword. Wanna see it? The movie, not the sword. It's in the RV. Mom has to work till three."

"If your mother doesn't mind. Sure. But we got to have popcorn for a movie."

"Yeah! The RV has a microwave. Mom?"

Nell sighed again, and Orson applied himself to the sandwich so she wouldn't see his silent laughter. "You call your friend Emmett. If he can come over, the three of you can watch DVDs together. Long as youns stay outta my hair so I can work."

JJ looked at Orson. "Youns is Tennessee talk. It ticks off Grandmother Stevens, so Mom and I say it all the time."

"Good for you," Orson said.

"And Mom wants Emmett around so I can be safe around you." JJ rolled his eyes and Nell blushed but didn't refute the statement. "She thinks you'll try to kidnap me and play grown-up games like sex with me."

"JJ…" Nell said, sounding embarrassed and amused, and uncertain which emotion held more sway. To Orson, she said, "I'm sorry."

"Don't be. You're being a good mom."

"But," Nell said, amusement winning out as she banged her soda can against her head in mock frustration, a smile pulling at her mouth, "he's giving away all my secrets.

"The Stevenses are okay," she said, taking them back to more socially acceptable topics, "but I'm glad they live in New York and not closer. And I really don't *try* to annoy them."

"But she's really good at it," JJ said, his voice proud.

Orson laughed, staring at the sauce-smeared, amazing kid. He had made the acquaintance of Joseph Stevens's mother. He figured anything that ticked off the old biddy was worthwhile. If he'd known that saying *youns* was all it took, he would have dropped into his native vernacular seven years ago. And maybe he'd have the chance later on. Fate was good about giving you second chances to do the right thing. Or to tick off old biddies.

17

Nell shook her head at the voices shouting on the other end of the cell call. Trophy had fired a guide for showing up drunk for work. Standard procedure was to give six sick days a season, and most guides took them for drunk or hungover days. Buster, aka Roger Pennings, had used all his sick days in the first two months, and when he clocked in for work drunk, he was fired on the spot.

Buster wasn't willing to let it go and had showed up at the Nantahala shop this morning making a stink. Trophy had called the cops and they had hauled Buster off to jail for being drunk and disorderly. Then his father had showed up, also drunk, and so Trophy had called the cops again. Now Mrs. Pennings was in the shop, wailing in the background about how she couldn't afford to bail them out and how her life was ruined and how she was going to burn down the shop if Trophy didn't get them out of jail.

"Is she drunk too?" Nell asked.

"As a skunk on moonshine."

"Call the cops," Nell sighed. "Again." She stepped from behind the counter and paced the length of the customer-service and retail part of the shop, using the phone time to check inventory on T-shirts. Multitasking. She had to order more shirts with the phrase Paddle Faster. I Hear Banjo Music silk-screened on back. She jotted the order number on a scrap of paper and began to count the shirts with the silhouette of a kayaker on the back, Rocking River in graphics beneath.

"Jason's calling 'em now. Oh, crap, that drunk old woman just knocked over the postcard rack."

Nell heard the clatter over the phone. "When the cops get there, tell her that if she goes home quietly we won't press charges. But if she cuts up, we'll throw the book at her and her entire family. They won't get outta jail till Jesus comes. And if the shop happens to catch fire, remind her that the cops now know where to find the culprit. Let me know what happens. And Trophy? You jist earned yourself a bonus." Nell grinned at the whoop on the other end and hit the end button.

"You are certainly generous with my brother's money."

Nell whirled, phone in one hand, pencil and paper in the other. Robert Stevens stood in the doorway, the heavy double-paned glass door propped open, heat and the sound of eighteen-wheelers seeping in, cool air and Nell's good mood seeping out.

"Robert." Nell stomped back to the desk, slapped down her paper and pencil, and set the phone to the side. Robert had been drinking. She could smell the fumes from across the room. "Shut the door, Robert. You're lettin' out my cool air. What are you doin' here, anyway. It ain't Thanksgiving."

The door banged shut, and Robert was inside with her. "We need to talk."

"If it's about money, my answer's still the same. Anything Joe left to his kids is JJ's. Period. I haven't touched a dime of the trust money and you know it. Louis Berhkolter sends youns reports every year. I know 'cause I pay him outta my own pocket."

Robert visibly recoiled at the word *youns,* but recovered quickly. "Mother and I are willing to accept that Joe is dead, have him declared deceased and have his estate probated. In return for half."

Even though she had long ago accepted it as truth, Nell's chest tightened and twisted at the cruelty of hearing that Joe was dead. Fury at the simple declaration whipped through her. She picked up the guest book on the counter. Slammed it down. A vicious sound, sharp and cracking. Robert's head jerked with the racket. "Well, that's mighty good 'a youns. Seein's how the seven years'll be up in October anyway. Louis Berhkolter and I won't be needin' you to agree to anything, to have my husband declared legally dead. And JJ can have his own money within a year after that."

Then his words sank in. "Half? Are you two outta your minds? That's my boy's birthright. His legacy from his daddy." Nell bent slightly and gripped the baseball bat. Robert couldn't see it, but it felt good in her hand. Security in an old-fashioned Louisville slugger.

"We can make this hard on you," he said. He wiped his mouth as he spoke the threat. His hand shook. There was something in Robert's eyes Nell had never seen before. Something far worse than the pest he had been in the past. Now there was desperation, fear. And fear could turn a spineless coward into a true menace. "Don't make us take steps to handle this."

The threat in the words and that amorphous something in his eyes triggered a cold chill through Nell. Behind the counter, she pressed the silent alarm button with her knee. Up the hill, under the interstate, the alarm was ringing at PawPaw's, bright lights flashing, the siren going off. The alarm could be heard inside, and up in the hills behind PawPaw's house. It was her ace in the hole at the shop. Backup. Nobody messed with PawPaw or what he claimed as his. While Nell hated to bring the old man's wrath down on Robert, no one threatened her boy. Not even his own family.

Her grip tightened on the bat as she scanned Robert's face. It was thinner than last fall. His eyes were bloodshot, his nose more pinched than she remembered. His hair slid forward, his six-hundred-dollar haircut giving him an expensive, coddled look.

But the new expression had carved lines into his perfect skin, his nostrils were inflamed, his skin was flushed and his fingers quivered. Desperate. That was it; that was what she saw in his face. Maybe more than desperate. Maybe hooked on something besides booze. Louis Berhkolter said the Stevens money was running out. Profligate living, he called it. High-fashion hell-raising, Claire called it. Nell was beginning to see that it might be trouble, no matter what it was called.

When she didn't reply, Robert shifted his shoulders back and added, "We'll sue to get Joseph Junior."

Nell laughed, a dangerous lilt in the sound. She lifted the bat across her body, to pat it in her other palm. Robert's eyes widened. Fear-sweat circled damply through his expensive shirt. "You idiot," she said. "You really think you can walk in here and threaten me? Threaten my *son?*"

Robert's head came up and he squared his shoulders. "Mother and I are not threatening Joseph Junior. We're offering him a life of opportunity and affluence and the breeding a Stevens deserves. New York, in place of this backcountry, hillbilly hole in the ground."

Steam started boiling in the back of Nell's brain. The AC compressor and fan went off with a wheeze, leaving the shop silent. Nell stepped around from behind the counter, her flip-flops snapping. She was so mad her skin flushed hot and her vision shrunk into tight focus with red sparks across it.

Robert maneuvered back, bumping the glass door. "You can intimidate all you want, Nell," he said. "We have money to hire the best lawyers. We can take Joseph Junior and gain control of his portion of the estate. And we will. But it would be easier on you to simply give us custody."

"Take JJ?" Her voice dropped an octave and her speech slowed. "Take my son?" Nell walked toward him, lightly slapping the bat in her hand. The delicate *pat, pat, pat* of the bat against her flesh, and the sharper smack of her flip-flops seemed to fill the small room like the sound of a beating. Robert's eyes followed the bat's motion. "Nobody threatens my family," Nell said, hearing the growl in her voice. "Nobody."

Robert slid a hand behind his back and opened the door, stumbling down into the covered shed at the front of the shop. "Really, Nell. This violent approach will only convince a judge that we are best suited to raise Joseph Junior."

Nell followed him out the door, spotting the sharpened hoe they kept on a nail for poisonous snakes, but it was too far away for her to use as a weapon. "What judge? One from this backcountry you're so ready to insult? This hillbilly hole in the ground? Here's where any trial will be held. Here. With a backcountry, hillbilly judge. Not in New York." Through the equipment shed, Nell saw PawPaw's old truck accelerating down the road, but she was so angry she might not be able to wait on backup. She grinned, showing teeth.

Robert took another step back, stumbling across the gravel of the equipment shed. "No Tennessee judge'll be taking a kid away from his good, Christian, churchgoing, upstanding mama. He'll take one look at you and that dried-up old crone you call a mother and toss you both back on a plane north."

"Old crone?" he said, horrified. "You *like* Mother."

"I put up with her. Jist like I put up with you," Nell said, anger rising, making her speak too plainly. "Not because I like or respect you. Because even if youns are a couple of limp-wrist weaklings, youns *family*." Her head came up at the word. "Same reason I let JJ go visit youns once a year. *Family.* So's you and Yvette can show him another life, the life he can have someday if he wants it. But not...*not*... because I like you or your mother or your city and not because I intend to let him live there before he's grown. Not gonna happen."

The truck slewed to a stop in the gravel. PawPaw stepped down from the cab, wearing hogwashers and work boots, no shirt, his shotgun cradled across his skinny forearms.

Orson heard the irregular roar of a misfiring engine and looked out the RV window. A battered blue truck skidded to a halt and a grizzled old man stepped out, carrying a shotgun over his arm, the action open. A lightning adrenaline surge brought him to his feet. He wasn't carrying his weapon. It was in his personal vehicle and the truck was between him and it. *Son of a bitch.*

The man strode toward the equipment shed at the front of the shop. JJ craned over the bench seat and looked out the window. Orson grabbed his head and shoved him to the floor.

"Ow!" JJ howled.

"Stay down," Orson said.

"Why? It's just PawPaw. Mama musta pulled the alarm."

He didn't know what was happening inside, but if Nell had pulled an alarm and a mountain man had come on the run, armed and looking determined, there was trouble inside, or was about to be.

Emmett jumped to the window. "There's gonna be a fight!"

Orson shoved him down too and glanced from the scene outside to the boys JJ sitting on the floor rubbing his head, Emmett looking mutinous. On the other side of the RV he spotted a rental car, a Lexus. Someone had gotten past him and into the shop while he watched Arnold Schwarzenegger twirl a sword. He muttered a curse and looked hard at the boys. "Stay here."

JJ's eyes narrowed and he crossed his arms over his chest. "You said a word Mama don't like us to hear."

Images of how he could make the kids do what he wanted flashed through his mind, but there wasn't time to tie them up. "Please, stay here," Orson said instead. Marginally more agreeable, JJ plopped back onto the bench seat of the dinette and turned so he could watch out the window. Emmett took the other seat, but was eyeing the door.

The old man disappeared into the shed. PawPaw. That would be Nell's grandfather, Orson remembered from his father's notes, Waylon Gruber. Former moonshiner. Multiple arrest records from the fifties. Nothing violent. So far.

Orson stepped down from the RV into the sunlight, closing the door behind him. Squinting against the brightness, trying to preserve some of his dark vision, he sprinted to his small SUV and dived inside, unlocking the glove compartment, leaving the keys dangling in the glove-box lock. Close by, he heard the familiar metallic snapping of a shotgun action closing.

He sucked in a breath. Fear and training warred within him for an instant, fighting with a cold sweat and images of the night he killed a kid and held a dying cop in his arms.

For a moment he was frozen in the past, in the cold dark, snow on the ground, ice slick with his friend's blood. Overlying images flashed through him.

Kneeling on the asphalt, firing position. Tightening his finger on the trigger.

The image of the kid, his own gun extended.

The sound of gunfire deafening as the kid fired at him. And he took the kid down. Multiple shots. Pain.

The cold hand gripped in his as Jamie Rozenfeldt died. The sound of sirens.

Daylight crashed in, shattering the nighttime vision. The cold, clear, ingrained reactions of training and experience took over. He retrieved his service weapon, wrapped his hand around the weapon butt and removed it from the lockbox. Disengaged the safeties. Checked the magazine and the action. Injected a round into the chamber. Rolled from the truck cab. Ignoring pain from his wound.

Leaving the vehicle door open, Orson slid along its side and sprinted to the side entrance of the shadowed shed, perpendicular to the shop door, at right angles to the door PawPaw had used. He whipped inside and placed his back to the wood framing, a huge stack of rafts to his right offering partial concealment but no protection against bullets. His body in deep shadow, his position as secure as he could make it, he shifted forward and took in the tableau in a heartbeat.

In the doorway of the shop, up two short steps, stood Nell, a baseball bat held across her middle. Hostile. Her face enraged. Her small body vibrating with fury. Facing her, the old man held the shotgun tight against his shoulder. Positioned for firing. Aimed at a pale figure cowering only feet away. Situated between them.

His back was to the old man and the shotgun. Black suit, mussed hair. Caucasian. Slender frame. Apparently unarmed.

If the old man fired and missed, he'd hit Nell. Orson had to defuse the situation, fast. But before he could speak, the pale figure facing Nell looked behind him. Saw the shotgun and the grizzled old man. He jerked down to the ground. Moving as if he'd been hit. Cowering. Orson got a flash of his face. A man. Early thirties. Familiar.

"I said, are you armed?" the old man said, warning in his voice.

"No. *No!*"

"PawPaw, it's okay," Nell said, her voice strained, her mouth turned down in a complex mix of emotions.

"Who is he and what's he done?" the old man demanded, settling the aim of the shotgun firmly on the man quivering on the ground, arms up over his head.

"It's Robert Stevens," Nell said, all but spitting. "Drunk and acting the fool. I'm sorry I had to call you. But JJ's uncle is just leaving."

"Him," PawPaw snorted and narrowed his aim fractionally, directing the business end of the shotgun on the younger man's backside, which took Nell out of the spread pattern.

Orson took one step closer. He really didn't want to shoot Nell's grandfather. But if the old man pulled the trigger... His focus tightened on the old man, midline, torso. He opened his mouth to identify himself as a police officer. But he was on leave. Not exactly an officer on duty. The thought made him hesitate.

PawPaw spat to the side. "Is he armed?"

"I don't think so. But then, I didn't actually get close enough to touch him," Nell said.

"What's he doin' here?"

"Threatening to take JJ," Nell said.

"She's lying," Robert said. "I just offered to help her get Joseph's estate settled."

"Nell don't lie," the old man said, his scratchy voice dropping lower. Orson caught a whiff of alcohol the stench of unwashed male, cologne, and something that smelled like wet dog. He didn't know which man stank. Maybe both. "And nobody takes what's mine."

"She misunderstood. I'm sorry," Robert said. "I didn't...I didn't mean anything by it. Please."

"We take care 'a our own up here, boy. And nobody takes JJ away from his mother."

Nell blew out a breath, and with it her anger. She lowered the bat and propped it against the wall. The tension in the shed decreased dramatically. "I don't guess we oughta shoot him just cause he's a drunk fool. What with him being unarmed and all. PawPaw, put down the gun. Robert, you get on outta here. I guess maybe I overreacted. A tiny bit."

The old man huffed a breath and a curse and moved his aim from Robert to the side. Slowly, his fingers fluid despite his age, he opened the shotgun's breach and rested it across his arm. He lifted his chin in stubborn resignation and a half challenge. Orson lowered his own weapon. Remembered to take a breath. Groaning, the old man sat down, his knees cracking like rifle shot. Robert flinched.

"Orson, you can come out now," Nell said. "And put that gun away 'fore somebody gets shot."

PawPaw whipped his head into the shadows, finding Orson. For a moment, violence again trembled through the equipment shed. Then it passed, like the aftermath of a lightning strike. "Who's he?" PawPaw asked.

"My new kayak instructor," Nell said, as if it were commonplace for a kayak instructor to be standing in the shadows holding a handgun. Hell. Maybe it was.

"Nice gun," PawPaw said conversationally.

Orson, feeling like he had just entered a twilight zone of slightly twisted reality, ejected the round in the chamber and set the safeties. He was drenched in sweat. A faint tremble sizzled through him. Holding the handgun low and to his side, he stepped into the light. "Did he hurt you?"

"No," Nell and Robert said together. Robert flicked his eyes at her, then at the old man, at the bat leaning against the wall, and at Orson. Carefully, Orson eased his weapon into his waistband at his spine.

Seeing the gun put away, Robert's arms fell slowly to the gravel and he pushed himself upright, standing in a crouch, like a kicked dog. Orson wasn't sure, but it was possible he'd pissed his pants. The cop crossed his arms and leaned against the raft at his shoulder. He was beginning to enjoy this. He'd have stories to tell when he got back to the department. It was like being back in the Hatfields and the McCoys, stuff his dad saw on a regular basis in the small towns where he worked, but that Orson had seldom connected with.

Nell wrapped her arms around her middle and glared at her brother-in-law. "He didn't hurt me. But when I told him I wasn't interested in pushing up the date to declare Joe legally dead, and when I told him I wasn't giving him and Yvette half of Joe's estate, he told me that him and her were prepared to take me to court and get custody. They've pushed before, but this was an out-and-out threat."

"Not a threat," Robert said, standing straighter, visibly struggling to shift the veneer of sophistication back in place. "An opportunity for the boy to live as a Stevens should, not in this—"

"—backcountry, hillbilly hellhole," Nell finished sourly.

"Not precisely what I said, but close enough." Robert brushed off his clothes, pulling the tattered remains of his dignity around him.

Two shadows darkened the opening to the shed. Orson started, pivoting around, one hand on his gun butt.

"I told you there was trouble," JJ said. His hand was held firmly by a bearded, shirtless, tattooed man, river sandals strapped on his feet and baggy water pants resting low on his hips. JJ tugged his hand free and raced to his mother, wrapping her in his arms, burying his head in her middle.

"I'm okay, JJ darlin'." She rocked him slowly, her hand stroking his hair. She raised her eyes to the newcomer. "It's okay, Tom. It was just JJ's uncle getting ready to try and get custody."

"Over our dead bodies," Tom said, rounding on the hapless Robert. "Nell and JJ got friends. You try to take him away and you'll be so full of buckshot you'll rattle when you walk."

Orson grinned at the image, a bitter taste in his mouth and an ache in his stomach as adrenaline broke down. He recognized Turtle Tom from old file photos and from the SAR for Joseph Stevens. The river guide had gained full sleeves of tattoos on each arm, a few across his chest, back and neck, and put on pounds of pure muscle in the intervening years. He was still pretty, however, his face slender, brown eyes wide and usually somnolent, now flashing with defensive energy.

The sound of sandals and running shoes slapping pavement at a dead run filled the air. Someone shouted, "Who's hurting Nell?"

"Who's car's zat?"

"I don't recognize that SUV."

"Watch out for the old man. He carries a gun."

"Nell? Where are you?"

Within seconds, the cramped space between rafts and the equipment-shed wall was full of river guides, the reek of reefer and beer, the stench of males in need of baths, and a lot of protective testosterone. Orson was shoved into the rafts. An elbow hit him in the stomach, driving the air from his lungs. His wound sent shafts of pain through him. He grabbed his middle and scuffed his feet, trying to find his balance. Emmett squirmed past him, breathing hard. Orson ground his teeth against crying out.

"We're okay," Nell shouted over the voices, pulling JJ back to her. "We're fine. Youns be quiet." When the shouting increased in volume and more river guides crowded in, she shouted louder. "Be quiet! Hey!" She lifted her head and raised her voice, *"Shut up!"* The words reverberated under the tin roof.

The guides quieted, craning to find her in the shadows. Most of them were carrying a weapon, one man with a butter knife, a teen with a hoe, a woman hefted a hockey stick. One guy was holding a can opener and an empty beer bottle. When he caught his breath, Orson stifled chuckles.

"Thank youns for coming, but we're fine. So, get on outta here," Nell said, stepping up on the stairs to raise her above the guides. "I'm fine, JJ's fine. PawPaw showed up in plenty 'a time." Stress made her Appalachian dialect and accent sharper but her presence stronger. She was… He sought for a word. Commanding. Yeah. That was Nell Stevens. All five feet two and a hundred twelve pounds of her.

Orson watched her from the shadows. His first impression had been right. She had grown up since he'd first seen her nearly seven years ago. She wasn't the grieving little wife now, and having a child and running a business had brought her into her own. Or the image of six years ago had been an act to cover up a murder. Now, Nell Stevens was tough as shoe leather. And pretty. Orson cursed under his breath. He had no time for a woman in his life, especially one who might have killed her first husband. No, not first. Her husband, one and only. And he was here to try to prove it, he reminded himself. She had kept on speaking while he woolgathered, and Orson, his priorities back in order, struggled to catch up.

"It was sweet of youns for showing up to help, but I'm fine. JJ's fine. We're all fine. But if youns see this here fella show up without an invite—" she pointed to Robert "—you can deck him for me. He threatened to sue for custody of JJ." A silence had taken over as she spoke, chill and absolute. Every head turned to Robert. The sense of threat went up a notch, heating the shed.

"Mama. What's custody?" JJ asked into the hush.

"It's where you get to come live with Grandmother Stevens and me in New York," Robert said.

"Live? Forever?" JJ squeaked.

"Yes," Robert said, a hint of smugness in his tone.

"No way," JJ said. "No freaking way. I'm not going, Mama, and you can't make me."

"Ow," Robert said, and bent over fast. Orson was pretty sure JJ had kicked him, and by the strangled sounds Robert was making, it hadn't been his shin that took the hit. Bodies shifted as something short and solid shoved through them. Orson reached for JJ as the boy headed for freedom. PawPaw caught him first, one bony shoulder in one knobby fist. In a panic, JJ struggled against the iron grip.

"Ain't no city boy takin' what's ours," PawPaw said, his voice like rocks tumbling from a hillside. "You ain't goin' nowhere, son." The old man swung him up in his arms and carted JJ out of sight. The sound of sobs filtered back into the shed and all the guides turned back to Robert who was once again trying to stand upright.

Emmett nudged Orson's thigh. "He can't do that, can he? Steal JJ?"

Orson shook his head. "I don't think so." Especially not with a cop as witness to…well, to whatever had happened here.

"I think you better get your scrawny butt back to New York City," a voice said.

"If you show up here again you might not make it back out."

"Stop that," Nell said smartly. "I may not like him, and JJ may not like him, but he's family. Him and his mama'll be here at Thanksgiving just like normal, if they still want to come. But I think the days of JJ visitin' youns in New York just came to an end," she said to Robert. "You can tell that to your mama when you see her next. Let him through, boys. My drunker-than-a-skunk brother-in-law is going home."

"This is not over," Robert said, regaining his breath and voice, though it was a bit higher pitched than moments before. "I intend to bring up charges against you for threat-

ening me with that bat. And for JJ kicking me. I have witnesses." He looked around the group.

"Yeah, yeah. Like we're gonna say we saw him kick you,"
a guide said, grabbing Robert by the back of his collar.

"What bat?" another said.

"I don't see no bat."

"Alls I see is a city fella trying to cause trouble." Robert
wobbled, possibly as a result of the man shaking him. Orson
couldn't say for certain. He had a feeling he should have left
sooner, but his position at the back of the crowd meant that
he hadn't seen anything with absolute certainty. Only by
guesswork and inference could he say that Robert had been
manhandled. Not adequate for court, he decided.

"That's enough," Nell said. "Let him go. And Robert?
Next time you show up , you better be sober. I ain't letting
JJ around you with you drinking."

Robert stumbled past Orson into the sunshine. Orson was
pretty sure he didn't see him get shoved. Was pretty sure he
was looking the other way when the man fell. And he was
certain he couldn't say which man shoved him if he did get
shoved. But they all got a good look at the state of Robert's
backside and the wet pants covering his crotch. The crowd
laughed and someone made a ribald remark.

Robert flushed, but had at least some sense in his head.
After scanning the crowd with angry, desperate eyes, he
pushed to his feet and pulled keys from his pocket, beeping
his car open. He climbed into the leather interior without
dusting himself off or putting anything on the seat to absorb
the aromatic moisture. It was a rental, after all.

18

Orson invited himself to supper in the guides' ramshackle, two-story, communal house, an eighty-year-old dwelling with termite-damaged stairs and foundation, one bath with old-fashioned iron-stained fixtures under the stairs, a battered sofa, chair and floor lamp in the living room, and clothes, trash and bare mattresses littering the warped hardwood floors. The solid brass floor lamp was probably originally a Tiffany, but now was dented, the stained-glass shade busted out to reveal two bare bulbs.

Wiring from the thirties and the overhead light fixtures, also made of solid brass, illuminated dirty windows and tattered movie posters on the dark, stained, beaded-board walls. A dripping air conditioner sat in the kitchen window, wheezing tepid air. The place was a dump, just marginally better than a crack house. At least there were no syringes or used condoms in the corners.

He brought two cases of Coors to lubricate his acceptance, and though there were some sliding glances and carefully tucked baggies, no one complained, thanks to the beer, a better quality than the no-name beer they usually could afford. Turtle Tom ripped open both cases and toppled the Coors cans into a cooler of ice on the back porch. Someone else put on head-slamming, neo-punk music and turned up the volume. It had been years since Orson had spent any time in a guide house, but the routine came back fast and he kicked back in a yard chair, putting up his feet as dinner cooked. Though he wasn't eager to eat anything cooked in the spare, painted-after-the-last-world-war kitchen, at least the mousetraps had all been emptied and reset, the hot water worked for washing dishes, and last he remembered, cooking killed most germs.

The guides ate organic, primarily from their garden, with a good early harvest of summer squash, cukes, leaf lettuce, early tomatoes, small red potatoes and beans. It all sounded great on the surface, and the food looked and smelled wonderful as it cooked, but Orson was more than half-afraid that "organic" meant that the guides didn't wait for the bathroom if it was in use when they needed to go. Small camper shovels lined up on the back porch said they used the backyard. Where the garden was.

Sunset meant food, and as the sky streaked pink and pearly gray and a soft shrimp tinted the clouds, a woman rang a dinner gong. They all grabbed paper plates and bent metal forks, dished up hearty helpings in the kitchen and headed back outside to the lawn chairs and more beer. The meal was vegetarian, with homemade butter and fresh-baked bread from the oven, hand-kneaded by Juliet, a river guide in her twenties with aspirations to live off the earth leaving no carbon footprint. She was six feet, two inches tall, with thick brown hair and a Minnesota accent. Orson liked her instantly, and decided that the smell wafting from her wasn't weed. No way.

Word had passed that Orson was either a cop on leave or a former cop, and the guides kept marijuana out of sight and underage drinking to a minimum. He was aware that he put a cramp in the guides' carefree routine. Their lives were typically the communal, free love, sex, drugs, rock-and-roll lifestyle of the sixties and seventies, and guides who complained or didn't partake were a rarity, and were usually ostracized or run off. Or they brought their own tents and set up summer camp in the backyard. There were three tents there now, circling the garden, and rafting and kayaking gear was stacked near each one. Orson counted ten guides, which put seven living in the two-bedroom house, three outside. And he guessed that they took turns bathing, though no one showered while he was there. It was…earthy. And oddly, Orson liked it.

He knew some of the guides from the SAR, Turtle Tom, Harvey, Hamp, Stoned Stewart and RiverAnn, who never moved off a long lawn chair. Each of them had been questioned by law enforcement six years ago. One, Turtle Tom, had been a person of interest. Others here were strangers, some young and new to guiding and the white-water lifestyle.

None of them seemed to recognize him as Junior from the SAR. He knew he had changed over the years, the long hair, loss of muscle mass and pasty skin giving him a different, and not particularly attractive, look, but still, he was surprised. He had expected at least someone to know him, or to figure out who he was. And sooner rather than later.

When most of the food was gone, and each guide had at least two beers, and the music had been turned down enough to make conversation possible, one of the guides brought up the raid on Nell and the attempted kidnapping of JJ by the "evil New Yorker moneybags" who had "pissed his pants." Orson sat quiet for most of it, listening as the truth was quickly mangled into something that bore no relation to what he had seen. Eyewitnesses. Worthless as usual. But informative in a totally different way.

By listening carefully to the banter, he added to his knowledge of the people in the guide cabin. Though he still spoke like a typical river guide, Hamp had graduated Furman University and had applied to be a schoolteacher in the local school system in the winter months. He'd been accepted and would start work in August. He still wore a hat with F.U. on the front.

Stoned Stewart, who got his nickname honestly, might have a patch of weed in the hills somewhere, though that topic was quickly squelched.

Turtle Tom had money in a trust fund, which was news to Orson and not in the old case files, some of which he had written. According to the ribbing he endured over the veggie meal, the tattooed back-to-the-earth guide had inherited "buckooes of green" several years ago. He had invested in Rocking River, made a few more bucks and let himself be bought out when Nell had made a go of the business. He was planning to buy the house the guides were using and upgrade it. If the deal went through before the termites totaled it, that is.

Jedi Mike wasn't present at the dinner, but Orson learned that the older guide was the river manager of all the Rocking River enterprises. He spent his summers guiding, training guides for the various rivers where Rocking River had a presence, and knocking heads when necessary.

RiverAnn was eight months pregnant and taking the summer off. She and Harvey were dirt poor and had set up housekeeping in one of the tents out back. They planned to get married eventually, though the two had a tempestuous relationship, as RiverAnn had with all her beaus over the years.

Orson also learned that Claire, Nell's mother, had sold her beautician shop and, like Turtle Tom, had invested in Rocking River. She lived with Nell and JJ up Stirling Mountain in a house they had bought when Nell sold Joseph Stevens's New York bachelor pad. At least, according to the rumor mill. And Orson had firsthand confirmation of how accurate that wasn't. One fact emerged from it all. River rats were still a community unto themselves, and Nell was one of them. He would have to be careful in his investigation to remember that these were her friends and protectors. The day's demonstration had been proof of that.

When they all had a few beers in them, and the sun had dropped below the horizon, Orson set his empty plate on the ground and asked a general question about Nell. "So, the owner, Nell, she married?"

"What, you thinking about testing the waters?" Turtle Tom asked.

"Sweet. You go ahead and make a move, dude," Harvey said as RiverAnn braided his hair into dozens of tiny braids. "Lotta guys have tried."

"She's in love with her husband. Can't compete with a ghost, man," Juliet said.

"She don't date, yeah, yeah. Ferget about it. Not gonna happen," teacher Hamp said.

RiverAnn patted her bulging belly resting on her thighs. "She's got JJ. She don't need no man."

"You'll always need me, baby," Harvey said. He waggled his head, swinging the braids.

"She's nice looking," Orson said.

"She's a mama grizzly. Got thoughts about the business and her kid. No room for anything else," Juliet said. She handed a bowl to Orson. "Scraps go in here. Paper bag is for trash." He scraped his paper plate and tossed his trash in the bag they passed around. No plastic in sight except for the boats. Earth conscious.

"So what happened to him? The husband? He run off?" Orson asked.

"No way, man. They were on a paddling trip down the South Fork of the Cumberland and he disappeared," a young man with blond dreadlocks said, stirring the scraps. Orson hoped he remembered it was compost. "Left her after she got caught in a strainer and got a concussion. Went for help. They found his boat and his PFD but not his body."

Macon, Orson remembered. One of the newbies.

"Yeah, yeah. Some folks say she offed him for his money," Hamp said, nodding with the cadence of his words, "but she didn't."

"Yeah?" Orson said. "Rich dude?"

"You see the dude in the Lexus today? That's Joe's brother," Juliet said. "His Rolex is real and his address is Park Avenue. Yeah, Joe was rich, though nobody knew it till after he went missing."

"Gimme the bowl, Macon," she said. "Compost barrel needs rotating." Juliet took the bowl and rolled out of the hammock. She disappeared into the falling night. From the dark she said, "The Stevenses have money, but they never offered to help Nell and JJ. Not once. They keep coming by trying to get her to sign over JJ's inheritance. Money. That's all they think about."

"Not all," Stoned Stewart said. "Guy wanted me to set him up. Nose candy. I told him I couldn't help him. That stuff'll kill you, man."

"Old lady Stevens is a lush," Juliet added. She entered the communal area and stretched out near Orson. She rested a cold can on her bare stomach between her skintight, midriff-baring tank and her tighter shorts. She was ripped, her abs a well-defined six-pack. Orson was glad he was wearing a loose tee that hid his flab. He had to get back in shape if he was going to hang with these guys.

"I got nosy once and Googled them," Juliet said. "They had a *lot* of money at one time. Forbes money, you know? Gossip columnists think they've run through their liquid assets and only have the trusts left." She drank, her glistening belly catching the light from the kitchen window. "Good beer," Juliet said. "You'll have to come by more often." Her eyes said she hoped he'd come by to see her.

"Thanks for the invite," Orson said, lifting his can and clinking it to hers. "I may just do that. But Coors is a little rich for my guide salary. It may be cheaper next time."

Juliet shrugged. "Beer's beer. Long as it's cold."

"Supposed to rain tomorrow. Anybody up for creeking?" Hamp asked. "Big Creek'll be running high enough to start at the top."

"Count me in," Turtle Tom said.

"Not me," Juliet said. "Creek runners are nuts. Psychos."

"Psychos do it in class Vs, dude," someone said from the shadows. Everyone laughed as if it was expected.

"Last time I ran it, I shot fourteen feet in the air at the Midnight Hole."

"Fish story," someone shouted, deriding. General laughter followed.

"What's Big Creek?" a girlish voice asked from the dark.

"Big Creek starts at the top of Stirling Mountain and plunges down to the Pigeon at the powerhouse," Juliet said. "And some idiots run it at high water."

Talk settled into the intricacies and accident stories about creeking, and Orson couldn't think of a way to weave the conversation back to Nell. He popped a second beer and sipped, silent, as he listened. The moon rose and night birds started calling. Orson learned that Big Creek ran at a precipitous angle over boulders and bigger boulders and a few massive boulders, between trees and through a park with campsites. He had no intention of running it, but he might mosey over and watch the carnage.

The black sky glittered with millions of stars rather than the few he could see in the city. The night wind was soft and damp. The sound of the river across the road and the trucks on I-40 was soothing. Turtle Tom pulled out a harmonica and played a mournful tune. Someone started a fire and the lawn chairs were rearranged around it. The flames were fitful in the strengthening breeze and smoke blew in restless patterns.

Orson felt tension and anger ease from his shoulders. Something that might have been peace rested across him, tentative and delicate as silk. This was the way he had lived his life until he went to the police academy, going to school by day and running rivers before dark, sitting with other paddlers as night fell. And then he became a cop.

And killed a kid.

In the dark, where no one could see, he slipped his hand beneath his shirt and touched his scars.

He had no right to peace. None at all. Yet, for this one moment, hidden in the night, with the moon bright between the trees and paddlers all around him, he felt serenity drifting so close he could almost take it in hand. Almost.

Nell tucked JJ in and kissed his forehead in the dark.

"Did you really tell Jedi that I could go on the Ocoee?" he asked.

"Yes. I told him." Nell's heart twisted with a familiar pain, a habitual fear. JJ was growing up and growing away from her. Like his daddy, he wanted to paddle anything that had water in it. And that meant danger. She pushed away her worry and said lightly, "Next week he has a training run up that way and you can go with him, camp out, help him with the training. After that, you two can take the Ocoee in his raft."

JJ grinned, his teeth shining in the meager light, and threw a fist in the air. "Yes! You coming with us?"

Nell shook her head, knowing he could see better in the dark than she, but not well enough to see the tears gathering in her eyes. "Not this time, JJ baby. This time it's just you and Mike. Three days and two nights away." Mike had lobbied long and hard for this. For her to start cutting her apron strings. For her to let JJ have some time with adult men, men who would protect him with their lives but give him a different vista on the world, just as Joe would have done. But it was hard. "You gonna miss me?" she asked, pleased when her voice sounded light and teasing and not tight with misery.

JJ raised up from the pillows and clasped her to him, his small body hard and wiry and fierce. "I miss you already. I want you to come."

"Enough to stay home?"

"Heck no! Jedi and me been wanting to go off and do man stuff."

"Don't come home with any bad habits or I'll skin Mike alive." Nell stroked his hair behind his ears and kissed him again. "Go to sleep."

"Bad habits like what?" JJ asked.

Nell could think of several, but it might not be wise to mention them to her curious and adventurous son. "Night, JJ darlin'."

"Night, Mama."

Orson had rented a room in old lady Fremont's house, and when the party broke up—when they ran out of beer—Orson drove under the interstate, up the hill, and settled in. He hadn't brought much with him: a few free weights to start getting back in shape after sitting around moping for so long, his kayaks and river gear, a satchel of river clothes, two pairs of jeans, one pair of hiking boots, a few new T-shirts, his laptop and cell phone.

In his room, with the door shut and snoopy old lady Fremont locked out, he booted up his laptop and went online. There were cell towers all along the valley, close to I-40 and the heavy traffic, so he had dial-up available if he got desperate, but he found a cable signal, which happened to be Rocking River's, and piggybacked it onto the Internet.

In the tiny room, its only cooling provided by the open windows, he Googled the Stevens family by individual names and by "heirs of the Stevens fortune," which was something he hadn't bothered to do before coming to Hartford. Juliet was right. There was a lot of stuff in print about them if you looked in the right places. There was even a photo of Joe Stevens glaring into the camera, a kayak cockpit over one shoulder, a PFD slung across the other, his hair wet, standing up in tufts, and beads of water on his face. He was smiling, but also annoyed, anger flaming in his eyes, intense and violent. Like he was about to rip out the photographer's throat. In the background stood RiverAnn and Nell, Ann looking tough and capable, Nell looking impossibly young and fragile and dainty near her.

Orson remembered her black eyes and bruised face from nearly seven years ago. And stared at the violence latent in Joe Stevens. Had the man hit her? Had she struck out and killed him? By accident? In self-defense? The narrow wooden chair cut into his thighs and he shifted in the dark, the laptop on the small table in front of the windows. Chin in hand, he stared into the night, over the roofs on the hillside below him. Could Nell Stevens have killed her husband? There was that letter his dad copied. Had Stevens written it? It was sloppy police work that his dad had lost the letter and not gotten it back. Sloppy and totally unlike his dad.

Returning to the Internet, Orson went deeper and found a snide, catty article in a New York online publication that mentioned the Stevenses' last holiday in Martha's Vineyard. Yvette had tried to purchase plants at a small business and her gold card was refused. According to the gossip columnist's *reliable sources*, the Stevenses were in financial trouble.

In another online site, an article posted several months later claimed that they had since sold the cottage in Martha's Vineyard, and a 75,000-square-foot home in the Pocono Mountains. There were shots of them, alone and together, coming out of restaurants and art stores, and three showing Robert weaving from a bar and throwing up in a gutter. Not a pretty sight.

Though Orson hadn't Googled the Stevenses before coming to Hartford, he had called a friend in the department and run a search through the databases. The Stevenses were clean except for a couple of DUIs for Robert. Nothing major. But his dad had left a few question marks by Robert's name, indication that he wasn't entirely satisfied by the man's responses when he was questioned. He'd have to call the old man and ask about that.

He studied his dad's suspect list until he knew it by heart. It was short. Nell Stevens. Claire Bartwell. Robert Stevens. Yvette Stevens. Mike Kren. Joe's slighted fiancée, Brigitte Boseman. All of them had alibis of one kind or another. A river guide who had a beef with Joe had once been on the top of the list, but the guy had been in the drunk tank at the time Joe went missing. As alibis went, it was pretty ironclad. A school pal Joe had turned in for cheating and who had been kicked out of Yale turned out to be in Vermont at the time. Very few names. And only Nell had motive, means and opportunity. She had been at the top of his father's suspect list. She was at the top of Orson's too.

Satisfied he had done all he could tonight, Orson closed down the laptop, cut off the bedside lamp and stretched out on the lumpy mattress, hands behind his head. Light and shadow played off the ceiling, a combination of the headlights on the interstate, a security light in a neighbor's yard and the curtains moving in the night breeze. Fully dressed in river clothes, shorts and tee, he fell asleep.

19

Nell was up early, rising when her PC dinged. She had it set to notify her whenever the local powerhouse changed its scheduled water releases and it posted a change at 4:00 a.m. to open early, beating the previous scheduled release by two hours. Walters powerhouse, part of Progress Energy, controlled the water level on the Pigeon River, and water level was the lifeblood of her company. There was a time when power companies opened their sluices whenever they wanted, but American Whitewater, a powerful nonprofit group, had lobbied with power companies all over the nation and, one by one, got them to agree to post releases so that the water could be used by enthusiasts and other water-dependent sport companies, like Rocking River. However, nothing said they couldn't change the schedule to open the sluices early or more often than the posted water releases. Nell thought they changed things in the middle of the night just to annoy her.

Up at four, an hour earlier than usual, she sat at her desk in the kitchen as rain pattered outside in the morning dark. Fuzzy socks on her feet, she was wrapped in a fleece robe against the chill, spending the extra hour doing books and checking over the accounts. Nell hated bookwork, but math was part of building a business, and she forced herself to spend at least an hour a day on math and money and responding to her accountant's queries.

She was making enough money to consider opening another Rocking River. It was that or pay too much in taxes. Maybe on the Chattooga, though that river was rain-dependent and recent droughts had put two other companies out of business. Which left it wide open for Rocking River to take a slice of the tourist trade, but didn't decrease the chance that continued droughts would ruin her like it did the others. To make a profit, a rafting company had to run at last four months a year, and if it stopped raining in July, as it had the last few years, she could run only three, maybe three and a half spring and summer months. She played with figures and possibilities until JJ came down the hall, rubbing his eyes and yawning, his baggy Batman bottoms hanging on his hips. There were times when she wished her son's sleeping habits took after her mother rather than her. He leaned against her, smelling of soap and sleep.

Nell enfolded him with an arm, hugging him to her. "Morning, sleepyhead."

"Morning," he said around another yawn. "I heard the ding. When's the water starting?"

"You heard the computer ding? At 4:00 a.m.? On a cloudy morning when it's dark and wet out and you should be sleeping?"

"Woke me up. And then you turned on the light. And I heard the keys clacking. What time we leaving?"

JJ had better hearing than she ever had. "What time *are* we leaving."

"Yeah," he said with a smile in his sleepy eyes. "'At's what ah said."

Playfully, Nell swatted his bottom for mangling his English. "You want some oatmeal?"

"*Do* you want some oatmeal?" he countered.

It was a game they played before work every morning. Nell didn't mind the fact that she spoke with a strong Appalachian accent, but she wanted her son to fit comfortably into both of his lives, his current one on the river, and his potential one. In New York. If he decided to make a life there. Someday. Not anytime soon, of course. Not for years and years. "Yes, I want oatmeal for breakfast," she said, standing and moving toward the stove, starting breakfast to dispel the funk brought on by thinking about New York, and therefore the Stevenses' threat to take JJ from her. Over her dead body. Over her dried-out, buzzard-eaten body. *Damn it!* She slammed a pot down on the stove.

"Mama?"

Surprised, Nell focused on her son, standing close, his eyes wide, but a hint of Joe's smile at the corner of his mouth.

"You're gonna wake Mama Claire banging the pots like that."

Nell looked at the pot and the sloshed water on the stove. She sighed and reached for a towel. "Not possible. Not even if I banged four pots on the stove."

"You mad at me?"

"No!" She set down the pot and towel and hugged JJ, bending so her face was close to his. "I'm mad at your uncle Robert, iffn you wanna know."

After a moment, his voice carefully blank, JJ said, "Could he really take me away from you?"

Nell tightened her arms around him. She'd kill Robert for scaring her son. "No, baby." She prayed it was true. With all her might, she prayed it was true. "He was drunk. Couldn't you smell it on him? And drunks can't be trusted for anything. Thank God."

"So why're you mad at him then?"

"'Cause—*because*—he comes here and messes up my week, making threats and acting all—" Nell stopped herself. She had tried to make it a point not to condemn JJ's family in front of him. She wasn't all that successful.

"Acting all rich and snobby and like he's got money and we're nothing but hillbillies. Right?" he asked.

Nell pushed JJ away so she could see his face. Carefully she said, "Appalachian Americans. Direct descendants of the Scotch-Irish immigrants who came to this country for freedom. Not hillbillies."

"PawPaw's a hillbilly. Everybody says so."

Nell picked up the pot she had banged in her anger. "Yeah. I reckon PawPaw's a hillbilly. But only 'cause he wants to be."

"And we want to be Appalachian Americans. Right?"

"Right." Nell wiped up the water and turned on the stove, setting the pot atop the flames.

"If he tries to take me away from you, we'll run away. Okay? To some river we can run all year. And start a new business," he added.

Nell knew the tagline was for her, an encouragement for her to go along with his grand plans. She was careful not to let him see her smile. "Okay," she said adding salt to the water as it heated. "It's a deal. Go get your river clothes out. We'll be leaving by six-thirty."

Though the sky was drizzling a thin rain when JJ and she pulled the RV into the parking lot, there were vehicles waiting: three cars and a tourist family in a fifth wheel—a tri-axel travel trailer attached to a dual-wheel, long-cab pickup truck. The RV was connected to the truck bed via a heavy-duty, gooseneck, hidden hitch. It was a rig for people who wanted to cover a lot of territory while carting along all the comforts of home. They had been in Rocking River's parking lot long enough to set up camp. The unit's slides were out, providing more inside space, and the interior lights were on behind closed blinds. The glow of a laptop screen was visible through one. The cable she had installed was better promo than almost anything else she did and it cost a lot less.

A dog on a long leash, tied off to the fifth wheel, wagged its tail and barked as she cut the engine and considered the RV. She eventually wanted to lease or buy land and open an RV park for tourists, but that was a few years down the road. Unless some land came up for sale cheap enough to use this year's profits.

"Mama," JJ said, breaking her reverie. "Uncle Robert's here again."

Nell didn't swear, but it was a near thing. Robert was walking through the meager light from one of the cars toward them. He was wearing high-end Stolquist river shorts and shirt, and a top-of-the-line PFD was slung over his shoulder.

"He's got gear," JJ said, sounding surprised and not particularly happy. "Think he's gonna go on the river?"

Nell smiled grimly. "Looks like he's thinking about it."

JJ laughed, the tone odd and almost unkind. Nell looked at her son in surprise. "Jedi and I can take him out," he said. "It'll be fun."

"You will not dump him on purpose. You understand?"

JJ grinned at her, innocent and crafty at once. "Yes, ma'am. I hear you."

It was Jedi Mike's tone and phrase, used when he fully intended to disobey a direct order. Nell huffed and opened the Rocking River RV door into the warming, damp morning.

Robert's expensive cologne blew to her on the wet breeze. When he saw her hop from the RV, he tossed back his well-styled hair and grinned at her as if they shared a secret. He walked gingerly, new river sandals unsteady on the gravel, but his eyes were clear and he appeared and smelled sober, which was a nice change. "Good morning, sister-in-law and nephew," he said. "I come bearing apologies and an olive branch. I was an ass, I was drunk and I was out of line. May we start over?"

At Nell's narrowed eyes, he bobbed his head as if to say, "*Yeah, I deserve that*." Instead, his tone ingratiating, he said, "I realized last night that I've never been on a Rocking River tour. You run the Pigeon even in rain, don't you?" He grinned, a ghost of Joe in the rueful gesture.

Nell hesitated, evaluating her brother-in-law while fighting her reactions to the grin. She decided that the vague resemblance to Joe was no reason to be nice. She'd rather knock out his teeth, but then again, there was something to be said for picking her battles and keeping her enemies close.

Nell ran a hand through her short, stiff hair, considering how she wanted to handle her recalcitrant son and this new, friendly Robert. A Robert in river clothes, evidently intending to poach on her territory. Since the other alternative— knocking out his teeth—could get her landed in jail, polite it was. "Sure, Robert," she forced out. Nell put a smile on her face. "You're welcome to take a tour."

JJ hung out at an angle from the RV door's security handle and glared, his tone belligerent, "Only if you're sober."

"JJ!" Nell said, coloring, her hard-taught manners leaping up fast. "I'm sorry, Robert."

"Why are you sorry?" JJ asked, his mouth growing stubborn. "It's a rule. You don't let anyone raft if they been drinking. Not even him."

Robert shrugged easily and smiled. "It's a good rule, JJ," he said. "Your mother is a smart businesswoman to enforce it. But I promise—" he crossed his heart, clearly determined to be charming "—I haven't had anything to drink since yesterday at supper. I'm as sober as a Baptist preacher."

JJ glared from Robert to Nell, jumped to the ground and stomped to the equipment-shed entrance of Rocking River. Robert looked from JJ to her in puzzlement.

"JJ knows you threatened to sue for custody, Robert. He's afraid," Nell said softly.

"Oh. That. I apologize," he said, placing his hand over his heart. He must think the heart gestures made him look sincere. And it did, sorta. Which ticked Nell off. "I had a few too many on the flight down, and, as Mother often tells me, I'm not a congenial inebriate. Mother and I have no intention of suing for JJ to live with us full-time."

Congenial inebriate. Fancy words for a happy drunk. But Nell didn't say it. Maybe the best way to stave off a custody suit was to be nice. "Yes, Rocking River runs in the rain. It fact, the extra water can make for a better run." She shut the RV door and fished in her pocket for her shop keys. "Come on in, Robert. And remind me to tell the guides not to kill you on sight." She got real satisfaction when he blanched slightly.

Nell unlocked the shed as JJ lifted the sharpened hoe from its hook near the door. There were two black snakes curled in the corner and another draped over the door frame over their heads. The presence of black snakes generally ensured that there were no poisonous snakes inside, and Nell went on through to open the office door.

Using the hoe as a snake hook, JJ picked up the sleek black snakes one by one and carried them into the trees near the river. Nell noticed that Robert stood back, mouth slightly open, watching. "You don't kill them?" he asked.

"Not black, king, green or garter," Nell said, working the lock and turning off the alarm. "They eat rats, field mice, and have been known to keep out thieves. Copperheads we kill. And once a rattler. Ticks off the environmentalists, but liability insurance is high enough as it is." She looked over her shoulder and laughed silently as Robert backed away from her son and the six-footer that curled irritably over the hoe handle, climbing toward JJ. "Black snakes kill copperheads," she said casually, "so when they spend the night in here, we don't mind."

"Do copperheads come in here too? JJ could be bitten."

Nell stared at her brother-in-law. Was that an accusation he might make to a family-court judge for custody? Maybe she should have brained him with the bat after all. "Sometimes," she said. "JJ is pretty good at killing them." She accented *killing* hard, and Robert flinched just the tiniest bit. Good. She hoped he thought his nephew was a bloodthirsty little savage, too untamed to keep permanently in New York.

Inside, Nell booted up the laptop and checked the day's reservations for all three Rocking Rivers. The Pigeon River wasn't a destination point for river runs, which meant that, unlike the Nantahala, which had numerous advance reservations from church groups, youth groups, local summer camps and families, the Pigeon relied more on drive-by traffic. Rafts on the rapids, visible to kids from the interstate, were the best advertisement in the world. Add on a few billboards and traffic was guaranteed. But today, four different church groups had booked tours, and the early water release meant that the first group could leave before ten if everything worked out right. If the first booked church group showed up early, if enough guides were sober early. If, if, if.

Nell had long learned to live on if—which meant being instantly adaptable. The black snake coiled atop one of the T-shirt racks was a case in point. "JJ," she called. "We got another one in here." Robert, peeking in through the door, visibly shuddered. It brought Nell all kinds of joy to see it. Which made her somewhat ashamed, but not ashamed enough to censor the joy.

The day was slammed. The first tour bus showed up at eight, and Mike and the new kayak instructor followed them in, walking the hyperactive kids—who had already climbed a muddy mountain for a cloudy, rained-out sunrise service, eaten breakfast, climbed back down through the mud, and who were still filthy and wet and about to get wetter— through the safety speech while Nell took care of liability forms and paperwork. Falling into a natural rhythm, Orson, Mike and JJ got the rafts checked out, taught paddling 101 and helped with the business of Rocking River. Mike crossed the street to the guides' house to roust them awake, but they eventually showed up, too. Two full busloads of paying customers headed out long before the other rafting businesses were ready to start, rafts piled and strapped on top of each bus, Mike and a sleepy guide starting their spiel to entertain the clients.

As the buses took off, Nell heard Mike's voice boom through the loudspeakers, "How many of you have never done this before? Okay, let's hear it for the newbies—first time on a bus!" Laughter sounded through the open windows.

Orson watched Jedi Mike as he handled the customers, joking and chiding as the guide learned the experience level of the clients and decided how to split up the large crowd among the boats. Family groups went into boats together. The others were divided up by experience. Skilled paddlers were evenly distributed throughout the boats with at least two capable paddlers and the guide per raft. The rank beginners he divided among boats. Strong-looking athletes who looked like they would learn fast were assigned to bow positions, and doughy couch potatoes who looked afraid of their own shadows went in the stern.

Each boat was assigned a guide based on his or her level of training and expertise, and the guides immediately began to learn the names of the people who would be on their boats, starting chatter calculated to increase the chance of tips at the end of the ride.

Orson was assigned to Mike's boat with JJ, Robert and a family of three from Des Moines, which was perfect for Orson. He had never paddled the Pigeon and it was a good chance to learn the river from the best rafter in the Southeast, who also happened to be still close to the top of his dad's suspect list.

When the buses reached the powerhouse, water was boiling through the sluices, rushing downstream, filling the cool morning air with mist that mixed with the rain and decreased visibility. Not ideal conditions, but not the worst Orson had ever seen.

Mike set the couple in the middle of the raft, the young girl in the back beside JJ, and assigned Robert and Orson the front as the power paddlers, Robert on the right, starboard side, Orson on port, to the left. Which was going to be funny if Robert proved to be useless, making them paddle in circles. However, JJ's uncle had listened to the safety speech as if his life depended on it, and though he took the single-bladed paddle in hand as if it might bite him, he gripped the T-grip properly and shoved his feet into the pressurized crease between raft side and bottom like a pro. When Jedi Mike pushed off from shore—the last of eight inflated Rocking River rafts, Robert dug into the water with a good, easy-to-track rhythm. Orson matched his paddle strokes when Jedi called out, "All ahead paddle," as they headed for the first class IIIs, unimaginatively named the Powerhouse Threes.

As they took the drop at the BFR—Big Friendly Rock, likely referred to as something else by the guides when the clients weren't present—Mike called out the river's tourist features. He knew a lot about the ecosystem, from plants that treated poison ivy to plants that were poisonous, to the changes in tree life over the last hundred years: the loss of the American chestnut to disease, the widespread death of hemlock trees, and the way accidental Oriental tree imports were taking over the terrain. Orson was informed about the effect of DDT on native wildlife and the reappearance of hawks, bald eagles and ospreys nesting along the water.

Mike gave them the history of the land from the first appearance of the white man to the Revolutionary War to the present, with special commentary on the way the government, especially the Department of Transportation, used and abused the land and watercourses, blasting trees and rock and even bridges and dumping all the waste and debris into rivers without proper thought. He pointed out the rusted remains of old trains and huge chunks of twisted rebar and concrete, discarded by the DOT, deliberately dumped into the river. "Mankind, particularly the U.S. government, ain't been too good to Mother Earth, and the idiots at the DOT are right up there with the worst of the troublemakers."

Orson hadn't known Mike long, but he figured that if a contingent of DOT VIPs came for a rafting trip, the spiel wouldn't change except to get more rabidly antigovernment. And maybe the raft would accidentally-on-purpose flip a couple of times. Orson's old man would hate this whole routine. Though Orson voted Republican and considered greenies to be shortsighted most times, he enjoyed the rough semipolitical commentary and had to agree with Jedi's take on the river. The government had done blessedly little to save the planet and her natural resources, and a lot to mess it up.

The water spray combined with the mist and rain was colder than Orson expected, his skin chilling fast and goose bumps pebbling his skin, even with the strenuous paddling. It made him wish he had worn a water-repellent shirt. Maybe water-repellent pants too. The sun stayed hidden by the clouds, the day gray and the air over the river a good ten degrees cooler than on land. But it was beautiful country and Mike was informative, well versed on the history of Tennessee and the river. He managed to be entertaining and educational all at once, and JJ and the girl sitting in the rear were shouting and laughing from the first rapid.

By the time the rafts reached the class III rapid named the Vegamatic, the team had settled into a comfortable tempo, the paddling cadence called by Mike, who steered the raft from his seat up high in the stern. He used his paddle as a rudder, guiding the craft while the water current and the paddlers provided the power. Each small waterfall, called a drop, allowed the stern of the raft to ride up high, giving Mike a clear view of the water ahead.

Lost Guide came up on them fast. Lost Guide was a significant, S-shaped drop of about four or six feet, with a squirrelly shifting current that often dumped a raft or dumped an inexperienced guide into the drink, leaving his paddlers without a rudder. The class IV wasn't technically dangerous, but it could be difficult, and people who had swum the rapid after being dumped often came away with some pretty major bruises and the occasional broken bone.

Orson saw the falls coming, read the water and picked the line. A VW Beetle–size rock just under the surface of the water created a huge pillow left of the drop. He shoved his river-shoe-shod toes hard into the tight crevice created where the raft's inflated sides met the floor.

Mike yelled, "Paddle right," to set their line into the center of the drop. But the water was feeling spiteful. In a smooth, easy slide, the river sent them toward the pillow. The Ranger rose up, half on the pillow, half off. They tilted.

Orson had time to think, Son of a *bitch*.

The water lifted the paddlers on the right of the raft up high. Robert was poised at the top, silhouetted against the gray sky. Time slowed, moving in stop-action video. The rock bent the boat in a partial, vertical taco. It threw Robert back like a bucking bronco. Dropped the raft down, hard, and bent it in a taco, left trying to fold over right. A screaming, rabid surge of river tore by Orson's left ear.

Robert bent. Dropped into the floor of the raft as it folded over. Rolled into a ball at Orson's right leg. Cradled his paddle and gripped the side wall of the boat. He didn't hit the water.

The woman behind Robert bent at her waist. Hard right. The boat snapped her entire body hard left. She was catapulted forward, over Orson. Into the water.

20

The man shouted, "Gina!"

The child behind them screamed. She threw herself toward her mother. JJ caught her and wrestled her into the floor of the raft, paddles flying. Orson took a blow to his kidney. Dropped a knee into the floor beside Robert, shoving the other man over. The father, Jim, thrust his daughter down with one hand. Screaming his wife's name, the man tried to stand, to search down the rapid. The boat plunged over the drop and the man nearly went over.

Orson banged the man's knee with the T-grip of his paddle. "Sit down," he yelled. "Hold on to your kid. We'll find her." Reluctantly, Jim sat, repositioning his feet under the thwart in front of him. Mike shifted his paddle, altering the direction of the raft into the lee of a rock at the bottom of Lost Guide, where the current backed up. He blew his whistle, three piercing beats. The signal was repeated from downstream and Orson saw heads start to turn. Someone downstream would rig safety lines or be ready to throw rescue lines to a swimmer.

The reality was, Gina would have to swim the rapid. Even experienced guides didn't care to swim a class IV. Orson didn't know if there were undercut rocks or sieves—narrow grooves between huge rocks that sucked water and debris in and let out only water—that might trap her. He didn't know about holes that might suck her in and hold her under, rolling her over like a washing machine until she drowned, letting her go only when the river was ready to release its kill.

Orson turned back around and searched for signs of the woman. Gina. Robert pointed with his paddle. "River-right. Eyes on her," he shouted. Orson spotted the woman clinging to a rock across the river from them, her Rocking River vest blue and red against the stone gray. Robert and Jim did a high five, touching paddle tips. All the other rafts ahead of them were clearing the river. The raft was downstream of her. The woman was clearly terrified, white faced, her mouth turn down in fear. Crap. She wasn't letting go of the rock. She wasn't going to swim.

Mike shouted over the nearby roar of white water, "We'll portage the boat back upstream, secure the raft to a tree onshore, and set up a Z-drag. From shore, we'll let out line and let the water carry the raft to her. Understood?" They all nodded.

"Paddle hard all," Mike shouted, "and we'll eddy out." Orson and Jim dug in. Orson's breath was harsh, audible over the river's voice as he used muscles he hadn't worked in months.

The river was a beast, clawing at them from below. Then the Ranger raft bumped a rock onshore, cutting off some of the river's voice.

They scrambled out. Above them on the interstate, trucks rumbled by, competing with the river for loudest voice. "Okay. Everybody lifts. Let's go," Mike said, making a path along the water's edge

As portages went, with four adults and two kids carrying a heavy-as-hell raft across a narrow, stony track on sloping ground, moving fast to rescue a swimmer, in a misting cold rain, it wasn't bad. The crew had to pass the raft over a pile of rock, skidding the boat's underside across the top, and

Orson, who was in front, had the pleasure of holding the boat's balanced weight until they all got around. He really had to get in shape.

Suddenly, Mike said, "All stop." They stopped and set the raft on the uneven ground. Orson, his heart hammering from exertion, craned around a rock to spot Gina, still on her boulder. Mike handed Robert two biners, a pulley wheel and a throw rope, and pointed from him to a tree. "Pulley Z-drag," he said. "That one."

Robert raced to the tree, tied off the rope and set up a pulley. He laced the rope through it, then around another tree, wrapping a bit of flex into a circle around the lines and passing one of the lines back through it, creating a Z-shaped lever system called a Z-drag. It wasn't a complicated system for a mountain climber or a rafter, but the average Joe off the street would have no idea how to set one up. Orson would have had to think about it a bit himself. Robert set it up as if it was second nature to him. Glancing from Robert to Mike, he caught a flash of satisfaction on the guide's face.

"You set this up," Orson said softly.

Mike shifted his attention to Orson and back to JJ's uncle. "Nope. Stop thinking like a cop. But it says a lot, don't it?" Using biners, he attached one end of the rescue rope to another. Orson watched and worked to catch his breath as Mike tied the rescue rope to the raft and played out some of the line. The spatter of rain increased, the malicious sky spitting at them.

Robert set up with his back against a rock and one leg against another tree, the pulley Z-drag system between his hands and the trees he was using to secure the rope. He let out a bit of line and called out, "Ready when you are."

"JJ," Mike said, "you and Beverly stay onshore."

"No way," JJ said. "I want to help."

"Not on this one. You have to protect Bev. But you can

both sit on this rock and watch. Go." Mike swatted him on the butt with his paddle.

JJ's face twisted in that stubborn expression Orson had come to recognize as characteristic, but he walked to the rock Robert was using as a brace and started to climb. From the top, he shot a look of retribution at Mike as he helped Beverly up. Orson couldn't help his grin. Up high, Beverly shivered with wet and cold and JJ put his arm around her. It was cute, but Orson knew better than to let the kid see his amusement.

Mike nodded at Robert but spoke to the others as he tossed all but three paddles to the ground. "We'll ferry across current to the rock. I'll try to bump us next to her, against the rock. I'll hold our place in the current. Orson, you or Jim pull Gina in, whoever is closer to her. Kneel on the boat side, grab the shoulders of her vest, turn her to face the boat and fall back into the boat, pulling her in with you," he instructed. It was rescue 101, and he had gone over it in his safety speech, but repeating it grounded them all in what was about to happen.

"If the current takes us left or right of the rock, we may have to work it. But we don't want one of you going in, or Gina dropping from the rock and having to swim the rest of the Lost Guide into the pool below, scared as she is. It would be better to have Robert pull us back upstream and try again.

"Robert?" The man looked at him. "If for some reason you can't see us, I'll blow one short note per foot of extra line we need." Robert nodded, looking oddly competent. "And if we need to go back upstream, I'll blow long notes for each line foot. When we have her, I'll blow one very long blast."

Mike pointed with his paddle at the boat. "Get her on the river."

The three men lifted the boat by the straps and walked

from shore. The raft rested atop the water, rocking gently, held in place by the rope Robert controlled, the current flying by underneath. The three paddlers climbed in and set their feet to secure their positions.

"Okay," Mike said. "Let's do it." He nodded at Robert and the lithe man released rope, muscles bunching beneath his river clothes. When did Robert get muscles? He had looked so doughy in a suit with piss-wet slacks.

The Ranger slid into the current. The surface of the river was foamy and dark, ringed with falling rain. "Paddle hard all," Mike shouted. They dug in. Orson's back and shoulder muscles were burning like fire.

The river growled louder as they pulled from shore, sounding angry. The current shifted, suddenly helpful, dragging them into the center. "Jim, you paddle," Mike shouted. "Orson, I think we'll be river-left of the rock when we hit. You get Gina. Jim, I want you in the middle of the boat to paddle."

Orson set his paddle in the bottom of the boat, out of the way. He shook out his shoulders, ready to lift Gina by the straps of her PFD. Jim crawled over the thwart, into the bow of the boat where he could paddle either side with a simple shift of balance.

With Mike's paddle as a rudder, the raft eased more river-left, centering on the rock Gina clung to, the river beating against her legs. The current caught the raft and spun it again and Mike compensated, his face tight with concentration. Orson glanced to his left and right, reading the water. Unpredictable, squirrelly. This wasn't going to be easy.

Onshore, Robert eased out line a few inches at a time. The river raced beneath them, tugging hard, pushing them, slapping them around.

Brilliant light exploded overhead, half blinding Orson. An instant boom shook the raft. They all ducked hard. The sky opened up in torrents. Lightning hit again, this time on the ridge near the interstate, white light shocking. Wind swirled along the river's course, pushing the boat around in a half circle. Rain beat into the Ranger, pelting their skin, stinging like nettles. A third lightning bolt stuck. Hit a tree river-left. The trunk exploded. Bark blasted into the air. A tree limb shot into the water. Visibility dropped to a few feet.

They had just left a man and two kids onshore. Under trees. In a lightning storm. It would have been safer in the boat on the water.

Icy rain hammered them. Orson's skin tightened into hard pebbles of stress and cold.

"Ready!" Mike shouted over the maelstrom, his voice tinny beneath the bellow of the storm. Lightning struck again, and Orson felt the tingle through his body, the electric current carried through the water current.

Orson spotted the blue and red vest. Gina was only about six feet in front of them. Either she had slipped or the water was rising. Her fingers were a bloodless white, curling into the river stone. Orson glanced back to shore. Robert was invisible through the pounding rain. He would have no idea how much rope they needed.

Mike blew five quick blasts on his whistle. A moment later the boat began to move again. One foot closer. Two.

Orson stretched out his arms and leaned out over the water as if he could will himself closer. "Hang on, Gina!" shouted, his voice lost in the rapid and the storm. Orson thought she might have screamed back, into the teeth of the cutting rain.

The boat moved another foot. Another. They were close enough to see blood trailing, watery and thin, across Gina's right hand. Jim paddled hard, arm muscles straining under his wet T-shirt, his fingers digging into the handle.

Mike blasted another note on his whistle, sharp and

quick. The current caught them, spinning them in a half circle. The rope went slack and the boat lunged forward. The spin intensified, reversed, and hit Gina's body square on. Orson and Jim were thrown against each other. There was no traction and they scrambled in the bottom of the boat. The raft rose and fell. Trapping Gina between boat bottom and granite.

Mike was beside them in the bottom of the raft. "All lean in hard right!" he shouted.

Orson had no idea which way was the stern or the bow. He followed Mike's example, leaning far over the side of the raft, Jim beside him, so close their feet were intertwined.

The raft eased back off the rock and settled uneasily on the river surface. Not bothering to turn her to face him, Mike reached hard and grabbed Gina's vest. He fell back, into the bottom of the raft. Gina landed on top of him. Even over the storm, Orson heard Mike's grunt as she landed.

Orson found a paddle. Mike swiveled upright and took his seat up high in the stern. Jim and Gina held each other in the bottom of the raft, rain plastering hair and clothes to their bodies. Mike blew one long, echoing burst on the whistle. A second passed, and slack line sent them spinning past the rock.

This time Mike dug in with his paddle-rudder and Orson provided power, paddling hard. They took the Lost Guide rapid in a series of fast drops. The shore came into sight. Moments later, they were beached, just downstream of where they had beached before.

With unsteady fingers, Mike released the tie on the boat. Orson stepped ashore on quivering legs and tied the raft off to a small tree. Mike blew the "all safe" on his whistle and pulled a Ziploc bag containing a radio and a cell phone. From downstream came his long note, repeated several times, barely heard over the storm and the Pigeon.

* * *

The cell phone rang just as the storm opened up overhead. Clients rushed into the shop. Melissa hit the brew button on the coffee machine and started working the crowd, hawking T-shirts, coffee, colas and the sweets in the rack behind the register. All to make a profit, of course. Nell answered the phone, talking fast while ringing up two tees and a halter top. "Rocking River. Take a rocking good trip down the Pigeon. This is Nell. Can I help you?"

"Mike here," his static-filled voice said. "We lost a customer on Lost Guide and did a rock rescue." The connection broke up for a moment and then Nell heard "—all's well. JJ's fine. But this storm—bad." Static took his voice away again, and then she heard "—soon as we can see more'n ten feet in front of us, we're—ing in with all speed."

Thunder rumbled in the background of the phone. A moment later the sound rolled over the shop, rattling the walls. Her hand clenched on the cell. "River's rising fast," he said. "The radios you make us—useless in a storm and the resc—I needed my hands free and the whistle worked—head back—visibility improves."

"I'll watch for you," Nell said.

The connection broke. Lightning shattered the sky overhead. Her baby was out in the maelstrom.

When the storm blew over, leaving only a patter of raindrops and patches of blue sky overhead, the crew pushed back into the river from the relatively still water of Bomb's Lake, where they had taken shelter, and headed downstream. Though the water level was higher, the Pigeon seemed calmer now, almost serene. The current lifted them gently over rocks and dropped them into troughs. JJ and Bev were shouting back and forth about river monsters and magic wands and lightning.

They quickly caught up with the other Rocking River rafts, the guides shouting insults and encouragement to one another. From his perch, Mike took a bow for the successful rescue, and Gina called out, "My hero," pointing to the guide.

"Yeah, yeah! Be sure to tip him," Hamp shouted. The crews all laughed, the sound of relief and release echoing along the river as they headed into the final rapids of the Upper Pigeon River.

21

Mike looked up from the coffee counter at the BP station, meeting Orson's eyes as the cop entered the food section. Mike's jaw was at a pugnacious angle, but the expression in his eyes was thoughtful and unsurprised. Almost as if he had been waiting on Orson. On the fly, Orson adjusted the tack he would take. Rather than attack and question, he would see what the older guide had to say.

While Mike watched silently, waiting, stirring his coffee with a plastic straw, Orson ordered a slice of deep-dish pizza and a Coke. Almost as if they had planned it, they went to one of the tiny booths and slid in on opposite sides. Considering one another and the coming conversation, they sipped. The guide was calm, wearing a T-shirt, jeans, and sandals. A do-rag printed with stars and stripes like an American flag was tied around his head. His skin was leathery with decades of tan and he needed a shave, but his eyes were bright, hard and determined.

A bell dinged and one of the employees brought Orson's huge, steaming pizza slice to the table. "It's hot. You be careful now, you hear?" she said, before disappearing back behind the counter.

Orson shifted the paper plate away from him, letting the slice cool. Mike blew on his black brew and sipped, watching him through the steam wreathing his face from the cup.

Orson sipped his Coke. When it looked like the guide wasn't going to speak first, Orson asked, "Did you set up the dump today?"

Mike's lips lifted a fraction of an inch. "No," he said. "But the universe was in a revelatory mood. You notice how Uncle Robert handled himself?"

"He did everything right."

Mike nodded and set down his cup. "Everything. Never let the T-grip of his paddle fly around, dug into the water at the right time, with the right amount of power. Rested his paddle twice even before I called it. Set up the Z-drag faster than most experienced guides could have. Understood the whistles. I never had to tell him anything twice." Mike leaned in and set his elbows on the table. "Uncle Robert knows white water. Knows it a whole lot better than he ever let on. You may be out *on leave*," he said with peculiar emphasis, "but you're *still* a cop. You had to think it was strange."

It wasn't the first time Mike had called him a cop, in the present tense. Orson cut into the pizza tip with his plastic knife and speared the tip of the slice with the plastic fork. Thinking, he carried the bite to his lips. Taste exploded in his mouth, tart and spicy, the bread a yeasty counterpoint to the Italian cheese. He chewed. He swallowed. He cut another piece. "And?"

"And I've done some research. Robert and Joseph Stevens traveled the world in summers when they were growing up, climbing mountains, hiking the Alps, taking rivers in touring boats. No mention in the gossip rags of white water kayaks, I grant you that. But he knows white water. It was obvious. And he comes here and never lets on he's been on a river?"

Orson took another bite and said through the cheesy mouthful, "And?"

"And he has two kayaks in his hotel room. Beat-up kayaks. River gear. And Robert don't strike me as the kind to buy used."

Orson stilled. "I won't ask how you know that."

Mike's eyes lit with amusement. "Good. I got a friend who checked the GPS on Robert's rental car yesterday. Don't ask who or how. I won't share."

Orson shook his head, laughter lurking in his thoughts as he ate another bite. It was surely the best pizza he had ever eaten. Either that, or he was hungrier than he remembered ever being.

"A guide punched in the coordinates and went to see what he could see. Ended up at a swank hotel last night, asking around."

"A guide," Orson repeated, still amused. "You?"

Mike didn't reply. "As it turns out, the joint has archived records back for more'n ten years. A twenty got the night clerk to check a few dates." Mike's eyes took on the intensity of focus. He sipped, squinting through the steam, holding Orson's gaze. "Uncle Robert's nearly a regular. He was a guest six years ago, him and his mama. But Robbieboy checked in several days before she did. Robert Stevens was a guest not fifty miles away, two days before Joseph Stevens disappeared."

Orson swallowed down a half-chewed bite of pizza. "He was already here? When his brother disappeared."

"Yeah. I'm thinking he mighta been on the river the day Joseph, the elder brother, the one Daddy loved best, the one with the bigger trust fund, went missing."

A flush went through him. Orson bit, chewed, but he forgot to taste the pizza. Since 9/11, airlines kept pristine records. It might be possible to discover if Yvette Stevens arrived alone.

"Where was he staying?" He had the interview documentation; he could check it out, compare the info Mike gave him with his dad's notes. Mike passed him a folded piece of paper. Written on it was the name of a three-star hotel not far from the park and campground where Nell and Joe had stayed six years ago. Orson needed a subpoena for the hotel records.

He took another bite. He also had to spend some time with the case file. See what had originally been turned up about Robert. The investigation might not have been very far along on the family connections. No body. No evidence, beyond the bloody PFD, pointing to murder. Except possibly at the battered wife's hands. Little time or resources had been spent looking at the brother, with his alibi of being in New York. Not then. Orson drank Coke, and asked his original question. "Did you intend to dump us today?"

Mike sipped his coffee, grinning. "I coulda. Part of me wanted to see how Robbie-boy looked swimming. But I was being nice. Besides. My sister was aboard."

Orson was drinking his Coke and spluttered. Nearly choking. He coughed into the napkins Mike passed him. "Sister?" he said when he could talk again.

Mike nodded ruefully. "Think I'd have risked dumping anyone with JJ aboard? With my family aboard? When we got back to the shop, Gina nearly tore me a new one for scaring Jim. But on another, completely accidental level, it was worth it. A cop working the cold case got to see how Uncle Robert handled himself."

Orson's suspicion was confirmed. Mike knew all there was to know about him working a cold case. More than Orson could deny. He wondered fleetingly if Mike had been in his rented room, and decided that the guide probably knew what brand underwear he wore.

Mike paused a moment to let that settle in before he continued, "A cop who took part in the original search and rescue on the Cumberland, back when he was a rookie and his dad was handling the case. Back then, we called you Junior."

For a long moment, Orson chewed, put all sorts of scenarios together, and took them back apart. He swallowed and said, "Have you told Nell?"

"Not yet. Even though she thinks she knows you from somewhere. And I'll hold off a day or so, unless you get stupid and try to arrest her for the death of her husband. Nell did not kill Joe." Mike leaned in. "The letter he wrote to her after the Double Falls, when he left her to get help, is hanging in her hallway where the kid can see it every day, framed in a fancy shadow box. She used it to teach him how to read when JJ was practically still in diapers."

Orson didn't respond. But he knew his old man wanted the letter back. And he wanted to see it himself.

"It matches Joe's handwriting. Nell's no forger. She can't draw. Her writing looks like chicken scratching. She didn't fake the letter. Joe went for help. Whatever happened to him happened between the Double Falls and where they found his boat.

"Joe's PFD was cut. And bloody." Mike drank his coffee, now too cool to steam. "And Robert just happened to be close by, a fact I bet was never disclosed to the cops. I bet he claimed a New York alibi."

Orson didn't react, but he didn't have to. Without a doubt, Mike Kren had been though his case notes.

"The rich brother hadn't announced his marriage to his family," the older river guide went on. "But if Robert had found out about it, he might have hoped to stop any transfer of monies away from the family. Or he might have just been pissed."

Orson ate the last of his pizza, chewing steadily, thinking about the one place on the South Fork of the Cumberland where the rescue crews hadn't searched. And it was pretty damn stupid that they hadn't. But then, they had been looking for a wounded man, not a murder victim. Silence settled between the men like a wet wool blanket, humid, too close and a bit itchy.

Orson wiped his mouth and drank the last of the cola. "Okay. Say I agree with you. What do you think I should I do?"

"I got no idea, cop. Not one. But I figure you'll come up with a few." Mike stood and went to the coffeemaker, calling to the staff, "I'm getting a fresh cup to go. You moneygrubbing capitalist pigs gonna charge me again?"

"Not this time, Jedi," the woman who had brought Orson's pizza to him said. "But we'd take it out of your mangy hide if the boss was here."

"Yeah, yeah, yeah." He waved them off. "See you in the morning, girls." And Mike Kren was gone, the sound of his voice echoing off the walls.

Orson sat with his greasy plate, empty Coke can and plastic cutlery. Thinking about the one place on the stretch of river where no one had searched, at least not with any concentrated effort. And not looking for a murdered body.

Nell was sitting at the kitchen table near the backdoor, eyes glued to a laptop. Beyond her was the den, with a leather couch on the left facing two upholstered chairs, and the flat-screen TV against the far wall on a shelf of an armoire, its doors parked wide. JJ and Claire were stretched on the couch, the woman with her feet on an ottoman, JJ with his head on her stomach, a brightly lit Star Wars light saber across his body. An animated movie was on, and JJ's carefree laughter floated to him through the screen door. Pawpaw was in a recliner on the right of the room, snoring softly.

Orson knocked. Nell raised her head. JJ looked over his shoulder. PawPaw came up like greased white lightning, closing the breech of a shotgun, and an orange and cream fluff ball with teeth threw itself off the couch at the door, barking hysterically, skidding to a halt at the screen door and jumping up and down. Orson took two steps back. The long-haired dog was maybe six pounds and looked as if it had spring-loaded legs; it reached the height of the door handle with each bound. Orson was just glad it wasn't something with a few more pounds like a chow or maybe a pit bull.

"Be still, Butchie," Claire said, dropping her legs from the ottoman. PawPaw moved to the side so his line of fire was clear.

Nell stood and a light came on, hitting Orson in the face. He shaded his eyes against the glare. "Orson?" Nell said when she spotted him through the screen.

JJ shouted, "Hey, Orson. Come on in!" He leaped from the couch to the door in a skipping run, gangly limbs swinging, the light saber in one fist. PawPaw broke open the shotgun, picked up a foam cup and spat into it, the action so filled with derision and insult, Orson wanted to smile. The old man didn't like nighttime visitors.

Nell glanced away and back. Orson figured she had a baseball bat nearby. He ducked his head so they wouldn't see his amusement. It was weird, but since coming to this little town, with its earthy, backcountry populace, he had remembered how to smile, and now he was having trouble keeping one off his face. Or he was having trouble when he was around JJ. And maybe around Nell too.

JJ slid back the latch at the middle of the door and bent to unfasten the lower latch. A two-lock screen. Good enough to keep out honest men. Not much good if a burglar had a knife and didn't mind taking out the screen. Of course, there was that shotgun… JJ opened the door and leaned out. "Whatcha doing all the way up here?"

Nell, JJ and Claire lived near the top of Stirling Mountain, a long, curving drive, several miles up a gravel road. In winter, with snow and ice, it would take a four-wheel-drive vehicle and a driver with nerves of steel to manage the mountain road. "I came to talk to your mama, if she has a minute."

"You coulda called," Nell said, still inside the house, her mother standing behind her.

"I could. But you mighta said no. It's easier to ask forgiveness—" he started.

"Than to get permission," JJ finished, pushing the door open all the way. He brandished the light saber like a baton, the glow turning his skin an ugly, neon green. "Come on in."

Orson stepped into the house, into the kitchen which opened up to his right. He took in the space, automatically searching out every hiding place, each piece of furniture, the position of the four humans and the little dog quivering at his feet, sniffing his bare toes in his river sandals. He could smell dinner beneath the scent of popcorn. Dishes were sitting in the dish strainer near the sink, and the faucet dripped with a faint plink. The windows were open, letting in the night breeze. He absorbed it like a cop, fast, with a rush of adrenaline.

"What do you need, Orson?" Nell asked.

"About a half hour. I know it's late." PawPaw walked up beside her, panther quiet, his very presence menacing. He stared at Orson.

Nell glanced at the clock. "We got church in the morning. I hafta get JJ's suit out."

"I'll take care of the church clothes," Claire said, speaking for the first time. Orson realized he hadn't heard the woman speak since she lambasted his daddy nearly seven years ago. She still looked young enough to be Nell's sister, her hair shoulder length and blond, figure still trim in jeans and a long-sleeved shirt. "You're welcome to come to church with us," she added.

"Thank you, ma'am. I might just do that." The words came from his mouth before he could check them. Orson hadn't been to church since he was a tot. And there was no telling what kind of church these people attended. He had a momentary image of JJ dancing a jig while holding a rattle-snake. "I don't have a suit," he said quickly.

PawPaw grinned, almost as if he could see inside Orson's head, and was laughing at Orson's discomfort.

"Lucky you," JJ said, rolling his eyes. "Mama makes me wear a suit. And a tie too."

"No suits needed," Claire said, her blue eyes laughing like her daddy's, as if she knew his mind held images of people shaking with the spirit and rolling in the aisles. "JJ has the scripture reading, so Nell likes him to wear a suit. Dress pants or even jeans will be fine for you. We attend the Church of Christ." She handed him a laminated card from a stack on the kitchen bar. There was a map on one side, and on the other, the words "Why I attend the Church of Christ," with a list of reasons below. "Services start at eleven sharp," she said. "I'll save you a seat."

"Cool," JJ said. "Orson can sit next to me."

Orson, not quite sure how he had let it get this far, bobbed his head. "Um…sure.". He turned his attention to Nell, who was grinning too. He hated being so transparent. "You got a half hour?" he asked.

"I do now," she said.

"Come on, JJ," Claire said. "Let's get your suit ready, and you can read the scripture again. You still stumble over the middle part, and with Mr. Orson coming, you need to be letter perfect."

JJ thumbed off the light saber, propped it in the corner and started speaking scripture as they disappeared into the far hallway. "I am the true vine, and my Father is the husband-man. Mama Claire? What's a husbandman?" Their voices became a blur in the background.

PawPaw and Orson stared at one another, each measuring the other. "I'll be in the RV, Nellie. You have trouble, you holler. I'll hear." He speared Orson with a threatening look.

"PawPaw, Robert won't be coming back up this way. You don't have to sleep over."

"Yeah, I do," he said. He moved out the door into the shadows, footsteps silent as a panther.

Nell sighed as if resigned and pointed at a chair. She closed the laptop. Without asking Orson, she put ice in a glass and poured tea, setting the glass in front of him. She topped off her own glass and sat down, folded her hands on the table and waited.

"I always seem to catch you working," he said.

Nell nodded. "Claire wants me to slow down. Lie in the hammock. Play with the dog. Rest. I'm not much good with doing nothing."

Orson had never seen her sitting around, having a lazy moment, not even after Joe disappeared. She had joined the search and pulled her load, even when her own injuries suggested she would be better off sitting on the sidelines. He wasn't very good at relaxing either. Look at what had happened when he took off time to recuperate. He'd gone from working sixty hours a week to a lazy slob. Beneath his T-shirt, he touched his scar, raised and knobby and ugly. "I have a confession to make," he said.

"I hear it's good for the soul," Nell said, a smile playing about her mouth.

"You may not like it," he said. Her brows went up and her amusement faded. "You know I'm a cop," he said. "But you don't remember me from Joe's search and rescue." Still she waited, that raised brow crinkling her forehead. Patient. "I was a rookie, and I was working undercover, to be there, on the scene, if we found him. Able to hear and see whatever I could pick up. Able to talk to people, ask questions."

Nell's expression didn't harden or shift into anger. In fact, it didn't change at all, which made him uncomfortable for reasons he didn't quite understand. She leaned back in her chair, resting her laced fingers on her stomach. Voice calm, she said, "You went by the name Junior. You were in a Perception ProLine. Purple and green. You helped me rescue the swimmer. I forget his name. Did you figure out anything while you was snooping into my life and my grieving?"

He opened his mouth and closed it on words he instantly decided not to speak. Cautiously, he said, "Not much. Not enough to make a case."

"A case against me for murdering Joe."

"A case against anyone for anything relating to Joe," he amended.

The little half smile returned to her lips, but it wasn't amusement so much this time. Some other emotion, something he couldn't quite put his finger on, but it made him feel like squirming in his chair. He drank some tea and put it back down. The glass made a little thump in the quiet room.

"Hamp told me who you were," Nell said. Orson looked up fast. She rocked back on two legs, making her chair creak slightly. "He recognized you at dinner yesterday. Made a few calls. Hamp's uncle works for the highway patrol. We knew you were still on leave but looking at the case for the Cold Case Unit. I told Claire and PawPaw this morning. JJ doesn't know." Her voice, like her eyes, held no expression at all. A factual, reasonable tone, offering nothing.

It really bothered Orson. He lifted his glass and leaned back, mimicking her posture, his glass on his stomach.

"I called Mike," she continued, "and he verified it through his sources. I'm assuming that you asked for a job because you're really back undercover, sticking your nose into my life. Trying to find reasons to arrest me for Joe's disappearance. While I pay you to work." Her smile widened, but there was no pleasure in it. "Sneaky little bastard."

"That's not it," he said, knowing it had been, when he applied for the job of kayak instructor. "I'm still recuperating. Not fit for active duty. But there were a few cold cases. I was given this one."

"I didn't kill my husband," she said evenly.

"I'm not saying you did," he said just as evenly.

Nell cocked her head. Her calm self-possession made her seem much older than her nearly twenty-seven years.

"In my report, written after the search, I stated that there was no evidence to suggest you were anything other than a grieving, injured spouse. But the case is still open because—"

"Habeas corpus," she interrupted. "No body. I got that. So what'er you wanting from me?"

"I want you to come with me, and let's us kayak down the South Fork of the Cumberland."

Whatever Nell had thought she expected from the lying undercover cop, it wasn't that. She dropped her chair legs to the floor and stretched across the table to see his eyes up close. "You want *what?*" she said, incredulity pitching her voice high.

"I want us to take the river now, while there's been some rain and it's runnable. Rocking River is closed Sundays and Mondays. We could go tonight and be back in time for the shop to open on Tuesday."

Shock went through her like lightning, burning and breath-stealing. *He's serious. My God. He's serious!*

"I've run it a couple times since, with some friends, but I want you with me, to walk me through every moment you can remember of the trip where Joe went missing. I have a feeling we can find—well, I think we can find Joe."

"No." The breath was cold in her lungs, a counterpoint to

the heated shock still raging through her like floodwater through a sieve. "I'll never—*never*—go back to that river." She shoved back from the table, rocking it with the force of her refusal. Her throat closed painfully, as if a hand clasped about her, stealing her breath. Smothering. "That river stole my husband from me," she whispered, her tone labored. "Left me alone and pregnant, with no daddy for my baby." Tears she hadn't shed in seven years filled her eyes. "That river *nearly destroyed* me."

Blinded by the glare swimming in her tears, she walked to the door, legs unsteady, and opened it, standing aside. "Now, I'd be most grateful if you'd get the hell outta my house."

Through her tears, she saw Orson Lennox rise, pushing back his chair. "I handled this all wrong," he said. "I'm sorry."

Tears spilled out over her bottom lids and raced down her cheeks. Nell lifted her chin, almost defiantly.

"But think about this. Finding Joe's body would put an end to old rumors that you killed JJ's father. It would let his estate pass to JJ without question or taint. Finding his body would mean that JJ can grow up free from the mystery and any possible scandal."

He stepped nearer, feet silent on the kitchen floor. Nell wanted to recoil from the words and the man. And the fear made her lock her knees and stare him down.

"And lastly, it would possibly point a finger to the killer. Think about it," Orson said as he stepped from her house and out onto the small landing. She could feel his body heat as he passed, so close they nearly touched. "We could do it in a day."

Nell closed the screen and then the solid paneled door. Setting the locks and the alarm, she leaned against the door, resting her head on one arm. Tears streamed down her face, to hit the kitchen floor. In the sink, the faucet dripped, a steady, arrhythmic counterpoint. She really had to get the tap fixed. The thought made her tears fall faster and she cried silently into the protection of her arm.

"Orson, when you screw up, you screw up royally," he said to himself as he followed the white concrete stepping stones back to the road and his SUV. He had parked down the mountain in the curve of a turnaround and walked up silently, unannounced, to their house, in the dark. He wanted to see how they lived, get the feel of the house and the grounds and their financial situation. He had wanted to look in on Nell and JJ, a surprise visit. Wanted to see if they were as innocent in their lifestyles as the financial statements from Joseph Stevens's trust fund indicated.

Cars more than five years old, the aged RV, old leather furniture, possibly from Joseph's New York apartment. Wood floors in the house with a few rugs, some masculine enough to have been Joe's. Stoneware in the kitchen hutch, not china. Stainless, not silver, though he hadn't gone through the china hutch to be sure. Same old dog as in the reports, Butchie. Orson grinned and glanced back at the closed door. At least she had locked the door. He'd heard three distinct clicks.

He moved through the night and almost reached his car when he heard the distinct clacking-ratcheting sound of a shotgun breech closing. His skin reacted, tightening into chills. Softly, Orson said, "Wondered when you'd want a chat."

A soft snort came from the dark and Orson placed it to his right. "You got wandering eyes, boy."

When the man didn't go on, Orson asked, "Wandering?"

"You got eyes that think one thing one minute, and another thing the next."

The voice had moved behind him, though not a single

twig had snapped, not a whisper of sound had indicated that a man was walking through the night. Orson's spine between his shoulder blades itched. He fought the urge to dive into his car and pull his weapon. Or run.

"You think Nell's guilty of killing Joe. Then you think how soft and sweet she is. How good she'd feel in the night."

Orson's breath hitched, and the old man laughed, a slow, malicious chuckle. "You hurt mine and I'll make you disappear. You remember that."

Long moments later, Orson realized that he was alone. PawPaw—if he wasn't a figment of Orson's own imagination—was gone. He had to wonder if Joseph Stevens had threatened or harmed Nell in any way. And if he'd been made to disappear.

Orson found his car in the dim light and opened the door, sitting inside with his eyes closed so the car's security light wouldn't steal his night vision. He turned the key in the lock and the engine came to life. The security light went off. In the dark, Orson lay his head back against the headrest.

He had made her cry. He tried to convince himself that it had been the right thing to do. That her tears had shed light on the case. If there *was* a case. If Joseph Stevens had been killed by human hands and intent, and not by the river.

"That river nearly destroyed me."

Orson eased off the parking brake and let the mountain pull him backward, spinning the steering wheel so that gravity made the turn for him and pointed him down toward the Pigeon. Shifting into gear, he headed down. He had nothing to do and nowhere to go. Not until Tuesday when he had a kayaking lesson for a party of four starting at 10:00 a.m.

He passed a small herd of deer feeding on the steep edge of the road at a driveway that curled out of sight. They were

unafraid, staring at him without curiosity, jaws chewing as
they decimated one of Nell's neighbor's flowering plants.

He wondered if he could find the Church of Christ.

22

Nell drew a bath and added bath salts, the crystals shushing into the hot water. As it steamed into the tub, she got out her nightgown and clean socks, folded down the bed, and found a skirt and top to wear Sunday morning. She was pretty sure she had worn pants, a blouse and a lightweight sweater last Sunday, and her only dress the Sunday before that. She didn't care what she wore, but Claire cared, and JJ seemed to think she looked great all dressed up.

Her son was in bed and the house was silent and dark except for the faint light seeping under Claire's door. She was reading her Bible, studying for her Sunday-school lesson. Her mother still taught Bible study to junior high–age girls every week. Nell went to church now, but didn't read the Bible except during the services, and she hadn't studied for a lesson since her father died.

In her heart of hearts she still blamed the church for her father's death. Which she knew was a sin. And stupid on top of that, and to her, stupid was far worse. But she couldn't seem to help it. Her father disappeared from her life, leaving her alone, with only Claire to love her. Like JJ was alone, except for her and Claire to love him. And in some way, that too, seemed like God's fault.

Back in the bathroom, she turned off the water, dropped her robe, and slid inch by inch into the hot water, hissing at the pain, her skin turning bright red. When she was buried up to her neck, she sighed and rested her head on the bouffant pillow attached to the tub by suction cups. Like the kitchen sink, this faucet dripped too, plinking to the water, the sound magnified by the tile walls to a harsh, pitiless tone.

"JJ isn't alone," she whispered to the room. "Not like I was." But some small part of her knew she was lying, knew JJ was alone with an old scandal. Just as the sneaky, cheating cop had suggested.

The church itself seemed to be singing, four-part harmony bouncing off the walls and out the open windows, notes dancing around the cars and the huge oaks that lined the gravel parking area. Though he had a feeling that dancing might be considered sinful to these folks.

Orson stood at the back of the brick church, having slipped in without being seen, to stand in the shadows between the outer doors and the inner ones in the vestibule. There was a baptistry behind the pulpit, softly lit, a table to the side with things stacked on it, a cloth over it all. No choir, no organ, no musical instruments in sight or sound. No special seat for the reverend, or father. He had no idea what they called their preacher. But most importantly, no snakes, poisonous or otherwise.

It was a simple church. Just the white-painted walls, a narrow aisle between wooden, unpadded benches, heart-of-pine floors and colored glass windows, but without scenes of shepherds or angels or a dying Jesus. There was a full house, all standing, singing like angels. Some of the men were in suits, some in dress pants, and two or three men wore jeans, as Claire had said. The man leading the singing couldn't have been more than twenty years old, and his suit was too big, hanging on his shoulders, but he sang with gusto, his face all smiles.

Orson spotted PawPaw on the aisle seat, about a third of the way to the front. The old man was dressed in his usual hogwashers but wore a clean, plaid shirt beneath it and his hair slicked back, wet-looking. Orson couldn't see the shotgun, and was surprised the old man didn't have it propped in the seat nearest.

Beside him sat Claire, down from Nell. JJ stood at an angle at the front of the church, beside a man. JJ tugged at his tie, pulling his head to the left, then to the right, as if to relieve a choking sensation. His hair, too, was slicked back, giving him an earnest, worried look, so different from his confident river persona. Claire wore a dress and Nell wore a yellow skirt and blouse.

When the singing stopped, the congregation sat and JJ walked up two steps to the podium, which the song leader lowered, adjusting the microphone. JJ started reading, serious and intent, his tone grave.

Orson had no idea what the kid read. He just watched the solemn face, listening to the boy's halting but clear tones. He knew from Nell's body language, tense and fidgeting on the hard bench, that she was worried and proud all at once, and that JJ was doing a good job.

When he was finished, JJ closed the Bible, handed it to the minister and walked down the aisle to his mother. But when he reached her questing hand, he sidestepped and came on back, his eyes finding Orson's in the dim light of the vestibule and holding them. Grinning ear to ear. Startled, Nell turned in her seat and followed her son's progress. PawPaw turned too, staring at him standing at the back of the church. PawPaw spat into a foam cup, expressing his opinion of Orson's presence. Nell pressed her lips together when she saw him.

"I did it," JJ stage-whispered. He took Orson's wrist and tugged it out from beneath his shirt. "Come on. Mama Claire saved you a seat with us."

A strange feeling rose through Orson, up from the small hand through his arm and into his body. A warm flush of…something. He looked from JJ's head to Nell as he let the small boy pull him down the aisle, their feet loud on the wooden floor. She was fuming but trying to hide it, sparks in her pale brown eyes. She was wearing makeup, mascara and pink lipstick. Her hair was scrunched and gelled into curls. She was…pretty. Just as he had thought when he saw her in the shop on his first day in town.

He felt slightly sick. Dizzy, like he had the day he walked, trembling, weak and nauseous, into his house after the shooting. And closed himself off from the world.

His eyes were drawn from Nell back to the hand holding his.

The warmth from JJ's small palm reached into him, filling him, touching…something. Touching the pain he carried. Pain centered around the wound and scar on his chest and abdomen, held tight to him like a fouled treasure. The warmth slipped around the foolishly cherished wound and squeezed. Pressure grew in his chest. He breathed through his mouth, a near gasp of shock.

Following the kid, Orson stepped past PawPaw, past Claire and Nell, and slid onto the bench, JJ on his right, Nell on his left. He leaned back. Took the songbook JJ handed him. And he…relaxed. Tension he hadn't known he carried evaporated like mist under a hot sun.

He wasn't sure what was happening, but whatever it was, Orson didn't want to fight it. Not anymore. He was letting it happen.

There were no snakes and no people frothing at the mouth and rolling in the aisles. Just a simple lesson on living right, the Lord's Supper—which he vaguely remembered from his youth—and a lot of singing in a cappella harmony. Then it was over, leaving Orson with a heated numbness inside, and with what he was sure was a silly smile on his face.

He stood with JJ, Claire and Nell, and shook a lot of hands, faces and names a blur, the only reality the presence of the family beside him. He was welcomed and invited back, and made to feel like he was the most important person in the world. He wasn't sure what was happening to his heart and body, but Orson knew one thing. The cop's soul, beating in his chest, had been compromised. He was no longer a disinterested observer, there to bring truth to light in a cold case. He was now a part of the case, part of the disappearance of Joseph Stevens. He needed to find out what had happened to the man.

And if Nell really did kill her husband? Orson pushed the thought away. Because he knew what he would do with that knowledge if it proved to be true. He'd arrest her and put her behind bars. And he didn't know if he could live with himself if he did that.

JJ invited Orson back to lunch at their house and the man accepted, despite the irritation Nell deliberately shot him every time she caught his eyes. He seemed oblivious to her ire and followed their vehicle back up the mountain, eating their dust all the way. But it was small satisfaction for her, and miserly guilt poked her all the way home. Claire's glee didn't help. She seemed to find the man's attention to her entertaining, while Nell knew his interest was as a cop looking at his best suspect. And PawPaw, well, PawPaw found the entire situation funny.

Claire bustled around the kitchen while Nell got JJ's Sunday best put away. She could hear her mother chatting to Orson, talking about the Lord and the church and the town and the river, Orson's laughing rejoinders, and PawPaw's rare laconic comment. Her mother could talk the copper off the top of PawPaw's still. When JJ joined them, the talk turned to paddling and kayaks. Everybody was so freaking happy. Even PawPaw unbent enough to laugh at something Orson said. Nell just wanted the cop gone.

He wanted her to paddle the South Fork of the Cumberland...

Nell shuddered and tossed her Sunday clothes across the rumpled covers and the dip where she slept, to the far side of the bed. They landed in a heap. On Joe's side.

There was no dip there. They hadn't had the king-size bed long enough for his side to carry evidence of their marriage. Or evidence of his passing. He was just gone, and all she had left of him was his boat, bits of his gear, his letter to her the day he disappeared and his clothes.

And his lies, a small, mean part of her whispered.

Nell pulled on wrinkled jeans and a ratty T-shirt and slid her feet into bright, neon-yellow flip-flops, the bottoms air-padded in lumps to massage her soles. She looked in the mirror on the back of her bedroom door and stopped. Her hair was up in spikes, her eyes ringed with liner and mascara and blush on her cheeks. Stuff Joe would have teased her for wearing.

Joe. Who had lied to her. For whatever reason, he had lied to her. About his money, his life in New York, his apartment. His trust fund. His family. About everything. She had come to terms with the fact of his lies long ago, but she had never accepted them, never made peace with them. And never forgiven him for them.

Had he not trusted her enough to tell her the truth? Had he been ashamed of her and her Tennessee roots and accent? Her chin came up and she stared hard at her reflection. Why? Why had he kept it all a secret?

When he disappeared, he had left her with the facts of his hidden life to deal with, his belongings to sell and his property to handle. And she had done it, turning the eighty thousand dollars she got when the New York apartment sold into a thriving business and a home for their son. Everything else had already been paid for—Rocking River, its gear and bus and the land the shop sat on, their small house, which she had added on to to make room for Claire, and the RV. Paid for. With just a signature, according to Louis Berhkolter. When she thought it had all been financed. Lies.

Because of Joe, she had given up paddling for fun.

Stopped kayaking down class III and IV rapids, stopped working the currents with her body and boat. Stopped feeling the excitement of taking an eight- or ten- or twelve-foot drop, clean as cutting it with a knife. Stopped searching out new, exciting rivers and creeks to run. Started taking to the water only when she had to, when she had to give a lesson. Stopped being the person she had been.

Of course, JJ came along, making her huge, filling her time and changing her empty life into something new. There wasn't time left to think about rivers except as they applied to her growing businesses. Running Rocking River Enterprises and caring for her son took up all of her life and time. But that wasn't why she had stopped running rivers. She had stopped because… She took a deep breath and continued with the thought.

Because she was afraid.

Nell cursed under her breath. Her reflection cursed with her, a hissing sound. She was afraid? Yeah. Nell Stevens was afraid. Afraid of paddling white water.

She opened the bedroom door and stalked to the kitchen, her shoes slapping the floor in anger. The four were laughing and looked up fast when she stepped into the room. Guilty expressions, laughter hanging on the air. Laughter that excluded her. PawPaw's brows went up at the expression on her face and he started to grin. Dang the old man. Nell narrowed her eyes.

The room smelled exquisite. Chicken and dumplings. Her

favorite. The silence in the room was growing. She looked from PawPaw to Claire's curious face, her son's laughing one to the odd look worn by the cop, to the plates. Theirs were half-empty. Her own plate looked slightly congealed. How long had she stayed in her room?

Nell took a slow, deep breath, her chest suddenly tight, her heart an uneven cadence. "Claire? Can you pack up some dinner for us? Orson and me—" she stared hard at the cop and then glanced pointedly at JJ "—we're heading north in the RV. We'll be back, maybe tomorrow night. The next night, latest."

Nell's look said, clearer than words, "Don't tell JJ where we're going." So Orson didn't. He simply stood and carried his plate to the sink, then hers. "I have to get some supplies," he said, meaning his gear and boat. She nodded stiffly, understanding, face white, hands trembling. "The meal was good, Mama Claire," he said. "I look forward to leftovers at dinner tonight."

"Can I go?" JJ asked.

"Not this time," Nell said, her tone brooking no argument.

JJ opened his mouth to argue anyway, but Orson placed his hand on the boy's shoulder. "Remember what we were just talking about? About women and stuff?" JJ poked out his bottom lip. Orson barely kept from laughing. "Well, this is one of those times." JJ huffed and glowered, crossing his arms across his narrow chest. "We'll take the Upper Pigeon together later on, just you and me and Mike, paddling. Okay? No girl stuff." JJ didn't reply, but his shoulders relaxed slightly.

Claire looked from Nell to Orson, uncertainty on her face, but she didn't question them. She merely stood and began to dish leftovers into plastic containers. PawPaw grunted and went back to eating. Nell didn't ask what "women stuff" they had been talking about. Which was good, as it involved women and their moods and how you just had to live with them but could never expect to understand them. Like this mood swing and Nell changing her mind.

One minute Nell was refusing to consider paddling the South Fork of the Cumberland, and the next she was looking like a thundercloud, clearly furious with him but agreeing to run it. No explanations.

Living with the mercurial Janine had taught Orson two things: don't argue with success, and take what you can get. "I'll meet you down the mountain," he said.

Nell nodded stiffly, shoving her hands hard into her jeans pockets. "I'll be down in half an hour. If we boogie, we can be in place today."

He wasn't sure what "be in place" meant, but he nodded and turned to Mama Claire. She hugged him. "Take care 'a my baby," Claire whispered, her arms tight around his shoulders, pulling his ear down to her mouth. Before he could promise, she added, "You hurt her in any way, and I'll hunt you down and carve out your heart with my brand-new boning knife." She patted his cheek and pushed him away, a feral glint in her blue eyes, her mouth in a sweet smile. Orson was pretty sure she saw him shiver.

Next, JJ hugged him, a short tight hug, one armed, almost manly.

PawPaw pursed his lips, chewing and thinking. Orson wasn't sure what his expression meant, but he was pretty sure the old man wasn't happy about something. Or maybe he was just naturally dyspeptic.

Before Orson could get himself in trouble, he got in his vehicle and drove away.

While JJ sulked, Nell tossed clean sheets and towels into the RV and stuffed a few clean clothes into a plastic grocery bag for herself. She hooked the hose to the water intake, kicked the tires and ignored her son, who was still sulking, sitting in the shadow of the back stoop petting Butchie. She wanted to ask what they had been talking about at the table, but was equally afraid about the potential subject matter.

She checked the supply of canned food, brought cereal, tea and coffee, and a thermos of milk out, and turned on the refrigerator. She added a few food essentials, enough to make one meal if needed, and put Claire's chicken-and-dumpling bounty in with it. Nell looked around the small space. Everything else was already in the RV, pillows, dishes, river clothes.

Claire stepped into the RV, blocking the door with her body, creating a shadow and a barrier to JJ hearing their voices. She handed Nell the dark blue and tan fishing-tackle box where Nell kept makeup and toiletries. Not much of either. They rattled in the bottom, even after adding hair gel, deodorant and insect spray. Nell set the box into the cubbyhole where she kept it on the road.

Her boat was in the shop, along with her PFD, helmet and paddle. Nell popped her knuckles, a habit she thought she had broken.

Claire said, "Is this a date or police business?"

Nell's head came up fast. "Date? No! The idiot cop wants me to paddle the South Fork of the Cumberland with him and find Joe's…" She took a breath that shuddered her air passages in her chest. "Find Joe."

"Do you trust him?"

"Trust?" Nell frowned and thought about the cop. The way his hand strayed to his torso when he was worried or thinking, an unconscious gesture. His dark hair curling slightly on the ends, framing his face, the beard he hadn't bothered to trim or shave since she hired him. The way he had looked that day in the shop, his gun drawn, pointing it at Robert. Protecting her. His eyes today in the church, so full of hope. She was certain he didn't know he had looked so lost and so buoyant all at once. "Yes. I trust him," she said grudgingly. "Which is weird, because he's here to prove I killed Joe."

"Or to prove you didn't." Claire stepped down to the concrete of the driveway. "Your water tank's overflowing."

She stepped aside as Nell raced out, to the back of the RV, turned off the water spigot, then coiled the hose into a neat set of concentric circles resting on the hook on the house wall. She was sweating when she finished.

Kneeling, she looked over her shoulder at her family. Claire was standing near the RV with Butchie. PawPaw looked irritated, but then he always did, especially when he was dressed up in his church shirt. JJ was scowling, still in the shade of the porch over the stoop.

Nell's heart broke when she looked at her son. This was the first time she had ever left him. Except for his yearly trips to New York, they had never been apart. But there was no way to take him with her, not on a trip to find his father's body. Nell looked helplessly at her mother, wanting to back out, cancel the trip. Nothing mattered if it upset her baby.

Claire glared at JJ. "Your mama's gonna be gone overnight. You come show her how much you love her or I'll tan your backside with my hairbrush."

"The river guides say it's illegal to beat a kid," he said, his mouth still in a pout, his arms wrapped around his middle. "They say the gov'ment will put you in jail for it. And 'sides, you never beat me before."

"Illegal never stopped a Bartwell or a Gruber or any other Appalachian American from raising a kid right. And there's always a first time for a good fanny smack." Her eyes narrowed in on his face and he flinched the tiniest bit. "*Get* over here."

JJ dragged his feet to the RV and halfway fell against Nell.

She gathered his deliberately limp body against her and hugged him, blinking away the tears burning her eyes. Half-heartedly, JJ hugged her back.

She stroked his hair behind his ears, fighting not to change her plans, fighting not to promise him the world if he'd just not be mad at her, both of which would surely be signs of weakness and foolishness of the highest order. JJ was too spirited to be given so much influence over her. He *needed* her to be strong and independent; he needed to be separate from her, in order to grow up capable and self-reliant. And she knew she needed to face this fear. To make *her* strong. "I love you, JJ."

Sensing something out of the ordinary, Butchie pranced over and raised up on his hind legs, balancing a moment before placing them on her shin. She stroked the dog and looked up at her mother. "I'll be back two nights from now at the latest." To PawPaw, she said, "You'll be here?" Asking him to watch over them for her. He nodded fractionally.

"Youns be careful," Claire said, her tone conveying much more than the simple warning.

JJ finally realized something more important than him missing a trip was up. He cocked his head against her, looking at Mama Claire and back, considering, and lifted his arms to hug her. The sun in his eyes, he squinted up at her. "You're going somewhere dangerous, are'n'cha?"

Nell nodded. "A little bit."

His arms tightened. "Youns be careful," he said, echoing Mama Claire.

Tears still bright in her eyes, Nell clutched him tightly once, released him and climbed the short steps into the RV. She closed and locked the door. Strapping in, she turned on the ignition and started down the mountain.

Nell was halfway to the shop when Mike's truck came around the bend. The guide dropped an arm out his truck window and Nell slowed. Dust swirled up around them as they idled, blocking traffic, if there had been any. Mike searched her face, his eyes tender, and Nell wondered what he saw in her expression. "Your mama called me. Says you're going to run the South Fork of the Cumberland with the cop."

Suddenly not sure she could trust her voice, Nell nodded.

"It's time to deal with that river. You been running from it a long time."

She nodded again, pressing her lips together, holding in tears or cussing, she wasn't sure which. Right now they felt like the same thing.

"You need me to come along?"

A breath burst out, sounding like a gasp of surprise or disbelief, or maybe grief. Nell laughed softly. "No. I got this one, Jedi."

Mike studied her a moment, seeing more than she wanted him to, she knew. He always did. He reached into the cab and then back across to her, extending folded papers. "You need to see this. Don't ask me where I got it."

Nell took the papers, opened them along the fold. On top was a photocopied sheet of lined paper. The header read, Short List, and a date from nearly seven years ago. Below that was a hand-written list of names, each with a short paragraph of comments and observations to the side.

"That was Orson Lennox's daddy's suspect list," Mike said. "You see what they've been thinking. From the very beginning."

Nell's name was at the top. Beside it were three short lines:

Motive: Money. Passion (beating.) Revenge?
Means: River.
Opportunity: Last seen with vic.

Nell refolded the pages and nodded to Mike.

"You be careful," he said. "They still don't have cell coverage in the gorge. But if you need me, get a ranger to call me on a landline. I'll come."

23

By the time she heard the sound of a truck engine, closer than the interstate roaring nearby, Nell had slung her gear into the undercompartments and strapped her boat on top of the RV. She stood straight, the nearly twelve feet of RV height giving her a clear view down the road. It was Orson, his SUV coated with a film of white dust from the gravel roads.

He pulled up in the parking lot and killed the engine. A moment later, he stepped out and squinted up at her. He looked as uncertain as her son in that moment, drawing a perturbed smile to her lips. He might be just doing his job, but his intent was to put her in jail for something she hadn't done. And she didn't intend to make it easy on him.

"How many vehicles are we taking on this jaunt?" he asked.

"Just two. Hand up your kayak," Nell said, her voice and words peremptory. She tossed one end of the rope down. She was making this trip against her will, but she'd do it with her in charge, not him, and Nell wanted him to know that right off the bat. Nell saw the understanding in his eyes, his disagreement in the thinning of his lips, but after a moment, Orson turned to his SUV and began to unstrap his boat.

While she pulled it up and placed it in position, he tossed most of his things into the RV. His movements were fluid and controlled, but she could see the frustration simmering beneath his skin. Nell fought a grin as she adjusted the lengths of the tie-downs and hooked his boat in place.

Satisfied that both boats were secure and that Orson'd had enough time to get good and mad, she made her way across the roof of the RV to the back and climbed down the ladder. If he was gonna get irate, she wanted it over with now, not later on the trip.

And, always honest with herself, Nell admitted that she was itching for a fight.

Orson had expected her to object to the pile of gear and his suitcase in the middle of the floor. Instead, she stood in the doorway, silent for a long moment, surveying the mess, and laughed. A hooting, derisive laugh that changed after a few notes to something almost appreciative. He wasn't sure why, either, and that disturbed him. He had expected her to object to his position in the RV, too, the passenger seat leaned way back, his feet on the dash, and a cold cola can on his belly. She seemed to find that funny too.

She stepped over his mess and got herself a cola from the small fridge before sitting in the driver's seat and cranking the engine. She was still laughing, the tone oddly self-deprecating, when they wheeled onto I-40. Orson was chuckling by then too, aware that she was casting quick glances at him. Making up her mind about something.

An eighteen-wheeler blew by them. Nell concentrated, changing lanes, a smile hovering on her mouth. Finally, to break the silence, he asked, "We need gas?"

"Yep. We'll stop at the junction of 40 and 75, near Knoxville. This things gets a whopping ten miles to the gallon, making this an expensive trip." She glanced at him and grinned, pure wickedness in the look. "By the way, you're paying for it."

"Lucky me," he said. Feeling just a bit guilty, he added, "I'll stow the gear away when we stop."

She snorted, a totally unladylike sound that suited her perfectly, and turned on the radio, a country station. Keith Urban was playing, and Orson relaxed back in the seat, humming along. After that, things seemed to ease between them. They didn't talk beyond noting the occasional billboard or vehicle. But maybe that was best.

Orson watched Nell surreptitiously as she drove, handling the RV with ease, changing lanes, following big rigs up and down the mountains. The world looked different from the RV. Sitting up so high meant he could see over concrete bridge railings and down into rivers in gorges far below, could see into cars they passed, spotting sleeping babies, kids fighting, couples holding hands, and once, sexual activity of a decidedly erotic nature. It was a unique experience to him to be so high above the roadway and yet so much more a part of the lives of the people they passed. And more and more, he enjoyed Nell's company. Which wasn't so good.

He paid for the gas at the truck stop and used the men's room inside, while she used the tiny bathroom in the RV. He wasn't comfortable with the idea of using her private space. In fact, he wasn't comfortable with a lot of things. He had seen that wicked smile cross her face a few times and knew it meant trouble for him, but he could handle anything she might toss his way. He hoped.

She said nothing provocative as he stowed his gear, pointing to cabinets or the closet as needed, and suggesting that he put his river gear in one of the lockable compartments beneath the RV. The small vehicle had more storage than he had expected and most of the compartments were empty. He hoped her being so agreeable meant that she had decided against giving him a hard time, but he wasn't betting on it.

Back on 75 the RV rode heavier, the gas giving ballast he hadn't expected. His wallet and credit card were decidedly lighter. The RV held eighty gallons of gasoline and Nell had filled the empty vehicle to the gills. Once past Knoxville, Nell drove past the usual intersection for the South Fork of the Cumberland, turning off at the next exit. Orson lifted a brow at the street sign. "Stinking Creek Road? You have to be kidding. What kind of name is that?"

"You never been on Stinking Creek Road?" she asked, that small smile playing on her lips as she made the sharp turn, then another, sharper turn onto an unpaved road. Driving down at a steep angle that had the wheels locked and sliding, they passed a small, dust-covered sign that said No Turnarounds From This Point. The road narrowed, pressing in toward the wheels, trees nearly scraping the sides of the RV.

No Trespassing signs were nailed to the trees. One stated Trespassers Will Be Shot and Questioned Later. Ruts that might have been wide enough for a compact car, if the driver didn't care to keep the paint unscratched, turned off Stinking Creek Road and disappeared into brush and trees. The road swerved and dropped into what looked like virgin territory. Or moonshine territory. The kind of places where grizzled men with shotguns stood watch and bodies were buried in hidden graves.

Nell seemed unperturbed.

Orson grabbed onto the armrests. His palms started to sweat. The RV bounced over ruts, jarring along his spine. He was glad he'd stowed his gear, or it would have been rolling all over the RV.

"Believe it or not, this road is marked on the state atlas," she said casually. "I saw a huge black bear here once. Biggest bear I ever did see."

The RV shuddered as if it was about to break apart. Orson

sat up, raising the chair-back up straight and tightening the seat belt.

"It was in the fall and mast was plentiful. Bears were putting on more pounds than usual. Musta been a record-size bear." Without taking her eyes from the narrow track, her grin widened. "Relax, *Junior*. It's only a few miles long. And it's a dandy shortcut."

Junior. She was getting him back for the SAR almost seven years ago. And for pushing her to come on this trip.

When she finally turned back onto a paved road, Orson was so happy he wanted to dance. He managed to keep his face unperturbed, but he knew she wasn't fooled. Not Nell Stevens. Her pretty little mouth was bowed in sheer delight. They toured through several small towns as his blood pressure settled and his sweat dried. Nell smiled the entire way.

The sun was setting when they turned into the Big South Fork National River and Recreational Area, and headed to Bandy Creek Campground near the South Fork of the Cumberland. As the forest closed in around them, the smile Nell had worn all day evaporated like the morning mist, leaving her looking wan and reserved and far more distant. Orson noted the change and wondered at her detachment, but didn't think it was the right moment to question her. Not just yet.

After Stinking Creek Road, the paved, winding, curving *S* turns were a piece of cake. Orson stared through the orange light of the setting sun at the magnificent scenery, the tumbled boulders, the dense forest, the water falling in tiny rills down cliff faces and creeks bounding through narrow beds. He hadn't been to Bandy Creek since the search for Joseph Stevens had been called off, but he remembered it as one of the best parks in Tennessee. It still was.

There was a lighted board at the entrance of the campground, showing two vacancies, each for one night. He stayed put and watched Nell as she signed them in. She held her body tight, arms stiff and close at her sides. She looked tense. Worried? The cop within flexed his muscles.

Silent, Nell pulled the rig through the campground and found their spot. Keeping her eyes on the job at hand, she expertly backed the unit into the space. He sat in the passenger seat the whole time, observing. Waiting.

In the gloaming light, she pointed out the spot for his tent. Orson unstrapped from the passenger seat and set about snapping up the high-tech tent and inflating his air mattress, watching Nell as he worked. She hooked the RV up to electricity and cable and piled their river gear in a safe spot for morning. She was capable and competent and clearly needed no masculine help. Which impressed him again. As she worked, she looked up once, staring into the trees, listening, body tense. Orson left her alone now that the laughter and bonhomie had vanished. But he didn't like the transformation.

Prickles rolled across Nell's skin as she stared into the night. She was going to run the South Fork of the Cumberland. Nell had promised herself she would never come back here.

In their assigned site, she looked around at the dark trees, hearing the soft rustle of animal life, the faraway call of owl, hunting or claiming territory. Forest smells and the scent of horse—hay, sweat and manure—permeated the campground. Joe and she had camped here. Not in this specific campsite, but close enough that she could find it in the dark if she wanted. She and Claire had taken a spot only a little farther in during the SAR.

Nell shivered and climbed the steps to the RV. Standing in the doorway, she watched Orson in the dim light. He was laying deadwood in the fire pit. Nell gathered up some of JJ's scrap paper and brought Orson a lighter. Without speaking, she returned to the RV and heated bowls of chicken and dumplings for supper. Microwaves were a lot faster than trying to heat food over a fire. But the smoke smelled good when she brought out bowls and spoons and two cold beers. Soothing. Orson had discovered the folding chairs in one of the storage compartments and set two up in front of the small fire. She took the empty one and they ate as true night fell.

Except for logistics for the morning run, they didn't talk. Turning in early, Nell went inside and locked up the RV for the night. She curled up on the queen bed and unfolded the pages Mike had given her. She studied everything the cops had on the case when it went dormant seven years ago. From the notes, Nell knew she had been the best suspect back then. But now she knew who else was at the top of the list. Someone, maybe Orson, had made additional notes in the files. Robert Stevens had moved up, way up, in the list of suspects.

Eyes dry and burning, her mind full, Nell turned off the light.

Nell knew she wouldn't sleep. But suddenly she was underwater, froth and bubbles and a swift current sweeping past her. Trapped in her kayak. Upside down. Her arms and helmet banged against boulders and her boat whirled slowly in a whirlpool, sucking her down.

Her paddle was gone, her hands whipping the water in a panic. She snapped her hips hard, but the boat didn't right itself. Desperate, she looked down. Into Joe's face.

He was far below her, in the murky deeps. Crying. Holding out his hands to her. "Help," he said, lips moving in the water, bubbles rising from his mouth. "You should have found me."

She threw herself at him. Reaching. "Joe!" She took a deep breath. Water flooded her lungs. Reaching for her husband, Nell drowned.

Gasping, Nell came awake. Grabbing at the empty air. "Joe?" She looked around, frantic. "Joe," she whispered.

Night pressed against the screens. A cool breeze floated through the window blinds. She hadn't dreamed about Joe. Not in years. Nell lay back in the bed she had shared with her husband only a few times. "Joe," she said softly. "I tried. I really tried."

Morning was still far off in the sky when Orson smelled coffee. And fresh horse manure. He rolled over, looked out the screened window of the tent, and saw a horse with rider clip-clopping slowly across the road, dark shadows upon the darker sky. He had forgotten that horses were a big part of the park, with trails for riders as well as hikers.

Feet wearing yellow sandals appeared in a spot of light in the screen. Her voice pitched low, Nell asked, "You awake?"

Orson, glad he had slept in sweatpants even with the residual summer heat, pulled on a tee, unzipped the tent and crawled out. He accepted an insulated mug from Nell and sniffed appreciatively. He had slept well and hard, and stretched out the kinks between sips.

It looked as if Nell hadn't slept at all. There were dark rings under her eyes, and her hair, which she usually wore in spikes, was lank and drooping. But she was moving economically as she arranged their pile of equipment into easy-to-carry groups.

As he watched, coffee warming him and bringing him awake, she climbed the ladder up the back of the RV. Standing with her small body outlined against the dark gray sky, she said, "I spoke with a park ranger and he sent me to one of the campers who might be willing to transport us upriver." Her voice was soft in the early dawn, but he could hear the strain in it. "I've paid for us to get a ride with our gear to wherever you want to start."

She knelt and began to untie the boats. Her skin looked pale in the slowly brightening light. She was wearing river shorts made from wet suit material and a sleeveless shirt. "We can start out at Burnt Mill Bridge on Clear Creek or at the confluence of the New River, just above the Double. It's up to you. Catch."

His boat slid down the side of the RV, tied off and handed down at the bow. He took it, steadied it against the RV and untied the rope. "Okay," he said. The rope slithered back up. A moment later Nell's boat came down. Orson hadn't noticed during the job interview–kayaking lesson, but it wasn't the same boat she had used on the SAR. This was a top-of-the-line pearl-white LiquidLogic Remix 59, with the best lumbar-supporting seat. But then, owning Rocking River, with access to salespeople who wanted to impress her and get her business, Nell would have the best.

"You and Joe started at Burnt Mill," he said. "We'll start there." It would be tough paddling down the creek in water that flowed sluggishly, but he couldn't ignore the mostly still water in the first few miles before Double Falls. Nell said Joe had been alive at the Double. She might have killed him much sooner.

"Fine," she said, and climbed down the ladder.

Nell stared at the water pouring under the new and old bridges at the Burnt Mill put-in. There hadn't been a mill at the site in who knew how long, but the old rusted bridge was still standing, though blocked off from traffic, and the new bridge curved nearby, high-tech and sleek, spotted with graffiti. A bit downstream was the concrete water-level gauge, a relic like the older bridge. The water was still high after the unusual spring rains. It swirled around the bridge abutments in trails of white foam and up across the sandy beach to the grassy verge. Turkey, raccoon, opossum and deer had tracked the beach. A low mist hung over the water and up into the trees.

It was warm and humid, but Nell shivered as she stepped into her white water skirt and pulled it up to her waist. She tied her yellow flip-flops into the boat's webbing and yanked river shoes onto her feet. Carefully, deliberately, she didn't look at the cop. She wasn't certain that she could look at him this morning without cursing or hitting him with something. Probably not the smartest thing a murder suspect could do. Robert's motive, means and opportunity notwithstanding, her husband was missing. She was still the suspect at the top of the list.

Orson extended her paddle and Nell took it, tugged on her helmet strap, checking the fit, and touched her safety rescue knife, secure in its sheath. She had remembered to bring a charcoal and UV water filter, so they could drink directly from the river without worrying about contaminants. She tightened her PFD straps and slid into her boat. With a well-practiced pull of her forearms, she snapped the white water skirt over the open cockpit, snugged her knees under the knee pads and tested her feet against the bulkhead.

She glanced at the cop and pushed off the bank, knuckles to the ground, her paddle balanced across her boat. She slid into the river with a nearly flat seal launch, her kayak entering the water at a perfect angle, dipping low and bobbing back as she dug in with deep, hard paddle strokes that peeled her into the current. Not thinking. Not thinking about anything. Because if she did, she would cry.

He felt like an ass. And yet, he couldn't afford to be swayed by his feelings. Firming his mouth and his resolve,

Orson imitated her launch and followed her down the river. Though he had known it was a waste of time, he had checked the Burnt Mill picnic area for anything that might have remained of their stay nearly seven years ago. There had been extensive renovations to the park; he had seen nothing useful. Nell had watched him, her eyes both knowing and accusing, then staring away, into the distance. She had looked so…so numb… Was it because she was facing arrest if he discovered her secret? Or was it still grief?

Six times in the few miles before they reached the confluence of the New River and Clear Creek, Orson called a halt and paddled to the bank, looking at likely spots. Each time Nell watched from the water, silent, her face giving nothing away as he unhooked his skirt and climbed up the bank, plowed through underbrush or scuffed through old leaves.

She wasn't stupid. She knew what he was doing. Looking for burial sites. Or bones.

The last time, she didn't even watch. When he paddled river-left, she paddled into deeper water at a pool just ahead and practiced her rolls. Settling her paddle along the side of the kayak, rolling over to hang upside down in the water, she repositioned the paddle. Bending her torso in a C shape to one side, then kicking her hip and knee, turning her body into a C on the other side, Nell executed a basic roll, rising to the surface as the boat rolled over, righting itself with the snap of her body.

Tucking her paddle into a brace stroke, she sat up. After several successful C-to-C rolls, she worked on sweeps, the roll similar to yet significantly different from the C-to-C. She was clearing her mind of everything but the Zen of rolling, of survival, of making her body and the kayak one.

Ignoring the cop. That was how she thought about him now. The cop.

24

It was noon by the time they reached the confluence. Though it wasn't a cakewalk under ordinary conditions, it wasn't usually a particularly gnarly meeting of currents. But today, the recent hard rains had carried away cut trees and brush from upstream on the New River. Trees, ends sawn flat and smooth, branches lopped off, had piled up against boulders and were jammed into crevices between rocks, making it more dangerous than usual to run the confluence.

In unspoken consent, they beached just upstream, river-left, and stood on the bank considering the logjam. After a moment, Orson climbed up the bank for a better vantage. He could hear Nell behind him, brush sliding and slipping on the incline. He caught a handhold on a sturdy tree, aware of her beside him, her breathing steady but hard. When his hand let go of the support, Nell's took its place, pulling herself up.

The logs, fresh cut and green, strained by the press of water, groaned and rumbled against the overlying roar of white water, like undead voices on a horror-movie sound track. The scene of churning water and boulders, trees and wild froth, was beautiful and deadly. If one of them came out of the boat, the chance of becoming entrapped was dangerously high. Pointing at the highest pile of logs across the river, he said, "Looks sorta like a beaver dam."

"If the beavers were two hundred pounds and had teeth like diamond saws," Nell said.

"Movie title. *Attack of the Monster Beavers*."

Nell turned red and stifled a giggle.

"Uh, that didn't come out right. No porno intended."

She slanted him a look and then quickly away. "The worst of it is river-right of the New, in the angle between the New and where they become the South Fork. If we stay river-left we should be fine."

After a moment, he said, "We can take the cheat."

In his peripheral vision, he saw her fingers tighten on the tree limb, skin white and water-wrinkled. A moment later they relaxed. "We need to scout ahead." She moved away from him, along the shore, through brush that had yet to reach its full summer thickness, pushing through and stepping over rocks and trees. He watched as she moved, her skirt hanging to her knees in front, much shorter in back, revealing well-shaped thighs and calves and rounded bottom in skintight river shorts. He shook his head to rid himself of thoughts a cop shouldn't be having and followed her.

Nell reached the shore at the top of Double Falls, the rapid marked by house-size boulders, and stopped. Silent, they contemplated the falls. One of the cut logs was stuck at the water line at the top of the first drop, mostly above water. They could run the Double if they rode the falls hard river-right, and bent backward over the stern of the boats as they crossed under the tree. If they hit the current perfectly. But there wasn't a lot of wiggle room.

The cheat was running, water roaring around and between the boulders. Nothing blocked the passage and the pool at the bottom was debris free. The cheat was runnable. The water was a steady roar, making normal speech nearly impossible. They didn't speak until they were back at their boats. Silent, they skirted in, Orson knowing it was no time to start asking questions.

"Go ahead," Nell said.

Startled, as if she had read his mind, Orson said, "Go ahead, what?"

"Go ahead and ask me why I didn't scout the Double before Joe and I ran it. Ask me why I didn't know there was a tree blocking the cheat. Ask me why I was so stupid as to kill my husband."

Orson's head came up fast, nostrils flaring. She was staring at her hands, fingers loosely holding her paddle, back bowed, head drooped so he could see only the top of her helmet.

"'Cause that's what I did. I killed Joe just as surely as if I held his head underwater. If I hadn't been such a Miss Know-it-All, I woulda been in proper position to take the current down the middle. Instead, I was so sure I could handle myself no matter what, I let myself get out of position. Was forced to take the cheat without scouting it first."

This was more information than his father had gotten at the time of the disappearance. Some memories had come back, it seemed. Or she had decided to embellish the truth in hopes of throwing him off. "What happened?" he asked, tone neutral.

"I don't 'member much," she said, her Tennessee accent hard. She took a breath, steadying herself, and her voice firmed. "And what I *do* remember comes to me in bits and pieces, all jumbled together. Confusin'."

Orson said nothing, waiting.

"I get this flash of a picture of the falls from hard river-left. If I had tried to run it starting from there, I was likely to hit the rock. Rock was undercut and water was running under, pulled under. I coulda been pulled under with it. I remember digging in hard with a perfect stroke, sweeping to turn the stern into the current and the bow into the cheat. The main flow whipped me around and I leaned forward."

She went silent, fingers limp. She inhaled, and they clenched spastically on the paddle. "I don't remember seeing the tree. Or hitting it. Or getting tangled in it. But I do 'member...*re*member my fingers in the branches. Pushing against the main trunk. Pain in my chest, stabbing. Water roaring, pulling my boat under the tree. Forcing me against the branch pushing up under my vest. I was hung."

When she fell quiet again, he asked, voice low, wishing he had a tape recorder, "How'd you get out?"

After a moment she exhaled, seemed to relax. Her voice dropped, barely a whisper. "I remember seeing some red flex."

"Flex?"

"Webbing. I'm not sure if I was tying myself to the tree or trying to cut myself free of it. I remember seeing blood on my hand, my knife in my fingers. I remember fighting panic, trying to stay calm and think it through. The tree was starting to shift. My boat was being pulled under it. But I couldn't get out of it." Her voice dropped, her breathing sped up. "Couldn't get the skirt to pop free with the tree on top of it.

"And then I see Joe. In the tree. His face right next to mine. Shoutin' for me to hold on." Tears splattered onto her hands and rolled between her knuckles to disappear. "I see his hands near my face, pulling my vest up by the shoulder straps like he was trying to pull me from the river. Then bubbles, like I'm underwater. This weird glimpse of a tree passing over my face. And Joe near me, on the surface, white water everywhere. And then I wake up, the next day."

"What do you think happened?" She looked up, confusion writ large on her face, tears standing in her eyes, trailing down her cheeks. He clenched at the sight, but his voice was steady and he clarified, "How do think he got you free?"

She stared into the distance, visibly recalling a painful memory, her body language suggesting she was not fabricating a new scenario, but remembering, her thoughts turned inward, into the past and possibilities she had worried through a hundred times. A thousand.

"I dreamed about it for a long time. I think mosta the branches underneath the tree had already broke off. I think he cut the rest away and popped my skirt free. Let my boat go on under. Pulled me up, maybe with a rope in a dragline. Maybe the tree shifted and he dropped me. Don't know. But I went under the tree, through the last half of the curve on the cheat. Mostly underwater. And I think I pulled him with me, maybe when he wouldn't let go 'a the rope. Or it tangled him and he had to jump in to follow me." She shrugged helplessly. "And I hit my head and he hit his knee before we dumped into the pool at the bottom of the Double. That's what I think."

"How did he get to you? In the first place?"

Her eyes shifted the other direction, into possibility. "I'm guessing he made the Double and waited in the small pool beneath it, and when I didn't come on through, he beached his boat river-left and walked upstream. Came onto the cheat from on top of the boulder nearest the shore. I figure he stabilized the tree with line first, then walked along the tree to me."

Her voice dropped even lower and Orson strained to hear her. "But when he cut me free, the current caught me and pulled me under. And he came with me. Off the tree and under, still holding on to the shoulders of my vest. I hit my head." She touched her temple, a place on her skull unprotected by her helmet. "He hit his knee." She inhaled and Orson saw her collarbones move, the breath strained and painful. "That's what I think happened.

"If I had checked the cheat first or been in proper position to take the Double Falls he'd still be alive." She lowered her head again. "I killed him. By being stupid, I killed him." She looked at Orson, her eyes so caught in the past that she wasn't really with him. "That's manslaughter, ain't it. To be stupid and kill someone."

Orson licked his lips. "Sounds like an accident," he said carefully. And it did. It sounded *exactly* like an accident. Well thought out, well planned, with nearly seven years to work out the kinks. The cop in him didn't believe it. "Let's take the cheat."

Nell blinked. Her eyes focused on him, still confused. "What?"

"Let's take the cheat. You point at the spots where the tree was stuck. Okay?"

She nodded once, quick and jerking, her face tightening, a hint of anger in her eyes. "Fine. That's what we're here for, ain't it. For you to poke holes in a story I can't half 'member." She pushed into the current, peeling out, too hard, too fast. She dug in with her paddle, not exactly reckless, but damn close to it. Orson followed, his paddle strokes controlled and easy, his pace slower, more thoughtful. Just how good an actress was Nell Stevens?

Nell shot through the water, her strokes hard and deep, propelling the kayak through the current, using the river to power the craft, her body, legs, and feet guiding the small boat through the churning white water, but not at its mercy. Never again at the mercy of this river.

Of course, "Never again" was what she had said about ever running the South Fork of the Cumberland. And here she was. On the river. With a cop on her tail. Hitting the confluence at high water. With strainers and hazards everywhere.

The currents smashed together, rising up high in a cresting wave, two rivers mingling and merging but neither ceding control to the other. Logs jammed the river throughout the confluence, piled and broken and jagged, waterlogged just under the surface in twisted, shattered masses, splintered ends visible and dragging against her hull. She pushed off one cluster, detectable only by the faint swirl on the surface water, to propel her toward the cheat.

Using her body to push against the current, she circled river-left around the massive boulder and entered the cheat dead center. The next boulder forced the water to swirl hard back river-right to rejoin the main current, making a fast-moving, C-shaped mini-canyon. Nell reached the center of the curving cheat and dug in deep with stabbing, forward strokes. A young poplar grew into the clefts of the rock, roots tight in the crevices, trunk leaning with the flow. She hadn't seen the small tree while scouting. She was pretty sure it hadn't been there seven years ago.

Just in front of the poplar, she pointed quickly with her paddle, right and then left, where she vaguely remembered the strainer tree being caught. If the cop missed her signal, too bad.

The drop was quick and furious. Her boat disappeared beneath the roiling surface, the water level riding chest high. She jerked up hard with her legs and the kayak broke the surface, water splashing from her skirt. She paddled into the pool below Double Falls, did a sweep-turn, facing back upstream to see the cop make the drop. It was only a few feet. But his eyes were bright and tight, searching out every part of the cheat and the pool. Without acknowledging her, he ferried across the current, river-right. He beached his boat, jerked his skirt free and pushed out with his hands. He pulled his boat up the shore. He began to search, his feet kicking at under-brush. Right in the spot where Joe had left her so long ago.

Fury geysered through Nell. With a sweep of her paddle and a quick rotation of her body, she took her boat downstream until tears and the sound of the next drop forced her closer to shore. She pulled up under the hanging branches of an oak, its roots undermined by the river. It leaned out over the water, limb-arms dragged by the current, trunk not quite ready to release the land where its roots still clung.

Heedless of snakes that might be nesting in the branches watching for prey, she grabbed a trailing limb and held on. Her boat whirled with the current, turning her backward, facing upstream. But she couldn't see the cop on the bank, searching for signs of Joe. She couldn't see anything. She could barely breathe through the sobs.

Joe was dead. She had known he was dead for nearly seven years. But *damn* the cop. She hadn't had to look at that fact. Not until now.

Orson directed his anger into thrashing the underbrush. A lot of scrub had sprouted in the intervening years, the smooth place he remembered from the SAR mostly overgrown. There was nothing left of the campsite where Joe Stevens had allegedly left his wife to go for help. He re-skirted, made a quick seal launch into the water and ferried back river-left just below the Double. He unskirted and searched the shore there, aware of Nell waiting and watching.

Satisfied that there was no grave there, Orson positioned himself in the pool for the next drop, an easy class II called the Washing Machine. His eyes found Nell, riding a slower current in the branches of a tree. She had been crying.

Something inside him solidified into a hard knot, painful and intrusive, just beneath his breastbone. With his paddle, he pointed downstream, demanding, waiting, for her to precede him. She blinked to clear her features, and closed her mouth into a firm line. Expressionless, she paddled into position and entered the class II.

Orson stopped several times between the Washing Machine and the El and searched the shores. He found nothing but animal scat and tracks. Once he startled several copperheads lying coiled together. One sprang at him, a warning. He backtracked fast. But he found nothing, not one sign of Joe Stevens. No bones scattered by scavengers. No grave site hidden by fallen leaves. Nothing.

The rock ledge of the El, with its swirling plunge, appeared, the water flow making it into a huge curl and drop. Orson watched as her boat dipped into the hole just in front of the ledge. She propelled herself forward with steady, fluid strokes, pushing the boat toward the drop-off. The backward-moving water tried to suck her boat back upstream. Moving with the fluidity of a ballet dancer, or a water mammal, she guided the boat through the hole.

Again his body reacted in ways that had nothing to do with being a cop on a case.

She bobbed and leaned downstream, shoulders strong and muscular. She worked her way out of the hole, defeating the invisible current that tried to trap her, and broke free.

Her boat went over the ledge. Orson positioned himself for the rapid. Nell appeared in front of him, below the drop and out of the way. He followed her line through the current, paddling hard against the diagonal curler trying to spin him sideways, and boofed over the ledge, wrenching up his legs and the bow, gaining some air, taking the drop.

He hit flat at the bottom of the vertical drop, landing in a spine-jarring thud of boat bottom against horizontal water. He leaned into the strokes, lashing the river with the paddle blade.

He broke the current with a whoop of delight, saw Nell in an eddy in the Long Pool, paddle resting across her cockpit. Grinning, he angled his boat through the water to her. But her expression didn't change, her face frozen, gaze distant. She seemed lost in the past again, staring away. He rested his paddle.

"I need to search along the Long Pool. It's gonna take a while. You want to wait onshore?"

"Sure. I'll eat lunch." Without looking at him, she dipped her paddle and stroked gently to the shore. She beached her boat, popped her skirt and pushed herself out. He paddled after her. He popped his skirt too and eased out of his kayak, stepping into shallow water. Though she didn't ask, he said, "I have to eat too. And I can start my search here."

It took an hour and a half for him to eat and then search the river-right side of the Long Pool. He got better at the technique, leaving his skirt loose, paddling through the nearly still water from place to place, sliding out to search the shore, sliding back in and paddling on. The skirt technique wasn't hard, but he was tiring. His chest was hurting from the unaccustomed activity and his still-healing wound. And he had a long river yet to paddle.

At one spot, however, near to the bottom of Long Pool, he found bones in low brush, bones so old and scattered he couldn't tell what species they were. He didn't think they were human. Maybe a large dog? Or even a small bear? There was no skull, and he was no anthropologist. He didn't disturb them, but backed away, fixing the location in his mind, and continued searching.

When Orson was certain that he had been as thorough as possible after so many years, floods, droughts and spring rains, he ferried across the river to the site where a strong hiker could make his way up to the Honey Creek Overlook. He pulled his boat high off the water, leaving it beached, and started to search the ground. He moved slowly from his boat up the beach, circled into the trees and back to the water. He retraced his steps a yard farther out from his boat. Then a yard farther, making his way up the incline and into the trees. He had searched for half an hour when he saw it.

A shallow depression scattered with needles from a dying fir.

25

The ground in the depression was different from the surrounding earth, more sandy, as if it had been turned in the not-too-distant past. It was approximately four feet long, less than two feet wide. Nothing grew on it.

A grave. Possibly. Not certainly, but possibly.

Careful to avoid tracking a potential crime scene, Orson backed away and returned to shore. He pulled his cell from a waterproof bag and checked the signal. Nada. Zilch. Of course. He closed it and stored the pouch back in his boat. How was he going to alert the authorities? How was he going to get a crime-scene crew in here? The logistics sucked.

More importantly...what was he going to do about Nell? He looked across the water. She was sitting on a rock, looking his way, her body relaxed. She hadn't rushed him, pushed him or complained that he was taking too long. Once, he had looked over and seen her stretched out. Maybe asleep. Would a killer fall asleep while a cop discovered the resting place of the body? Somehow he didn't think so. But then, he didn't *want* to think so.

He scanned the Long Pool, then upriver and down. They were in an isolated part of the river basin. Twice they had been passed by other boaters and commercial rafts, but right now, the river was empty and they were alone. Without a cell

signal, he could either hike out or run the river to the O &
W bridge and hope there was someone hanging out there
who would give him a ride back to civilization. If not, then
he'd have to hike from the O & W. Or they could run the river
to the Leatherwood Ford takeout. Orson sighed. Or he could
do the responsible thing and keep searching the riverbanks
for another burial site. There was no guarantee that this
possible grave site held the body of Joseph Stevens.

He checked his watch, climbed into his boat and ferried
back across the water to Nell. As he neared her, she stood
and went to her boat. She had removed her helmet and skirt
and PFD. She pulled the gear back on. He didn't want to do
it this way, but he didn't have much choice. He needed to
keep searching the banks. Just in case.

It was darker than the underside of hell when they made
it to the Leatherwood Ford takeout. Orson was so tired his
bones ached. So tired his teeth ached. So tired his hair ached.
He was in pitiful shape if a day on a river of class IIs, IIIs
and IVs wiped him out.

Nell had spent the day in her boat, waiting as much as
paddling. She looked fresher than he, and she didn't stumble
when she pulled her body from her cockpit. Orson flopped
like a dying whale to the beach beside his kayak. Knowing
that now he was going to have to tell her about the grave at
Long Pool. If he could find the energy to talk.

"I'll hike up the road to the RV. Be back in a few
minutes," Nell said.

She disappeared into the gloom to get the RV from the
upper tier of parking, where they had left it for the day, and
he let her go. If she had figured out that he had discovered
something—several somethings, but the Long Pool's
possible-grave was the most interesting—would she run?
Leave him here and take off in the RV? If she did, he was in

no condition to chase her. The image would have made him chuckle if the pain hadn't been so bad. Orson rolled over to take the stress off his ribs. Even gravity hurt.

His stomach rumbled with hunger. He hadn't brought enough provisions. Nell had shared hers with him, some high-calorie tropical trail mix that gave him a short- and long-term sugar boost. But it hadn't been a meal.

Lights sliced the dark. The RV bounced along the road, curving slowly through the day camp. A flashlight beam picked across the ground from farther right, but closer in. A park ranger was attached to it. The ranger reached him first, a woman, trim and spiffy in her uniform. Orson forced himself to his knees and then to his feet. "You folks okay?" she asked. "We've been watching for you, trying to decide if we needed to call out a SAR."

"We're alive. Just barely. I'm an investigator with the state police, working a cold case." He reached in the kayak for his waterproof pouch and handed her his ID, aware that he had, in the last four hours, turned a corner in his mind. Had left behind his old life of an active-case investigator and accepted a new one, in the Cold Case Unit.

Now he wanted to get some things set in motion before Nell was back in earshot. The RV was easing through the dark, drawing close. "Were you working here seven years ago?" he asked. The ranger nodded. "You remember a search and rescue? Man by the name of Joseph Stevens went missing on a trip with his wife?"

She nodded again. "I remember."

"I was running the river with the wife today. Spending a lot of time searching the shores for a grave or bones. That's the wife coming this way in the RV. I don't want her to know what I found. Not yet."

"What did you find?" she asked, the question far more than idle curiosity. Like Orson, she knew that murder in a state park meant overlapping jurisdictions. Too many chiefs fighting over responsibility and territory.

"Two locales with surface bones, scattered, probably not human, but strewn by scavengers and hard to tell. One possible grave site that gives me pause."

"You think the wife did it?" she asked.

"If the surface remains are human, she's a suspect—*if* there's enough left to positively identify a victim. If it's Stevens in the grave, though, that assures us it's murder."

He flipped open his cell and saw that he had sufficient bars in the day camp. "I need to call this in. Can you distract her?" The RV was right on them. It slowed, tires crunching gravel.

"I can do that," the ranger said as the headlights cut strips of shadow through the trees. "But I remember that little girl from the search. She didn't kill her husband. You better look somewhere else."

Orson grinned in the illumination from the RV. It was bright enough to read her name tag. "I said she's the most likely suspect, Brenda. I didn't say she did it."

The ranger nodded and walked to the RV. Nell stepped down to the bottom of the stairs, the door open behind her, soft yellow light spilling out. "We were worried about you," the ranger said.

"Blame the cop," Nell said, her voice tired. "He's a certifiable nutcase. In one day he paddled the South Fork *and* hiked it."

"You haven't paid for the night at the park," Brenda said.

Orson could hear Nell sigh from where he stood. He turned his back to them and flipped open his phone. He called the Knoxville field office of the state police and asked for the investigator in charge for the shift. After a short conversation, he made one other call, to his father. When Nolan answered, Orson said, "I got something. Bones in two sites

Rapid Descent 291

and what looks like a grave. I called in a team. It'll take us a few days to see if it's him."

"You got any gut on it?" Nolan asked, meaning did his instincts tell him anything about the scene and about Nell.

"No. Not a thing. Could be a pet, or someone else buried there, or most anything."

"And the girl?"

Orson's gut tightened. "Not a thing," he lied. "Not a thing."

Nell wasn't stupid. She had watched the cop, studied his body language. He was relaxed for most of the trip, his limbs loose and his paddling easy, except for a few moments. He had found something three, maybe four different times. Something that worried him or piqued his professional interest. He had sent the ranger, Brenda, to keep her busy so he could make some calls now that they were in the park and had cellular reception. And to think she had begun to think of him as…as something more than a river guide and employee. Could she be any more stupid?

Disgusted with the cop and with herself, Nell informed the ranger that she didn't need to be kept busy while the cop called in reinforcements, which made the woman laugh. Instead, Nell made arrangements with the ranger to stay over, this time in a different campsite, a cancellation giving her a two-night stay. If the cop expected her to take off and go home, when he might have found evidence of Joe, he was stupidly mistaken.

While he talked, his cell phone to his ear, his voice too soft to carry, she loaded her kayak up on top of the RV and stowed her gear, leaving his in an untidy pile on the beach and dumping his tote containing a change of clothes and toiletries onto the parking lot. To the ranger's amusement, she tossed his tent, air mattress and sleeping bag onto the ground,

making a heap. Crossing her arms, fully aware that the ranger
was entertained and enjoying the drama, Nell waited the
cop out.

When he finished his last call, he closed his phone and
ambled over, a shadow against deeper shadows, stopping just
outside the pool of light from the RV door. "I won't be going
back with you," he said. "Something came up in Knoxville.
I have a ride picking me up in about an hour."

"Reeeeally," she said, drawing the word out, her tone dry.

"Yeah. Really," he said, standing straight, as if surprised.

Irritation shot through her, hot and prickly. She said the
first thing that came to her. "Liar, liar, pants on fire."

His head came up, half-offended. In the dark, the ranger
let out a bark of laughter.

"That's what JJ would say to that, and since it fits, I'll say
it too. You're not heading home. You're not heading back to
Knoxville. And you're sure as heck not heading back to the
Pigeon. You're sticking around here for a few days, checking
out some sites where Joe might be. So, I dumped your camping gear in the parking lot, Mr. Liar Cop."

"Nell—"

"There aren't any more campsites available. I took the last
one. But the rangers might let you pitch your tent behind their
residence, you being *undercover law enforcement* and all."
She imbued the words with all the derision at her command.

"You're staying over?" he said, his body doing that
uptight, law-enforcement tensing thing.

"Yep. Mike and Melissa can run the business for a few
days. You think you mighta found something that points to
Joe. So I'm staying. Not that I have to tell you, and not that
you can do a blasted thing about it."

The cop stared at her through the gathering night. She
stared back.

When she realized he had nothing else to say, Nell went

to the RV and opened the back hatch, tossing the last of his personal and camping gear onto the gravel parking lot of the day camp. She tossed each piece with unnecessary roughness, slamming them into one another, sending them tumbling. Including his little cooler, which somehow came open and scattered colas and beer all over the place. Tough.

Orson said nothing, just watched. Which just made her madder and madder. When she had the last of his things out of the RV undercompartments, she slammed the hatches and marched into the RV. She slammed that door too. And roared off, to locate B-21 in the dark. Leaving the insufferable, sanctimonious, lying *man* standing in the dark with his things to tote up the hill and down the road to the ranger's house.

Orson stood in the dark and stared after the taillights. He wasn't quite sure what had just happened. But whatever it was, it pulled an unwilling smile at his mouth.

"Feisty," a voice said from the night.

Orson turned to the sound. "She takes after her mother. I've seen them both in action. Brenda, may I pitch my tent behind the ranger residence?"

"It's against park rules, but I guess I can make an exception." The flashlight beam came on and he watched it pick across the ground and center on his gear. "Gimme some 'a that. We'll see if we can cart it to my backyard all in one trip."

Orson loaded a lot of his equipment into his boat and lifted the bow by its strap, letting the stern drag across the ground and grabbed a load of miscellaneous equipment in his other hand. Brenda was stronger than she looked and carried his tent over one shoulder, his suitcase strap over the other, and his cooler in one hand. "Speaking of breaking rules," she said mildly, holding up the repacked cooler, "alcohol is against the rules in the park."

"If I offer you a beer, will that mitigate my punishment?"

"Low-level beer bribery is usually welcome. The government don't pay us diddly squat."

He slept like a log on his air-mattress sleeping bag, waking early when his cell phone rang. Before he could speak, the caller barked, "Lennox. The CSI van will leave at eight. They'll be there no later than noon. Get them cracking and get back here by midnight if you get negatives. Time is money and I got the governor on my ass for the Dickerson case." His boss, Mohasil Ibrahim—Mo to his investigators—was known for machine-gun-fire instructions, complaints, questions—and for being a skinflint. Occasionally, he stopped to take a breath. "If they need more than one day to process the sites, we have a deal with Motel Six for whenever we have to stay over someplace. Make sure all the guys bunk together. Sheila can stay in the van overnight."

Orson chuckled into the slight pause between orders, his voice hoarse with sleep. "This is a wilderness refuge. Tell them to bring sleeping bags and tents. We'll all be sleeping behind the ranger's residence."

Mo cursed explicitly and colorfully, and then brightened. "They'll bitch, but we'll save on hotel bills." He hung up. Orson rolled over and snuggled back into his bag. He could sleep in.

Nell phoned her mother at eight, knowing that JJ would have her up early. It was one of the many changes her mother's life underwent when Joe died. Claire had sold her shop and her small house and moved in with Nell, helping with the baby, working in the shop in Rocking River, manning the store so Nell could work the river as a raft guide, saving a bit on guide fees. She had done the books, and taught Nell how, kept the house clean, searched on the

Internet for deals on rafts, kayaks, gasoline for the buses, and had invested the eighty thousand dollars Nell got from the sale of Joseph's apartment and the investment from Turtle Tom, so that Nell could open Rocking River Nantahala. The early years had been a strain on all of them, but by far the most difficult change was Claire learning how to live with early risers, Nell and JJ.

Nell had called her mother last night when she got settled, to check in on JJ and any business problems, and to tell Claire about the day's search for Joe, though she hadn't mentioned a crime-scene team or the cop's interest in certain sites on the river. No need to worry her. Claire had been alert and lively sounding, David Letterman talking in the background. This morning she sounded a bit less perky. "What?" Claire croaked into the phone. Okay, she sounded completely asleep.

"You and JJ have a good night?"

"Oh, my God," she groaned. "Remind me to never let that kid sleep with me again. He kicked me so hard I got bruises on my backside. And don't gripe at me for letting him sleep with me. He couldn't go to sleep with you not here and it was the only way either of us was gonna get any rest. Anyway, he's not here. Mike picked him up about a half hour ago, muttering under his breath. It seems some of your loyal guides called in sick so they could go up to the South Fork and see what was going on. They there yet?"

"No," Nell said, her heart sinking. "I haven't seen them. How did they find out?"

"Jedi Mike called me after 1:00 a.m. He knows a ranger at the park who notified him about the search, and the crime-scene team your *kayak instructor* called out. I'm guessing Mike told one person too many and the word got out."

Nell closed her eyes. The world of river enthusiasts was fairly small, and she wasn't surprised that Mike had been contacted by a ranger. He was the Jedi, after all, the old man of Tennessee rafting.

A knock sounded on the door of the RV. Nell stood and peered out, spotting Turtle Tom. She sighed. "They're here. I'll call later today when I know something."

"Love you, honey."

"Love you too, Claire." Nell punched her phone off and glanced around the RV. It looked like a storm had struck it, clothes everywhere and dirty dishes in the sink. But then, she knew the conditions under which the guides lived. They'd likely think it was the Taj Mahal. She opened the door and peered out. Turtle Tom, Stoned Stewart, RiverAnn, Hamp and Harvey stood on the concrete parking pad, expressions tense and angry, as if they had been arguing and the disagreement still hung in the air among them.

"Morning," she said, tone neutral. "I hear youns called in today. Too sick to work?"

"We're not sick," Turtle Tom said, his voice soft. "We heard they might have found Joe's body."

"Which means that you killed him," RiverAnn said.

Shock zinged through her at the words, tingling in her fingertips, tightening her chest muscles.

"That's *not* what we heard," Tom said, shooting his friend a hard look. RiverAnn put her hands around her pregnant belly, the motion protective. "We heard that your kayak instructor, who claimed to be on leave, was really undercover," Tom said, "and that he found something. That's *all* we heard."

Turtle Tom had liked Joe. They had often eaten lunch together, brainstorming ideas for a family-oriented rafting business. And then she had married Joe. Had become Joe's partner. Had Tom wanted to be his business partner? Nell had never thought about the possibility that she had come between them in some way. "Thanks, Tom," she said softly.

"I don't know exactly what Orson found yesterday, but it was enough for him to stay. So, it was enough for me to stay too."

Tom said, "Joe was my friend." He shot another look at RiverAnn. "He was a friend to all of us. We're here for you."

"Nell? You got problems?"

Nell looked over at Orson, standing in the shade of a young oak. One hand was under his T-shirt at his waist, in that characteristic pose. But Nell had a feeling that sometimes he kept it there to secure a gun.

"No problems," Tom said, stepping back from the RV door.

"We hear you found Joe," Harvey said.

Orson blew out an irritated breath. "I found some sites with a few indications that there *might* be human remains. But we don't know whose. We don't even know yet if they are human. So how about you boys and lady head back to the Pigeon and take Nell with you. You're not needed here."

Turtle Tom blew through his nose, laughing softly.

"I thought you weren't a cop now," RiverAnn accused. "Heard that you quit. Then we hear that you're here *undercover*. Living with us to see who killed Joe."

"I'm on leave to recuperate from an injury," Orson said after a moment.

Nell studied the cop, wanting to be mad at him, wanting to hate him for his duplicity. But he looked so conflicted that she couldn't. She kept her mouth shut.

"Nell and I thought we could maybe retrace the trip down the South Fork of the Cumberland. See if we could look at things from a new point of view. I found something that might be interesting. That's all. No body."

Turtle Tom lifted a hand. "Well, whatever. See you on the river, man." The five moved closer together, as if closing ranks, and moved away.

Orson looked over his shoulder at her, his long hair

brushing his collarbones, his eyes somber, with a hint of steel beneath. "Call Jedi Mike and tell him to keep his mouth shut for once, would you. Last thing we need is the press all over this. I want this to be quick and easy and done before they get wind of it."

Nell nodded once, but didn't speak.

He turned and moved into the morning shadows. Nell stood in the doorway, open to the morning heat and humidity. A fly darted in to buzz at the front windows. Orson Lennox walked away, his lanky frame looking assured and self-contained, back down the road to wherever he had come from. Watching her? She needed to remember that Orson was here to do a job. Not take care of her. Not comfort her. Not ease her pain. He was the man who would arrest her in a heartbeat.

The river would be closed if the cops discovered a body. If she wanted to be there while they worked—or at least close by—she needed to decide which one of the sites that Orson had shown an interest in was the most likely to be examined first, and hit the water. She was going to have to run the river alone. Again.

26

Orson walked away from Nell's RV. He didn't appear to look left or right, but he knew instantly where the five had congregated. They stood near the showers in a tight clump, watching him, silent.

He didn't know why they had decided to show up or what they had planned, but they would bear watching. If Nell had killed her husband... His gut tightened. He remembered the way Nell had looked during the original SAR for Joe, eyes black, lacerated skin. The later image of her in the small church overlapped with the wounded one, followed by the vision of Nell, confident and assured in her boat the day he auditioned for the job of kayak instructor. Which one was the real Nell? Was it possible that all of them were real?

He shook his head and went to shave and change clothes. He needed to look like a cop again.

Nell dropped her PFD, helmet and paddle and bent over, hands on knees to try to catch her breath. Beside her, a pimply-faced kid set down her boat and did the same. Sweat dribbled down his pale, pasty body and his knees looked wobbly. This was likely the most strenuous hike the boy had ever been on. Her own legs felt unsteady and she hiked often.

She had paid the kid thirty bucks to drive her to the put-in at the confluence and help carry her equipment down to the river. It wasn't an easy trek down to the basin, and it was downright hard when dragging a boat, all her gear and supplies. She didn't know how long she would have to be on the water today and had come prepared to last until sunset, which meant they had carried the forty-pound boat, and maybe another forty pounds of equipment, down the sharply inclined, muddy, rocky, slippery trail. They were both panting by the time they reached the water, and Nell figured the kid had earned a ten-dollar tip, which she held up with her thanks.

He took it without a word, but rather than start back up, he collapsed against a tree and rocked his head back to open up his airway. "You all right?" she asked.

"No. I'm pretty sure I'm gonna die, lady. But you go ahead and paddle on off." He flapped his fingers at the water and closed his eyes, mouth open like a carp, sucking air.

Nell hid a smile and knelt to store her gear in the kayak. "I used to walk up hills like that all the time when I was your age," she said. "Carrying all my own gear."

"Yeah," he said. "I heard the stories. In ten feet of snow. Barefoot."

Nell laughed. He grinned with her, but didn't open his eyes. "Watch out for ticks and chiggers," she said. He flapped his hand at her again. Nell skirted up and tucked the extra gear into the boat, strapping equipment and supplies into place. If she had to do a wet exit, she wasn't gonna lose the binoculars. Twenty minutes after they reached the gorge, Nell was on the water, sticking close to shore as she maneuvered through the waterlogged trees. After due consideration, she had decided to stake her claim to the most upriver of the sites Orson had shown an interest in. She could always let the water take her downstream, but it would be tough hiking upstream, carrying her boat, if she started at the bottom of the run.

The water level today was running at fifteen hundred, too low to take the cheat, but low enough to duck under the log blocking the upper drop of the Double Falls. She hoped. Nell approached the Double and calculated the exact spot she wanted to enter the rapid. She ferried a little river-right and took a steadying breath.

She peeled into the current, leaned downriver and speared the water with paddle strokes. White water roared like a thousand engines, bouncing off the wet rocks. The current jerked her forward. Toward the log obstruction. Time slowed, allowing her to see everything in slo-mo, like a series of perilous snapshots.

The bow of her kayak passed beneath the tree, out over the edge of the falls. Nell whipped her body back, lying down over the back of the kayak in a water-limbo.

Her heart rate doubled. The log passed an inch above her chest. She tilted her head. The bark of the log passed so close she could feel it against the hair of her cheek. Watched it as it slid beyond her head. Gravity caught her boat and tilted the bow down, arching, stretching her body to a sharper angle. The boat fell with the water down the drop.

Time snapped into fast-forward. Nell contracted her abdominals and slung her torso forward, shoving with her feet as she entered the water between the two drops. The kayak submerged. Bobbled. She braced with the paddle, left and right and left again as the water rocketed her over the second drop. "*Whoooo!*" she shouted with the rush of adrenaline.

The sound shocked her, sending a thrill of knowledge and pain through her body. It had been years since Nell had shouted with joy. Seven years since she took a rapid and…loved it. Tears gathered in her eyes and her breath came in a gasp. Seven years since she did what she loved. Fear had held her away from white water. Fear and grief and guilt and aching misery.

Knowing she had to be in place before the cops got to the

river, she didn't pause, didn't think about the revelations that were coursing through her. Instead, she set up for the Washing Machine, positioning the kayak with her paddle. Time for self-revelations later.

Nell paddled slowly around the Long Pool. She was alone. Just her and the barely moving water, five buzzards wheeling overhead, a deer drinking on the far shore, near the site where Orson had undergone a transformation from paddler to pure cop. Until then he had been having fun between treks into the brush. Here, at the Long Pool, he had changed.

He had stomped around, kicking at the brush and deadwood, hands on his hips, looking around. Then…his body had grown taut, tense. His concentration seemed to sharpen. When he knelt in the brush, it was with an almost agonizing slowness. His focus changed. Totally changed. He had morphed into a cop. And she had known…

Just watching it had given her a bad case of the willies. And that was why she had chosen this site to stake out. Though there had been other places downstream where he had shown an interest, this one had been the first, had created the strongest reaction. And it was upstream from where they had found Joe's cut PFD and his boat on the SAR.

The deer's head came up. Its body tightened, drew down, locking power into its haunches. It leaped sideways, over a log and again over a car-size rock, and it was gone. Nell rested her paddle, waiting. Voices carried over the water, high-pitched female, lower-pitched male. Orson appeared through the foliage, carrying his boat to the shore. He stopped, staring out over the water, shock triggering a reaction, drawing in just as the deer had done, preparing himself for flight or fight.

Nell had debated whether she should hide, drag her boat into the brush on the far shore, find a comfy place to wait out the day and use the binoculars to keep up with the cops.

Assuming they showed up here. But she wasn't much on hiding and sneaking around, and was even less apt to be successful at it. So she just parked herself in the middle of the pool and waited. If it ticked off Orson, well, then, it ticked him off.

He peeled off a dress shirt and jeans, revealing a wet suit that covered only the torso, thighs and shoulders down to midbicep. Perfect for temps like today. It was easy to move around in and fit well under clothes, it seemed. He skirted up, moving with erratic intensity, anger or some other emotion making his body less fluid. He shoved himself into the boat, his voice carrying over the water, though pitched too low to make out words. She waited, knowing he was coming to her. Knowing he was ticked off.

Orson's paddle technique was choppy and rough, his boat skittering too far right and left with each stroke. His mouth turned down in reaction, and Nell permitted herself a small smile. She figured it might be her last for a while. Orson visibly collected himself and smoothed out his motions. When he was ten feet away, he rested his paddle, letting the momentum of the boat carry him the rest of the way to her. Their boats bumped and did a little dance, swirling around each other, maintaining contact.

Orson stabbed her with his gaze. "You want to tell me how you turned up here?"

Nell frowned at him, and then understood. He thought she knew to come here because this was where Joe was, because she had put him here. He really thought that. "You're an idiot," she said baldly. "I've got a six-year-old kid." At his confused look she said, "When JJ discovers something new and tries to hide it from me, he gets these herky-jerky body movements. Just like you did here yesterday. Any mother would have known you found something." At his look of disbelief she added, "You found something at two other places too, but this one was upstream. I figured if you didn't show at this one by noon, I'd paddle on down to the others."

He started to say something then closed his mouth on it, saying instead, "You're paddling alone."

"My paddling partner is a cop on business."

"You can't stay here, Nell."

"Stop me."

"Nell—"

"I'm staying. You can arrest me or do some other cop thing, but that's the only way you'll get me to leave."

He rubbed his face, leaving water-wet prints. He had gotten some sun in recent days and his fingers left white spots in the sunburn. He dropped his hands and met her gaze, seemed about to speak, when a shout from upstream drew his attention. He stuck his paddle in the water and turned upriver. A kayak came over the ledge of the El. Another followed. And another. "At least you won't be alone," Orson said disgustedly. With a sweep of his paddle, he turned back across the Long Pool.

Nell pivoted her boat to study the new arrivals and huffed out a breath. Turtle Tom, Hamp, Stoned Stewart and Harvey, already below the falls. No RiverAnn. Too pregnant to take rapids safely.

She could ask them to leave, but Nell figured they would react much as she had with Orson. But maybe with language a bit more pointed. The guides had been friends with Joe. They deserved to stay, if that's what they intended.

The four men regrouped at the bottom of the El, looked her over, and, without exchanging a word, paddled closer. She waited on the water for their judgment. The paddlers' body movements were tense, edgy, uncertain emotion displayed in the less-than-smooth forward progression of the kayaks and the diffident expressions they wore.

When they were close enough to exchange words, Tom tapped Harvey's boat with his paddle, an indication for the guide to speak. Harvey looked at him, an uncomfortable emotion—maybe anger?—moving under his skin, but he was too far away for Nell to read it for certain. He called, "Mind if we join you? We brought supplies." The others bobbed heads, helmets moving up and down, eyes on her.

"Sure. Company's welcome."

Heads bobbed again and Harvey said, "That was a sweet run. I'd fergot how sweet." His paddle pointing back at the El, he added, "But that kid nearly died back there. He was breathing when we left him, but it sounded like his lungs might bust open." Nell smiled slightly as the guys laughed, their tension vanishing.

Tom said, "We could head to the beach over there and start a fire. I brought a lighter and chips."

Harvey said, "Sweet. Plenty of deadwood around to get a fire going."

"Yeah, yeah," Hamp said.

Stoned Stewart, usually silent among his more gregarious friends, said, "I brought beer." The guys chortled. Stew always brought beer.

Turtle Tom had turned his boat to watch the shore. "We searched the banks around this pool half a dozen times during the SAR and didn't find anything." He cocked his head "Why're they so far up the bank?" he asked.

Nell shook her head. "I don't know. But that's where Orson was yesterday when he got all squirrelly. Whatever he found, it's high off the water. Way higher than flood stage the day Joe went missing."

"Who searched that bank on the SAR? Anyone remember?"

"Too long ago to remember," Harvey said. "Let's get a fire going. I need a beer."

Nell and the guys watched from the far bank, passing the binoculars back and forth, keeping a constant eye on police activity, little of which made sense without being a lot closer but which all the guys commented on, having been *CSI* fans over the years. Nell was silent, not joining in the camaraderie, her thoughts and worries focused on the distant shore. However, just having people nearby was a help to her fraying nerves, and the fire, while not needed for warmth, was comforting. Especially when the cops brought out shovels and started to dig.

Just after two, the paddlers all noted something different on the far shore. A change in body language. The cops had found something.

27

Almost frantically, Nell reskirted, not bothering with helmet or vest, which she tucked into her boat. She was only half-aware that the guys with her were putting out the fire and sliding into kayaks. She was first in the water, paddling steadily across the Long Pool, bisecting the slight current with sure strokes, and eddying out near the shore. The guys paddled up behind her, spreading out in a long, uneven line.

The cops were standing around a pit high above the waterline, its depth not easy for Nell to judge. Rocks had been placed around it, dirty, removed from the pit as they dug.

A woman cop ran yellow crime-scene tape around a large area. Another cop saw the paddlers and started to the edge of the water, watching them, arms akimbo. Other cops brought out a body bag. Orson never looked her way.

Orson was still hot, sweaty and filthy when he entered the interrogation room in the Knoxville office of the state police. He should have taken the time to clean up; it might have given him a more dominant position, an edge over the woman. But then, he had a feeling that Nell wasn't the kind of woman who noticed things like clean clothes or dirty, so maybe not.

He had been watching her through the one-way window in the next room, and she hadn't reacted the way he expected.

Most people paced or sat and stared at the table during the softening-up time prior to questioning. Nell Stevens, still in paddling garb, hair plastered to her skull, had indulged in a crying session, and then stretched out on the interview table, where she closed her eyes and appeared to take a nap. Her bare feet were crossed at the ankles, hands laced on her stomach. He had a feeling it was PawPaw's influence. Anything to throw off the revenuers. If not for the tears that occasionally trickled down the side of her face into her hairline, Orson might have really thought she was asleep.

Sweeping into the room like a hard wind, Orson threw open the door and set down a cup of coffee near her head. His partner followed. Nolan Lennox, OIC—officer in charge—of the original case, strolled into the room after him. Having his dad here made him feel itchy. Already they had fallen into good-cop, bad-cop, with Orson as Nell's angel.

Nell opened her eyes and rolled her head their way.

Nolan slung a chair around, the clatter banging off the walls, and stood in front of it, hands on his hips. "Get off the table and sit in a chair like a normal human being."

Nell slid her eyes over him in a lazy perusal and slowly sat up, her back straight, legs tensed, in a fluid, athletic move that looked effortless. She swung her legs off the table and dropped to the floor, taking the chair. She never once looked at Orson, and that bothered him more than he wanted to admit. Nell frowned at the coffee. "Is my lawyer here yet?"

"Why do you need a lawyer?" Nolan asked. "Usually it's the guilty ones who cry for a lawyer."

"Really? I thought it was the smart ones. Is. My. Lawyer. Here. Yet?"

"He's on his way in," Orson said. "But you need to tell us the truth, Nell."

"You found Joe, didn't you?"

Nolan leaned over the table and over Nell, crowding her but not touching her. "Oh, yeah. We found Joseph Stevens. Buried in a three-foot-deep grave, under river rock. Shot in the head with his own gun."

It wasn't the complete truth, but cops didn't have to tell the truth; only suspects had to tell the truth. It was one small part of the system that was skewed in favor of law enforcement. But this once, Orson wasn't happy to see partial truths used on a suspect.

Nell's eyes closed. Her face paled. Orson was pretty sure she stopped breathing.

After that, it got ugly.

Nell was shaking with hunger and exhaustion by the time Jacob Smith, of Berhkolter, Smith, Rector and Associates, led her out into the night. "What happened? What do you know?" she asked, her voice dull with fatigue. "Why did they let me go?"

Taking her elbow, Jacob escorted her down the steps and to his car, a black Cadillac sedan that he beeped open. He held the door for her and she slid into the passenger seat, the leather warm and supple beneath her, the door closing with a solid, soft thunk. He didn't speak until he had the engine running.

"Not enough evidence is the usual reason they don't charge someone," he said, stating the obvious, pulling through the parking lot. "The cops had records from Joe's dentist on file already—the benefit of working a cold case, where all the legwork has already been done—so the ID was fast. They also have adequate forensic evidence for a preliminary COD." When Nell looked the question at him, he said, "Cause of Death. The M.E. thinks he likely died from a gunshot to the head. They recovered a bullet from the cranial cavity." He wheeled the car into traffic and said, "That sounds like a lot of evidence, but it's all circumstantial, and nothing specifically points to you as the murderer."

Nell closed her eyes. "All these years," she whispered. "All these years." Thinking Joe had drowned while trying to save her. Carrying the guilt of that around on her shoulders. And Joe had been murdered.

Smith went on. "Seven years ago, a river guide told Lennox Senior that Joe always carried a gun when he boated. Something about wild pigs?"

Nell nodded, her dirty hair rubbing against the leather headrest. "He was attacked by a boar once on a river run. It was in the middle of the water, half submerged. He thought it was a rock. When his boat came at it, the boar shot up out of the water, onto a rock and leaped at him." She smiled, a half twitch of her lips. "Said it scared him so bad he nearly pooped his britches." She breathed out, the sound whipped. "He had a permit. They know all this."

"All they know at this point is that preliminary-test results indicate that it's *possible* the bullet they found with his remains was fired with his own weapon, which was buried with him. I'll be honest with you, Nell. Even with nothing but circumstantial evidence, there may be enough for them to charge you."

"I know," she said. She closed her eyes. They were burning with unshed tears against the glare of oncoming headlights. "I didn't kill my husband." Her unwavering tone, her quiet certainty, filled the car.

Jacob, maybe mid-forties, trim and muscular with the gym-maintained body of a man in the prime of his life, said, "That may not be enough. In a courtroom, your word isn't going to measure up very well against a prosecutor pushing a crime of passion or a black-widow murder for money." When she didn't reply, he said, "Right now, all we have in your favor is the medical records that prove you had a concussion, bruises, lacerations and contusions consistent with being caught in a strainer, and the police report stating that your gear and clothing, confiscated by law enforcement, appear to corroborate your story of what happened on the South Fork of the Cumberland. But a good prosecutor is going to tear that to shreds in a courtroom. Especially since they have the lifejacket that was found with cut straps and Joe's blood on it. Considering your injuries, it might be best to plead self-defense," he finished softly.

Nell opened her eyes, staring out into the night. "I didn't kill Joe," she said quietly.

"The cops aren't going to look for someone else," he said, pressing the point home. "They have you." When she didn't reply, he said, "I'll have someone in the office trace the money trail. Maybe we'll find something." But Nell could tell he didn't expect to find anything that might point to someone else. Even her own lawyer believed she had killed her husband.

"Killing for hire is out for several reasons. One, because no one could have known Joseph Stevens would be at a certain place on the river at a certain time." Nolan drank from a mug and made a face. "Cold," he said, and poured himself a fresh mug of swill.

Orson shifted his own cup over to see his father's notes from seven years ago. Nolan went on, nailing Nell's coffin down tighter. "Two, I bet the number of contract killers who can kayak to a kill site or who would be willing to hike in to one are nonexistent. Three, if the wife had hired a professional, she would have made sure to have an unimpeachable alibi, and the body would have been where we could find it so she could get the money. Therefore, it wasn't for his money. That brings us back to our starting point. He beat her and she shot him."

"Which makes it self-defense. Unless the brother did it, not knowing Joe had married and changed his estate. He was in the area at the time of Joe's murder."

"You're reaching," Nolan said. "Making it more complicated than it is. The case isn't complex or convoluted. It's simple and clear cut. You should charge her. And you know it."

"She's a single mother with a business to run and not enough money in the bank to make her a flight risk. It's already been nearly seven years. We have time to look around." He turned a page, but in his peripheral vision saw his dad shake his head.

"According to the original case files," he said, skimming, "both Stevenses expressed shock and outrage that Joe had married. Both denied it, saying he had a fiancée in New York. They hired someone to look into the marriage records and into the estate. They were not happy with what they found out. The original investigator—you—" he said, his tone even.

"Yeah," his father interrupted. "I contacted the fiancée, who stated that they had broken off the engagement. She hadn't heard from him in months. But—" he sipped and made another face "—if the brother or the ex-fiancée hired it done to get the estate, not knowing Stevens had married, we'd still be back to having a body and an alibi," Nolan said. "What we got is a skeleton in a grave on the bank of a river. A grave everyone missed during the search and rescue." The accusatory tone was a hair more fervent.

"I was on the SAR," Orson said, still not looking up, and not knowing why he was defending Nell Stevens. Okay, he knew why... He just didn't know what to do about it. Cops weren't supposed to be interested in a suspect. Not and stay on a case. "We were looking for an injured man or a body in the water or on a bank. Not a grave. And it was October, before the leaves fell, when the underbrush is at its thickest. The grave was above the flood line in the brush. No one saw it. But no one was looking for it, either." He pushed his chair back from the desk and rubbed his eyes. "It still could be the brother."

Nolan snorted, full-throated and full of derision. "Walk me through *how*."

Orson dropped his hands and stared at his father. "He hears about the marriage," he said, "drives down, follows them down the river. Meets up with Joe after Joe got Nell onshore. They argue. Struggle. Robert shoots him. Shocked, panicked, he doesn't know what to do. He buries the body. Maybe he even wrote the goodbye note you lost."

Nolan grimaced. "Damn hippie."

"We don't know where he spent the next day or so." Orson tapped the case notes. "But we know he met his mother at the airport after her flight from New York. A fact you missed in the original investigation?" It was intended as a verbal spear, but Nolan looked too happy at the thrust.

Orson sat up straight, suddenly realizing his father was making him defend his position, making him dig into the facts. Making him enjoy the process of working through the cold case. "You son of a…gun," he said. "You knew all this. You're just being a pain in the ass to get me into the Cold Case Unit."

"Is it working? And watch your mouth. You're talking to your father. Have a little respect. Anyway, I didn't know it all. I just put it together faster than you because I'm a better investigator than you." Nolan shot his chin out at a pugnacious angle. "Always have been, always will be."

Orson laughed, a single bleat of sound, stunned at his father's transparency and deviousness. How could one man have so much of both?

Nolan went on. "Robert told me they had flown down

together. We got him in one lie right there. Why did he lie? We know he has experience on white-water rivers, we found evidence of it on the Net. Pictures of him and Joseph on rivers in India and South America and the Northwest when they were teens. Another lie, if only by omission. Freaking gossip mags," Nolan said. "That'll look good in court."

Dragged back into the trail of evidence and logic, Orson said, "He still says he doesn't have white-water experience. Another lie. According to the gossip mags you don't want to trust, he's coked up. We know he needs money and has tried to get Nell to sign it over to him. We know he has a temper. I witnessed the aftermath of that."

"Reaching," Nolan said. He stood and looked at Orson across the desk. "I still think the wife did it. But I'll give you forty-eight hours to find something. After that, I'm taking a circumstantial case to the D.A. And I can guarantee he'll move on it."

Forty-eight hours was more time than Orson had expected, so he nodded and stood. But as he walked from the building, he could feel Nolan's triumphant eyes on his back.

Nell pulled into the Ingles grocery store and cut the engine on Claire's car. It had been an impossible twenty-four hours and she was worn-out. She had driven the RV back alone through the mountains in the pitch-black dark. It was after 2:00 a.m. when she drove up in the driveway, and Claire was still awake, sitting in front of the TV, watching news reports about the murder of Joseph Stevens. She had asked no questions, but Nell had seen them lurking in her mother's eyes. PawPaw had risen from the recliner he claimed when he visited, hugged her hard and left the house without a word, his shotgun over his arm.

Nell hadn't slept, spending the night staring at the ceiling as the minutes glowed by. She had risen several times to check the house and look in on JJ, her baby, sleeping the active sleep of childhood, tossing and turning as usual with his dreams. She often wondered if he dreamed of whitewater when he thrashed.

The morning had been strained and cold, with Claire getting up surprisingly early and making breakfast but not making small talk. After that, the day had quickly become worse. At the shop, the guides had been less ebullient than usual and a lot more watchful, with several throwing her odd glances, as if she was guilty of murder. She was fresh out of a kayak teacher and had to refund four people their money; she was too upset to teach them herself. They were pretty ticked off about losing the lessons. She figured they wouldn't be back, which was never a good thing.

And then Mike walked in. Nell hadn't seen him since the news broke, and he didn't look happy. He stood in the open door, the muggy air flowing in, her cooled AC air flowing out. Silent. Totally silent. Just staring at her. Nell had never seen Jedi Mike with nothing to say. Or maybe with so much to say it was all crammed up inside, like a pileup on I-40, so tightly packed with carnage nothing could get out. Either way, Nell didn't like it.

"Do you want to tell me something?" he said finally.

"Nothing to tell," Nell said. She looked away from him, back to the laptop and the letter she was composing to her managers, so they would know how to respond if—or when—the media connected the discovery of bones on the South Fork of the Cumberland to Rocking River and came calling. It was a "No comment" response, but couched in "She is innocent and has our total support" terms. Nell read it aloud to Mike, figuring it would loosen the logjam in his brain. When she got to the end, she kept her eyes on the screen and said, "So. What do you think?"

"What do I think? Good Lord a mercy, girl. The guides are ready to quit 'cause they think they're working for a cold-blooded killer. The media is gonna show up and massacre us. We'll be ambushed by reporters every time we turn around." He stepped inside, the door swinging shut behind him.

His voice went up a notch, growing louder and more strident. "We went through all this crap last time, when Joe first disappeared. None of us want reporters hanging around asking questions.

"And how in hell did the cops find Joe's body, anyway? With you on the scene. How, Nell? After all these years? Crap, girl, do you know how this looks? Did someone send them some kinda clue? Call Crime Stoppers? What in hell happened?"

Nell looked up, straight into Mike's eyes, stopping the tirade in his throat. "There's only one question that really matters. You've known me since I was a baby. Do you think I killed Joe?"

The small room went silent. Mike's face underwent a series of changes, each distinct and eloquent and full of pain. *He did.* Her oldest friend in the world, the person who had shown her the glory of white water, who had sheltered her from her own mother's condemnation of her lifestyle and the sport she loved, who had stood by her for all her life, the one person she trusted most, believed she had killed her husband and buried him in a secret grave.

Her throat spasmed with pain. Tears sprang into her eyes. Slowly she hit the send button on the e-mail. Then the shutdown button on the laptop, moving by instinct because she couldn't see the keyboard. The screen went black. "I didn't kill my husband," she whispered, the words tearing up through her throat.

She squared her shoulders against the ache throbbing

through her. "But even if I had, and had managed to keep it secret for almost seven years, do you really think I'd have been so stupid as to take a cop there?" She blinked and tears fell, one over each cheek to splat onto her shirt.

Mike opened his mouth, all sorts of things passing through his eyes, his face unguarded, his emotions exposed and raw. And surprised. He hadn't considered that.

"If I did the crime, and was waiting for the seven years to be up so I could get Joe's *money*—" she imbued the word with loathing "—why would I have taken a cop to the river and let him get near the grave? Why would I do that?"

Beyond the equipment shed Nell spotted a white van. It pulled up at an angle exposing a logo on one side. NBC Knoxville. "Crap," Nell said. Mike turned and looked out front as a man in casual clothes stepped out of the van and stretched, looking around. Mike's response was much more succinct. A man in jeans stepped from the driver's side and opened the sliding side door. Camera equipment was inside. A lot of camera equipment.

"You're right," Mike said. "You're too smart to be that stupid." He sighed grumpily and plopped into a plastic chair. "I'm the stupid one for all of the last ten minutes. You can shoot me later for it. Just know this. I'll defend you to the death, Nellie baby. Now get outta here. It's only going to get worse. Probably a lot worse. By nightfall we'll have more news vans than we can deal with."

A shadow appeared from the side entry of the equipment shed. Melissa, peeking out before scuttling into the shop, pushed Mike out of the way. "Boss, we got all sortsa problems. Whatcha want me to say to people when they ask dumb questions? And whatcha want me to say to the press?" A second van pulled up beside the first. "Cripes. They're everywhere."

"Tell 'em our boss loved her husband," Mike said, again

talking loud and fast, "and that the cops did a piss-poor job of searching for Joe when he first went missing. Nell Stevens told them he had enemies, and finally the cops listened. She acted as a guide to show the cold-case cops the South Fork of the Cumberland. And finally one cop, smarter than the rest, found him. They have a suspect list and Rocking River believes the murderer will be apprehended with all speed."

Nell stared at him openmouthed. "You sound like a lawyer."

"I'm too frigging smart to be a lawyer." Mike wiped a thumb across her cheek. "I ever see you crying because I'm a stupid idiot, I'll beat your ass. Hear me?"

Nell nodded and hiccuped, relief pouring through her. Mike believed her. He really did. She squeezed his shoulder and the Old Man of the River hugged her one-armed.

He said, "Furthermore, Nell Stevens of Rocking River is actively working to help law enforcement solve the murder, but is in hiding at this time due to threats on her life."

"Really?" Melissa said, her eyes wide.

"No," Nell said on top of Mike saying, "Yes."

"Get outta here, Nell," he said. "Fast."

Nell said, "Melissa, you just got promoted to general manager of Rocking River on the Pigeon. We'll talk money later."

Melissa, whose eyes had been huge when she entered, got bigger. "Totally rad."

With that, Nell grabbed her bags and slipped out the door, sliding through the narrow passage between inflated rafts and the shop wall just as a cameraman hefted a camera. Nell had the feeling she would be spending a lot less time at the shop, and a lot more time planning a legal defense. As she ran to her SUV, she put away any plans of opening a new Rocking River. She would need that money to pay legal fees.

28

Orson rocked back in his chair, in his office in the Cold Case Unit, a windowless, stifling nook under the stairs, so distant from any air-conditioning vent that the place was almost hot. It was 1600—4:00 p.m.—and he had just spent forty minutes setting up interviews with several guides who had been on the original SAR, and who were still working for Nell: Stoned Stewart, whose brain had long been fried with drugs and who wasn't likely to tell him anything new, short of drugged ramblings, Hampton, Harvey, RiverAnn and Turtle Tom. They were people who had known Joseph Stevens, and who might able to shed some light on the man. When the phone rang, he picked it up. "Cold Case Unit. Orson Lennox."

"You done messed with mine. I told you what I'd do iffen you did."

Orson dropped his feet to the floor. "PawPaw?" *Crap. What was the old man's name?*

"You keep my Nellie and Joseph Junior safe. You know she didn't kill Joe. You know it in your gut. Now get off your ass and prove it." The phone went dead.

A slow grin split Orson's face. "Good idea, old man. I'll do that." Slinging his suit coat over a shoulder, Orson left the office nook and trudged up the stairs.

* * *

Nell hid out in the house all day, watching TV news and working on the Internet, once again tracking down the mystery man who had been Joseph Stevens. News vans cruised up and down the dirt road all day, sending dust flying, searching for the address of the notorious black-widow killer who had murdered her husband and buried him on the bank of the Cumberland. Or the maligned innocent widow who was being framed for the murder of her husband by her evil brother-in-law who wanted her money. Depending on which news you listened to.

To avoid the media vans, Claire had removed the address numbers from the mailbox; the neighbors followed suit. Nell figured they either preferred the reclusive life to one on TV, or believed the staunch defense raised by Melissa and Jedi Mike and televised nationwide. Their interview had run on CNN and Fox all day, her two friends calling the news reporters stupid and libelous for suggesting Nell was the killer, a super-smart black widow who had then somehow become stupid enough to lead cops to the grave.

Melissa, looking like the healthy, all-American girl, informed the news crew that a police officer had let it slip to her that they had another suspect who they liked a lot better than Nell for the death of Joe Stevens. Melissa leaned into the camera and said almost conspiratorially, "I think they're following a whole different angle entirely. I think they're hunting for the money."

Mike had chimed in, "I think they're going for the passion angle, an angry fiancée."

Melissa leaned back in and said, "Nah. The brother-in-law has been trying to get his dead brother's money for years. I think it's him."

The reporters, scenting a juicy story, were now doing some digging themselves, taking the focus off of Nell and

Rocking River. The stories emerging about Robert Stevens weren't pretty. The man was a drunk and a druggie and had lied to the cops about all sorts of things.

By nightfall Nell was feeling a bit euphoric. JJ, who had been driven home by Mike and let out at the road to scamper down the driveway before the news van caught up with them, had had a wonderful day. He informed her that Rocking River had the busiest day on record, even counting Labor Day and Fourth of July in 2006.

In the middle of the mother-son celebrations, Claire walked in and informed them that they were out of groceries, which meant a nighttime trip to Newport, some ten-plus miles away. Nell had thrown on a jean skirt and a T-shirt, and here they were, in an Ingles parking lot at 10:00 p.m., her head on the steering wheel.

"Mama? You got a headache?" JJ asked.

Nell smiled without opening her eyes and put out a hand. JJ took it. "Yes, I got me a headache the size of Montana. But I'll feel better as soon as we get the groceries and get back home. Come on. Let's get it done."

"Git'er done," JJ said, laughing, copying a comedian. He turned his light saber off, secured it between seat and floor and pushed out of Claire's car, slamming the door. Nell followed, pulling a hat down over her forehead. Together they strolled the aisles and loaded up a buggy with necessities.

During the summer, fresh produce was purchased or traded for locally, but it was still early in the growing season, and so Nell bought fruit, lettuce, tomatoes, root and vine veggies, and stocked up on meat and oatmeal. One problem with living so far from a city was that if she forgot something, it meant a long drive back or doing without. Clare didn't make the trip anymore, which meant Nell had to. She consulted the list Claire kept taped on the fridge, and sent JJ scouting for the products he liked: Cap'n Crunch, grape soda, his favorite trail mix, sweets she let him have only rarely but which he adored. It took over an hour, and was near midnight by the time they were done.

Beneath the blue glare of the security lights, Nell loaded the groceries into the trunk, situating the bags so they wouldn't slide, and putting cold and frozen things in insulated bags she kept in the back just for that purpose. Her eyes were gritty with fatigue, and she had bought a cold Coke from a glass-fronted fridge in Ingles, to give her a caffeine and sugar boost, enough to get her home safely. She hoped.

When she had the groceries loaded, she handed JJ the Coke and the keys. "Okay, monkey. Start the engine and put the drink in the holder." He crawled in between the seats, and Nell slammed the trunk. Feet dragging, she took the buggy to the cart corral.

Behind her the engine turned over. JJ loved being old enough to start the car, and was already bugging her about being allowed to drive.

Pain slammed into her. Nell lurched, hurled across the buggy. It rammed into her middle. She heard the pained *woof* as breath shot from her lungs. Time snapped and stretched. Pain thrummed through her. The world tilted. The parking lot rose toward her face. Her hands hit, skidding hard. Instinctively, she bent her elbows. Pushed off with her foot. Rolling. Bare knees scraping on the asphalt.

The buggy landed. Someone fell over it. A silhouette of a body tangling with a buggy.

She sucked air to scream.

A boot came at her. Fast.

The belly kick landed. A one-two punch of pure agony. Air shot from her lungs. She gagged and kept rolling, tucking her legs and arms around her middle. Two forms followed. Boots striking pavement. Male. Backlit by the security lights. Faces and heads covered.

Jackets, in spring.

An alarm went off. No, a horn. Blaring. Headlights and a roaring engine. Again she saw a boot coming. It bounced off her thigh.

A vehicle slammed on brakes, screeching. People were running up. Shouting. Booted feet ran, the sound diminishing. Nell uncovered her face. Time seemed to recede and darkness wove in to form a tunnel.

It was over? What…?

A man knelt to her, his face concerned. "Are you okay?"

It took a moment to make the two visions of him merge into one. "I'm…" She didn't know what to say. "What happened?" JJ's arms went around her, squeezing. Hurting her bruised stomach.

But she held him close because he was crying. And so was she. "It's okay, baby. I'm okay."

"Can you get up, lady?" the kneeling man said.

"Let her stay down. An ambulance and the police are on the way." Nell looked up at the second voice, seeing a man. The name badge pinned to his white shirt said Neil. Store Manager.

Sirens sounded in the distance. "Don't tell the cops, Mama," JJ whispered in her ear. "They might arrest me. I drove the car at the bad guys and blew the horn. And they ran off."

"My hero," Nell whispered, hugging him again and then easing him away, trying to focus on the strangers standing around her. "It'll be fine, sweetheart. The cops will understand. Honey, will you find my cell phone? I need to call Orson."

"Why you wanna call him?" JJ said, belligerent. "He's a sneak and liar. Mike said so."

"Got your bag, lady." The man who had knelt beside her first handed her the tiny purse she carried clipped to her belt loop when shopping. It was just big enough for a wallet, keys and cell phone. It was still closed, and she wondered why the muggers hadn't taken it.

"Orson is a cop, JJ. And even though he's a sneak and liar, he's the only cop I know." She had input his cell number when she hired him, and dialed it quickly. While it rang, she brushed off grit and inspected her knees in the security lights. She had some pretty major raspberries, but nothing was broken.

When Orson answered, Nell told him what had happened. And, God bless him, he said he would be right there.

"Why do you think you knew them?" Orson asked.

The local cops had finished taking her report and the reports of the bystanders, but because she wasn't hurt badly enough to require hospitalization and nothing had been stolen, they had dispensed with her quickly. Bigger crimes awaited, Nell was sure, crimes with blood and mayhem and police chases down city streets or through vacant lots. Things a lot more interesting than the petty crime that left her disoriented and abraded.

The only thing that had interested the uniforms in the least was her contention that she might know the assailants. But, when she couldn't say why, the cops had left, leaving her their cards.

"I don't know," Nell said. "But they seemed…familiar." JJ snuggled up in her lap in the front seat of the car, for once not caring if he looked less than the little man, his body pressing against her, seeking comfort. They were in the passenger seat, Orson in the driver's seat, his body swiveled around to face her, one knee canted out, close enough to touch. The overhead light was on, casting harsh shadows on them.

Nell tightened her arms around her son and breathed JJ

in, his little-boy smell rich with the river. He hadn't taken a shower before they left and the odor of the Pigeon was strong on him. Nell tensed.

"Did they use your name?" Orson asked. "Did they speak at all?"

"No," Nell said, again breathing in her son's scent. "That's it," she whispered. "The way they smelled."

"What smell?" Orson said.

It was gonna sound stupid, Nell knew it. But she had to try to make him understand. "Every river has a scent. A smell peculiar to it. Ever noticed?"

Orson shook his head. "No. Can't say as I have."

JJ twisted, not moving from his perch to look at the cop. "Mama says the Cumberland smells like iron. The Green smells like wood," he said. "The Nante smells like shadows and cold and fall. The Pigeon smells clean and smoky, and like gasoline."

"Ozone," Nell corrected. "Not gas. But this smelled different. Not like the Pigeon. Or even like the Cumberland. But it was a river smell. And beer."

"Which river, Mama?"

"I don't know, baby. But I've smelled it before."

"River guides?" Orson asked.

Nell didn't want to say it, not in front of JJ. She settled on, "I don't know. I just don't know." But her eyes said, *"Yes. River guides."*

Orson looked at the delicate woman with the small boy clutched in her lap. Unreasoning anger steamed up through him at the sight of her bloody hands and knees, an anger that he recognized and tried to force back down. On its heels, twined with the anger, tenderness welled and grew. *Damn.* It felt suspiciously like he was… Crap. He was falling in love with her.

* * *

Orson followed Nell and her son back to Hartford with the intent to help her unload groceries at her home. Instead, she had stopped at Rocking River, while the news vans were elsewhere, to pick up paperwork she needed for the next week.

Deprived of the opportunity to see her safely home, he had checked back into his room at old lady Fremont's. His stuff was still there. So was the lumpy bed and the small table and chair in front of the window. He opened a few drawers and was pretty sure someone had been through his things. His landlady? Probably. Jedi Mike? Probably, again. In fact, his room and scanty belongings had likely been pawed over by several locals in the last couple of days.

He dropped his laptop on the bed as he stripped out of his suit coat and looked out at the night view of Hartford and the lights in Rocking River. Nell's vehicle was still there. Even from here, he could see a human form moving in the security light, bending once and rising. Nell cleaning up trash from the lot? She did everything for the small business, so it shouldn't surprise him to see her picking up trash at nearly 1:00 a.m.

He pushed open the window, the wood stiff and dragging. The tire and engine roar of the I-40 was a soft white noise overlaid with the stutter of Jake-brakes on the big rigs. He imagined he could hear the soft babble of the Pigeon over the sound of modern life, although there was no way the river-voice could compete with eighteen-wheelers.

Orson sat at the table, night breezes brushing him, staring at his clasped hands. A faint tan had darkened his pallid, sallow skin. He made a fist, feeling the muscles in his arm contract.

The tan was because of Nell. Getting more physically fit was because of Nell. Getting back on rivers and out of his depression was because of Nell. Finding his joy of investigating cold cases was because of Nell. Hell, everything seemed to come back to her. Especially this case. So why had someone attacked her tonight? Could it be because of the crazy stories Jedi Mike had been dreaming up and planting in the press? Was someone worried about Nell *not* taking the blame for Joe's death?

He sighed, the breath easy, moving without pain through his lungs. He froze, staring into the night, almost afraid to breathe deeply again. But his body demanded it, and his rib cage expanded. Painlessly. How long since that happened? To take even one breath without pain?

His physical therapist—the one he walked out on after only two weeks of agonizing exercise—had told him movement and stretching would likely give him complete freedom from pain. Seems the guy had been right. He straightened, thinking.

Orson had a decision to make. Either he was a cop, or he was Nell's...supporter? Victor? Champion? Boyfriend didn't work, especially when she had no interest in him. But he was honest enough to admit that his feelings for the woman had changed. What in hell was he supposed to do?

A knock sounded on his door and Orson turned, gripping the butt of his weapon strapped atop his shirt. "Yeah?"

"Your light's on. Got a minute?" a voiced called through the door.

It was Mike Kren. Orson paused in surprise, looking from the door to the window. He had been here all of ten minutes, and back in Hartford for less than half an hour. His lamp was giving him away, it seemed. "Sure," he called back.

The door opened and Mike stuck his head in, his braid swinging across his shoulder and dangling. "Three things. First, my pickup is missing." He extended a slip of paper to Orson. The cop could clearly see the make, model and tag number of the big pickup Mike drove. "Would you call it in?"

"I can do that, but you need to make a report to the sheriff's office."

Mike waved the necessity away. "One of the guides probably got toked up and went for a drive. If it ain't back by morning, I'll do it tomorrow. Few things you need to know, bro."

"I'm listening."

"First, Nell didn't kill Joe. Girl can't lie worth crap, you know? She says she didn't do it, then she didn't. Second, Harvey was the one who suggested that the guys follow Nell on this last trip to the South Fork. And Harvey never had an original thought in his life. You might want to figure out why he suddenly had an idea all his own. If it was his own. Third?" Mike grinned, showing all his teeth. "Brother Robert was on the water yesterday, too. Don't know where. But his rental with a kayak rack went missing from his Knoxville-hotel parking lot. And it's back tonight. A little bird told me Brother Robbie's been checked in for a week. Sweet dreams, dude." The door began to close.

"Mike?"

The guide stuck his head back in.

"I believe that Nell didn't kill Joe."

"Good. Because I made the mistake of doubting her. *One* of us should believe she's innocent all the way." The door closed and Orson heard soft footsteps as Mike descended the stairs.

Orson wondered how hard it would be for a man like Robert to hire a couple of thugs to attack Nell in an Ingles parking lot. For that matter, how hard would it have been for him to kill his brother? As he sat thinking, considering, his cell phone rang, a tinny, soft buzz of sound. It rang again as Orson looked around the small, dank room. He spotted it on the bed beside his laptop and fell across the bed to answer. "Lennox here," he said.

"Orson." The panic in Nell's voice stabbed at him. "JJ's missing."

He made it to Rocking River in less than two minutes, his SUV screeching to a halt on the pavement and skidding across the gravel. PawPaw's truck with the missing headlight pulled to a stop right behind him. Mike Kren was standing in the pale security light, his hands on Nell's arms, steadying her, his mountain bike lying on its side, discarded. Orson could hear her sobs over the sound of the interstate and the voice of the river. He gathered the small group and quickly ascertained that Nell had been in the shop, working late, while JJ played around the building. She had heard him laughing about ten minutes past, and the sound of a rubber ball hitting the building. When Mike biked up, moments ago, he was gone.

"Were you outside—" he checked his watch "—twenty, thirty minutes ago, picking up trash or bending over for some reason?"

"No." Her eyes widened. "Why?"

"I saw someone," he said. *Robert? Did Stevens made good on his threat to take JJ?* Orson looked at Mike. "In the parking lot, bending over. Just before you knocked."

"JJ was gone when I got here," Mike said. "We're talking five, maybe ten minutes. They have to be close."

"I'll get my dogs," PawPaw said. "Nellie, I need something 'a JJ's for them to take a scent." Nell nodded.

"I've called in an Amber Alert," Orson said. "How long does it take sheriff's deputies to respond?"

"Damn cops ain't gone do nothing," PawPaw snarled, cranking up his truck. "We take care 'a our own around here." He whipped his old truck around and headed back up the hill.

A wailing siren broke over the sounds of eighteen-wheelers on the interstate. *Five minutes. Maybe ten. That's how long JJ's been gone.* In five minutes, with the I-40 and access to dozens of smaller roads so close, the kidnapper could be miles away already. Cold fear slithered through him.

Orson stepped from the shop and punched in his dad's cell number.

"Nolan Lennox," he said, sounding all business.

"I just put out an Amber Alert on JJ Stevens. I need you to issue a BOLO on Robert Stevens. Seems he's in the area." Orson gave the rental-car tag number and the hotel Robert frequented. He heard keys clicking and voices in the background and recognized the familiar sounds of his father's office.

"I see the Amber Alert," Nolan said. "It just went out statewide. You think Robert took the kid?"

"I don't know. But I once heard him threaten to take him. And I don't like to screw around with coincidence."

"Yeah," Nolan said. "I'm on the BOLO now. Later." The connection ended. Orson dialed the sheriff.

Each time she raced up the bank Nell saw PawPaw and his dogs, the hounds on long leashes, noses to the ground. The best tracking dogs in the county, they were sniffing, excited, their ruffs up, visible even in the security lights. But JJ's scent would be everywhere in the town. There would be no way for the dogs to pick out what was recent. Terror spiked through her like a thousand knives and she moved back to the water. When she called JJ, her voice was breathless, breathy. Desperate.

Heart pounding, Nell crossed the river. She had already searched the side close to the shop. Now she negotiated the shallow flow, her flip-flops sucking at the bottom, sliding over round river rocks, the slight nighttime current washing away sweat, blood and grime, to the other side, which was the bank of an island. The underbrush was thicker here, untouched by tourists, walking more difficult. The heavy-duty flashlight, the kind used by road-construction crews doing graveyard-shift repairs, penetrated to the ground with difficulty. "JJ!" she shouted. "JJ!"

Flashlight bobbing, her heart racing and breath so tight she thought she might pass out, Nell continued searching up and down the riverbank, shouting JJ's name, while Orson, Mike and PawPaw organized something with more punch. Orson, working with the deputy, had gotten out an Amber Alert, and Mike had rousted the guides from their beds, sending them to help Nell. Within half an hour, ten searchers had joined her along the river, shouting for her son.

She scanned right and left with the big lantern flashlight, pushing through brush, shining the beam over the water and back. Jumping over logs that might hide snakes, she imagined scenario after scenario where JJ had been snake bit; fallen and broken a leg, banged his head, broken an arm, been attacked by a wild boar, pounced on by a mountain lion, slipped and landed in the river, unconscious. Stolen, forced into a trunk, screaming for her. Each scene was vivid and soul stealing.

Mike called her name and Nell crashed back across the river, through brush, finding Mike fast, her breath aching in her chest. Whatever he was going to say evaporated when he saw her. "You're bleeding, girl," he said.

Nell looked down. Her arms and hands, and her legs below her denim skirt were gouged and scratched, and the raspberries she had acquired when the mugging took place were bleeding again, trickles down her shins, blood smeared all over from her torn hands. "Later," she said, sucking in great gulps of air, her voice hoarse. "What?"

"Your mom brought the RV," he said. "You need water and a break."

Claire, who hated to drive after dark, had driven the RV down the winding, dangerous, mountain road and parked it in the gravel lot. Nell batted away tears. Her breath was heaving, her body flushed and slick with sweat. "No. Gotta—"

"What you gotta do is take a break. Now." He took her arm and pulled her up the riverbank to flat ground and into the gravel lot at Rocking River. Nell was too exhausted to resist. She didn't want to stop, even for a moment, but Mike had a firm grip, and, even in the midst of panic, Nell knew he was right. You didn't do a SAR without water and breaks. You might miss something.

Mike dragged her to the RV and knocked. Claire opened the door, welcome light spilling into the night. He pulled her inside and sat her down. Claire placed an open bottle of water in her hand, brushed a hand over her sweat-damp hair and dropped a kiss on her head.

Mike accepted a bottle and drank before saying, "I got the guides rousted and searching upstream. PawPaw's dogs are working the road—"

Nell's cell phone rang. She pulled it from her pocket and looked at the readout. Unknown Caller. She opened the phone and said, "Nell Stevens."

"I got your boy."

Nell froze, her breath blocked off as if a huge hand grabbed her throat.

Terrified, she focused on her mother. Claire's eyes widened, seeing something in Nell's face that frightened her. Paling, she pulled her own cell phone and speed-dialed a number.

"I want a hundred thousand dollars dropped off under the I-40 bridge at 10:00 a.m. tomorrow," the muffled voice continued. "That'll give you plenty of time to get the money from JJ's rich uncle. You don't tell the cops. And don't move from where you are. I'll know if you do."

"What—"

"Mama?" JJ said.

"JJ?"

"Ten a.m.," the voice said. The phone went silent.

"Hello?" Nell whispered. "You there?" her voice rose. "You there?" she screamed. "You there you there you there you there?"

Claire's strong arms wrapped around her. Nell fell against her into the warmth of the embrace, her own body so cold she feared she might shatter and break.

Someone had her baby. Someone had JJ.

29

Orson slammed on brakes. During the ransom call from the kidnappers, Claire had used her cell to phone him. He had heard the final words. And Nell's breakdown. Her wailing fear.

Smothering his own fear and shock, he shoved through the gathering crowd in the predawn dark and hustled the two women back into the RV and onto the bench seats of the dinette. He locked the doors, pulled the privacy curtain over the huge windows and closed the blinds. "Tell me," he said hoarsely.

Nell was frantic, her face raw and swollen with tears, her limbs shaking, and she hyperventilated with shallow, rasping sobs. "They have JJ…and they want…money," she said. She wrapped her fingers around her throat as if it pained her to speak. "They want a hundred…thousand dollars…tossed under the I-40…bridge at 10:00 a.m. And they're watching the RV." Suddenly she thrust up from the dinette. "Get out! They said no cops. They'll know you're here. Get out!"

Orson grasped her shoulders and shook her. "Nell! Stop it. Listen to me." She raised her head, her eyes wild and unfocused. His own heart wrenched with pain at the sight.

"They have JJ," she whispered, her voice pained, rasping like rusted steel against wet wood.

"If they're watching the RV," he said, "then that means

he's close by. I want you to stop, calm down and *think* about the call. *Think*," he commanded.

Nell looked into his eyes, her pale face streaked with tears and blood from where she had torn open the wounds on her hands, her eyes so dilated she looked drugged. "They knew about the Stevenses. They said I could get the money from JJ's rich uncle. They know Robert's been here…" She jerked away from Orson and stared at the RV door. When she wiped her mouth, her hand looked wrinkled and dry, desiccated. A fine tremor ran through her. "It's somebody Robert knows, isn't it? Or someone…" She wheeled to him. "It can't be Robert. He wouldn't ask himself for money. Did someone follow Robert from New York and do this?"

"We can't assume—"

"I'll kill him," she whispered, soft and almost surprised sounding. "I'll…kill him." The words held an infinite finality, dark and breath-stealing as the deepest reaches of space. She took a breath, and Orson watched as something new and fearsome formed, evolving inside Nell Stevens. "Whoever took my son, I'll kill that son of a bitch," she said, her words filled with amazed resolve.

Orson knew without a doubt that this woman had never killed. Not yet. But that if she caught the person who took her son, she could kill. And she would.

Long minutes later, when she again took a breath, Nell set up a phone relay and issued radios to the searchers, the same thing she would have done in a dicey rescue on the river. She followed the searchers' progress, keeping track of the crime-scene cops who were dusting Rocking River for prints. But Nell couldn't go back to the river to search. JJ wasn't there. He was with someone who wanted to use her son to get money. Instead, she sat, frozen, staring into the night along the road.

* * *

Orson, back out in the parking lot, spent twenty minutes organizing the deputies and calling in the FBI. Between calls, he answered his phone. Mike Kren's number was in the display. "Harvey's missing," the river guide said. "No one seems to know where he is. He went out for a walk when he and RiverAnn got into it over her drinking a beer, her pregnant and all. He left about the time my truck went missing. If he was drunk enough, it coulda occurred it him to do something stupid like kidnap a kid and ask for ransom."

Orson swore. Mike said, "Also, his boat's gone. River's running one-sixty-five, enough for a drunk, fool hothead to run it by moonlight. I'm heading up to the put-in in case he took JJ. I took Claire's car. The keys were still in the ignition."

Orson looked around. In the circus of searchers and media vans he hadn't noticed the car was missing. The thought of the groceries crossed his mind, melted and spoiled in the trunk, and he pushed it aside as irrelevant. "What if JJ went on the water with him?" Orson asked, whirling to the equipment shed, picturing JJ in his kayak, trying to navigate the river by the light of the moon. The lights in Rocking River spilled out over the parking lot, and Orson ducked inside, ignoring the garter snakes and one huge black snake that slithered into a dark corner. JJ's gear was all in place, kayak hanging on the wall, his dry PFD and paddle untouched. "No," he said, stepping back into the night. "His gear's all here."

"I'll be back in twenty or thirty minutes," Mike said.

"Call my cell if you find anything," he said, spotting the sheriff's car coming down the hill. "Gotta go."

"Will do."

The sheriff stayed only long enough to deputize any searchers who were sober, send the drunk ones back home

and call for a city cop to check out the hotel Robert was sup-
posedly staying at. He assigned Deputy Wales to Orson as
his personal liaison. The kid was wet behind the ears, and
though Orson knew babysitting detail when he saw it, he was
happy for the extra set of hands, ears and the kid's radio.

When his cell rang moments later and Mike's number
again appeared, Orson held up a finger to the deputy and
answered the phone.

"Orson," Mike Kren said without greeting. "Getchyer ass
up to the put-in at the powerhouse. Harvey's up here, and I
think he's dead."

Orson reached the put-in ahead of Wales who followed
with siren and lights flashing. Mike, fists on his hips, wet to
the waist, was standing onshore illuminated by the headlights of Claire's car. He pointed as Orson slid from the cab,
and the cop swung the beam of his flashlight over the
rippling water. Fifteen feet out, a rock shaped like the
humped back of a sea turtle had snagged a lump of flesh and
cloth.

"I went out there. Touched the body enough to see who
it was and if he had a pulse. It's Harvey for sure, and he's
got a purple knot big as my fist on his head." Mike made a
fist to show the size. "His face was underwater. Don't know
if he drowned or what, but he ain't staying on that rock too
much longer. We need to get him off it."

Mike pointed into the shadows up the bank and along the
road. "Truck tracks through the gravel and into the mud on
the other side of the road, like someone turned around."

Orson followed the direction of the finger and held up a
hand to stop the deputy from driving through the tracks and
destroying the evidence. The kid had been a sheriff's deputy
for three months' worth of break-ins, drunk-and-disorderlies
and vehicle accidents, and this was the twenty-one-year-

old's first real excitement. His adrenaline level was running at flood stage, his hands were twitchy, his body jumpy with tension, and his eyes showed white all around like a panicked horse.

Orson leaned into the deputy's window and said, "Get the sheriff and the M.E. on the horn. Tell them we got a body in the water. It may or may not be related to the Amber Alert, and may or may not be related to an assault in Ingles earlier tonight and may or may not be death due to natural causes. That may or may not be important, understand?"

The deputy nodded his head up and down so fast he looked like a bobble-head doll, and reached for the radio.

"Good. Then get up to the powerhouse and get that water cut off."

The deputy nodded again. "Yes, sir. Yessir. I got it."

"What assault?" Mike asked from behind.

Orson hadn't mentioned the incident when Mike came into his room. Now, he explained about Nell's assault outside of Ingles as he dug equipment from his SUV and set up a second set of paperwork in less than an hour. When he finished with the story, Mike cursed with explosive force and strode off into the night. Orson wanted to join him in a rant but couldn't. He had a possible crime scene to secure. He checked his watch. "Mike," he shouted over the sound of the power plant. In the dark, the river guide turned back. "Was the body warm or cold?"

"Not cold as the water, but not warm either. Why?"

Orson shook his head, wondering how long it took a body to go cold in the Pigeon. Wondering if Mike had known the body was here, had killed Harvey and left him in the water, then returned to *discover* it. It was a ploy the guilty had been known to use, hoping to throw off suspicion and play hero too. But hell. Why would Mike kill a river guide? Why would anyone? The death didn't even have to be related to Joe's death. It could be an accident.

Heedless of watching eyes, Orson reached into the back of his SUV for his wet suit shortie and stripped off his outer clothes, stepping into the suit and pulling the tight neoprene up over his legs, torso and shoulders. He zipped it closed and tucked a body tarp beneath his arm. Grabbing camera, flashlight, river shoes, his PFD and a rescue rope, he headed to the water.

Mike, his rage controlled if not truly spent—assuming it had been real and not feigned—followed, watching as Orson unfolded the tarp, a specially designed sheet used at crime scenes when the body had to be moved, and placed it on the ground. Understanding what was intended, Mike helped him set up a recovery line. With biners, Orson clipped the line to his vest along with the flashlight and the camera, pulled on his river shoes and strode into the water. It was a lot colder than he expected and Orson smothered a series of high-pitched squeals, breathing deeply until his body adapted to the temperature.

He got ten real good shots of Harvey before the current threatened to lift the body away. Clearly, he couldn't wait for the water to stop. He had to get the body to land now or they'd be chasing it. Orson hated to screw with a possible murder scene, but the alternative was to lose the body. Once he was satisfied he had documented the body in situ as well as he could, Orson ran the rope through Harvey's vest and towed him toward shore. The body bobbed facedown in the current, likely washing away any trace evidence, but again, there was nothing he could do about that.

The current wasn't ferocious, but it wasn't still water, either. It took muscle to balance against the flow, keep the camera and flash out of the river and drag the body. He was almost to shore when a faint glow up on the bank caught his eye. He noted the position in relation to the security light.

"Take this," he said, handing the rope to Mike. "Ease him to shore. I don't want him scraped over the rocks."

Mike stepped into the water. He lifted the river guide by the shoulders and Orson slid his hands beneath the dead man's knees. Together they lifted his weight from the Pigeon and placed him, dripping, on the tarp. Orson knelt beside the body. Harvey's blondish hair and beard was plastered to his head, which rolled in the shadows to reveal a nasty bruise and lump on his temple. Orson was reminded of the bruise on Nell's face almost seven years ago. There were eerie similarities to the wounds. He put a hand on the man's abdomen and registered faint body heat, but the water had stolen much of it.

Mike rose and stepped back, his expression shuttered. Orson looked up. "Sorry, man. I know you knew him."

"Worked with him for going on ten years. He was one of the good ones." Mike shook his head and walked away. Orson rose from the tarp and turned on the flashlight again, moving up the shore, trying to find whatever it was that had caught his eye. He found it more quickly than he expected. The batteries were almost dead, but the greenish glow alerted him. A Star Wars light saber rested in the weeds.

Jedi Mike's pickup was found abandoned a mile downriver under the bridge that crossed the Pigeon. They had passed within a hundred feet of it getting to the put-in. Inside, in the floor of the passenger seat, were JJ's shoes, the laces still tied as if he had toed them off in a hurry. Orson wondered if whoever had stolen the pickup had intended to set Mike up for the kidnapping, or if it all was accidental.

In other circumstances, Mike would have been the most likely suspect, but thanks to his visit to old lady Fremont's and the timetable of JJ's disappearance, he had an alibi. He had been with a state police investigator during JJ's disappearance. It would have been nearly impossible for anyone to put all these elements in place in the short timetable. Lucky Mike. Too lucky? Orson wondered. Two people had attacked Nell in a parking lot. If Mike had an accomplice… But then again, why kidnap JJ? Or attack Nell? Maybe there *was* more than one thing going on here.

He pulled out all the stops, calling in a medical examiner to estimate Harvey's time of death, calling in a crime-scene team from Knoxville to supplant the efforts of the county's crime team, and woke up his boss at 2:00 a.m., informing Mo that the cold case might be taking a weird turn. It was looking more and more likely that the death of Joseph Stevens—or rather, the discovery of his body—had resulted in someone going into a full fledged panic and committing additional crimes.

While setting everything in motion, he got a call from the Knoxville PD. Robert Stevens was missing from his hotel room. His vehicle was not in the parking lot. Orson issued an APB for JJ's uncle. And Deputy Wales discovered a splatter of blood in the cab of Mike's truck.

Added to the disappearance and Amber Alert, the night now became a full-scale murder investigation. Fortunately, this wasn't his gig. Not his jurisdiction. Turning the investigation over to Deputy Wales, Orson returned to the RV and Rocking River.

Nell rocked back on her knees and pushed away from the toilet in the RV. She had emptied her stomach in a painful heave, her bruised abdominal muscles protesting the action. She flushed, but the stink lingered on the air.

Claire handed her a wet, cold cloth. "Here, Nellie baby. Wipe your mouth." Nell, unable to go home, unable to rest, unable to eat or drink, sat in the driver's seat. Outside, the entire town of Hartford was up, searching for JJ. Though word had reached them that a ransom demand had been received, they hadn't stopped looking. In fact, they had re-doubled their efforts, going door to door, rousting anyone who had managed to sleep in, sometimes even bullying their way inside to look for a trussed-up kidnapped kid.

Cars moved up and down the streets, high-powered flash beams scanning the bushes. The guides had taken over the river search, scouting both sides of the river and all around the island. PawPaw was still on the streets, the dogs on long leashes, but the hounds looked dispirited and the old man grim.

It was nearly 5:00 a.m. Nell was exhausted, her eyes gritty with tears, her stomach so sore she couldn't breathe without pain. If it hadn't been for Claire, she was certain she would already have gone insane.

Her mother, who was suffering her own torment, had washed and bandaged Nell's knees and the scratches she had suffered on the banks of the Pigeon. She had bullied her daughter into taking a shower and donning clean clothes. She made tea and coffee for the searchers. Informed that JJ's light saber had been discovered, she had marched over to the nearest news vans and given an impromptu interview.

It was mostly threat and bluster, what the citizens of Hartford would do to the kidnapper when he was caught. But a cameraman captured it, to the delight of the CNN reporter.

"My grandbaby's been kidnapped and a river guide's been killed and the whole town's looking for him. And I got this to say to the kidnapper. 'You good-for-nothing, useless, hunk of human refuse. When we find you, we're gonna skin you alive and hang your bleeding body up for the crows.'" And that was just the start.

It was a great news byte, the distraught blond woman de-scribing torture in her hillbilly accent. The heir of Joseph Stevens was missing. Thanks to Claire, the story hit the airwaves a little after 4:00 a.m., and made the national feed long before the early morning news.

Unfortunately, the reporters also pointed out that Nell was the last person to see her son alive. The innuendos that she had killed and buried her husband, and now had done away with her son were not long in coming. Not that Nell cared. If it got people looking for JJ, she would have confessed to the murders of Hitler, Marilyn Monroe and both Kennedys. Anything to get help in the search for her baby.

She made her way to the passenger seat and swiveled it around so the news crews perched outside her RV would have trouble getting a clear shot. Claire handed her a cup of hot chai tea with whipped cream and lots of sugar. Holding her stomach with one arm, she sipped and watched Claire prop herself on both elbows and lift her own cup. Lips hidden behind the rim of the mug, Claire said, "You do know they's taking a picture of us."

"I know."

Orson knocked and Claire let him in. But he had nothing good to report. Not a single solitary thing. Instead, he came close and hugged her. In full view of the camera outside, he gathered her up in his arms and cradled her, her face in his shoulder. Nell shuddered hard, gripped him fiercely, and burst into tears.

She knew she was losing her mind. If she lost JJ, there would be no reason to live. Not one.

Orson knew he shouldn't offer comfort to Nell. It went against everything he had ever been taught or done. But he couldn't stand seeing her looking so lost. His dad called him ten minutes later and asked him what he was doing hugging a murder suspect. Orson told him what he could do with his question and hung up. Nell hadn't killed her husband. And she hadn't kidnapped her son. No way.

30

Just before sunrise, a tattoo of knocks rained on the RV door. A voice called from outside. "Mama!"

Nell's head shot up, nostrils flaring. Her body so still it might have been stone. "JJ?" she mouthed, her lips moving soundlessly. "JJ!" she screamed. She shoved Orson and he fell into the passenger seat as she ripped open the door. Nell slipped to her knees on the steps. And lifted JJ into her arms.

Outside, cameras flashed like lightning, catching the moment in vivid flares of exploding light. Reporters and cameramen pushed and shoved, crowding the doorway. A cacophony of raucous questions and demands filled the RV.

"Is that the kid?"

"How did he get away?"

"Looks like his picture."

"Are you sure?"

"Nell, is that JJ?"

Tears in his eyes, Orson slowly righted himself and stood, watching mother and son. Nell rocked JJ back and forth, holding him so tightly it looked like she wanted to pull him inside her chest. Against her heart. JJ's arms were tight around his mother's neck, squeezing off her air, his legs around her waist, gripping. Both were crying.

Something inside him twisted at the sight. Coiled around his heart and constricted. Gently, he pushed the reporters back. "We'll have a statement for you in a minute," he said, not knowing if they even heard him over their own clamor. He shut the door.

A steady knocking began as the reporters banged for attention. Nell stood with JJ, rocking, swaying, both of them sobbing. Claire sat, her mouth open, staring, breathing in short gasps, tears rolling down her cheeks.

He wiped his face so he could see them clearly, unable to take his gaze off the pair. When he could speak, when he could force his eyes away, Orson opened his cell phone, punched in Deputy Wales's number and requested assistance, his voice strained with tears. "Get the sheriff to cancel the call to the FBI," he said. "Cancel the Amber Alert. Tell the sheriff the kid just came in the door. No. I don't know anything. I'll call you in a minute."

JJ was damp, as if he had recently been in the river; his clothes were filthy. There were scratches on his arms and legs, wounds that looked fresh and others that were half scabbed over. Orson's body stiffened. His relief burned through with a silent, hot rage. There were ligature marks on JJ's wrists. The kid had been tied up. And he had bloodied himself getting free.

It was suddenly stifling in the RV, airless and close. Orson fought to control his temper. Fought to find the distant, cool, observant part of himself that had once made him a good investigator.

Orson took Nell by the shoulders, lifted her to her feet, steering her to the seat she had vacated. She sat at an angle, her feet pointing at the door, JJ on her lap, still rocking. Orson was sure she intended to never let JJ go again. But he needed to ask the boy some questions. Fast.

"Nell," he said softly, prying at JJ's arms. "JJ, I need to ask you a few questions. Nell, I need to talk to you both. So the kidnappers don't get away. Understand?"

Outside the RV, blue lights flashed. The knocking on the RV door stopped, the resulting silence seeming as loud as the previous din. Orson could hear Wales's voice as the deputy cleared a space around the RV. Promising a statement soon. Agreeing that things seemed to be happening. Babying the media. In the distance, a siren sounded. Likely the sheriff, on the way to handle things from wherever he had holed up. There wasn't much time. "JJ," he said again, pulling at the boy's arms. "Nell…"

JJ eased back, still keeping a hammerlock on his mother, but looking at Orson. He was crying, tears and mucus running down his face, his eyes dilated. His mouth was red and abraded in a two-inch strip where tape had sealed him from ear to ear. His lips were torn and bleeding, swollen and parted. He was mouth-breathing like a fish onshore. His expression was as wild as his mother's.

"Calm down, son," Orson said. "Take a slow breath"

JJ seemed to gather himself and took the commanded breath, clearing the detritus of terror away. He blinked, his eyes focusing.

"Right. That's good. Just breathe," Orson said.

The boy blinked again, his pupils constricting slightly. He was clearly still frightened, yet underneath the panic there was something else. Something sturdy and strong and resilient, a strength of a different sort from his mother's determination and fortitude. The boy pulled himself together, breathing in deeply, as if he had been underwater, oxygen deprived, and now was safe. He relaxed his fingers around his mother's neck one finger at a time until his hands rested on her shoulders. As he watched, Orson had the feeling that he would have liked JJ's father. And whoever had taught the kid Zenlike relaxation techniques. Nell? Mike? It was remarkable to watch in a child so young.

JJ eased back against the power of his mother's hold.

"It's okay, Mama." He patted her cheek and wiped her tears. "I'm okay." He looked at Orson. "Whatchya need to know?"

Orson, not sure why he was so emotional, batted away his own tears. "Did you see who kidnapped you?"

"No. I was playing with my ball and my light saber and then this blanket went over my head. They picked me up and carried me off. And dropped me in a truck."

"Did they…hurt you?" he said, not knowing how to ask a young boy if an adult had abused him. JJ held out his wrists as evidence the cop could see and further evidence that the question had been stupid, and looked at Orson quizzically.

"He wants to know," Nell said, understanding, "if the people who took you—" Nell took an anxious breath "—touched your privates, JJ. Like we talked about, when bad people touch little boys wrong."

"No way," the boy said, indignant. Orson felt some of his tension dissipate in an unexpected grin, and saw Nell's shoulders relax a fraction. "They wouldn't even let me go to the bathroom. And I hada pee like a racehorse."

Orson chuckled, and touched the boy's head to reassure himself that he was really here. "How did you get free?" he asked. "Did someone let you go? And where were you?" He stopped himself. *One question at a time*, he reminded himself. "How did you get free? That question first."

"I heard 'em coming back. I'd been pulling at the ropes. And I finally got the mask offa me."

Orson noted the faint abrasions on the boy's tanned neck. A hood had been tied there. He wanted to rip someone's head off for that. Outside, a car door slammed, additional blue lights flashed steadily against the RV windows. The press started up with their shouted questions again and Orson heard the sheriff saying, "No comment," over and over as he tried to make it to the RV.

"I could see lights," JJ continued, "and I ripped my hands loose." He looked at his wrists, turning each one over so he could see both sides. The left one was actively bleeding, blood smeared up his arm and all over Nell's clothes, a rose-colored sweatshirt Orson hadn't even noticed until now. "And I ran."

Orson heard a car door shut again and the blue lights went off. The sheriff had retreated to his cruiser. Unobtrusively, Orson turned off the ringer on his phone.

"Do you know who took you?" Orson asked. "Did you recognize any voices?"

"I thoughted I did one time. But I wasn't sure. One of them shined a light in my eyes and blinded me and another one put a tape on my mouth and then a bag over me and he took me and put me into a truck. And I could hear two of 'em talking, mad kinda. Whisper-yellin', like Mama used to do when I was little and made noise at church." He looked at his mother. "It wasn't Jedi Mike whisper-yellin', but it was his truck, I think. It smelled like it."

JJ looked at Orson. "Mama says everything has a smell and that we can smell a lot better than we think we can because we ain't hunter-gatherers no more and we forget how to use our noses. So I smelled the truck and it smelled like Mike's. But it wasn't Mike yelling."

That would have been a stroke of luck, for the kid to recognize his kidnapper. But if Orson had to chose between JJ recognizing the kidnapper and getting away, he'd take the boy's freedom in a heartbeat.

"I'm hungry, Mama. I ain't had nothing to eat."

Movements jerky, as if she were on automatic pilot but her joints didn't work properly, Claire stood and removed peanut butter and jelly from the cabinet over the sink and a bag of bread from the microwave where they stored it. Sniffing, she began to make PB&J for the boy.

"I'm starving, Mama Claire. Can I have two? Please?"

"Sure, baby boy. Tonight, you can eat till your belly busts open, iffn you want to."

"When you got free," Orson said, "where were you?"

"Inna woods. I could see lights from the tree where they tied me. When I got my hands free, I ran into the woods and stayed quiet for a long time. Pulling off the stuff on my mouth hurt." He touched his bleeding lips with blood-caked fingers. "And then I started working my way down the hill to the lights."

"Go on," Orson said softly, controlling his mounting rage by force of will.

"It was hard 'cause it was so dark and I hada be quiet. So they couldn't hear me and find me again. And then I reached 'em. The lights."

"And," Orson prompted, wanting to shake the story out of JJ, but knowing he had to go slowly, so he could get it all.

"And it was the BP station. And I stayed in the shadows and got to the road under the interstate and then I saw the RV and here I am." He turned his palms over in a shrug that said, "How about that?"

Orson rose and peered out the RV's curtains at the green and white lights of the BP station. Behind him, JJ said, "Mama, you ain't mad at me 'cause I crossed the big road under the interstate all by myself, are you?"

"No, darlin' boy," Nell said, ducking her head and touching her cheek to her son's. "I'm not mad at you for nothing. You got free. Sometimes when you're in danger, you hafta break rules to save yourself. If you ever need to—" Her voice cut off and her throat worked as she swallowed, unable to continue. "I'm not mad," she finished in a whisper.

Orson said, "You came out of the woods, where? At the back of the BP, near where the truckers park at night, or at the side near the Dumpster?"

"At the back," JJ said.

"Someone we know," Nell whispered. "Not from New York…"

"You came down *that* hill?" Orson asked. It was a steep hill. From one angle, the hill ended up at the BP, from another, it ended up in the backyard of an old house. And that house overlooked the guides' garden. And he understood what Nell was saying. It had been river rats who attacked her in the grocery-store parking lot. And Joe had been killed on the bank of a river.

"Yep," JJ said. He held up a foot, his sole bleeding and muddy. "I hurted my foot on a stick, I think. Or maybe it was a rock." He pushed away from Nell and looked in his mother's eyes, his voice firming, "What are all the TV people doing here? Are they making you cry again?"

Nell hiccuped and laughed. "No, baby, the TV people aren't making me cry. Getting you back is what's making me cry. It's a happy cry. And the TV people want to interview us. You most of all."

JJ perked up. "I'm gonna be on TV? Cool!" Nell laughed, a quaking, breathy sound.

"Nell?" Orson said, drawing her attention to him. "I need you to think back. To seven years ago. I need to know if anyone you know ever had a pink rabbit's foot. Like a good-luck charm."

"Harvey carries a pink rabbit's foot," JJ said.

Orson went still.

"It's how he got his river name," Nell said, her chapped lips barely moving, her voice rough with shouting and crying, colorless. "He's always carried himself a pink rabbit's foot. So the guides named him after the invisible rabbit, Harvey, from the old movie. His real name is Dean Anthony Haver Why do you want to know about the pink rabbit's foot?"

"Because the crime-scene investigators found one." His eyes added, *"In Joe's grave,"* but he didn't say the words aloud. Not in front of JJ. Nell's gaze sharpened, understanding. "And Harvey isn't with us anymore," he said. Nell's mouth fell slowly open and Orson nodded. "Up at the powerhouse."

JJ looked back and forth between them. "So where'd he go? Him and me was gonna run part of Big Creek in the morning, iffn you wanted to let me, Mama," he added.

"In a minute, baby. Orson?" she asked and stopped, not able to phrase whatever question she needed to ask. She shook her head. "Later," she said instead.

"I want you to look at something," Orson said. "But I have to go back outside to get it, and that means dealing with the press, which I don't want to do. They all saw JJ come home," he said, and Nell's smile flashed at the words, her sudden joy warming him. He smiled back. "So there'll be no getting away from them unless I get someone to make a statement. Okay?"

"Sure," Nell said. When JJ started to interrupt, she said, "You can be on TV in a little bit. Not just now."

The boy sighed, a long-suffering sound, and shook his head, "I never get to do nothing."

Orson opened his phone, saw the sheriff had called him five times in the last five minutes. He punched the send button and the sheriff's number rang. Orson stood and walked to the back of the RV. There were a few things he wanted the sheriff to say to the press. And he didn't want JJ to hear any of it. Not yet.

Nell carried JJ to the bathroom to clean his wounds. She had a feeling Orson would have insisted that a crime-scene tech should work him over first, but the cop was busy on the phone and her baby was bleeding. She closed the door behind her and sat JJ on the bathroom sink, on the narrow ledge that most RVs offered. He balanced himself with both hands as Nell dampened a rag. Tenderly, she removed the filth from his face, broken twigs, traces of leaves, fine gravel and mud. Around his mouth, where the tape had kept him quiet, his skin was inflamed. Here she used a bit of baby oil, soothing the adhesive away, rolling it up in little balls as it came loose. She saved all the mess, shaking it onto a clean towel which she spread over the toilet seat, the only other flat surface except the floor or the shower. Her motion banged the cell phone in her pocket against the wall and Nell pulled it out, setting it on the ledge by the sink.

She couldn't help the tears that fell. There was no way to stop them. Once, JJ hugged her hard, seeming to understand that they were tears of joy. Nell hugged him back, the tears mixing with laughter. "I love you, baby boy," she whispered. Then, "Thank you," she whispered to God. He had answered a lot of prayers in her life with a no. But this one was the most important, and this time he had come through. She rested her forehead against JJ's. "Thank you for bringing my baby back to me."

JJ hugged her close, not minding her tears, letting her cry all over him, which she had never done before. He kept whispering, "It's okay, Mama. I'm okay."

When she had herself under control again, Nell returned to cleaning up her son. Minutes later, as she was applying Band-Aids with cartoon characters on them to his legs, a knock came. Orson opened the door and stuck his head in. "What are you doing?" he said, irritation and dismay in his tone. "I needed to collect trace evidence from him."

"Tough. I'm bandaging my son," Nell said. She folded the towel with the trace in it and handed it to him through the crack in the door. "Here's your evidence."

"I can't use this—"

Nell turned her back and shut the door in his face. Frankly, she didn't give a good flying darn what he could or couldn't use. She bent over again and tore open another bandage and applied it to JJ's wrist.

When they emerged later, it was to find the sheriff and Orson sitting in the driver and passenger seats, the chairs swiveled around to face the common area.

"I still say we need to clear out the street and take this down to the department," the sheriff said.

Ignoring him, Orson said, "Can you look at this?" He extended a thin file folder and Nell took it, curling up with JJ on the only vacant seat, facing the two cops and her mother. She opened the file, finding, not the police report she had somehow been expecting, but an old, faded photo, one she had seen before, not long after Joe had died. Just after she found out that Joe had once been one of New York City's most eligible, rich bachelors.

The photo was of Joe and her, snapped soon after Joe wandered into Hartford. It had been taken through a telephoto lens, and her own face had ended up slightly blurry, the photographer clearly focusing on Joe and uninterested in her. Joe's face was crisp, his jaw chiseled, skin taut and deeply tanned, the photo so clear that water droplets glistened on his lashes. His eyes flashed, looking black in the photograph; his dark hair was wet, finger-combed back from his forehead. And he was laughing. Nell shivered, remembering his laugh, so devil-may-care, so alive. JJ sounded like that when he took a drop in his tiny hard boat, the notes ringing off the water.

Nell brushed the photo with the tips of her fingers. She had a copy of this at home, in a photo album where she had collected all the bits of Joe's life she could find, hoping his son could use it to get to know his father. In it, she looked impossibly young and totally infatuated.

Orson leaned down and tapped the edge of the photo. "Do you recognize this person?" The figure was even more out of focus than Nell.

"It's RiverAnn," JJ said.

It *was* RiverAnn, in one of her weightier times, her curves and stance proclaiming her identity. "Yes," Nell said. "RiverAnn."

"Look at her. Tell me what you think," Orson commanded.

Nell studied the shot, the fisted hands, belligerent position of her feet and the shape of her torso. She looked up surprise. "She's pregnant!"

Back before Joe disappeared, RiverAnn had been pregnant. And she was pregnant now, only much further along than in this photo. Nell studied the grainy reproduction. RiverAnn was facing forward, her body turned at an angle. She appeared to be watching Joe and Nell. And there was a strange look on her face.

Nell looked at her mother. "Take care 'a JJ."

31

Nell opened the door and walked down the steps. A reporter thrust his mic at her, "Nell, can you tell us how JJ got free?" That was the last thing Nell heard as the entire pack of nearly rabid journalists converged on her.

The sheriff and Orson took her, each one by an arm, and pulled her into Orson's SUV. As if they had rehearsed it, the sheriff raced to his unit and blasted the lot with lights and siren, driving his car through the mass of cameras and up to Orson's truck, where he whipped the wheel, turning the car in a tight U. Orson followed and reached the road, the two vehicles moving up the black asphalt, away from Rocking River. Nell leaned her head against the headrest, startled to see that the sky was bright.

"You want to tell me what the hell you intended to do just now?" Orson said, his tone mild in comparison to his word choice.

Nell wondered if he was one of the men who got progressively quiet the angrier he got. Joe had been a shouter. The madder he got, the louder he got, making it fairly easy to tell when she had ticked him off. She glanced at the cop, whose eyes were on the road, and who looked less than irritated.

"I was going to talk to RiverAnn and the guides. If there was a pink rabbit's foot in the grave with Joe—that was what you were trying to say to me, wasn't it?" When he nodded, she continued her first line of thought. "Then the guides, Harvey at least, had to be there when he died. Right? And now Harvey's dead. So, one of his friends has to know something about his death, and it has to be tied in with my baby getting kidnapped."

"It's plausible."

"Plausible?" Nell felt her blood pressure rise at his tone, which was on the verge of patronizing. "Of course it's *plausible*. It's more than just *plausible*, it's *likely*. To the point of being a near *certainty*." She crossed her arms and looked away. "And don't smile at what I'm saying. I'm not stupid, you sanctimonious...cop."

He chuckled, which made her want to hit him, but she didn't want to end up in jail if he decided to arrest her for it. "I know you're not stupid, Nell. But this is an ongoing police investigation and I can't let you interfere." When she snorted, staring at the sunrise, he said, "I'll drop you off at your house. Claire can bring the RV and JJ. Okay?"

"Whatever." A moment later, she said, "I need you to take me back to the shop. I need to do some paperwork. And I got a kayak lesson to give at ten."

"Nell," he said patiently.

"Don't *Nell* me. I got a business to run and my kayak instructor up and quit on me without notice. Now, take me to my place of business or arrest me."

"For what?" he said, the patient tone morphing into irritation.

"For whatever you dang well please, I reckon."

The SUV lurched forward when Orson hit the brakes, throwing Nell against her seat belt. The screech of tires announced they were turning around and Nell grabbed the arm support with one hand and the loop-style handle over the door with the other. The tension in the vehicle went up about 150 percent, but Nell didn't back down. When Hartford came into sight, she said, "Stop here. I'll walk around behind the post office, along the river, and up to the shop to avoid the reporters."

Orson braked hard in the middle of the road and Nell undid the seat belt, opened the door and climbed into the street. "Ain't no call to be snippy." She slammed the door and walked off down toward the river, satisfied that she had ticked him off enough not to pay attention to where she was for the next half hour or so.

Nell made her way along the river, watching for snakes out for their morning sun, moving upstream, behind her river-running competition, The Bean Trees, which was open for business, selling coffee to the media and the locals, and past the post office to Rocking River. But she kept going. Twenty yards upstream of the shop, Nell came up from the water and crossed the street to the guides' house without looking back down the road, hoping that the remaining reporters wouldn't see her. She was in luck. No one shouted or gave chase.

Without knocking, Nell climbed the three front steps, turned the front door handle and went in. It was early yet and, after the excitement of the hunt for JJ, everyone was, oddly, either hiding in their rooms or back in bed. Nell could hear three people snoring, two radios playing competing stations and a soft thumping sound she really didn't want to investigate. Fans hummed quietly from upstairs and down. The house smelled of river, unwashed bodies, cigarette and marijuana smoke, beer and cooked cabbage.

Nell remembered it all from her eighteenth year, when she had run away from home and signed on as a guide. She'd taken a private room on the second floor and had installed a lock to ensure her privacy. Now, she looked up the stairs, trying to decide which room RiverAnn and her now-dead boyfriend might have chosen.

The cadence of soft voices floated in through the open windows from the back. With nothing better to indicate a direction, Nell followed the sound through the living room and the kitchen, to the back. Standing on the rickety porch, in the doorway to the kitchen but still hidden in early-morning shadow, Nell spotted a gathering in the backyard near the edge of the porch.

RiverAnn lay on the hammock, which was swinging slowly. Wearing shorts and a thin yellow tee stretched across her pregnant belly, she was curled on her side. There were scratches on her arms, and a swath of what looked like poison ivy on one ankle.

Hamp sat facing her, his bare feet on the grass, his eyes full of misery and longing. It was that longing, so full of tenderness and desire and pain, that stopped Nell, made her pause just out of sight. The helplessness in Hamp's eyes. And grief. Utter, total grief.

Turtle Tom, dressed in cutoff jeans and sandals, shirtless, sat in a deck chair, bent over, his head hanging forward, his laced fingers dangling between his knees. His back was bowed with worry and tension, his long hair unbound from its tie, draping forward to obscure his face. "You can't do it, Annie. You got to turn yourself in," Tom said.

"For what?" RiverAnn asked. "They can't prove Harvey took the little shit. Brat never saw us, not once. Besides. It wasn't like I was gonna hurt him. All we wanted was the money so we could go away. The family's rich. They wouldn'a missed the money any."

"The cops are involved. It's daylight." Tom lifted his head and, for an instant, Nell feared she had been seen. She stepped deeper into the shadows and his eyes looked away. "Won't be long till they head up the hill. They'll find Stewey's crop. And the place where you tied JJ up. If the old man and his dogs haven't already found it." Tom looked up the hill behind the garden, a darkly shaded path curving into the trees. "For all you know, JJ's PawPaw has a hunting rifle trained us all right now."

"Yeah, yeah," Hamp muttered, looking uneasily up the hill. "They'll put it all together. And they'll come here."

"No," RiverAnn said. As if the huge bulge itched, she rubbed her stomach over her T-shirt with the tips of her fingers, a nervous, angry scratch. "I am *not* going to jail."

Nell closed her hands into fists, her breathing sped up. In the distance, a mourning dove cooed, a plaintive "Who, who, who?"

"I'll get you the best lawyers," Tom said finally, his head hanging low, his eyes not meeting his friends'. "The best in the state."

"I'm *not* going to jail," the girl said, her pregnancy-swollen lips snarling. "I'll get away. I just need money, and you got some. We all know it, Tom. So just give me a couple 'a thousand, to get to a new place and get a new start."

"If you run, they'll figure out about Joe," Tom said, "and then you'll go to jail for a long time. But only if you run. If you go to the cops, with a lawyer who knows how to spin it, it can make the difference between life in prison and just a couple years."

RiverAnn raised up, her face twisted with hate. "I. Am. *Not*. Going to prison."

Nell shrank back again. *Prison? For kidnapping JJ? For…Joe?* She put a hand on the doorjamb to steady herself. She needed to get Orson. One-handed, Nell patted the pockets of her sweats. Her cell was in the RV bathroom, where she had left it when she cleaned JJ's wounds.

"Come with me, Tom," RiverAnn said. "We'd would have us some good times."

Hamp's head drooped lower and, from her place in the kitchen, Nell saw tears fall from his face to the ground. When he spoke, his voice was pleading, vibrating with pain. "Where'll you go, Annie?" He put his fisted hands together, white knuckles touching. He raised his tear-stained face. "Where?"

"I'm not going with you, RiverAnn," Tom said, his voice heartrendingly sad, but calm. "And I can't let you run away from this."

"You gonna turn me in?" she asked, rolling in the hammock to see Tom better in the brightening light. "After all we been to each other?"

Up on the hillside behind the house, a dog started baying, long, crying howls of success. PawPaw's hound had found JJ's trail.

"We slept together a few times, Annie," Turtle Tom said, still staring down.

Both men were watching their hands now, as if they couldn't bear to look at her or at each other. Stoned Stewart, sitting in the shadow of the porch, looked confused. Uncertain.

Tom sighed and said, "But then, you slept with all of us at one time or other." He shook his head. "No, Annie. I won't let you. I won't let you hurt Nell anymore. And now that I know about Joe…" He sighed again, his voice firming. "You got to turn yourself in."

"All this is *her* fault. I shoulda killed that bitch first time I set eyes on her," RiverAnn said viciously. "None 'a this ever woulda happened if Joe hadn't gone and married her."

Rage shot through Nell. The howling on the hill resolved into sharp barks. The dogs were getting closer. PawPaw was coming. His presence gave her courage. Spurred her anger. Before she could think it through, Nell stepped onto the porch, into the light. "Joe loved me, Ann," she said.

With twin jerks, RiverAnn and Hamp looked up at her.

Stewart turned more slowly, puzzled. Only Tom didn't look her way and Nell knew he had spotted her earlier. Spotted her and let her stay. Let her listen.

RiverAnn rolled to her feet, her back swayed, holding her belly. Fury flashed across Ann's face, her mouth snarling. "He was mine!" she said.

Nell stopped cold. RiverAnn lunged at her. Hamp caught Ann's arms, holding her back. The girl whirled and slapped him. His head snapped back. RiverAnn screamed. Balled her fists, raging, beating him. Hamp suffered it, ducking his head, stepping back as he absorbed the blows, blocking the ones he could.

Tom shook his head and looked up through his long hair. "I'm sorry, Nell. I just found out about it."

"Found out what?" She watched the four friends, her gaze picking from one to the other.

RiverAnn wrenched away from Hamp. "I was gonna have Joe's baby," she said, spitting the words. Climbing the steps. "All those years ago, back when you *stole him from me!* I was pregnant with *his baby*." Laughter split her face at whatever she saw on Nell's. "He was mine and you stole him away from me."

Nell backed away. Blood and strength seemed to leach out of her. "No." Nell retreated through the kitchen, her knees weak, her vision blackening. "No…" she whispered, "No, no, no."

"Yes," RiverAnn said, advancing. Her body was bent forward over her belly, her fists clenched and vibrating with anger.

"He was mine. We were in love," she said, following Nell into the living room. Light from the busted overhead fixture and the broken lamp cast strange shadows, harsh on the mud-brown walls. "And then *you* came in. And you waved your little ass at his face and he *left* me."

Nell bumped into a chair, the upholstery rough on her calf and knee. "No."

"Yes. But I knew I could make him come back to me. I knew I could make him love me again." RiverAnn kicked a chair.

Hamp, following her, caught it and set it upright. Behind him stood Tom, his tattoos like living things crawling up his arms. Stoned Stewart, confused, crowded into the living room, blinking as if he was trying to wake up.

"I could have," RiverAnn said. "He woulda come to me. Divorced you. And married me. I know he would. Soon as I told him about our baby."

"RiverAnn and Joe were together for a couple of weeks that summer before he met you, Nell," Tom said, filling in the blanks.

"How—" Nell stopped, blanching. It wasn't possible. It wasn't.

"He was gonna leave you," Ann spat. "That was what he was gonna tell you on that trip down the South Fork of the Cumberland. And we was gonna move back to New York."

That stopped Nell. "New York?" she said. "He was going to live in New York?" Relief spiraled through her, weakening her further. Suddenly she laughed, the sound shaky. "Joe hated New York. He *hated* it." Nell backed away, along the moldering couch, toward the door, her hands waving back and forth as if she were wiping away the girl's claim. And she began to put it together.

"No. You're lying." She thought back, putting the months in place in her memory. "Joe saw me on the Nantahala in early spring. He came to Hartford in April, looking for me. He drove into Hartford on a Friday, when the river wasn't running, and he found me in Wildwater, where I was working. Asked me if there were any creeks to run."

Nell sat slowly on the lumpy couch, remembering, her eyes out of focus, buried in the past. "He came into the

Smokehouse for lunch. And we took one look at each other and whatever had started on the Nante picked up and…and we fell head over heels."

Nell blinked her way out of the past and RiverAnn's face came clear. "There wasn't time for him to meet you and get you pregnant. You're lying, Ann. You're just plain old lying. You were still in school that year. He didn't even meet you till he and I had been dating for nearly a month."

The boys looked from Nell to RiverAnn, uncertainty on their faces. "It wasn't Joe's baby?" Tom said.

"That means it was mine," Hamp whispered. His face fell as horror grew in his eyes. "You got an illegal abortion," he whispered in growing horror. "You killed my baby. You… killed my baby."

RiverAnn screamed and rushed Nell.

32

Orson eased down the steps from the second story as RiverAnn bragged about being pregnant with Joseph's Stevens's baby. He had followed Nell into the house, and had thought she went upstairs. By the time he figured out that she was standing in the kitchen, the discussion had moved into the house, and he'd been caught on the stairs to the second story, one hand on the rickety stair railing. He could see Nell's face clearly, the play of emotion skittering through her. And then her denial. It made sense. It all made sense.

The two boys looked from Nell to RiverAnn, to each other and back. "It wasn't Joe's baby?" Tom asked.

"That means it was mine," Hamp whispered. His shoulders hunched, his hands clenched. "You got an illegal abortion," he whispered. "You killed my baby. You killed my baby."

RiverAnn screamed. Rushed Nell. Shock raced through him, electric. Without thought, Orson leaped. Over the railing. Landed on his right foot. Between RiverAnn and Nell. Caught the pregnant girl's forearm. Momentum carried him. He pulled her with him, knocking her off balance. With a hard nudge, he sent her spiraling onto the couch.

Nell leaped away. To safety.

Moving fast, he cuffed RiverAnn's hands in front of her belly. The girl screamed, crying in fury.

He whipped around to find Nell facing Hamp. The man's chin was gripped in her fingers. Her eyes holding his. But Ann wasn't done.

She pushed up from the couch. Bringing the brass floor lamp with her. Lifted it in a batting hold. Took a hard swing. Orson blocked it with a forearm. The thunk of metal hitting bone was loud in the room. He cursed and doubled over. RiverAnn swayed, off balance. Whirled. Orson caught a steel cuff in the face. He ducked away, pain ripping at his mouth. Blood gushed from his upper lip. The sounds of the room dropped on him like weights.

"Who killed Joe?" Nell screamed.

Orson looked from her to RiverAnn , struggling to focus though the pain. Shook his head. Nell advanced on RiverAnn, her voice dropping low. She growled, "Who killed my husband?"

"We don't know," Turtle Tom said, his mouth pulled down. Orson turned to him, keeping RiverAnn and Nell in his sights. Tom spoke to him, his voice changing from laidback river rat to something more upscale and self-possessed. "We weren't there." He guided Ann back to the couch. Eased her down onto the cushion. RiverAnn covered her face, crying softly. "Annie was having some problems at home that year. Her old man—" He stopped, stroked her head, clearly changing his mind about telling the backstory. "She was dating Hamp. When Joe came to town, she broke up with him."

Hamp was staring at RiverAnn, his heart in his gaze, tears spilling over. "She chased him all spring and summer. While he chased you," he said to Nell. The room went silent for a moment, the only sounds the uneven breath of them all and the distant call of a rooster. "Broke my heart."

Tom said, "I remember when she started to show, she told us all it was Joe's baby. That he had been with her for a few weeks before he settled down with you. That he got her pregnant and then said the baby wasn't his. We believed her." He shook his head and righted a folding metal chair that had ended up on its side in the melee.

"Harvey told me last night that RiverAnn and he followed Nell and Joe down the South Fork of the Cumberland. But he wouldn't tell me what happened. We just found out this morning, after JJ got away and the search was called off."

Orson, his pain under control, but still bleeding, took RiverAnn's arm and pried the lamp from her fingers. It clattered when he set it on the floor. Ann didn't resist this time, tears and mucus running down her face. Her eyes were darting from man to man in the room, as if seeking something she had lost. Or maybe never had.

"She shot Joe," Hamp whispered. "Yeah, yeah. She had to 'a. Harvey never woulda shot him." He ran his hands up and down his arms as if cold. "She shot him. And then she killed my baby." Hamp looked at RiverAnn. "We were together all that winter, in school, till you saw Joe. And suddenly I wasn't good enough for you. First it was Joe. Then Harvey. But that baby was mine."

Turtle Tom said to Nell, "RiverAnn and Harvey kidnapped JJ. And we think that when they argued, she picked up a rock and hit him. She killed Harvey."

"It was an accident," RiverAnn said. "He loved me. Joe did," she insisted, looking up at Orson. "And I loved him. And if I can't have him no one can."

Nell put a hand to her mouth.

It was close enough to a confession to bring her in. Orson pulled his cell phone.

"Oh, shit," Hamp said. "Oh, shit, oh, shit, oh, shit." He burst into tears. "Yeah, yeah. Yeah, yeah," he said, and turned away, closing his eyes in grief.

RiverAnn collapsed across the couch, cradling her belly, crying.

Turtle Tom stared between his friends as if his heart was breaking. As if his world had crumbled in front of his eyes. Into the emotional mess, came the ominous sound of a shotgun breech closing.

PawPaw and three dogs entered from the back of the house, the dogs lunging on their leashes, tongues hanging, PawPaw's shotgun on RiverAnn.

Nell watched through her tears as Orson called for backup. Mirandized RiverAnn. He wiped blood from his lip in angry dabs, keeping his back to her. Nell hunched in the corner, PawPaw's arm around her like a steel band, watching, ignored or forgotten. Her tears fell, hot and scorching, silent.

River guides gathered in the living room, whispering, asking questions no one answered. The smell of hot, wet dog, unwashed human, marijuana smoke and stale beer competed for dominance. Beneath it all, the clean smell of the river wafted through open windows, soothing.

A siren wailed down the street, the unit lurching from the road, through the ditch, and up to the front door, followed by a second unmarked cop car, boxy and ugly and with a blue light flashing, attached to the roof over the driver's door. Orson pushed RiverAnn out the door and into Deputy Wales's squad car.

The media still in the Rocking River parking lot followed the police lights, attacking like rats on dead meat, mics thrust into Orson's face, questions screamed. Silent, no longer the center of attention, Nell watched, standing with the gathering crowd of awakening guides as they continued to stumble in, bleary-eyed and hungover. Orson never looked at her once. Not even when his father, looking older and more wizened than she remembered, appeared from the unmarked car and pulled Orson into it and drove away.

And they were gone, heading to the sheriff's department

for questioning, Nell supposed. The news vans screeched after the squad car. Within seconds the media had disappeared. A strained silence settled on the sleepy guides.

"What the hell was that all about?" Juliet asked. She was standing at the top of the stairs, an orange towel wrapped around her, long legs damp with shower water, wet feet leaving footprints on the steps.

"I don't know," Nell said, shaking her head, thinking about RiverAnn and her hatred. And murder. "I just purely don't know."

Turtle Tom looked up at her from his place in the metal chair. "I'm sorry, Nell. I'm so very sorry."

She patted his shoulder once and left the guide house, moving stiffly down the termite-ridden steps, followed by PawPaw and his dogs. She stopped in the grass. Thought about breathing, about her heart still beating, steady in her chest. About her son. And her dead husband.

PawPaw touched her shoulder. "You'll be all right," he said. "You got my blood in you. And your ma's. You're strong. Strong as the hills and jist as full of iron." It was the longest statement she had ever heard him speak. He hugged her once, his grip bruising, then clicked once to his dogs. "Lessus go home, boys."

Across the street, between the weeds and the trees on the bank, she could see the river flowing sluggishly. Sunlight caught the eddies and sparkled. The mourning dove called, lamenting and sad, and was answered by another, nearby.

Nell squared her shoulders. By the sun, she guesstimated it was close to eight o'clock. Come ten, she had a kayak lesson to teach. With Melissa as manager, she didn't have to be in the shop. She could teach the lesson. And then... Maybe she'd take the Upper Pigeon. In her kayak. With her son. Nell considered that possibility.

For the first time since Joe disappeared, she could take a

river. She could and she would. With Joe's son. Her stomach growled, demanding attention.

First, she would find her baby and hug him. And eat breakfast. And put on clean, blood-free clothes and kiss her mom. And maybe drink a whole pot of caffeine.

Then she would get to work teaching kayak lessons at Rocking River on the Pigeon.

33

Orson turned off the key in his ignition and relaxed back in the seat. His engine tinged and ticked as it cooled. Butchie raced from the backdoor to his SUV, barking like a fool, long fur flying, tongue flipping up and down from his mouth. Eventually the backdoor opened. Claire stood there, in jeans and a smocklike top, studying the vehicle, drying her hands on a dark green towel. She seemed to make up her mind.

"Butchie," she called. "'Comere, you little idiot." Louder, she said to Orson, "You come on in, too."

Orson opened the door and followed the dog, obeying the woman as any sensible man would. He entered the house and stood inside the door, letting his eyes adjust to the dark. He heard her at the sink, running water. It shut off.

"You shaved and cut your hair," Claire said. "You look like a cop."

Orson lifted his mouth in a half smile. The statement had been intended as an insult. "I am a cop."

"Uh-huh." She moved closer, resolving out of the gloom. Or maybe his eyes were just adjusting to the dark. She put a glass of tea in his hand. "You arrested Joe's killer. As the mother of the widow, I'm grateful." She put three cookies in his other hand. "Ain't seen you around much this last month."

"I figured my father was enough Lennoxes to hang around the house."

"He's a pistol," she said. She leaned a hip against the counter and drank her own iced tea. Her glass was sweating in the heat, warm July air moving through the open windows. "Slow to get going—took him seven years to make a move—but a pistol."

"Yeah. He says pretty much the same about you. Of course, he thought that when he met you."

"So why'd he wait so long to ask me out?" Claire asked.

"I think he was scared to death of you."

Claire found that amusing, snorting, ladylike and prim. "He was scared that he'd have to arrest my daughter." Orson inclined his head in agreement with her observation. She stood straight. "Can you tell me why Joe had to die? Or not? Nell won't say, and for once, the guides are all close-mouthed."

"Can't," Orson said. "Not until the trial. If there is one. The suspect isn't all that stable."

Claire took him by the wrist, the one with the cookies, and led him into the den. She pointed at the couch and Orson sat, thinking that he was acting like a well-trained dog. To drive the point home, Butchie jumped up beside him and licked the condensation on his glass. He elbowed the dog away and it stared at him, panting in the heat, cute little button eyes that hid the soul of a killer pit bull.

"Nell will be home soon." Claire said. "You gonna tell *her* why RiverAnn shot her husband?"

"Nell knows," he said.

"I see." Claire hadn't known that her daughter had the information she sought. She didn't look happy at that. "You gonna tell my daughter that you're halfway in love with her?"

"Not planning on it," he said easily, not surprised at anything this woman might say or know. "Not today anyway. I thought I'd take her to dinner instead. You gonna marry my father?"

"He asked, but after seven years of lollygagging, he isn't finished courting me. He hasn't even brought me no flowers yet, the big boob. If he gets any good at courtin', we'll see about marriage later on. But it complicates things a bit if you and Nell get together. People will talk if I marry your old man and you marry my daughter."

"Why? And who cares?"

"Them's a couple 'a million-dollar questions," she said. Butchie started barking again and dived through the doggie door back outside. Orson heard tires on gravel and his heart leaped into his throat. He hadn't seen Nell in four weeks. Not since he arrested RiverAnn for Joseph Stevens's murder.

The story would come out at trial. If there was a trial. But Orson wanted to tell Nell himself, what he had learned and pieced together. And he wanted to see if he was as much in love with her as he thought he might be. He set the tea glass and cookies on the coffee table and stood. JJ raced into the house and threw himself at Orson. Startled, Orson just managed to catch the kid in his flying leap.

"Hey, Orson. Long time no see, dude," JJ said, his face so close Orson couldn't focus on him. He smelled like river and grape soda, and a purple ring circled his mouth. "Mama said to meet her on the Lower." He squirmed around to see Claire. "And she said to hold dinner, please," he enunciated the last three words carefully, as if repeating them exactly. "She's got some things to say to *him*." JJ squirmed in Orson's arms to face him and said, "What's Mama got to say to you?"

"I'm terrified to ask," Orson said, setting the boy on the couch.

"You should be," Claire murmured. Which did nothing good for his confidence level.

Nell slid into the kayak for the hundredth time this busy month. Rocking River had taken almost a thousand people down the Pigeon in the last four weeks. Not a record for the rafting businesses, but pretty dang close. She took the carpeted slide down the bank into the river, seal-launching into the water and peeling into the current with deft strokes. She had given forty hours of private kayak lessons and ten hours of group roll clinics. She was making money hand over fist, thanks to the free, if unwanted, publicity that came her way after RiverAnn was charged with Joe's murder. She'd also found time to run the Pigeon with JJ several times. Once, they had run part of Big Creek together, JJ at her side, screaming with glee at the ten-foot drop of Midnight Hole.

She heard a door slam and looked back and up, waiting. Ten minutes later, a purple-and-green Perception ProLine boat whisked down the slide into the water, landing with a neat splash. His old boat. Had he chosen it for her? To remind her about the SAR for Joe?

"Pretty," she said of his deft launch.

"Thanks," Orson said, sweeping to face her. "I never said, but I like your new boat."

Nell patted the LiquidLogic Remix, the pearly finish now scratched and scored by rocks and logs, feeling the pride of ownership. "My baby."

He nodded. "Nice. So. What now?" he asked.

"Now we make use of the last of the water today and paddle down the Lower Pigeon. And you tell me what happened the day Joe died."

He shrugged. "Okay. And if the powerhouse closes off the chutes early, and we run out of water onto rocks? Or if we dawdle too much and the sun sets?"

"Life is full of possibilities and danger."

Orson chuckled, and Nell laughed with him.

They paddled lazily down the Lower Pigeon, taking the long pools of nearly still water, dropping over the ledges as the sun set in the west. The golden ball turned the sky a vivid gold and pink, scarlet, purple and eventually cerulean, as Nell learned what the cop had to say about how her husband had died.

RiverAnn had confessed, a long and rambling tale full of self-deceit and teenage stupidity, but for Nell, Orson condensed it all down into the short and sordid story it really was. RiverAnn, though only seventeen and still in high school at the time, had been sleeping with Hamp before Joe Stevens came to town. Instantly smitten with the newcomer, she had hidden her pregnancy and later attributed the child to an affair with Joe.

Harvey, in love with Ann for years, but never her favorite, agreed to go with her when she followed Joe and Nell to the South Fork of the Cumberland for their belated honeymoon trip, to confront him. When the honeymooners didn't reach the campsite they had planned for at the end of the first day, the two paddlers had taken to the water.

They found the rescue X where Joe had left Nell when he went to get help, and discovered Nell, in a coma, on the shore. RiverAnn had wanted to kill the girl, but Harvey had forced her back to the water to go after Joe. They caught up with him at the bottom of the El, where he had taken a spill and had to swim to shore. Joe had denied that the baby was his and refused to leave Nell. In a fit of rage, RiverAnn had attacked Joe, beating him with her fists.

Joe should have simply gotten on the water. Paddled out from shore. Let Harvey cool RiverAnn down. Instead, he pushed her away. She crashed into him and his injured knee took him down. While he gasped and writhed in pain, RiverAnn raided Joe's overturned boat for the gun he always paddled with. And she shot him. Afraid that he would be part of any arrest and trial, Harvey had helped her bury the man.

And showed up with their friends later to help with the search.

In another version, one that RiverAnn came up with after seeing an attorney, Harvey had shot Joe. That would be her defense if it ever came to trial. And it was a good one, with Harvey gone, and his death ruled as a possible accident. It wasn't uncommon for a drunk paddler to slip, hit his head and drown, RiverAnn's story for his death.

Nell listened to it all, and then thought about it all. As she thought, she turned her boat in lazy circles at the base of the last ledge. The day was darkening, night creeping in. The water level had dropped in the last hour. As she turned, the shores spun around her, bringing Orson into the picture once every three hundred sixty degrees. Around and around. Thinking. Finally she stopped and let the boat continue its flowing turn until Orson appeared again. She stopped the boat's motion and feathered her paddle to bring herself closer to the cop.

"Thank you," she said.

"You're welcome."

"You weren't supposed to tell me all that, were you?"

"No."

She cocked her head to the side, curious. "Why did you?"

"According to your mother, it's because I'm halfway in love with you."

"You are?" Nell wasn't surprised. Wasn't too upset at the declaration. But, like knowing what happened the day Joe died, it made her feel weird.

"I was going to take you to a movie," he said. "Maybe dinner. Maybe lunch, too, before I told you."

"I like river dates better."

"Yeah. I just figured that out." He looked around, as if considering the site for date material. "Pretty hard to bring roses to a river date. And how in heck are we gonna get home anyway?"

"I called PawPaw from the shop. He'll be up there—"

Nell pointed to the shore and up the hill to the road "—in about half an hour."

"PawPaw?"

"Yeah. He's got a few things to say to you," she said, humor in her tone.

"Should I be scared?"

"Probably. PawPaw had a talk with Joe when he started dating me. I have a feeling it was…um…pointed."

"Pointed. You mean like, 'Iffn you hurt my gal, I'll skewer you.'?"

"Shoot you. Several times. And leave your body for the crows."

"Ah. Of course." He twirled his paddle, amusement lurking in his smile. "I should have realized it would be the shotgun. You folks don't leave much to chance, do you?"

Nell chuckled. "Nope. Race you to the takeout."

The cop grinned and dug in with his paddle. Nell dug in with hers.

A novel that could only be written by

RICK MOFINA

SIX
SECONDS

A VENGEFUL WOMAN WHO ACHES FOR HER
PLACE IN PARADISE…

AN ANGUISHED MOTHER DESPERATE TO FIND HER CHILD…

A DETECTIVE WHO NEEDS TO REDEEM HIMSELF…

THREE STRANGERS ENTANGLED IN A PLOT THAT COULD
CHANGE THE WORLD IN ONLY SIX SECONDS…

"Six Seconds…moves like a tornado."
—James Patterson,
New York Times bestselling author

*Available the first week of January 2009
wherever books are sold!*

www.MIRABooks.com

MRM2612

ANOTHER SHOCKING THRILLER BY

J.T. ELLISON

It was a murder made for TV: A trail of tiny, bloody footprints.
An innocent toddler playing beside her mother's bludgeoned
body. Pretty young Corinne Wolff, seven months pregnant,
brutally murdered in her own home.

Cameras and questions don't usually phase Nashville
Homicide lieutenant Taylor Jackson, but the media frenzy
surrounding the Wolff case is particularly nasty...and thorough.
When the seemingly model mommy is linked to an amateur
porn Web site with underage actresses and unwitting players,
the sharks begin to circle....

"Mystery fiction has a new name to watch."
—John Connolly, *New York Times* bestselling author

*Available the first week of January 2009
wherever books are sold!*

MIRA®

www.MIRABooks.com   MJTE2629

REQUEST YOUR
FREE BOOKS!

2 FREE NOVELS
FROM THE ROMANCE/SUSPENSE
COLLECTION PLUS 2 FREE GIFTS!

YES! Please send me 2 FREE novels from the Romance/Suspense Collection and my 2 FREE gifts (gifts are worth about $10). After receiving them, if I don't wish to receive any more books, I can return the shipping statement marked "cancel." If I don't cancel, I will receive 4 brand-new novels every month and be billed just $5.49 per book in the U.S. or $5.99 per book in Canada, plus 25¢ shipping and handling per book plus applicable taxes, if any*. That's a savings of at least 20% off the cover price! I understand that accepting the 2 free books and gifts places me under no obligation to buy anything. I can always return a shipment and cancel at any time. Even if I never buy another book from the Reader Service, the two free books and gifts are mine to keep forever.

185 MDN EF5Y 385 MDN EF6C

Name	(PLEASE PRINT)

Address	Apt. #

City	State/Prov.	Zip/Postal Code

Signature (if under 18, a parent or guardian must sign)

Mail to **The Reader Service:**
IN U.S.A.: P.O. Box 1867, Buffalo, NY 14240-1867
IN CANADA: P.O. Box 609, Fort Erie, Ontario L2A 5X3

Not valid to current subscribers to the Romance Collection,
the Suspense Collection or the Romance/Suspense Collection.

Want to try two free books from another line?
Call 1-800-873-8635 or visit www.morefreebooks.com.

* Terms and prices subject to change without notice. N.Y. residents add applicable sales tax. Canadian residents will be charged applicable provincial taxes and GST. Offer not valid in Quebec. This offer is limited to one order per household. All orders subject to approval. Credit or debit balances in a customer's account(s) may be offset by any other outstanding balance owed by or to the customer. Please allow 4 to 6 weeks for delivery. Offer available while quantities last.

Your Privacy: Harlequin is committed to protecting your privacy. Our Privacy Policy is available online at www.eHarlequin.com or upon request from the Reader Service. From time to time we make our lists of customers available to reputable third parties who may have a product or service of interest to you. If you would prefer we not share your name and address, please check here. ☐

BOB08R

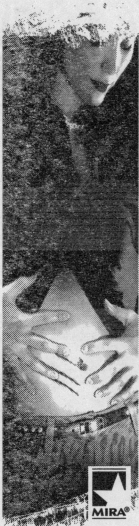

GWEN HUNTER

32221 BLOODSTONE ___ $6.99 U.S. ___ $8.50 CAN.

(limited quantities available)

TOTAL AMOUNT	$ _____
POSTAGE & HANDLING	$ _____
($1.00 FOR 1 BOOK, 50¢ for each additional)	
APPLICABLE TAXES*	$ _____
TOTAL PAYABLE	$ _____

(check or money order—please do not send cash)

To order, complete this form and send it, along with a check or money order for the total above, payable to MIRA Books, to: **In the U.S.:** 3010 Walden Avenue, P.O. Box 9077, Buffalo, NY 14269-9077; **In Canada:** P.O. Box 636, Fort Erie, Ontario, L2A 5X3.

Name: _____

Address: _____ City: _____

State/Prov.: _____ Zip/Postal Code: _____

Account Number (if applicable): _____

075 CSAS

*New York residents remit applicable sales taxes.
*Canadian residents remit applicable GST and provincial taxes.